THE REGIMENT'S WOMAN

Bob Kerby comes from Essex but now lives with his wife in Ontario, Canada.

THE REGIMENT'S WOMAN

Robert Kerby

THE REGIMENT'S WOMAN

Olympia Publishers

www.olympiapublishers.com
OLYMPIA PAPERBACK EDITION

A CIP catalogue record for this title is
available from the British Library.

ISBN: 978-1-84897-014-4

First Published in 2010

Olympia Publishers
60 Cannon Street
London
EC4N 6NP

Printed in Great Britain

For
Jenny, Jackie and Alan
with love.

Acknowledgements

I wish to thank my wife Jenny and our friends Kate Moore and Cassandra Haughton for their invaluable suggestions and help in proof reading and editing of the final document.

To all the wonderful staff at Olympia Publishers, I offer my thanks and appreciation for all your help and advice during the editing and production process of this work.

I would also like to extend my special thanks to Dorothea Helms (www.thewritingfairy.com). At a time when I was blocked by self-doubt, I attended one of Dorothea's lectures at the Oshawa Public Library. Dorothea's wonderful enthusiasm and advice for first-time authors; encouraged and inspired me to finish this novel. Without her, it may still be sitting on my shelf, unfinished.

PART ONE

CHAPTER 1

Tywardreath
1864

The pain was more than he thought he could bear as it surged through his face and head like a hot knife. His back ached and his right elbow and left leg were in severe discomfort, but he was unable to focus on its cause. A second thunder of agony swept through his head, overwhelming him, before it faded once again into the distance. He struggled to breathe. His mouth and throat were clogged with dust; and then the thunder returned in a new agonizing wave, and he drifted into oblivion.

Dreadful moans and the sound of someone crying came to him in the darkness and again the thunder overpowered his thoughts. He had no idea how long he'd been lying there or how many times he'd drifted in and out of consciousness. He only knew he was in serious pain and was extremely uncomfortable.

Very slowly he began to focus his mind. He tried to raise his right hand to his face but his elbow was trapped under his right side and he was unable to move it. His left arm seemed free, so he brought his hand to his face and felt a wet mushiness. He guessed he was blind but didn't panic. He was in too much pain to panic and he dearly wanted to lie in a more comfortable position. His body was painfully arched backwards over something under the small of his back. His left leg was twisted back and to the side, and his foot was pinned to the ground. He coughed and choked on the dust in his gullet, and struggled to regain his breathing. The thunder returned and for a few moments he could do nothing but fight against the incessant pain in his head.

When the wave passed, he felt down his left side and found he was lying over the legs of another man, his foot caught under the man's stomach. He grabbed hold of the man's shirt and tugged at him, but got no response. He guessed that he was dead. Ignoring the pain as much as he could, he rolled over onto his right side and pulled with all his might to raise the lifeless body off his foot. The pain in his head increased to the point where he was forced to let go, but he'd only moved his foot a couple of inches towards freedom. He inhaled heavily for a few seconds, took another deep and dusty breath and then pulled again, screaming as loud as he could to overcome the pain, until his foot was free. He collapsed back onto the man under him and straightened his leg. Thank God, he thought, his leg wasn't broken. He then found himself trying to laugh at the ridiculousness of it. He was probably blind, and yet all he was worried about was a broken leg.

"Bill, is that you?"

The weak voice came from beside him, perhaps no more than six feet away. He spat dust from his mouth and winced as some pebbles fell onto his bloody face clattering like rain on the floor about him.

"Yeh," he croaked. "Johnny boy, is that you?"

"Yeh," came the reply, "don't feel so good though."

"You'll be fine lad just you hang on there!"

Bill Rundel had no idea how long he'd been lying there. Perhaps ten minutes, perhaps an hour. He couldn't tell as he'd drifted in and out of consciousness. He remembered aiming the blows of his pickaxe at a small crack in the rock that flickered in the light of a candle in his hat. He remembered the familiar taste of the dust, the heat and the smell of men's sweat in the closeness. Then the roaring returned to his head and he remembered the flash that burned his eyes and being thrown about the cavern like a discarded rag doll. After that, oblivion.

For a few seconds everything was still, and then the screaming began. Those still conscious became aware of their injuries as the pain enveloped them. Men cried for help or screamed in panic when they couldn't see. Blood ran from their ears and eyes. Many lay silent and grew cold, their bodies torn apart. Others moaned and choked on the dust.

In the darkness and confusion, Bill slowly gathered his wits about him. He knew he was hurt badly, but the cries of his work mates diverted his attention.

"Fred," he gasped. "you's al'right?" A moan came in reply from the gloom. "Ted, Peter, Jimmy, where are ya?" The roaring came once again to his head and he laid his head back and groaned with pain.

"Jimmy's had it," said a raspy voice a few feet away.

Bill raised his hand to his face. It felt wet and sticky where the blood was fresh, dry and hard where it was crusting. His eyes were mushy with burns. He knew he was blind but couldn't be certain in the darkness of the mine.

Further down the shaft someone was sobbing. Cursing and screaming suppressed the moans of the others. Next to him, Bill could feel someone shivering violently, but after a minute or two he stopped, let out a long slow sigh and went quiet.

Despite his pain, and the almost certain knowledge that he would never see again, Bill felt strangely calm, as if he was ready to accept what fate had dealt. He felt no panic, just pity for his friends who cried and screamed in their agony. He slowly pushed himself off the lifeless body and propped his head and shoulders against the wall. It was excruciatingly painful to move, but once he'd managed to find a comfortable position his ribs didn't hurt him so much.

"Bet'll be upset when she sees me," he said out loud, as though talking to one of his mates. But nobody was listening, nobody replied.

In the darkness somebody struck a match and lit a candle. A thin glow appeared weakly in the dark, illuminating a pile of twisted bodies, but Bill didn't see it. He lay there in his own darkness listening to the roar grow and then recede in his head, and in the distance he fancied he heard the tolling of a bell.

Outside in the sun, a miner frantically hammered at a large warning bell. Clouds of dust bellowed from the mineshaft like the aftermath of dragon's breath, only to be picked up and spiralled into the sky by the sea breeze. Men ran toward the entrance of the shaft with stretchers and lanterns, while others barked orders and rallied workers into rescue teams. Two or three young lads working on the shod stamp press where the rock was crushed, were sent into the village of Tywardreath to spread the news to the miners' families.

****

There was a small row of pretty miner's cottages at Chapel Down, just north of the village of Tywardreath. Elizabeth Rundel stood outside Number 4, sharing local gossip with her neighbour, Martha Cory, when they heard the bell toll.

Martha was an attractive twenty eight-year-old miner's wife with a five-year-old son named William – after his dad. Although Martha was nine years younger, Elizabeth considered her to be her dearest friend. Despite the age difference, the two women were not unalike in appearance. They had dark shoulder-length hair parted in the middle and tied back into two broad loops that partially covered their ears; both had slight, trim figures. Elizabeth was still a beautiful woman. Despite raising six children she had managed to keep her figure, albeit with a little help from her stays, and was generally considered to be the most handsome woman in the village.

It was a gloriously warm summer's day and both women were taking time out from their household chores to take advantage of the sunshine. It was hot in the sun, made worse by their ankle length dresses, which should have been buttoned up tight to the neck, but were undone for several inches, exposing their upper chests. Their long sleeves were rolled up to their elbows exposing their forearms.

Four of Elizabeth's children sat on the wall at the front of the house, her two-year-old, Mary, clung to her gown sucking her thumb. There was only one child missing when the bell rang at the mine and that was her ten-year-old daughter Janetta. She was nowhere to be seen when the messenger boy arrived breathless, after cycling up the hill from the village.

He stopped at the gate and bent forward at the waist, supporting himself by leaning his forearms on the handlebar. He stared at the ground and breathed with a heavy asthmatic wheeze. Elizabeth and Martha stepped outside their gates to get the news.

"Accident at mine," wheezed the lad. "Been explosion!"

Elizabeth turned pale in horror and Martha supported her by the arm. Both their husbands were named William and both worked at the mine. Martha's Will wasn't on that shift, having strained his back, whereas Elizabeth's Bill was.

Mine disasters were common and everyone in the village dreaded the sound of the mine bell. Life was perilous and hard enough for a Cornish mining family, but the death of a miner meant possible ruin and starvation.

"Jane," Elizabeth ordered her oldest daughter, "go an' find Jan, we're all going."

"I knows where she is," piped up seven-year-old Lizzie, wiping her nose on her sleeve.

"Alright, then you go!" said Elizabeth, and little Lizzie jumped down off the wall and ran towards the village. "And bring 'er t'mine," she yelled after her.

The boy, having recovered his breath, cycled on to deliver his news to others in the village.

"Come on Bet," said Martha. "We'd better go."

****

To the east and west of Tywardreath the land rose up into high cliffs that curved around forming a horseshoe-shaped cove. A few fishing boats rode at anchor in the bay, sheltering from the winds coming off the English Channel. A small path led up from the village and climbed to the top of the cliffs where a copse of trees bent inland by the almost constant sea winds. Along the edge of the cliff and through the trees ran a low, moss-covered stone wall.

It had been a beautiful summer's day, bright and warm; the type of day that shows Cornwall at its best. There was no merging of land and sky, but a hard, clean line that defined the hills and cliffs. The sun made the meadows glow the brightest green, and the rocky outcrops and walls a sharp slate grey that defined the edges of the fields. Janetta leaned her forearms on the top of the wall, lowered her head onto her hands and watched the white caps on the deep green sea below.

This was her special place, where she came with her friends from the village, far from her mother's calling. It was a quiet secluded spot. Nobody ever went there except her friends, and of course, her sister, Lizzie.

Today she was with Mathew, who was twelve. He seemed so much older than her; so much worldlier! She was only ten, but determined to catch up to him as soon as possible.

"What do ya wanna do?" asked Mathew as he too stared out over Saint Austell Bay.

"Dunno!" said Janetta dreamily, which implied she had hardly heard or cared what he had said.

Mathew waited a minute or two, as if he couldn't think of anything he wanted to do. In fact, he knew exactly what he wanted. It was just a matter of getting the timing right. A few moments passed.

"Cummon," he said, getting bored with the ocean, "I'll be doctor!"

This was one of Janetta's favourite games. She played it often up here in the trees, but she was careful never to show too much enthusiasm for fear of being thought too easy.

"So what's the problem?" Mathew asked, imitating Tywardreath's doctor rather well, and making Janetta giggle.

"Got the ague," replied Janetta, although she had no idea what "the ague" was.

"A'right, young lady, take a clothes off."

Janetta giggled again, at his imitation of the doctor. She undid her laces and let her dress fall down around her ankles and stepped out of it.

"Lay down and we'll take a look shall we!" said Mathew in his most grown up voice.

She lay down on the grass and waited. Mathew knelt down beside her and looked at her nakedness. He felt a stirring in his groin and an excitement that was oddly different from previous occasions when they'd played this game. How pale and smooth her body looked in contrast to her dirty knees and feet, runny nose and tanned face.

He felt unusually nervous, far more than he normally did when he was playing this game with her. Something was happening to him. It was no longer an innocent game. He was beginning to find it very erotic.

But Janetta was so young. He doubted whether she knew what turmoil his body was going through.

He was wrong. Janetta may have only been ten but she was growing up faster than her body, and she lay there wondering when he was going to pluck up the courage to touch her. She felt both amused and frustrated at his shyness. They'd done this many times before. Why was he hesitating this time?

If there was one thing that Janetta was learning very fast, it was that she possessed a certain quality that other girls did not seem to have; something that gave her power over the boys. She didn't know what it was, but sensed its potency. Other girls in the village were playing doctor; but with them it was just a game they played and didn't really enjoy. They played it because the boys wanted to. Janetta, on the other hand, was always in control and made the boys she picked feel privileged to be with her.

Mathew wasn't the only boy she'd played doctor with, but he was the oldest. She sensed in him some indefinable difference that attracted her to him. He didn't usually stumble and fumble about like the others. Today, however, he seemed distracted. She decided to break the ice.

"My turn," she said sitting up. "I'll be the doc now."

Mathew was rather startled.

"Ya can't, you're a girl. Girls can't be doctors!" he said.

"Can too!" insisted Janetta.

"Can't!" replied Mathew indignantly.

"Alright!" insisted Janetta, "I'll be the nurse. Now where's it 'urt?"

Mathew paused for a moment, and it slowly dawned on him that maybe the game was going to take on a new dimension.

"Down 'ere," he said indicating his lower intestine.

"Drop ya britches then," insisted Janetta.

Mathew was quite taken aback by her forcefulness and found that he was obeying her without hesitation.

"Listen. What's that?" said Janetta turning her head away from the sea.

She fancied she had heard a bell, but the wind rustled the trees and the sound faded.

"Do me up," she said turning her back towards him. The game was over.

Mathew pulled his britches up and then fumbled with the laces on her back. He wasn't used to dressing girls and his hands trembled.

"Listen!" said Janetta turning to look down towards Tywardreath.

Through the trees and across the bay they could hear the distant sound of a tolling bell. It couldn't be the church bell, it wasn't Sunday. Mathew took a few steps forward toward the wall as if trying to get within range of the sound, and furrowed his brow.

"It's t'mine!" he exclaimed. The one bell he knew every member of the village dreaded.

"Come on, Jan!"

He took Janetta's hand and they ran together down the hill towards the village. Halfway down they saw a small figure running up towards them waving her arms. It was Lizzie.

"Mum says we gotta go t' mine. The whole village is there. Come on!" she yelled. Satisfied that they had heard her, she turned around and ran back the way she had come.

****

Outside the mineshaft a large crowd had gathered, and everywhere was a hubbub of activity. Dr Taylor stood to one side so as not to get in anyone's way. He was a handsome man in his early fifties and considered the best mine surgeon in the area. He didn't enter the mine. He was dressed in what appeared to be his Sunday best suit and wasn't about to get it dirty. He stood with his weight firmly between his feet, holding his elbow with one hand and stroking his moustache with the other.

"No point in going in. Won't be able to do anything in the dark anyway. Better to bring them out!" He was talking to Francis Puckey, the mine captain who had just arrived with the doctor in the doctor's buggy, and still had his table napkin tucked in his collar.

The doctor turned to look at Puckey. His eyes drifted down to his chest and he discreetly cleared his throat.

Puckey glanced down and quickly snatched the napkin away.

"Pity this, I was enjoying our lunch. Thank Mrs Puckey for me. Didn't get a chance, dashing out like that," said the doctor staring at the mineshaft entrance. "I thought Mrs Skinner looked particularly radiant this afternoon."

"Hmm," grunted Francis distracted by the day's events.

"Will we see you tomorrow Mr Puckey?" the doctor continued casually, "the village will be a fine spectacle, I dare say."

Francis Puckey was barely listening, He was not interested in the village's annual Bal Maiden festival.

"The Bal maidens," Dr Taylor pressed on in an effort to raise Puckey's spirits, "carry their fondness for dress to extremes. All the dresses exhibited in the plates of the monthly books of fashion may be seen in Tywardreath or St. Blazey on a fine Sunday afternoon, not even omitting the additional accompaniment of parasols, lace-edged pocket handkerchiefs, etc."

"Hmm! Why did this have to happen?" Puckey snapped, not expecting an answer. "We do everything we can to keep the miners safe and fit! Didn't we install the 'man machine' † for them? And a pretty penny that cost I do assure you."

Puckey was a short, round-faced and rather superior individual, and he fidgeted were he stood. Mr Treffrey, the owner, was in London and it fell upon Puckey to organize the rescue efforts. He felt completely stunned by yet another disaster at a mine already in serious trouble with depleted copper yields and a steadily decreasing work force.

"I know, damn shame! ...Ah! Here they come!" the doctor replied.

A solemn line of pale-faced miners came out of the dark hole carrying stretchers, burdened down with bloody men. Some had their arms hanging over the sides, which swung with the motion of the stretcher.

"I'm not good with suffering you see. I know how to run a mine, but I can't deal with blood!" fretted Francis Puckey.

The doctor wasn't listening but watched the line of men coming towards him.

"Over here lads!" he called.

One by one they filed up to the doctor and stopped in front of him with their load. The doctor looked down at the first injured miner and bent close to his face. He held his jacket and cravat close to his chest, so as not to get it bloody. Shaking his head, he gestured to take the injured miner to the left. The next, clearly still alive, he waved to the right.

† *The 'Man Engine' was the first elevator invented for mines in 1841. It was subsequently designed and erected in the Fowey Consuls mine by William West in 1850.*

On either side of the main track leading from the company office to the mineshaft, were the remains of a once well-kept lawn which was now a trodden and scruffy patch of muddy grass. Slowly, two lines of stretchers were laid on the ground; those needing treatment to the right and those to be mourned by their families on the left.

A group of village bystanders edged towards the stretchers, and a steady stream of families came through the main gates to find their husbands, brothers and sons.

"Let them see the dead ones, but keep them away from the others until the doctor's finished seeing to them," said Puckey solemnly to one of the foremen.

"I'm going to need some women to help me," shouted the doctor to the waiting crowd, "but not if you're squeamish!" Then turning to Puckey, "can't you shut that confounded machinery off, I can't hear myself think!"

The whole mine resonated with the low-pitched grinding of the rock into fine gravel through the iron shod stamps and the rumble of the ball mill where the gravel was further ground into finer particles. Further down the line the shaking table rattled as it washed, separated and concentrated the ore.

"Oh, oh yes!" said Puckey who skipped from foot to foot as if uncertain which way to go. He finally decided to head straight for the shod stamps and hastened across the grass to stammer his instructions to some workman standing around by the machinery. One by one the machines shut down and an eerie silence settled over the works. Oddly, the quiet made everyone uneasy. It was as though the ceasing of the roar emphasized the calamity. The noise was strangely reassuring for the villagers. The machines never stopped. They rumbled all night and the villagers felt easy in their beds. Everything was as it should be. Now there was silence. Only the doctor seemed relieved by the sudden quiet.

"Good, that's better!" he said to himself, then raising his voice to all the ladies. "Right! We'll need lots of bandages, use whatever you can find, as long as it's reasonably clean! Your petticoats will do."

One by one a handful of women came forward to offer their help, Elizabeth among them. She felt guilty that her reason for volunteering was motivated by her desire to find her husband, but she suppressed the thought and followed the doctor towards the line of bloodied patients.

Almost immediately she saw Bill about six stretchers along the line. It's not that she recognized his face, for that was covered with congealing blood; she saw his familiar red shirt and blue britches. She ran to his side and let out a great gasp when she saw him. His eyes had gone. Where once there had been two sparkling blue eyes – the eyes she had fallen in love with so long ago – now two blackened heaps of burnt flesh and dried blood.

"Bet, is that you?" came a harsh whisper from lips that barely moved under the crusting blood. He suddenly rolled onto his side, coughed and brought up the black sputa the miners call "old black trade".

"It's me Bill, it's me," she sobbed as she dropped to her knees beside him.

Two hands, gently placed upon her shoulders, came to support her as she cried. Martha knelt beside the stretcher and hugged Bet.

"Is this her husband?" It was the doctor who had just finished attending to the neighbouring injuries. Martha looked up at him and nodded. "What's his name?"

"Bill, Bill Rundel," replied Martha, since Elizabeth was still too much in shock to respond.

"Alright, let's take a look!" He bent over Bill and whispered to him. "I'm just going to take a look at you. I won't hurt you."

The doctor took his jacket off and laid it on the grass. Martha watched him methodically roll up his sleeves.

"I think it would be better if you took Mrs Rundel for a cup of tea," he said gently, gesturing to a makeshift tent that had been set up for the purpose. "I don't think she should watch this, do you?"

Martha was surprised at the sudden compassion in his voice. The aloofness he had earlier displayed, which was so common in his class, had vanished, and his eyes seemed full of pity for the suffering around him.

"Com'n dear," she said lifting Elizabeth to her feet, "let's get a cup of tea while the doctor sees to Bill."

Elizabeth's eyes, full of tears, looked helplessly at the doctor.

"He'll live Mrs Rundel, God willing, he'll live," said the doctor as he gave her a gentle squeeze on the forearm.

Martha led Elizabeth away, and as soon as they were out of earshot the doctor sprang into action to save Bill Rundel's ebbing life.

Janetta and Lizzie ran through the front gate of the mine complex and started looking through the crowd for their mother. Martha saw them first.

"Over 'ere Jan, Lizzie, over 'ere," she called above the clatter of the crowd. The two girls made their way across to the tea tent and stood by their mother's side. Elizabeth was still sobbing between sips of tea.

"It's your dad, girls," said Martha. "I'm afraid he's been hurt."

Lizzie immediately burst into tears and Janetta put her arm around her. "Will he live?" she asked.

"Yes he'll live, the doctor's with him now."

It had been a bad day at the West Fowey Consuls Mine; eleven dead, twenty-two injured with cuts, abrasions, broken limbs, perforated eardrums, and eight blinded.

It was the end of William Rundel's working life, and the beginning of a new era of potential hardship for the Rundel family.

****

The following week was one of gradual acceptance for Elizabeth Rundel. Bill remained in bed in a great deal of pain. For days he drifted in and out of consciousness and struggled with a high fever. Elizabeth sat by his side for hours while Martha looked after the children. Dr Taylor stopped by every couple of days and administered morphine for Bill's pain, and gave encouraging words to Elizabeth.

"We can only wait and pray, Mrs Rundel. He's a strong man, he should pull through."

Martha helped as much as she could, but Elizabeth threw herself into her housework on the second week, as a way of coping with her distress. She frantically scrubbed the front door step with soap and water every day, and Martha sat patiently and talked with her while she scrubbed.

Gradually the gravity of their situation began to fill Elizabeth's mind, and at the end of the second week she sat the children down for a serious family talk.

"Now then," she began, "Dad's on the mend, praise be to God! But he won't be working no more, so we don't 'ave no more money see?"

The six children sat around the fire with glum expressions and lowered heads. Jane and John, the eldest two sat opposite Elizabeth, while Janetta, Lizzie and the five-year-old Louisa huddled to keep warm directly in front of the fire. Elizabeth cradled little Mary on her lap.

"Jane and John, you're big kids now and you're going to 'ave to earn your keep. I'm going to take in laundry to do, and Janetta, you'll 'ave to look after little'uns."

"Ahhhh," whined Janetta, cringing at the thought of tending to her three younger siblings. Jane leaned forward and smacked the back of her head.

"That's enough out of you, young lady," continued Elizabeth. "You've had it too easy up'n 'til now. No more skiving off with ya friends. I want ya 'ere, where ya can be of use."

A knock came at the front door, and Bet was visibly annoyed by the interruption.

"Oh, oo's that! Go see will ya Jane!"

Jane got up and went to open the door. It was Mrs Shilling from number 5 standing on the step under a cape pulled over her head to shelter her from the rain.

Mrs Shilling was a lady of mature years, and although she lived in a miner's cottage, her husband worked in accounts thus she liked to put on airs. She dressed beautifully, buying all her clothes in Truro, and everyone pitied her husband, since they doubted he could really afford his wife's lavish wardrobe. But for all her shortcomings, Shilling was a kind-hearted woman and was by no means disliked.

"Hello Jane dear, I've got some news for your mother, can I come in?" Without waiting for an invitation, she edged her way past Jane, who stood aside so as not to get rain dripped on her dress. Amelie draped her cloak over the stair banister and walked quickly into the parlour, her cobalt blue gown brushing the walls as she went. Seeing the whole family gathered around the fire as if posing, and waiting for the flash of a Tintype portrait, she stopped, raised her hands in mock surprise and announced.

"Well I never did, what a handsome family you are, to be sure!"

Elizabeth, doing her best to be gracious, smiled and nodded to Amelie, who stood completely filling the doorway with her extravagantly wide gown, and blocked Jane from re-entering the room.

How grand she looked. Her blue gown was quite new, the fabric smooth and shiny like silk, although Elizabeth doubted that it really was silk. Her hair was parted in the middle, as was the fashion, but hung in tight ringlets down the sides of her face, which Elizabeth felt to be too young for a lady of her age. Over her hair, she wore a white delicate lace bonnet with a green ribbon.

"To what do we owe this pleasure?" asked Elizabeth, putting on pretend airs to parry Amelie's theatrical entrance.

"Well my dear," Amelie glided further into the room allowing Jane to sneak past and regain her seat by the fire, "I've solved your money problems. Well, almost anyway! Is there tea in the pot dear?"

"Would ya put the kettle on the hearth please Jane?" asked Elizabeth. and Jane, who had barely sat down again, rolled her eyes and disappeared into the kitchen.

Elizabeth turned to Amelie Shilling who had pulled up a chair and sat down.

"Ave ya? Ow did ya do that then?" Elizabeth replied a little bristly.

"Well now! I was down at Farraday's Butchers this morning and he told me that Mrs Jones said her niece knows some gentleman who's looking to rent rooms in Tywardreath."

"Really? An' why should a gentleman want to live in this little cottage?"

"Well there aren't many places to stay in Tywardreath are there? And besides, Mrs Jones said he wasn't fussy."

Elizabeth felt her face flushing and she fought to suppress her anger. After all, she reminded herself, Amelie meant well.

"Well it's a thought isn't it?" she said, her mind racing through all the practicalities. "I'm very grateful to you Mrs Shilling"

"Amelie my dear, call me Amelie; what are neighbours for eh?"

"Amelie," corrected Elizabeth, who had never been on a first name basis with her neighbour and didn't feel comfortable getting too familiar. "What exactly does this gentleman do? And how would I meet him?"

"He comes from Truro, and apparently he's a master coach builder. He builds coaches and chaises for everybody who's anybody. Don't worry dear, I've already talked to Mrs Jones. We'll arrange it all for you. Ah! Here's the tea! Thank you dear."

Jane laid a tray, containing their best teapot and several cups and saucers on the table.

Elizabeth didn't bother to raise the point. Still, she couldn't help wondering why a master coach builder of such renown should want to come to a small mining village like Tywardreath And if he was so successful, why would he choose to stay in such humble accommodation? Still, the money would be a great help. Now all she had to do was make room for him to stay.

She watched Amelie as Jane poured her tea.

Amelie Shilling took her tea and gossiped about everything and nothing for a whole hour before eventually retiring to her own cottage.

"Now I'll be in touch as soon as I've arranged for this gentleman to come and see you. No need to see me out."

When the front door closed behind Amelie, Elizabeth flopped back into her chair with a sigh of relief.

Janetta looked at her mother and sister with a bemused look on her small face.

"He comes from Truro," she announced, waving her hands in the air in mock imitation of Amelie, "And apparently he's a master coach builder." Her little voice worked hard to mimic the affectations of their neighbour.

Elizabeth and Jane looked at her in astonishment.

"Now I'll be in touch soon. No need to see me out." Janetta's eyes rolled to the ceiling and her head tilted back as she gave a regal wave as if she were leaving.

Her mother desperately tried to stifle a smirk.

"Now, Jan dear, that's not kind," she managed to say before letting out a giggle that quickly became a burst of laughter.

CHAPTER 2

The Lodger

The following morning was a bright sunny day but with a very strong sea breeze. It was so strong, in fact, that Elizabeth wasn't inclined to risk hanging her washing on the line in the backyard. She had made that mistake before and had spent half the afternoon running around the neighbourhood retrieving her petticoats and other items of clothing that had blown away.

Today, she arranged her washing over the furniture in front of the fire.

Shortly before lunch someone knocked on the door. Since she was in the middle of ironing and expecting it to be Martha, she didn't bother to go to the door but simply called out, "Come in, it's open!"

She heard the front door open, and after a short pause a man's voice tentatively called, "Hello, Mrs Rundel?"

"Oh!" she exclaimed. Wiping her hands down the front of her apron to smooth out any wrinkles, she walked into the hallway to greet her visitor.

There stood a tall, well-dressed gentleman in his early forties carrying a red-checked carpetbag. Elizabeth's immediate impression was that he was quite handsome. He had naturally curly hair, which he combed and gelled to force it to be straight and tidy. His sideburns extended down almost to the point of his chin, but he had no moustache. Around his neck was an uncomfortable looking, well-starched collar and a cream and green cravat that puffed up out of the top of his waistcoat. His jacket, done up by one button right under his cravat, matched his waistcoat in a deep brown wool, and his trousers were of neatly pressed gray checked flannel. "*All in all*," she thought, "*a very handsome gentleman*."

"Good day to you, ma'am," he said raising his right finger to his temple, "My name's Phineas Stone, I understand you have a room for let." Elisabeth was impressed. He sounded educated and she made an effort to improve her own speech.

"Oh, er, yes I do!"

She nervously straightened her dress and ran her hands over her hair to smooth any wayward strands.

"I'm sorry for the mess, I wasn't expecting you just now you see, and I'm in the middle of doing the ironing."

"Bless me ma'am there's no need to be embarrassed on my account. The Lord bestows special blessings on those who toil in the keeping of a good household."

"Does He?" replied Elizabeth a little awkwardly. "Yes, well you'd better come through."

She opened the door to the front parlour and hurriedly went about the room gathering up the damp laundry from the furniture.

"Sit yourself down Mr Stone, and I'll get some tea."

"That's very kind of you, very kind indeed!" beamed Phineas Stone as he sat in the armchair and made himself at home. "I can see I'm going to like it here, Mrs Rundel," he continued as he followed her out of the room with his eyes.

Elizabeth retreated to the kitchen.

"Jane, put the kettle on. Then John, you help her fold these sheets, don't get them dirty mind. Jane, put clean sheets on our guest's bed. Hurry now girl!"

She removed her apron, checked her hair in the mirror, took a deep breath and scurried back into the parlour.

"There now, that's better. Tea won't be long, Mr Stone!"

"Please Mrs Rundel, call me Phineas," he interrupted with a broad grin.

"Oh well, then Phineas, as you can see we're very small here and I..."

"Small is delightful, and very cosy Mrs Rundel, very cosy indeed!"

"...Yes, well, as long as you won't find us too crowded Mr er, Phineas."

"Not at all dear lady, not at all."

"I'm sure it's not as grand as you're used to. You must have had a much larger 'ouse in Truro, being a master coach builder an' all. I'm afraid living in a miner's cottage may be a bit 'umble for you."

Elizabeth found herself sounding overly apologetic.

"Mrs Rundel…"

"But for us, you see the money would be very welcome."

"Mrs Rundel," Phineas raised his voice just enough to ensure an interruption. "I assure you that I am very much at home in a miner's cottage. Why, my parents' house was not much larger than this. As for my accommodation in Truro, it was one extremely small room in a very dark, and rather damp back alley."

"But I thought that as a master coach builder you would…"

"A master coach builder, Mrs Rundel? I *worked* for a master coach builder, but I'm a carpenter," Then lowering his voice to emphasise his humility, "A very good one, I admit. But only a carpenter, Mrs Rundel I do assure you."

"Oh I'm sorry Phineas, we thought ya was going to be too grand for us. Amelie will be disappointed," said Elizabeth with a small grin growing on her face.

"Now how could anybody be disappointed in me Mrs Rundel?"

They both broke into laughter and Jane brought in the tea.

"It's six shillings a week bed and board, if that's all right wi ya, Phineas!"

"That's fine Mrs Rundel. That's more than fair!" replied Phineas as he took the cup offered to him by Jane.

"Well then, that's settled. Show Mr Stone his room Jane, and then you come down and finish your tea Phineas."

****

As the weeks went by William gradually got stronger. It hadn't been easy. Dr Taylor had shown Elizabeth how to change his dressings and wash his wounds. The first time the bandages were removed, Elizabeth nearly fainted. Bill's face was a dreadful mess. But in time the scars softened and she became used to his disfigurement.

Bill still insisted on having the bandage on though, even after they were of no medical use. He felt more comfortable hidden behind them – especially when he was with the children.

Elizabeth understood his concern. His face was still dreadful to see. His right eye, although blind, was intact, but stared unseeing.

There was no pupil, just white scar tissue covering the eye. His left eye, however, hit by some flying debris, was completely gone. The lid was sewn shut, but there was an unnatural hollow under the lid, which gave it a rather grotesque appearance. Much of his face was covered in burn scars, although they had faded in colour somewhat and were more acceptable to look at.

Bit by bit, Bill found the strength to come downstairs, sit in the parlour and listen to the family conversation. It wasn't physical strength he needed, but the strength to face his family again and to cope with his lot in life.

Little things made him lose his temper and he swore and cursed at anyone in the room. He tried to remember the positions of the furniture. Two steps to the table, one-and-a-half steps to the fire grate, and so on. Woe betide anyone who moved something so that he tripped over or bumped into it.

It was into this strained household that Phineas settled, but he seemed to have an instinctive understanding of Bill's suffering and was always there to lend a helping hand.

On sunny days, Bill sat in a chair outside the front door, laid his head back against the wall and allowed the heat from the sun to bathe his face.

"Call me if it rains or you get cold," Elizabeth would say, "and I'll come and help you in."

"I know where 'bloody door is woman," Bill would snap back at her, "won't move will it?"

Phineas, when he was at home, would sit and chat with Bill in the sun, and Bill became very fond of Phineas. But still he wore a thin bandage about his eyes and refused to let anyone see him without it.

One day as they sat chatting, Dr Taylor drove up in his horse and buggy and stopped outside their house.

"It's the doc!" said Phineas.

"Confound the man, now what does he want?" Bill moaned.

Dr Taylor walked up the front path."Good day t'you both", he announced.

"Damn it, doc, what is it this time? Brought me some new eyes 'av ya?" chided Bill. Despite his rough greeting, Bill had grown very fond of the doctor who had shown him a great deal of kindness since the accident.

"Almost Bill, in a manner of speaking," replied the doctor with a broad grin on his face and a wink to Phineas.

"I was in Truro last week," he continued.

"Good for you," mocked Bill.

"And I found something perfect for you."

"Oh ya! Wait for it! Here it comes!" said Bill, tapping Phineas' arm.

"I saw some perfect spectacles for you," beamed the doctor.

"Just what I could do with…spectacles!" mocked Bill

"Ah!" cut in the doctor, "but these are different. They have darkened glass in them, you see. That way you can wear them and people won't be able to see your eyes."

Elizabeth, hearing the voices from inside the house, came out to join the conversation. She had been making pastry and her hands were white with flour.

"Now that sounds a good idea, Bill," she said. "Then you won't have to have that damn bandage on all the time, will ya?"

Anticipating an objection, she pulled his bandage off and slapping away his protesting hands, took the spectacles from the doctor and placed them on his nose.

"Confound ya, woman!" protested Bill, but he allowed her to fuss over him anyway.

"There!" exclaimed Elizabeth.

"My that looks good Bill," agreed Phineas.

The three of them stood in front of Bill and studied him in his new spectacles. He really did look quite good. The dark lenses almost completely covered his eyes. You could still see the burn scars, of course, but they weren't so bad.

Janetta came out of the house to see what was going on. By now Bill was beginning to recognize the various members of his family by the sound of their walking.

"Well what's your opinion, young lady? Will I do?" he asked.

"Yeh," she replied. "You look very nice in 'em."

"Well then, if my Jan says they're all right, then I reckons they are!"

Everyone laughed and approved, and the doctor, not wishing any payment for them, bade them goodbye.

Late that summer, Jane found a job working in the local haberdashers as a sales assistant and John went to work on a farm as a general labourer. It wasn't a lot of money they earned, but with the laundry Elizabeth took in and Phineas Stone's rent money, the Rundel family got by. Janetta looked after her sister and helped around the house. Consequently she found it more and more difficult to get out of the house to spend time with the local boys. Whenever an occasion presented it self, however, she slipped away for an hour or so and hoped not to be missed.

****

1868

It was a beautiful summer's afternoon and the ocean was of the deepest blue and the sky of the palest shade. Phineas felt quite warm in his woolen waistcoat and tweed jacket. He walked along the cliff path with a determined energy, planting his rough-hewn walking stick in front of him and steadying himself on each stride. He breathed in the sea air and gave a contented sigh. Life didn't get much better than this; he was a happy man on a bright and cheerful day in the most beautiful corner of England. He enjoyed the quiet and the smell of the sea air on the cliff edge. All that could be heard was the sound of the gulls, the occasional large wave that hissed on the shingled shore and his footfalls on the gravel path.

Halfway up the cliff he stopped and sat down to rest and admire the view. A clipper ship was slowly making its way along the channel towards the Atlantic and two or three boats bobbed up and down on the waves fishing for pilchards. He turned and looked up the hill at the small copse of trees on the very top of the cliff. It wasn't far and he stood up, brushed the dust off the seat of his trousers and continued on his way to the top.

Janetta was leaning against a stone wall that ran through the copse trees. She was with two lads from the village, each a year or two younger than herself.

It was a shaded and secluded spot that she had frequented ever since she was a very young girl. It was her special place, out of view of the village, quiet and peaceful.

It was here that Janetta had played as a child and here that she had discovered her power over the village boys. She was accustomed to hearing the village ladies say how beautiful she was and she'd especially noticed the way boys looked at her, and she liked it! She had always been popular and learned very early what pleased the boys the most.

She was beginning to get a reputation in Tywardreath and her mother had spoken to her several times about "how to be a lady", but it didn't bother her. She wasn't going to change.

Nobody knew anything for sure, of course. She'd never been caught doing anything she shouldn't. Yet, somehow, rumours got around. Perhaps a careless remark uttered, a guilty look on some lad's face. Recently though, she'd been aware of a few disapproving looks from women in the street. She had also been the butt of jokes from some of her girlfriends. Someone had even called her a tart – to her face – but she didn't mind. She had a vision, a goal in life, a purpose, and she wasn't about to be put off.

She was becoming a young woman fast and it bothered her that she still had to hide in the trees to meet boys. Her body was changing, and her bosom, although not large, was beginning to become very noticeable. She had a new asset to promote, but she also felt frustrated at not being able to grow faster. She was a fourteen-year-old in a hurry.

"I got a penny, Jan," said Freddy, the older of the two boys, holding out a dirty hand with a copper coin lying in his palm.

"For what?" said Janetta, "it's a penny farthing from now on, see." She wanted to ask for more but knew they couldn't afford it.

"But why?" whined the boy with disappointment, as he only had a penny.

"Cause I got tits now, ain't I? I'm not a girl no more, I'm a woman, so ya have to pay for a woman."

The look on Freddy's face was heartbreaking and Janetta felt a pang of pity for him. She thought he was going to cry, but he didn't.

The younger boy also looked distinctly downcast, for this would have been his first time, but a penny farthing was out of the question. He stuck his hands in his pockets and scuffed the dirt with his bare feet.

"Ah c'mon Jan, just this once," said Freddy with the penny still in his outstretched hand.

Janetta turned to the younger boy, little Kit Farraday from the butcher's shop, "Av you got a penny an'aul?"

He nodded his head but didn't look up.

Janetta looked at the two dirty faces with their runny noses and sad eyes, and thought of the two pennies.

"Alright then, just this once, but next time it's a penny farthing each, right?"

"Yeh all right!" said Freddie and his eyes brightened at the prospect of what was to come.

Janetta undid the laces at her back and lowered the top of her dress. A small gasp emanated from the younger boy and Freddie swallowed hard.

Both boys stood before her, their eyes fixed on her breasts.

"Cum on then, give me ya 'ands."

Both boys offered a hand to her, Kit shyly following Freddie's lead. Janetta took hold of them, one in each hand and placed them firmly on her breasts. A small whimper escaped from the smaller lad and a big smile slowly grew across Freddy's face. He'd been here before. He hadn't been allowed to touch her though, only look at her nakedness. Now he had physical contact and was growing surer of himself. He started fondling her breast and squeezing it with delight in his eyes.

Janetta hardly seemed to notice him, however. She was captivated by little Kit who simply held his hand against her other breast, frozen to the spot. His eyes stared at her flesh; his pupils were surrounded by white and his mouth just hanging open, stupefied and overwhelmed by the experience.

Janetta was most amused by his reaction, and amazed that so little flesh could hold such potent power over a lad. If this much power brought her two copper coins, what limits could there be to her wealth? She'd already accumulated ten shillings collected from just about every boy in Tywardreath and the neighboring village of Saint Blazey. A penny here, a halfpenny there, it soon mounted up. Now she was becoming a woman and the older boys would start taking notice of her, and they had money, from working in the mines.

Gradually, as she stood there with these two little grubby hands on her body, she began to see a way out of this small village and her pre-ordained life of drudgery in the milliner's shop. She was going to be rich, live in a big house and have servants. She would show them all. Janetta was destined to go far.

Phineas reached the top of the hill and paused for a second to catch his breath before entering the shade of the trees. He heard some children's voices and curious to see who was playing, he slowly and quietly entered the copse. There, a few yards ahead of him was Janetta and two boys. Each was standing holding her breasts like two sentinels guarding a secret treasure. The sight struck Phineas as rather amusing and he stopped, leaned on his walking stick and gave a little smile to himself. He could remember when he was young and played these games; when life was simple and games were innocent.

Janetta hadn't seen him but she suddenly stepped back from the boys pulling away from their grasps.

"That's enough then!" she said, "Time you was off 'ome young Kit!"

"Ahhh," he whined.

"Come on! Do me up!" said Janetta turning her back to Freddie.

Freddie fumbled with the laces tying them up. Kit stood quietly to one side. Janetta glanced at him and snapping her fingers, "Didn't get your penny!" The boy shyly hesitated. "Cum'n, quickly!" she ordered, and the lad held out his coin to her. She pocketed the penny, and sensing the laces were tied, walked over to the stone wall and leant against it. The two boys turned and ran back down the hill; neither of them saw Phineas who stepped back behind a bush.

"Keep ya mouth shut, ya hear?" shouted Janetta as they ran down the hill toward the village.

After they had left the copse, Phineas came out from behind his tree and sauntered into the clearing where Janetta stood looking out at the sea.

"It's beautiful isn't it?" he said.

Janetta, startled, swung round to see who was behind her.

"Sorry lass, didn't mean to frighten yer."

Recognizing Phineas, Janetta relaxed and let out a sigh, "Blimey ya scared me!" she said holding her hand to her heart. "Ow long ya been standing there then?"

"Only a minute," he lied to spare her embarrassment. "I've just walked up the hill. It's a lovely afternoon."

"S'pose!" said Janetta.

"Mind if I sit down?" Phineas sat beside her on a tuft of grass and Janetta sat down and leaned her head against the wall.

"I used to play in a spot like this when I was a lad," Phineas said, resting his head against the wall and looking up into the trees. Janetta didn't respond, so he continued. "Used to play with the girls. I played with them a lot. Learned a lot of stuff about girls playing them games."

Janetta began to realize she'd been caught and felt uncomfortable; but still she said nothing. She wasn't sure if she was going to be scolded or lectured, so she decided to wait and see what he had to say.

"Came a time though," continued Phineas, "when I got tired of feeling up girls in a game. I wanted to go further. I wanted to fall in love. I wanted to roger them!"

He turned and looked at Janetta to assess her reaction to what he was saying. Was he shocking her or frightening her? Neither it appeared. Janetta sat quietly with little or no expression on her face.

"Comes a time when you're too old for kids' games, Janetta." Still she made no response. "I think you're old enough don't you?" he said and he placed his hand on her knee to attract her attention. She looked at his hand and then at him.

"It'll cost yer tuppence!" she said with as much assurance as she could muster.

Shocked, Phineas removed his hand and stared at her in disbelief. It took him a second to realize what she had said; and when he did, he roared with laughter.

Janetta was not at all pleased with this response and squirmed with discomfort.

"Wot!" she exclaimed, "Wot's so funny?"

Phineas tried to compose himself.

"You don't want my tuppence you silly girl!"

"I ain't silly!" she pouted.

"No, no of course you're not, girl," he fought to contain another fit of laughter. "You're becoming a woman, Janetta. How old are you, fourteen? And a real beauty at that! It's time you stopped selling yerself short, girl. A penny farthing indeed!"

"Oh yer mean I should charge sixpence?"

"No, I don't mean sixpence! Christ almighty girl, yer got to start thinking ahead. You're growing into a woman and you have to protect yer reputation."

"Don't have no bleed'n reputation!"

"If yer don't, yer soon will have, if yer go on entertaining the lads like this. You've got to learn to be a lady see." He fidgeted to find a more comfortable position against the wall.

"I ain't no lady, but I will be one day, you see if I ain't!"

"Well Jan, ladies are discreet and discriminating, and if you want to be a lady it's time to grow up."

"What do'ya mean discreet and… discrim-ating?"

"Discreet 'cause you'll break yer mum's heart if you go on this way, and discriminating 'caus you want to give yer favours only to the man you love, see? Not to every Tom, Dick and Harry who has a penny farthing to spend. Do yer understand me?"

"Sort of!" replied Janetta, although she wasn't sure she did.

Phineas gave a frustrated sigh. "Look!" he continued, "if yer go on the ways you are, you'll soon get the pox, and likely as not, see an early grave. Do ya want that?"

Janetta stared at the grass and shook her head. She wasn't sure what the pox was, or how you got it, but knew it must be something terrible.

"No, well then! What I'm saying is, a beautiful woman can go a long way in this world, but only if she uses her assets wisely and discreetly… but don't tell yer mother I said so!"

Phineas wasn't sure he was explaining things wisely at this point. He should have told her to stop playing with the boys and keep her virginity intact until she was married. He assumed she was still a virgin, but didn't like to ask. He recognized a fire in Janetta; a fire that could easily consume her if allowed to get out of control – especially in a small village like Tywardreath where half the population was Wesleyan. Yet it was a fire that would not be easily suppressed, and he considered it better to advise her on how to manage her appetite rather than lay down the moral law.

"So yer saying real ladies get rogered all the time but only by posh folks, is that it?"

"Yes!...No! I'm saying a lady acts with decorum at all times and is choosy about who she takes to her bed. It's usually their husband. Appearances are everything, Janetta, everything!"

He took a good look at Janetta with her dirty face, unkempt hair and badly creased dress. Under all that grime was a beautiful young woman screaming to get out, and he feared for her future.

"I think it's time you started behaving like a young woman Janetta. It's time to wash your face, brush your hair and try to get through the day without blaspheming."

Janetta nodded and smiled at him.

"And no more child's games with the boys, al'right? You're not a child any more."

She nodded again.

"Come on then, let's go home and help your mum prepare the tea."

They stood up, brushed grass and dust from their backsides and started their walk back down the cliff path. Janetta glowed inside. She suddenly saw Phineas in a new light. He understood her. He understood her power and desire to use it. He had reasoned with her like an adult instead of chastising her like a child. He hadn't lectured her on what nice girls do, or on saving herself for her husband. He hadn't threatened fire and brimstone in the depths of hell where her soul would rot in torment. He saw she was becoming a woman and had been kind to her. She found herself looking at him as an older, wiser and more handsome man than she had ever seen before. She began to feel something really special inside. She had found her first true love.

****

During the following weeks Janetta made an effort to be more presentable in her appearance and tried not to swear too much – that part wasn't easy. Swearing had become a natural part of her vocabulary although she toned it down in the house. Her mother and father didn't swear, and her mother would have thrown a fit if she'd heard the cussing Janetta was capable of. So she worked hard at expressing herself in a more appropriate manner and even tried to improve her diction.

Elizabeth Rundel couldn't help commenting with great pleasure that Janetta was turning into a "proper young lady." Bill couldn't see her but beamed with pride when Elizabeth told him how his Jan was growing up. Even the neighbours and customers in the shop where she worked were impressed by the transformation that was taking place before their eyes.

The local boys still hung round her and occasionally offered her copper coins for a feel, but although tempted she told them that they were too young for her now that she was a woman. Older boys of fifteen, sixteen and seventeen started taking an interest in her, but still she turned away from them with an air of indifference.

Janetta's interests lay in another direction and she made a special effort to be nice to Phineas, without being too obvious in front of her family. She became constantly aware of where Phineas was at any given time and often contrived to be in the same room as him on some pretext or other. She was committed to proving her womanhood to Phineas and watched patiently for the smallest sign of his recognizing her charms.

Naturally, Phineas couldn't help noticing her attentive behaviour. Her infatuation was so artless that at times he fought back laughter at her pathetic attempts to woo him. But he understood the growing pains of a young woman and did his best to keep her at arm's length. Always gentle, always friendly, yet with just the right amount of formality, Phineas managed to live in the house without instigating any embarrassing situations with Janetta.

For a couple of months life went on in the Rundel family with the same uneventful routine. Bill, by now, was capable of walking unassisted down to the pub where he met his mining friends to discuss the troubles of the world. Lizzy looked after the younger children, taking them to and from the local school and Janetta went each day to the milliner's shop and learned the skills of sewing, measuring and cutting cloth.

****

It was a bright sunny Sunday with a gentle sea breeze cooling the village. Bill had gone down to the beach to fish off the shingles with his mates and the children had all gone to the Sunday school bible studies at the village hall. Janetta had gone with them but had complained of having a headache and sniffled with a runny nose, so she went back home.

Phineas sat in the parlour stuffing tobacco into the bowl of his pipe and Elizabeth kneaded dough at the kitchen table. The house was quiet and still after the hubbub of children's voices. Bill rummaged about in the closet for his rod and bait box. A placid calm descended on the house, and Elizabeth sighed with relief. "Alone at last!" she said to Phineas, who smiled affectionately as he lit his pipe.

He got up out of his chair and walked round the table and stood behind Elizabeth. He wrapped his hands around her waist and propped his chin on her shoulder.

"Ey! Alone at last," he agreed, and Elizabeth laid her head back against his and smiled.

"Nice isn't it," she whispered.

"Shame to waste it really," grinned Phineas as he slowly ran his hands up the front of her dress to caress her breasts.

"Cheeky bugger!" said Elizabeth as she turned to meet his lips, initiating a long and passionate kiss.

"Jesus Christ!" wailed Janetta standing in the doorway. Phineas pulled away but it was too late, they'd been seen. Janetta turned and fled upstairs to her room.

"Oh God!" Elizabeth dashed out of the kitchen to chase Janetta upstairs.

"Let her go luv!" said Phineas, but to no avail. Elizabeth was panic-stricken and in hot pursuit of her daughter.

Janetta slammed the bedroom door behind her and threw herself face down on the bed in a cascade of sobs. Elizabeth opened the door and gingerly entered the room. She breathlessly sat on the bed beside Janetta.

"Go away, I 'ate ya!" screamed Janetta.

"Luv I'm sorry but…"

"Yer 'ad to steal him from me, didn't ya?" yelled Janetta as she sat up and glared into her mothers eyes. Elizabeth suddenly realized that her daughter wasn't distressed over the hurt to her father, but over the loss of Phineas.

"Shit Jan, he's much too old for ya! Can't you see that?"

“Don’t want ta hear no bloody excuses. Yer stole ’im!” With that she jumped off the bed and ran downstairs. Elizabeth didn’t follow.

Phineas leaned against the kitchen table with his arms folded and stared at the floor as Janetta ran out of the front door. He considered running after her but stayed rooted to the spot. What could he say anyway? In her eyes he’d betrayed her and the chances of being easily forgiven were remote.

Janetta walked the length of Chapel Down towards the village as if she were late for her own funeral. Tears streaked her face but she refused to cry, they were tears of blind rage.

“How dare she! How dare she! Bitch! Bitch! Bitch!” She spat the words out as she strode past neighbours standing outside their front doors chatting. Her chest became so tight she felt she would swoon or her heart would burst. When she reached the end of the road she stopped, leaned against a fence, slid down into a stooping position and burst into uncontrollable sobs.

Two boys walked up the lane and saw her sobbing on the corner. One was Freddy and the other was the blacksmith’s boy, Darren. They stood in front of her and watched her in silence, neither wanting to interrupt her distress.

Gradually her sobs turned into whimpers that subsided into sniffles and she raised her head from her knees to see the two lads in front of her. For a few seconds they just looked at one another, then she sniffed, wiped her nose across the back of her forefinger and said, “Got yer tuppence ’ave yer?”

The two boys nodded enthusiastically.

“Come on then,” she said as she pulled herself back onto her feet and the three of them walked together through the village towards the cliffs.

PART TWO

CHAPTER 3

Plymouth
1875

The street crowds never ceased to amaze Janetta. In Tywardreath you could walk down the main street and meet a dozen people at the most on a busy day, and see one or two carts or wagons slowly rumble past, but Plymouth was altogether different.

In 1871, she had worked for a while as a servant at the *London Apprentice Inn* in the little hamlet of London Apprentice, just a couple of miles outside St. Austel. If she thought Tywardreath was quiet, it had been nothing to the loneliness of London Apprentice. She liked her job there. The landlord, Mr. Williams, and his wife had been very kind and had helped her improve her speech a great deal. But the hamlet had been far too quiet for a young girl eager to see the world. The only people she met were travellers who stopped for the night before moving on, and the local farmers who drank there in the evenings. The country life held no attraction for her, so she moved on to Plymouth.

Here the streets were thronged with people, all jostling and elbowing their way from shop to shop. The roads, mostly in disrepair, were muddy and full of potholes and horse manure. When out walking one had to take care not to be pushed into the path of a horse by some impatient passerby, or worse, get splashed with excrement. Wagons of all descriptions frequently blocked the road and the noise and smell of the city was overpowering.

Janetta loved every minute of it. The town was full of life and excitement, and today she hurried along through the throng of people, her heart singing as she absorbed all the colours, noises and smells of the town.

She eventually stopped outside the butcher's and tried to remember what Mrs Atkin had asked her to get. Mrs Atkin had given her a list, but since she'd left it behind she had to rely on her memory. She'd never learned to read and write but managed to recognize a few words, especially for food items. *One moorhen and a pound of pork sausages,* she remembered just in time, and stepped inside. She never really got used to going to the butcher's shop. Seeing so much death hanging on the walls, and animals waiting their turn to be slaughtered in the pen just outside the back door made her feel uncomfortable. Beside the counter stood a small wooden wheelbarrow, which contained four or five hog's heads that stared up at her from their straw bed. The countertop was covered in blood and odd pieces of offal lay abandoned to one side. Chickens, geese and a variety of smaller fowl hung by their legs in the window, and a small collection of blood-stained knives and axes lay about the shop.

The butcher, Sam Weald, was a large red-faced man with a thick mop of unkempt hair and a roving eye. He had a bulbous nose, bright shiny cheeks and sleepy eyes. He gave you the impression you were addressing a drunkard, yet he was bright and jolly with all his customers. He very much enjoyed teasing all the women, and although the older ladies laughed and told him how "wicked" he was, the younger girls found him quite appalling. Janetta tolerated him because he was, without doubt, the finest butcher in Plymouth, and Mrs Atkin wouldn't buy from anyone else. He had a particular liking for Janetta, which she felt went beyond good-natured teasing.

"Now Mr Weald," she said getting in the first gibe as she entered the shop. "I'll take no sauce from ya today, just me shopping!"

Sam was standing in front of his counter spreading fresh sawdust on a pool of blood on the floor. He beamed at Janetta and then gave her a big squeeze on her bottom.

"You'll keep ya bloody 'ands ta yaself and give me ya best moor 'en," snapped Janetta as she sidestepped out of his grasp.

"Ah, Janetta my little darling, I've always said you've got the best rump in town," grinned Sam as he wiped his hands down the front of his stained apron.

"Bleed'n cheek!" squealed Janetta in pretended shock as she hitched her skirt round and craned her head under her arm to see if he'd left any blood stains on the back of her dress.

"A nice moorhen is it then, and a kiss to go with it? Mrs A always likes one!"

"Git awf wi ya!" said Janetta, "and I'll 'av a pand of porkers an'awl!"

The door opened and a gust of wind blew the sawdust about the floor until the door closed again. Janetta didn't turn round at first, but could tell by the heavy boots on the wood floor that it was a man.

"Morn'n sir," said Sam looking up from tying a string round the wings of the hen. Janetta glanced over her shoulder to see a soldier in his blue, tight-fitting jacket and black trousers, standing behind her. She looked back at Sam, not wishing to appear rude by staring at the stranger.

"There ya'ar me dear," said Sam. Janetta held open her basket to receive the hen. "Wot no kiss!" Sam winked at the soldier.

"Ya'll git a kiss when ya give me a full pand of sausages, an' not alf measure," grinned Janetta.

"Cheeky wench!" laughed Sam as he cut some sausages off a chain and wrapped them in brown paper.

"Mrs A 'il git ya account then?" said Janetta.

"Right you are my sweet. See ya Thursday."

Janetta placed the sausages in her basket, turned, and after squeezing passed the soldier, stepped back into the street. She was met by the sounds of wagon wheels, squealing axles, sheep bleating in a pen across the street, and the cries of several hawkers selling their wares. She hadn't gone more than a few steps when she heard someone with a slight Welsh accent calling out behind her.

"Miss, oh miss, wait a moment!"

She turned and found the soldier hurrying to catch up with her. She assumed that she had left something behind and quickly glanced down at her wicker basket containing the hen and sausages. She appeared to have everything and looked up at the soldier now standing in front of her. He wasn't particularly handsome, yet he possessed an honest face. His swarthy, sunburned look made his face stand out in contrast to his blonde hair, pale blue eyes and bushy whiskers running down the side of his cheeks.

"Morning miss," he said giving a lazy and rather unmilitary like salute. "Hope ya don't mind me running after ya like this, but I might neva sees ya agin, and I thought well..." He looked about him nervously as if not wanting to be seen, "well can I see ya sometime?"

Janetta was quite taken by his apparent nervousness. It was a pleasant change from the usual approach soldiers used when meeting young women. He wasn't brash, coarse or obnoxious; best of all, he was sober.

She also noticed his uniform. Most soldiers tended to be rather scruffy; their uniforms were creased and mud splattered after a day on the town, but this young man was quite presentable. His buttons were polished, his deep blue woollen waist-length jacket smartly pressed, and his black trousers and boots barely dust covered.

"Sir," she said putting on her best lady-like air, "we haven't been introduced. Do ya normally go around stopping young women in the street?"

"No, I assure you miss," he replied apologetically, "I never do!"

"Well ya 'ave now, and I don't go round talking to men I ain't been introduced to, see!" Janetta had let her diction slip but couldn't help chuckling to herself at having made such a bare-faced lie.

"My name's Martin," he cut in hurriedly, fearing he was losing her. "Bombardier John Martin at your service, miss. And you are?"

"Janetta Rundel," she said, and instantly rebuked herself for volunteering the information too eagerly. She virtually had him begging and she'd let him off the hook.

"There, now we're introduced," he said with some encouragement, having acquired her name. "May I buy you a lemon water, before ya rush off with that hen?"

Janetta couldn't help smiling at his pretend grimace at the sight of a hen head hanging over the edge of her basket.

"A lemon water would be very nice," she said, wishing it could be a gin but feeling she should maintain her pretence at refinement as long as she could.

John Martin offered her his arm, which she took, and they walked slowly down towards the little café at the end of the street.

****

Ethel Atkin was becoming more agitated by the minute. She was trying to prepare the evening meal but found herself slamming cupboard doors and banging pots and pans down hard on the kitchen table. She wasn't concentrating on what she was doing.

"Where on earth is that girl?" she muttered as she sprinkled flour onto the table.

Ethel Atkin was the cook at the house of Colonel Francis Wentworth, Commander of the 10th Brigade, Royal Regiment of Artillery. Janetta was the maid. She cleaned, helped Faversham serve at table and Mrs Atkin in the kitchen.

Colonel Wentworth was a robust man in his mid-fifties. He was every inch a military man; always in uniform, punctilious, a stickler for detail, having lived his life to a strict regime. The Colonel was quite particular about his likes and dislikes in food and drink, about what time he came and went from the house, dined, and went to bed. For his household staff, it was a mixed blessing. They always knew where they stood with his precise timetable, but feared the day when the routine was unavoidably broken. When things went wrong, there was hell to pay, and today Janetta was late back with the Colonel's moorhen.

"I'll skin the hen, then I'll skin 'er," muttered Ethel, working herself into a state of panic.

Ethel's panic attack was interrupted by the sound of boots coming down the kitchen stairs. It was Faversham the Colonel's butler and third member of the household staff.

"Colonel's arrived, Mrs. A," announced Faversham with his usual superior air.

Ethel found it very hard to like Thomas Faversham. He was one of those young men who considered himself a cut above the rest of the world and looked down his nose at everybody. On top of that, he was far too young to be a butler in Ethel's opinion. He had the most unsettling eyes Ethel had ever seen; they seemed to be constantly scanning the environment taking in every detail, as if storing the information for future use. Even the way he spoke occasionally gave her the creeps. She could never be sure how sincere he was. He always chose his words carefully and skillfully so that he could never be accused of holding an unpopular opinion. In short, he was always careful to appear to be on the right side. The Colonel, however, was very content with Faversham because, for all his pomposity, he was extremely good at his job. Faversham had the ability to anticipate the Colonel's every wish and, to a military mind, that meant efficiency.

"Of course he has! It's six o'clock. Why shouldn't he have arrived?" snapped Ethel as she pounded a lump of doe on the mat of flour.

"Keep ya hair on Mrs A, I'm just letting ya know he'll be ready for his dinner in alf 'n hour, that's all."

"Well dinner'll be late tonight, so stall him." Ethel waved a dismissive flour-covered hand at Faversham.

Faversham eyebrows raised slightly, "Late, Mrs A!"

"Late, Mr Faversham!" she repeated.

"Is there anything I should know Mrs A?" inquired Faversham still maintaining his calm countenance.

"That bloody girl's not back with the moorhen is she?" Ethel was growing more agitated by the minute.

"It's Tuesday, Mrs Atkin, he likes his hen on Tuesdays," replied Faversham, knowing that Ethel was fully aware of the fact.

"Go away Mr Faversham and let me get on." Ethel pointed a rolling pin menacingly in Faversham's direction. She had finally had enough of the conversation.

Faversham was about to go back upstairs when the back door opened and Janetta entered the kitchen.

"Well now!" said Faversham, anticipating some form of showdown.

"Weren't you leaving?" Ethel straightened up from kneading the dough, placed her hands on her hips and fixed an icy stare on Faversham.

"All right I'm going!" said Faversham, giving in. He retreated up the stairs.

"Now my girl, where the bleed'n 'ell 'av you been?"

****

Dinner was started over an hour late. Faversham served as usual and Janetta went back and forth to the kitchen with dishes. The

Colonel sat at the head of the table in a sullen mood, acting as though he was host to a dozen invisible and unwelcome guests. Nothing was said. The room was empty of sound but for the clicking of knife and fork on china and the ticking of the clock.

Every time Janetta came down to the kitchen, Ethel would look at her and shake her head. Faversham was icy. It was as if the whole house were waiting for some great calamity to befall them.

By eight o'clock the Colonel had finally finished his meal. Scraping his chair back, he left the table and retired to the library for his cigar and brandy.

Faversham looked at Janetta and raised his eyes to the ceiling. She didn't care what he thought. "*Faversham is a prat*," she thought. Ethel's displeasure, however, bothered Janetta more because she really liked her. However, she wasn't going to give either of them the satisfaction of knowing she was sorry. She may have caused the atmosphere that filled the house, but she wasn't regretting her afternoon with the smart soldier.

She cleared the table of dirty dishes and laid the silverware on the top of the sideboard. Faversham brushed crumbs from the tablecloth.

As she was putting the condiments back into the sideboard cupboard, Faversham cleared his throat in an obvious attempt at getting Janetta's attention. She turned to see him standing beside the colonel's chair, frozen in the act of lifting his napkin off the table. He transfixed Janetta with his eyes and then directed them down to where the colonel had been sitting. There on the table where the napkin had been was the Colonel's small blue pocket book.

The abandoned pocket book was the Colonel's signal that he wanted an audience with the guilty party.

Faversham grinned at Janetta. It was a nasty, knowing grin that told her he knew what was about to happen and wished he could be there to witness it.

Janetta walked over to the table and looked Faversham right in the eye. With a nonchalant smile on her face, she picked up the little book and slid it into her apron pocket. She was damned if she was going to let Faversham gloat. She would show him that she was quite unconcerned about the treatment she would shortly be receiving. As she passed him to leave the room, she deliberately brushed herself up against him and felt his frustration, for she knew he secretly desired her.

Janetta left the dining room and closed the door behind her. She crossed the hall to the library fingering the book in her apron pocket. Faversham returned to the kitchen grinning slyly at the thought of what was going to happen. Ethel sat by the kitchen table watching him come down the stairs and wished he'd wipe the stupid grin off his face. They both understood what it meant when Janetta was summoned to the Colonel's library. Ethel felt very uncomfortable with the ritual, but had lived with it since long before Janetta had come to the house. Most of the previous maids had endured it and many had left the Colonel's service because of it; only Janetta took it in her stride. Faversham seemed to get pleasure out of it and delighted in making crude jokes at Janetta's expense. This angered Ethel a great deal and she frequently told him so.

Janetta stopped outside the library door and gathered herself. She'd stood on this spot many times before, always when she had committed some small misdemeanour and had come to receive her punishment. It was always the same routine and always the same part she had to play.

In truth she really didn't mind these punishment sessions. At first she thought them strange, even demeaning, but in time they became a sort of game between the Colonel and her, and an odd affection had grown between them.

She knocked on the door. From inside came a cough followed by the gruff command. "Enter."

She twisted the brass doorknob and entered the smoke-filled room.

The Colonel stood with his back to the fire. His feet were firmly planted at shoulder width and his left arm hidden behind his back. In his right hand he held a large cigar, which he raised to his mouth and sucked hard on before releasing a great cloud of blue smoke that rose above his head. He had replaced his dress uniform jacket with a green paisley smoking jacket.

"Come in, girl!" he demanded.

Janetta closed the door behind her, walked further into the room and stood before him. His manner was quite intimidating, and Janetta felt sure the men under his command would have been shaking in their boots if they stood before him witnessing this power. She felt quite calm though, seeing under his stern attitude the kind heart of a very lonely man.

"So you were responsible for my dinner being one hour and seven minutes late, were you?"

"Yes, sir," she replied with her eyes downcast and head lowered. She knew the form. She knew by heart what was coming next. "*We can't have this kind of slack behaviour...*" she could hear him saying in her mind. And then…

"We can't have this kind of slack behavior, can we? It will never do young lady!" yelled the Colonel in his most frightening voice.

Janetta imagined Ethel and Faversham listening from the kitchen stairs.

"No sir, I'm very sorry sir," she repented.

"Well you know what we must do!" he said, still with a great deal of sharpness to his voice. He turned and sat down on the easy chair by the side of the fire. Janetta walked close to him, dropped to her knees and bent forward over his lap stretching her arms out above her head.

The Colonel raised her dress and petticoat up over her back and then pulled down her bloomers. He looked at her bare buttocks for a second or two and then began to smack her quite hard.

These punishments puzzled Janetta. Being seduced by her employer didn't come as a shock to her. Indeed most of her friends were in domestic service and had been seduced or even raped by the master of the house. One of her friends had even married her employer and become the mistress of the house, but the Colonel had never tried to seduce Janetta.

As she lay across his knees and stared into the fire, she remembered that sunny afternoon on the cliffs so many years before, when Phineas had warned her against becoming a whore and had suggested that she could still prosper by using her talents more discreetly.

She was now twenty-one-years old, beautiful and shapely, and yet the Colonel only seemed interested in this perverted act of domination. Was this his only sexual outlet? Was he too shy to go further? Perhaps she could profit from this situation after all. Maybe she needed to take control and seduce him. Maybe she could make him love her.

Janetta winced at the first sharp sting, but then settled in to withstand the rest as best she could. After several hard smacks the Colonel began to dramatically soften the blows. Janetta knew that he had no intention of seriously hurting her. The blows became softer and softer until at last he was barely caressing her. His hand came to rest on her reddened and glowing buttock and for just a few seconds his fingers very gently stroked her. Then, as suddenly as it had begun, he told her to get up and he stood once more before the fire.

"Let that be a lesson to you my girl," he said. "You can go now!"

Janetta rearranged her clothing then stood before him and looked him straight in the eye. "*What a poor man*," she thought. In him she saw a man full of love and longing. He was a man who was only truly comfortable on the parade ground in the company of other men. A man who had no social graces, especially where women were concerned, who had never been married and, she suspected, had never really been with a woman, other than some whores in his early soldiering days. Perhaps, she thought, not even that.

He was sad and pathetic. His only outlet for a sexual relationship was his clumsy attempt at disciplining his maids. Yet Janetta quite liked him. God knows she was no angel. She'd lost count of how many men and boys she'd been with; so why should she judge him for his short moments of pleasure? He never hurt her. He was always apologetic the day afterwards, and he wasn't that bad looking. The fact that he was old enough to be her father didn't really bother her. What did that matter? She may only be a maid, but she was young and beautiful and quite possibly the only woman the Colonel had any sexual connection with. "*He was*," she thought, "*ripe for the picking*." If she could coax him into loving her, she'd gain status as his mistress. If she could manoeuvre him into marrying her she'd be rich, and she'd be the mistress of a beautiful house. Janetta felt confident she could seduce him.

She took a step towards him and placed one hand on his chest.

"I found ya pocket book on the dining table," she said, looking straight up into his tired eyes. "You're always losing that, aren't ya, sir?" She knew only too well it was left behind deliberately, but enjoyed the teasing.

"Very careless of me, isn't it?" he said to her in a low whisper. He knew he was being teased but allowed himself the pleasure of the moment.

"I think I should return it to you... later."

The Colonel stared at her, not believing his ears. Was she really seducing him?

"Shall we say your room at eleven?"

The Colonel swallowed hard and nodded.

CHAPTER 4

The Proposal

During the following weeks, Janetta led a double life. On her days off she met John Martin in town and went on picnics and walks in the country. He was always very attentive and for an ordinary soldier, quite the young gentleman. Naturally they had their moments when alone in some secluded spot and they'd kiss and cuddle against a tree. Occasionally she'd allow him to fondle her breasts, but for the most part John treated her with respect. He was surprisingly shy when it came to lovemaking and Janetta felt that if she wanted him, she'd have to do the seducing.

John was fun to be with, full of energy and charm, yet marrying him never really entered her mind. He was, after all, just a bombardier in the army. He'd never have any real money, and being married to a common soldier was not an easy life for a young woman, being dragged from camp to camp never knowing where you could call home.

Meanwhile, back at the house, she continued to pay late night visits to the Colonel's bed. It had started as just one night a week, then two, but very soon she was spending almost every night with him. She still received his occasional punishments for real or perceived misdemeanours, and she found herself being drawn increasingly deeper into his fantasy world. Her spankings seemed to give him special pleasure and he continued them despite having her in his bed on a regular basis. He kept the two activities quite separate. When she was in his bed he treated her tenderly as he would a loving wife, but the spankings were carried out as if he were in a whorehouse and Janetta was just another paid tart. Not that he frequented the whorehouses anymore. That was far too risky. He could have been spotted by one of the men in his regiment. His officers occasionally invited him to private parties where local women made themselves available, but his natural shyness prevented him from enjoying them.

No, his own servants were more to his liking, and Janetta was the best he'd ever had.

Despite his pretence at punishment he never hurt her and always ended up speaking kindly, almost apologetically to her. Later he would thank her with some small gift.

Faversham and Ethel Atkins went about their business in the house and said nothing, but Faversham secretly envied the Colonel and his frustration festered. Occasionally, he grabbed Janetta by the arm on the stairs or in an empty room and hissed at her that she was "*no better than a common whore*." Janetta would pull away from his grip and tell him to mind his own business. Ethel, realizing that Janetta had become the Colonel's mistress, sometimes gently enquired of her if she was all right, and was the Colonel treating her kindly? But otherwise she kept out of her business.

Everything was going Janetta's way. Life was good for her during the cold November of 1875. She was dating John Martin once a week, keeping up the appearance of a happy couple, while maintaining an ongoing affair with the Colonel at home. As long as she could keep from becoming pregnant she could look forward to soon becoming the mistress of the house. She knew only too well that a pregnancy would push the Colonel into a corner and spoil everything. There was a danger he might simply throw her out onto the streets. It happened to so many unfortunate girls in service who became an embarrassment. No, she must stay in control and he must be made to come to her on his knees, of his own accord.

Janetta had always known that she was good at manipulating men and this situation required all her skill. In his bed at night she slowly made herself as indispensable as possible. She advised him on matters concerning the running of the household, always careful never to step on Ethel's toes, and when he became frustrated with politics among the officers of the regiment she coaxed him in the ways of manipulation.

She quite surprised herself. So much skill came pouring from this young miner's daughter from Tywardreath. When she saw how impressed the Colonel was with her advice, she couldn't help giggling to herself and dreaming of all the nice clothes she would wear after they were married.

How easy it had all been. She remembered what Phineus had told her about using her talents discreetly, and how right he'd been. Being blessed with natural beauty and a love of the physical pleasures of sex was going to make her a lady. Oh, how deliciously wicked it was to have such power over men and how thoroughly she enjoyed herself at the same time.

****

Two weeks before Christmas, on a freezing Sunday afternoon, Janetta walked through the gray and white streets of Plymouth, her head bowed and her back bent forward into the wind. Her ears were red and burning with the chilly wind, and she held her scarf in front of her face to ease her breathing.

There were very few people venturing out in the cold. Only the occasional hardy soul braved the weather to carry on their trade. It had been a week since Janetta had seen John, and although her relationship with the Colonel was growing ever closer, she found herself missing her young soldier's company. She had been careful not to get too intimate with him for fear of the Colonel finding out, yet she was sorely tempted at times.

She arrived at the Swan Inn, stamped the snow off her boots and went inside, where she was met by the smell of stale beer, wood smoke and a gruff voice demanding that she, "close the bloody door."

Her eyes, watering from the cold wind, adjusted to the gloom in the bar. There weren't many people inside: a couple of local fisherman, half a dozen labourers, and a man with his back to her sitting in the shadows by the fire. She glanced around for John but didn't see him. The innkeeper's rotund and buxom wife waddled over to her carrying four pots of ale. Her nose was red and running and her eyes bloodshot. She looked as though she didn't have the energy to last the afternoon.

"Allo Jan dear, looking for ya young man are ya?"

"Is he 'ere Betsy?" asked Janetta in a half whisper.

"Oh yeh," replied her friend much too loudly giving a big sniff, "'e's in the back room waiting sort of anxious like."

"Ta Betsy!" said Janetta as she brushed passed her and made her way to the door at the back of the room.

The young man sitting by the fire looked up and followed Janetta with his eyes as she disappeared through the back room door. It was Faversham.

The back room was very cosy and quiet. A fire glowed in the grate and a beautiful bay window looked out over the harbour, but today there was nothing to see but driving snow. In the middle of the room was a table laid out in preparation for a meal. John was sitting on the window bench in his smart blue uniform; he stood up as soon as she entered.

"Jan, it's wonderful to see ya!" he exclaimed. "'Ere let me take your cloak!" He stepped forward and helped her off with her wet cloak and hung it on a coat peg. Janetta wondered why he seemed so unusually nervous.

"What's all this then, John? Private room? Meal? You're lashing out a bit ain't ya?"

"I wan' it ta be special see, Jan, I wan' it to be right."

John pulled her to him, and Janetta found herself being kissed hard and passionately, his two-day stubble prickling against her face. After a minute or two, during which Janetta thought she'd never breathe again, he let her go and walked to the table.

"Some brandy wine Jan?" he asked

"Blimey, brandy wine. You made of money or sumfing?" Janetta had never actually had brandy wine. It was the Colonel's favourite. She'd sniffed at the decanter when nobody else was in the library, but never dared taste it for fear of somebody smelling it on her breath.

"'Ere get this down ya," said John, handing her a glass of amber liquid.

The door opened and Betsy came in with a couple of pewter platters of lamb and potatoes.

"There ya'are me dears." Then lowering her voice to John only, "ya can lock the door if ya want."

"Thank you Betsy, you're a darlin an' no mistake," said John winking at Janetta, who did her best to hide a smirk.

Betsy laid the platters on the table and turned to leave, but not before receiving a good slap on her ample rump.

"Mr John be'ave ya self," she protested as she swiped her hand at the air behind her. Then turning to Janetta with a half concealed grin "ya better watch 'im deary, 'e's got a lot of hands that one."

“Go on, ya luv it Betsy, don’t say ya don’t!” laughed John.

“Cheeky blighter!” said Betsy, closing the door behind her and she disappeared back to the bar.

John sat across the table from Janetta and grinned like a mischievous child who’s just gotten away with a prank. After a few seconds of silence, they both broke out in a fit of giggles.

It felt good to be with John again. He had no money or prospects, but he seemed to be a good man who, Janetta thought, would make an ideal husband for someone. She’d consider him herself but she had her eye firmly fixed on the Colonel.

They ate their meal and enjoyed pleasant conversation for an hour in the glow of the fire.

“*How odd it is*,” Janetta thought, “*that I enjoy this man’s company so much and yet I’ve never had sex with him.*” Why that should have been, she had no idea. It certainly wasn’t for lack of opportunity or even desire on her part. John had always been a gentleman, or perhaps he was just shy. Either way it was unusual for a soldier to be so polite and hesitant in these matters. She’d had her share of drunken and amorous soldiers, and she had become quite capable of handling them. But John’s reticence unnerved her. What was it that kept bringing her back to see him?

At the end of the meal, John pushed his plate away from under his nose, leaned on his elbows and fixed his stare on Janetta. She felt uneasy as though she was being scrutinized and stared intently back as if in a showdown.

“What’s the matter wi’ you then?” she asked, trying to keep the atmosphere light.

John stood up and walked around to Janetta’s side of the table. She pushed her chair back and stood up in an effort to remain facing him. John stopped in front of her and looked down at her upturned face. There was a strange calm determination on his face that Janetta found quite exciting. Was he going to kiss her? She prepared herself for his advance, but was surprised when no kiss came to her. Instead he held her by the arms and then slowly dropped onto one knee, his face turning upward to stay focused on her.

“Jan” he swallowed hard and made an effort to gather strength in his voice, “will ya marry me?”

****

Out in the public bar Faversham swallowed down the last of his ale and wiped his mouth by dragging his sleeve across his face. He stared at the closed door to the back room, full of anger. The ale fogged his thinking and his chest ached. He recognized that it wasn't the soldier that made him angry; after all, he was a man and Janetta was beautiful. Of course he fancied her. No, it was Janetta who really angered him. She treated him with scorn, while giving herself willingly to the old Colonel, and having clandestine meetings with her soldier boy once a week.

"Oh yes!" he muttered to himself, "She's the whore. She's the one who needs bringing down a peg or two."

He stood up and thrust his arms into his greatcoat. After taking one last look at the closed door, he turned away and left the bar lowering his head into the wind and snow.

His walk through the town was a trial of bitter wind and hot temper. How he had longed to have Janetta in his bed, her breasts to kiss, her kisses showered upon him. He knew that would never be; he was nothing to her. He was less than nothing, and that made him furious. She'd never look at him, as long as she saw herself as the future mistress of the house, and he was damned if he was going to let that happen.

As he walked, his head slowly cleared and his mind focused. His way to Janetta lay in first bringing her back down to her rightful level. Down to a level where he would be above her in social standing, albeit below stairs. He found himself surprised by the fact that the more he planned the more his anger subsided. The lust for revenge slowly became a plot to redemption. He began to see himself as her saviour; the one who would catch her as she fell from favour. All he had to do was set the ball in motion and await events. It was going to be so very easy.

Faversham arrived back at the house and went down the steps to the servants' entrance in the basement. Once inside he removed his coat and shook it free of snow.

"Mrs A has the Colonel come in yet?" he called into the kitchen.

Ethel walked into the foyer wiping her hands on a tea towel.

“Not yet, fortunately you’ve beaten him,” she said. “Where’ve you been on an afternoon like this?”

“Out Mrs A, just out!” replied Faversham in a tone that implied it was none of her business.

He went upstairs to set out the Colonel’s nightclothes and make sure there was brandy wine and tobacco ready for him.

“Ave ya seen that girl while you were out?” called Ethel up the stairs after him.

“No,” he lied, as he disappeared onto the ground floor.

****

Janetta was quite taken aback by John’s formal proposal and rather flattered. She hadn’t expected it. Perhaps if she’d paid more attention to him during the previous few weeks, she may have seen it coming, but she had been far too preoccupied by her own manoeuvering around the Colonel.

“Oh John, ya are a dear to be sure,” she said as she looked down on his sweet, expectant face, as he knelt before her.

“Say yes, Jan, do say yes.”

Her head swam and she was tempted to say yes, but a common soldier’s wife was not what she had in mind at all. She decided to stall for time.

“Oh sweet John! Dearest John!”

“Yes my luv?” John interrupted like a child impatient to open a gift.

“John ya must give me a little time to consider. I’m flattered and honoured that you asked me, and I luvs ya, ya know that don’t ya?”

“An I luv ya too Jan, I really do. I’ll takes good care of ya. Promise I will.”

“I knows ya will John, I knows.”

John found himself becoming bolder than he’d ever been before. He didn’t press her further for an answer but laid his head sideways against her stomach and slowly ran his hands up the backs of her legs. He expected her to pull away from him, but she didn’t. Encouraged by her lack of objection, he proceeded up to her buttocks and paused for a minute with his hands cupping her cheeks.

Dare he go further? He was on the verge of destroying a perfectly romantic proposal. He could lose her at this moment, but Janetta didn't flinch.

She put both her hands on his upper arms and very slowly stepped backwards towards the table. She wasn't trying to get loose from him. In fact, as she backed up she pulled him forward on his knees. Presently she backed into the table and John had to lower his hands to avoid having his fingers pinched between the edge of the table, and her buttocks.

She reached back and slid the platters and wineglasses aside before lifting herself onto the table and lying back across it. John stood up, finding himself between her knees. He could barely believe what was happening. She lay on the table before him with her bright eyes sparkling and a slight smile in the corner of her lips.

"Well," she whispered. "What are ya waiting fer?"

John tried to swallow but found his mouth too dry. He lifted her dress and petticoats, reached forward with both hands, and pulled her bloomers down off her legs, and let them drop in a heap on the floor.

He tried to undo his britches, but his hands fumbled and trembled.

"Cum 'ere," said Janetta and she undid them for him.

For the next fifteen minutes John could hardly believe what was happening. He was like a man possessed. He cared about nothing in the world but the moment. He didn't think about the consequences, or about being caught by somebody entering the room. He just concentrated on how it felt and the expression on Janetta's face. He was in a different world, and nobody could have done anything to spoil it for him. She was his, and although she hadn't said yes to his proposal, her submission made it plain that she wanted him.

John suddenly grabbed Janetta by the shoulders and pulled her tightly into his groin. His body gave a great shudder and he collapsed forward on top of her. For a minute or two they both lay still, panting hard, with perspiration running down their faces. Janetta rolled her head to one side and grasped John's head holding it tightly against the side of her face.

Then her eyes met the clock on the mantel, "Christ John, I gotta go. The Colonel will be back soon!"

She pushed John away from her and rolled sideways off the table. She frantically pulled her bloomers back on, and grabbing her cloak headed for the door. But before opening it, she stopped and looked back. John had collapsed into a chair and was stuffing his shirt into the front of his britches; she hurried back and kissed him on the forehead.

"Gotta go!" she whispered in a soothing voice, then turned and hurried out of the room.

****

The Colonel arrived home uncharacteristically late that evening. Dinner was ready to serve, and Ethel was getting concerned that it would spoil if he didn't settle down to eat soon.

As soon as the Colonel came through the front door, Faversham could tell he was agitated. He snorted a "good evening" and threw his cloak on the hall table before storming straight into the dining room. His cloak slithered onto the floor and it was left to Faversham to pick up and hang on the coat hook.

"Is dinner ready?" the Colonel bellowed.

Faversham hastily followed him into the dining room and did his best to catch up with all the little niceties he performed for the Colonel on a regular basis. Tonight the routine was broken.

"Oh stop fussing man!" snapped the Colonel as he made for the drink decanter.

Faversham, seeing what he was about to do, stepped forward and attempted to take the decanter and glass from him.

"Leave it, I can do it!" The Colonel was in no mood to be waited on tonight. "Damn fine Christmas this is going to be!" he muttered under his voice as he poured a large brandy wine.

"I'll inform cook you're ready to eat, sir," said Faversham as he backed out of the room.

Faversham walked down the hall and when safely out of earshot, he bolted down the stairs to the kitchen.

"Mrs A, the Colonel's ready to eat and he's in a foul mood I can tell ya!" Ethel was already putting dishes into the dumb waiter ready to be hoisted up to the ground floor. "You know he wouldn't even allow me to pour his drink for him."

"Ooo, I say!" said Ethel. "Wonder what's got into him?" She gave a sideways glance at Janetta who was busily straightening out her apron.

"Don't look at me Mrs A, I dunnos, do I?" she said.

"Well come on girl," snapped Faversham. "Get upstairs fast."

Dinner was more quiet and hurried than usual that evening. The Colonel didn't seem to enjoy anything that was put in front of him, although he didn't complain. Depending on the particular offering, he either picked at his food or stuffed it in his mouth as fast as he could.

When he'd finished he stood up and, without comment, left the room for the library where he immediately lit up a cigar.

Faversham and Janetta proceeded as usual to clear the table. The Colonel's little pocket book lay under his napkin.

"Well you're wanted again!" said Faversham in a sly tone. "Quite a busy day for you!"

"What do ya mean by that?" Janetta bristled. Surely he couldn't know about her afternoon with John, could he?

"Nothing!" Faversham almost sang the word as though he wanted to tease her but couldn't really be bothered. "Nothing at all!"

He left the room and crossed the hall to the library to attend to the Colonel.

"Faversham," commanded the Colonel before he'd even closed the door behind him. "I want you to pack a trunk. I'll require dress and day uniforms and sufficient clothes for say, two weeks, yes, that should be enough. Plus my guns, of course!"

"May I inquire as to the reason for this sudden departure, sir?"

"Damned army, Faversham! They're splitting the regiment, confound them. Half of us are being stationed in Exeter for six bloody weeks. M'Lord Cornwall has asked me to go with 'em."

"Ah!" was all Faversham could think of saying.

"Damn and tarnation Faversham, this will utterly spoil my Christmas plans."

"Christmas plans, sir?" Faversham enquired. This came as a complete surprise to him. The Colonel never planned anything for Christmas. He was, above all, a quiet solitary man who usually spent Christmas in front of the fire with a book.

"Yes, Christmas, Faversham!" he half whispered in frustration. Then looking up from studying his cigar, "I was planning on holding a dinner party at Christmas for all my friends. I was planning on making an announcement." He turned away from Faversham and stared into the fire. Faversham remained silent.

"But now it will have to wait." The Colonel sat back into his favourite chair, continuing to stare into the flames. "You can pour me a brandy." He paused as if composing the next sentence. "I was going to announce something very important. Something that will affect you all." Faversham handed him his drink. "But now you will all have to make your own arrangements for Christmas. I won't be here. Won't be needing you!" Looking up, almost apologetically, at Faversham, "I shan't be taking you with me, Faversham. I'll have a battalion man to look after me. You can have Christmas off." He took a large swig of brandy. "You can go home, you can *all* go home! I'll shut up the house 'til January."

"Yes sir," was all Faversham could think to say. He had momentarily forgotten his plan to denounce Janetta. This turn of events was unparalleled and had quite taken him off guard. The Colonel waved a dismissing hand towards Faversham, but as Faversham got close to the door, he said,"Tell Miss Rundel to come and see me."

"Yes sir," replied Faversham in a slightly disapproving tone. He had been reminded of his plan for this evening, which had now been circumvented by the Colonel's sudden announcement to depart the next morning. He was now going to be far too busy preparing the Colonel's trunk to raise the subject. Besides the Colonel was in no frame of mind to receive bad news about his mistress.

****

Janetta tapped lightly on the library door and timidly entered. She wasn't sure what kind of reception she was going to get. Faversham had made it quite clear to her that the Colonel was in a bad mood.

The Colonel said nothing. He continued to sit and stare into the fire. Janetta slowly walked over and stopped a couple of feet in front of him. He held out his hand to her.

"Come here, girl," he said very quietly and gently, putting Janetta more at ease. She took his hand and knelt down beside him. The fire crackled and the flames warmed her face.

"I was planning a wonderful Christmas for you," he said. "It was going to be very special. But I have to leave with my battalion. I'll be gone about six weeks."

He paused and Janetta laid her head on his knees.

"Will you be alright while I'm gone?"

"Yeh, I'll be fine."

"I want you in my bed tonight, Jan. Six weeks is going to be a long time without you."

"What were you planning for Christmas?" Janetta asked, fishing for some concrete evidence that he was going to propose to her.

"A big dinner party Jan, a big lavish dinner party!"

He didn't want to tell her at that moment what his plans were, not now that they were cancelled. It seemed cruel to disappoint her. It would have to wait until he got back.

"You'd better get back downstairs now, but I'll see you later, about eleven?"

"I'll be there," said Janetta as she got up.

****

The next morning the household said their goodbyes to the Colonel and made their arrangements for closing down the house. In the afternoon Janetta walked down to the Barracks. There she joined the crowds gathered to wave goodbye to the seven hundred men of the Tenth Artillery Battalion as they left for the railway station.

When they marched out she saw the Colonel leading the column on horseback. He looked so grand and heroic in his blue uniform and black cap, but she took care not to let him see her. It would be undignified for a Colonel to be seen acknowledging a servant girl in public, and she had no desire to embarrass him. She also didn't want him to know that she was there to wave goodbye to one of his men.

Once the Colonel had passed by, she stepped forward to the front of the crowd and eagerly studied the faces of the troops. There was John, sixth line back and second in from her side. What luck, he would be able to hear her as she called out to him. She watched him march closer. How smart he looked in his blue greatcoat with the red collar, his firearm slung over his shoulder and, on his back, a black pack and rolled blanket.

"John, John," she called as he came near to her, and she was much relieved to see a slight grin come over his face and his head turned, so very slightly, towards her. He knew she was there and he felt a warm glow inside knowing his girl had come to see him off.

She stood there in the street and waved at the column, even after John had passed and could no longer see her. John and the Colonel were out of sight, the house was closed up for Christmas, and standing alone in the steadily thinning crowd, Janetta suddenly felt very cold and lonely.

CHAPTER 5

Christmas and New Year

Colonel Wentworth's carriage pulled up outside the main entrance of Elstram Hall, a large Georgian mansion on the outskirts of Exeter. The front driveway was congested with carriages as guests arrived for the annual Christmas Ball. The coachman expected the Colonel to remain seated in the carriage until he had, in his turn, stopped in front of the steps leading up to the main door. To his consternation the Colonel became impatient with the wait and got out.

There was a slight rain, but the Colonel didn't seem to notice as he walked the last few yards to the cover of the entrance. A doorman standing between the pillars at the top of the steps saw him coming and frowned, half expecting to be harangued about the jam up of carriages. He needn't have been concerned as the Colonel walked straight past him and entered the hall. A footman wearing green livery and an out-of-date powdered wig met him and took his cloak and helmet. A second footman asked his name before indicating that he should follow him into the main hall.

The vestibule was full of people and glowed with the light of dozens of ornate oil lamps and two enormous candled chandeliers. He could hear the orchestra playing a waltz and, for a few seconds, he was overcome by a sudden sense of panic. He wasn't used to these society functions and felt out of place. He dreaded the prospect of having to dance with some very stylish ladies. Undoubtedly, he would tread on their toes and confirm their suspicions that he was just another provincial clod of a soldier with no redeeming social graces.

The footman led him through two large and brightly gilded doors then stopped at the top of a short flight of stairs and announced, "Colonel Wentworth". Nobody seemed to hear or pay the slightest bit of interest in the new arrival, for which he felt very much relieved. He stood at the top of the stairs rather woodenly, looking out over a sea of glittering people on the dance floor, and wondered where he could get a drink.

"Viscount and Lady Hornchurch," announced the footman, The Colonel, realizing he was blocking the entrance of the new arrivals, mumbled his apologies and advanced down the stairs.

The ball was very grand with, he suspected, at least five hundred guests. The women all sported their finest and most fashionable gowns, and he had to admit to himself that there was an abundance of beauty and style in the room. The gentlemen were a mixed group. Many of them wore the usual evening dress of black tail suit and stiff white dress shirt, but at least half wore military uniforms. From the uniforms they wore, at least three regiments and the Navy were present. Red dress uniforms and gold braid were everywhere. Colonel Wentworth felt almost drab in his Artillery Blue, but he wore it with pride, nonetheless. He'd taken great care in making sure his boots gleamed with a mirror finish; his medals were polished and arrayed on his chest in just the right order.

A footman walked past him with a tray of champagne glasses and the Colonel removed one. He wasn't that fond of champagne but having swallowed a quick mouthful of the sparkling liquid he felt better. Two or three more gulps and he might actually feel confident enough to speak to somebody. He began to walk slowly around the outside of the hall trying to find someone he knew. He felt extraordinarily lonely in such a crowd and already began to wonder if coming had been such a good idea. He saw several of his junior officers laughing with some young, beautiful girls that reminded him of Janetta. As he ambled past them they politely acknowledged him but didn't invite him to join them.

He placed his empty glass on a side table and liberated a full one from another footman's tray. He wasn't sure he even wanted champagne. He much preferred brandy, but there didn't seem to be any choice.

"Fanny, you old rogue, how are you?"

The Colonel winced. He used to be called "Fanny" when he was a junior officer. The only person who called him that now was General Cornelius Cartwright. He turned around to meet his old friend.

"You never could get used to calling me Francis, could you General?" he replied somewhat stiffly.

"Cornelius old boy, please. No need to be formal here, eh?" The General beamed at him with a look that suggested he'd had at least four or five drinks already. "Still with the Tenth are you?"

The Colonel nodded, took another mouthful of champagne and idly watched a couple of young girls giggling behind their fans.

"With the Thirty-fourth myself. Rogues and rascals the lot of 'em, but fine fellows! Danced with that divine little filly in the blue gown yet, 'ave you?" He indicated the lady in question with a wave of his champagne glass.

The Colonel shook his head and shifted feet nervously. "I've just got here actually. You're the first person I've spoken to."

The General, who was a good four inches taller than the Colonel and as thin as a rake, looked down at him and gave a sympathetic smile. Then in lowered tone he said, "Never were one for society, were you? An army man through and through, eh?"

The Colonel smiled with embarrassment.

"Much prefer the company of your fellow officers than the idle chit-chat of the ladies, eh? I know!" The General took his arm and led him to a window alcove where they would not be so easily overheard. "Did you ever get yourself a wife my old friend?"

The Colonel shook his head. The General was one of his oldest friends and perhaps the only one he could talk to. Cornelius was brash and downright bawdy at times, but he was also discreet and sincerely mindful of his friend's problems. Francis Wentworth, by now on his third champagne and in the company of his oldest friend, now found himself thinking about Janetta.

"There's nothing like having a good woman in your bed, old man!" continued the General. "Oh sure! It's good to get ya leg over a whore now and then, but a steady wife is worth her weight in gold. Take it from me ol' boy!"

"Think I've finally found her actually," he heard himself reply.

"Stout fellow, knew you had it in you!"

"But there's a problem, you see, and I don't know what to do about it. Not had this problem before!"

"Somebody else's is she? Sticky!"

"No, no, that's not it. Not it at all!"

"Is the lady willing?"

"Oh yes!" Francis beamed. "She's willing alright!" He took another sip of champagne. Perhaps he liked champagne after all, he thought.

A short, bald and rather effeminate man in his mid-fifties came over to them with a buxom and rather overly made up lady on his arm.

"General, it's a real pleasure seeing you again – my word it is! May I present my wife, Joanna."

"My Lord," Cornelius clicked his heels together and gave a slight bow of the head. "Lady Pulham, the pleasure is all mine." He kissed her hand and smiled broadly at her. "And may I present to you, Colonel Francis Wentworth of the Tenth Brigade Royal Artillery."

"I hope you're enjoying the ball, Colonel," said Lady Pulham in a weak yet self-confident voice.

"Very much my Lady!" replied the Colonel rather nervously.

"Do dance with the ladies, gentlemen, it's a crime to have two such distinguished gentlemen not dancing," she pleaded, before gliding away into the crowd with her husband in tow.

"That was our host," said Cornelius in a slightly mocking tone. "Now back to your problem. The lady is willing!"

"Yes indeed! Yes." The Colonel wanted advice so much, but felt damned uncomfortable talking about it. "She's a real beauty Cornelius, she really is! But she's not… well she's…"

"She's not," interrupted Cornelius in an attempt to help the Colonel spit it out. "as wealthy as you thought, eh?"

"No she's not wealthy… but I knew she wasn't you see." He took another swallow of champagne. "In fact, she has no money at all!"

"Ah, I see! Good family though eh? After all money's not everything. As long as the stock is sound."

"Damn it! Cornelius," the Colonel interrupted irritably, "she's my maid." There he'd said it.

There followed a short silence between them as Cornelius replayed what the Colonel had said in his mind. Then brightening up he slapped the Colonel on the arm and rocked with laughter.

"Well you old rogue. Good for you, what! If she's a pretty thing there's no harm in a kiss and cuddle with a domestic, is there? Does you good, in fact!"

"I love her," the Colonel whispered through clenched teeth, feeling himself becoming maudlin. "But I could never bring her out could I? She's been trying to improve her diction and she's very intelligent." He brightened up as he tried to convince himself, as well as Cornelius, but he knew what he was saying was madness. "She's very presentable when she's dressed up, and has a bright wit you know!"

"Yes, yes, I'm sure she's quite delightful," Cornelius tried to comfort his old friend. "It won't do tho', will it? Think about it. Plymouth is a small town and you know how tongues do wag. Take it from me old boy, the first time you have friends over for tea, there'll be gossip all throughout society. Best thing is to keep quiet about her and slip her in your bed whenever you fancy. Nobody'll be any the wiser, and if they are…well they'll just wink and nod and think what a delightful old rogue you are."

"She thinks… she suspects, that I'm going to propose to her after Christmas. What can I do? She'll be horribly disappointed. She's already started making plans about the running of the house an' all."

"Tactical retreat I think old boy, time for strategic withdrawal."

"Don't want to hurt her feelings you see. She's been good to me."

"General, you wicked man, you promised me a dance." It was a small delicate lady in her mid-thirties, the Colonel guessed, and she had clasped Cornelius' arm and was pulling him toward the dance floor. "Do excuse us, won't you?" she said to him, and the General shrugged an apology and handed him his glass to look after, as he allowed himself to be dragged away.

The ball held no charms for the Colonel for the rest of the evening so he excused himself early and retreated back into the rain and the gentle quiet of the night.

It had been a short discussion with Cornelius Cartwright, but the words of his oldest friend had put into focus what he already knew. And, although he didn't look forward to it, he knew he had to disappoint Janetta. He resolved to speak to her as soon as he got back to Plymouth.

****

On the cold and snowy morning of December 26th, 1875, Janetta and her sister Jane and Jane's husband, Thomas Vanson, boarded the hansom carriage hired to take them the mile from Chapel Down, through Tywardreath and on to Par Station. The goodbyes had been tearful. Her father was looking older and Christmas had been a bittersweet visit for Janetta.

Janetta's mother was still uncomfortable about her living and working so far from home and privately she had expressed concern about her lifestyle. An argument had broken out between them on Christmas Eve. Elizabeth, had called her daughter a 'little whore' and had railed at Janetta accusing her, amongst other things, of being the 'biggest hussy' in Tywardreath. Janetta hit back with, "Well you don't mind a bleed'n kiss and cuddle now 'n' then does ya?" An obvious reference to Phineas. It was lucky that most of the family were out for an after lunch walk in the snow. Only Phineas was in the house, and he had come into the kitchen to step between mother and daughter before they exchanged blows.

Elizabeth had retreated to her room in tears, and Janetta, red in the face and wild with anger had lashed out at Phineas accusing him of coming between her mother and father. Phineas had taken her outburst very calmly, although he denied nothing, he made conciliatory gestures designed to calm the situation before everybody came home from their walk.

Janetta had later apologized to her mother, but the accusations, once made, could not be forgotten. She had stepped into the coach that morning feeling that a rift had opened that would take a very long time to heal.

Her father had been as loving and emotional as always during the goodbyes, and it seemed he knew nothing of the fight. That at least was a blessing. Her sister Jane on the other hand had sensed the atmosphere, and fully aware of Janetta's appetites, somehow put two and two together.

There was a silence in the carriage as they pulled away from the cottages at Chapel Down. They all sat huddled in blankets and made themselves as comfortable as possible for the cold journey. The windows had frost on the inside and the two doors fit so badly against their frames that a freezing draft blew in around their legs.

Janetta wrapped her shawl about her face and stared at the white mist of her breath that pulsed into the air and faded like winter spectres. Opposite her sat Thomas who said nothing and avoided her gaze. He was caught between sisters and wished to avoid any personal involvement. He always secretly admired Janetta and envied any man who found her favour. He was careful not to let his wife know of this, as she was openly critical and disapproving of her sister's scandalous behaviour. Jane sat quiet and tense not wishing to engage in conversation.

The road was icy and full of ruts and potholes, so the carriage had to proceed very slowly. The coachman had his foot hard on the brake as they went down the steep hill into the village of Tywardreath. Once in the village, the road levelled out as they crossed the small creek and drove down to the station. Their slow progress down the hill had taken longer than they had hoped, and when they arrived at the station the train was already in view a quarter mile down the track.

"You two go on ahead, I'll get the tickets," said Thomas as they came to a stop outside the ticket office.

Jane and Janetta jumped out with their bags and ran into the station. Thomas came after, and stopped at the little ticket window. Bending forward to peer in at the elderly ticket master, he asked for three singles to Plymouth.

The train pulled in just as the girls arrived on the platform. Janetta had only been on a train a couple of times before and found herself staring up in wonder at the beautiful green and brass engine that glided past her as it slowed to a stop at the end of the platform. For some reason the sight of the train depressed Janetta and she felt cold and alone.

The Christmas at home had depressed her more than she cared to admit, but there was something else that worried Janetta; something that made her mother's rebukes far too real, and difficult to bear; something that she was going to have to face, and soon.

* * * *

In Plymouth, life was quickly coming back into the Colonel's house. Mrs Atkins had returned early from her Christmas visit to her sister and was busy readying the house for the Colonel's return. She might have cursed Janetta for not being there to help her, but in truth she was enjoying the quiet. Janetta and Faversham would be back soon enough, full of stories about their Christmases, and the house would resound with domestic activities. But for now all was peaceful.

A chill permeated the house and Mrs A's first job was to light a couple of fires to dispel the damp. Clean linen was placed on the beds and everywhere was dusted and polished until the house gleamed. It was remarkably satisfying to have the house single handedly ship-shape before everyone returned, and Mrs A felt triumphant.

****

The snow continued to fall – almost horizontally – carried by the chill wind that blew off *the Sound* and roared across the open ground towards Hoe Road. The great black gates of the Royal Citadel were dragged open leaving deep quarter circles in the snow. The first men of a long, frozen column, rounded the corner just a hundred yards away. The battalion was returning from Exeter, but the trains were cancelled due to a derailment, and so they had been marching for ten hours through snowdrifts.

Their return was far different from their departure. There were no waving crowds to welcome them home. The whole town was huddled in front of their fireplaces trying to keep warm. There was no proud march with boots beating time on the cobbles, but instead a slow, foot-dragging column that was frozen to the core. Most of the men wore blankets over their heads to cover their ears. Heads hung low and their shoulders bent into the wind. The officers also were far too cold to insist on military smartness as everyone just longed to get into the warmth of the fort. The whole column looked like Napoleon's retreat from Moscow, but they picked up their feet a little as they saw the Citadel ahead and the promise of a warm fire. Rank by rank they broke into a slow trot towards the gate. The Colonel sat on his horse, and shivered. His legs were numb. At least when you marched you kept moving. On a horse you froze to the core.

Before them lay the long gray walls of the Royal Citadel that guarding the entrance to the Naval Port. The impressive, Portland stone gatehouse was several storeys high and decorated with Grecian columns in relief, and the Royal Coat of Arms in the centre of the pediment. A lion and unicorn sat on the very top, flanking a great globe, each supporting a shield of St George. Just above the arch was the Coat of Arms of the Earl of Bath and the Greenville family motto, *Futurism invisible.*

As he rode over the bridge, the Colonel straightened his back as much as he could. He glanced up at the great arch and read the inscription over the gate, '*1670 -Carolus secondus dei gratia magnae Britaniae franciae et hiberniae rex, Charles II, by the grace of God, King of Britain, France and Scotland.'*

The two sentries snapped to attention and saluted as he rode past. For a few painfully short seconds he felt warmer as he rode through the shelter of the arch, and then, coming out into the central parade ground he was once again hit by the bitter wind.

He stopped his horse as two orderlies ran forward to take the reins. Dismounting was agony as every limb refused to move. He struggled to find his footing in the snow and to straighten to his full height before his men had all assembled. The column filed into the courtyard. Their disarray would normally have sent the Sergeant Major into torrents of abuse, but today nobody felt enthusiastic about military precision. The column slowly closed up into ranks and came to a halt in front of the Sergeant Major. A few stragglers limped through the gate. Even they didn't agitate the officers. Everyone was too cold to care.

The Sergeant Major made an attempt to bark his command, "Companyyyyy…shun!" His weakened voice would normally have given the men amusement, but not today. The column shuffled to attention.

The Colonel didn't wait for the wagons to catch up. He turned to the Sergeant Major and said loud enough for all to hear, "Extra grog ration for the men, Sergeant Major… you may dismiss them, if you please." A murmur of approval drifted through the ranks.

The Sergeant Major attempted to snap back "Su!" but the ice on his moustache cracked and pulled and his voice came out as a weak croak. He stamped his foot, which sent a flash of pain up his numb leg and pivoted round to face the column, "Companyyyyy diiiiiss….miss!"

The column disintegrated as the men made their way as fast as their frozen legs would carry them, to the barracks and the welcome fires.

Once inside, John collapsed onto his bunk, still wearing all his kit, and immediately fell asleep.

****

The Colonel's return to the house was uneventful. After settling his regiment back into their usual barrack routine, he rode home in a borrowed carriage with his cloak collar pulled up against his ears. He hated the cold and this winter was one of the worst he could remember. He rubbed at the frost on the window with numb fingers to peer out into the street. There was nothing to see, but he stared into the white gloom and thought of Janetta. Not for the first time during the last couple of weeks, he found himself looking forward to seeing her, despite his anxiety over what must be said.

Janetta had never left his mind while in Exeter, and he felt relieved at having confided his feelings for her to another officer. He hadn't wanted advice; he already knew what had to be done. But somehow, hearing the opinion of a fellow gentleman cemented what he already knew. He was besotted with her. He longed for her body beside him in his bed, but society would never accept her. By society's standard, she was simply an illiterate, working girl from a small fishing village and no amount of beauty or brains would make her a lady. If he tried to bring her into society his friends would be appalled and he would become a laughing stock. No, he would have to make it quite clear to her that her position would never change. He knew her ambition. How could he not see it? But without doubt she was going to be gravely disappointed.

****

Janetta had now been back a couple of days and had settled into her household duties. The Colonel's return filled her with anticipation, but also some misgivings.

At two in the afternoon the front door opened and the Colonel, covered in snow, entered the hallway gasping from the cold air. Faversham hadn't heard the carriage pull up outside, so he rushed upstairs to greet him with unseemly haste. The Colonel didn't appear to notice as he struggled to remove his cloak.

"Welcome home, Colonel," said Faversham as cheerfully as he could, while catching his breath, "let me take your cloak."

Snow fell to the floor as the cloak exchanged hands.

"I trust you had a good Christmas, sir," he continued.

"Mmm," replied the Colonel unenthusiastically. He stamped the snow off his boots onto the carpet and sneezed.

"I hope you're not coming down…"

"Don't fuss Faversham," interrupted the Colonel, "I'm quite all right. Is everyone back?"

"Yes, sir. May I get you some tea, sir?"

"No you bloody well can't!" the Colonel snapped as he entered his library. "Get me a brandy… a large one." He went and stood in front of the fire to warm his hands, and as they warmed they began to tighten and sting.

Faversham approached him with a brandy glass virtually full. The Colonel looked at the brandy and then at Faversham wandering whether he was being impertinent.

"Are you trying to warm me up or get me drunk man?"

"You look as if you need it, sir!"

"Mmm, so I do. Bloody weather!"

The Colonel flopped back into his chair and held one foot up horizontally, inviting Faversham to remove his boot. Faversham obliged.

"Now leave me," he muttered under his breath. Laying his head back against the chair, he closed his eyes.

Faversham picked up his boots and quietly left the room.

At five o'clock Faversham re-entered the library to light the lamps. The Colonel snored in his chair, but awoke when he heard Faversham in the room.

"What time is it, Faversham?" he yawned.

"It's five of the clock, sir. Dinner will be at six as usual. I thought you might be recovered enough to change for dinner, sir."

"Quite right Faversham, quite right." he slapped his knees and stood up, still a little groggy from his sleep.

Dinner that evening was, as usual, a silent affair. The only sound was that of Faversham and Janetta bringing and removing dishes and the Colonel's knife and fork clicking against the chinaware. After dinner the Colonel retired to his library and Faversham and Janetta tidied away the table things. They wondered if the Colonel's little book would be under his napkin, and were both surprised to find it wasn't.

Janetta found this oversight quite worrying. She thought the Colonel would return anxious to have a private moment with her, and she wished to be with him so that she could give him her news.

Faversham was also impatient to tell the Colonel about Janetta's other affair before he could make any public announcements or proposals to her. It seemed as though Mrs A was the only one in the house who was content not to have a private audience with the Colonel.

The Colonel, anxious to see Janetta again, sat in his library with his brandy, still unfinished from earlier in the afternoon, and fretted about what he was going to say to her. He'd forgotten the little book.

Finally, at nine o'clock, he stood up and pulled the bell cord that hung on the wall beside the fireplace. He turned and stood with his back to the fire, his feet apart and his hands behind his back. He took a deep breath, lifted his chest and raised himself up to his full height as he waited for Faversham to enter the room.

He didn't have to wait long.

"You rang, sir?"

"Yes, send Miss Rundel in," he said in his most business-like manner.

"Sir!" replied Faversham, and he turned to leave the room. *"This is not right,"* he thought to himself. *"If I'm going to have my say I should speak up now."* "Sir, if I might have a word with you about a matter of some delicacy?"

"Not now Faversham."

"With respect, sir I believe it should be said now before you speak to Miss Rundel."

The Colonel looked at him with some surprise. What could be so urgent that had to be said before he spoke to Janetta?

"What is it man?" he said with obvious impatience.

"Sir," started Faversham nervously, "Mrs A and I have been aware of your feelings for Miss Rundel for some time now and we wish you every happiness and would..."

"Get on with it man!"

"Well, sir, we wouldn't wish you to be hurt in any way; and we all love Miss Rundel sir, she's a good girl at heart, but our loyalty is first and foremost to you sir."

"Well...?" The Colonel was getting annoyed with Faversham pussy footing around the subject.

"Well, sir, it's like this, sir," he took a deep breath and tried to look as sympathetic as possible, "Miss Rundel has a man friend, sir."

There followed a very long pause.

"A man friend," the Colonel was trying to absorb this statement.

"Yes, sir," replied Faversham in a half whisper. "I believe he's a bombardier in your regiment sir."

The Colonel stared straight into Faversham' eyes. "In my regiment?"

"Sir," nodded Faversham. "I believe his name is Bombardier John Martin, sir. She's been seeing quite a lot of him recently."

"The devil you say! Well... thank you, Faversham." There followed an uncomfortable pause before he took a deep breath and continued, "You may leave me now!"

"Yes, sir, I'll send her in shall I?"

The Colonel nodded his assent, and Faversham backed out of the room closing the double doors behind him. In the hallway he gave himself a congratulatory smirk before heading down to the kitchen.

The Colonel sat in his chair, all his strength leaving him. He had to think fast before she came to him. He had to assess the situation.

As a military man he was trained to rapidly assess battlefield situations, the lives of his men depended on it; just now, however, he felt as if an artillery barrage had hit him. He was stunned and found it difficult to absorb what he'd been told.

This changed everything. At first he felt blind anger, jealousy even, but after a minute or two he began to realize that his problem was solved. He didn't have to remind her of her unsuitable status in society; she was dating one of his men. She'd been unfaithful to him. And this John Martin was an enlisted man; far more suitable for her. He was now in a position to back out of their relationship gracefully without being unpleasantly cruel to her. He resolved to be fatherly and understanding to her new 'true love' and would give them his blessing to marry. How he would miss her, but the situation had been getting out of hand and now it could be resolved to everybody's satisfaction.

****

It took Janetta ten minutes to arrive at the library. When Faversham had entered the kitchen Janetta was in the privy, but on her return, it was obvious that she would have to wash and change before going upstairs.

"What have you been doing, girl, you're wanted upstairs," said Faversham with some irritation.

"I'm cleaning out the fire from the copper ain't I," she replied.

Janetta made a futile attempt to brush off her apron but it was covered in soot and she merely smeared it. Strands of hair, once tied neatly back under a headscarf now hung down about her face.

"Go an' tidy yerself up girl," said Mrs A, as Janetta disappeared into the back room to find a clean apron.

When she was more presentable, she reappeared and started up the stairs. Faversham followed, but almost immediately she stopped and turned on him.

"I can manage to find me own way!" She glared at him and he stopped and took a slight step back down a step.

He raised his hands up in front as if to ward her off.

"All right off ya go then," he said, and turned to retreat to the kitchen.

Outside the library Janetta stopped, took a deep breath and smoothed her hair before knocking.

The room was dark but for one oil lamp and the glow from the fire. The Colonel looked stern. *"Oh, he wants a punishment session,"* Janetta thought as she approached him. But tonight she really wasn't in the mood for being playful as she had a serious problem to discuss with him. She would, however, have to be careful not to displease him, and would have to use all her feminine powers of persuasion on this occasion.

Janetta walked right to him, placed one hand against his chest and stretched her head up to kiss him on the cheek. He bent forward just enough to receive the kiss, but not enough to show any real enthusiasm for it.

"I've missed you," she whispered.

He took her by the arms and pushed her gently away.

"I must talk to you Jan." He sounded firm but not unkind, and Janetta suddenly felt that he was not going to fall for her charms tonight. "You know how I've felt about you for a long time,"

"Here it comes," she thought, *"he's going to give me up."*

"Well, I've given this a lot of thought over Christmas and…well it just won't do."

"Won't do?" interjected Janetta with some surprise.

"I was hoping to be able to carry on as we were… it was good wasn't it?" he continued sympathetically.

Janetta nodded.

"But I can't marry you and that's not fair on you."

"Why can't yer marry me? Yer luvs me don't ya?" Janetta had been trying hard over the last few months to improve her diction but now she forgot and slipped back into her common speech. It was a strong reminder to him that he was doing the right thing, but he didn't want to hurt her more by bringing up her obvious social inferiority. He changed the subject.

"I understand you have been seeing one of my men. John Martin, I think his name is."

Janetta was stunned by this revelation. How on earth did he know about John?

"I knows John, yeh," she said. She had no choice. There was no point in denying it. Her head suddenly spun and she had trouble focusing her thoughts.

"You realize that it puts me in an embarrassing position, Jan."

He spoke to her as if he were her father trying to make her see sense, "I can't be seen to be sharing one of my enlisted men's women! It would render me a laughing stock in the regiment." This didn't come out quite right and he felt as if he was hurting her more than he intended.

A silence fell between them and then, without thinking, Janetta quietly murmured,

"But I'm pregnant."

****

The snow blew hard across the parade ground and a lone warrant officer, wrapped in a thick navy blue cloak, waded through the drifts of snow towards one of the gray stone barrack buildings. As he opened the door a freezing wind blew through the Sergeant's ante-room, blowing papers off his desk.

"Close the fucking door can't ya!" screamed the Sergeant, and then looking up and seeing who had entered, he suddenly stood to attention, "Oh begging your pardon, sir!"

"At ease Sergeant. Hell of a day!"

"Sir!"

"Tell Martin the Colonel wants to see him, on the double."

"John or Sydney, sir?"

"What? Oh, John, Sergeant."

"What's the bastard done, sir? Something I should know about is it?"

"I don't think so Sergeant. Family matter I think."

"Right, family matter is it, sir," replied the sergeant not believing a word of it.

"So it seems Sergeant."

The warrant officer brushed snow off his shoulders onto the floor. "Now, if you please, Sergeant!"

"Yes, sir." The Sergeant turned and left the room. Inside the barrack was a long narrow room with wooden bunk beds down both sides of a central corridor. In the middle of the corridor three pot-bellied stoves smoked making the air thick, which stung the eyes. Men sat on bunks polishing boots or cleaning guns. They all looked up when the Sergeant entered.

"Martin!" he yelled. Sydney Martin stood up. "Not you, sit down."

John Martin stepped out from behind his bunk.

"Yes Sarg'?"

"You're wanted Martin, fall in, smart like, you're going to see the Colonel lad."

John struggled to put his tunic and cloak on. A murmur ran through the room. The Colonel didn't summon enlisted men unless they were in serious trouble.

"Come on you bastard get a move on!" snapped the Sergeant who was particularly put out about not knowing what one of his men had been up to.

John and the Sergeant went out to the anteroom where the warrant officer waited.

"Martin?"

"Yes, sir."

"Right, follow me."

The officer opened the door again and winced as he headed into the wind. John glanced at the sergeant, who glared at him, before he followed the officer out into the snow.

****

John sat on a bench in the corridor outside the Colonel's office and shivered. It only took two minutes to cross the parade ground, but that was twenty minutes earlier, and still he shivered. His tunic felt damp from the melted snow and his toes were cold in his wet boots. But his shaking was perhaps more from apprehension than the cold. He couldn't understand why he was there. What had he done? The warrant officer had left him on his own and he hadn't seen anyone since he'd arrived there. He felt strangely abandoned.

The door opened and the Colonel's aide peered out into the corridor.

"Martin?"

"Yes, sir." John stood up.

"The Colonel will see you now."

John followed the aide into the office and waited while the aide knocked and then entered a second office. Within seconds he was out again and holding the door open for Martin to enter.

John walked in and snapped to attention and saluted in front of the Colonel's desk. The Colonel was writing a letter, and didn't look up, but muttered, "at ease soldier."

John widened his stance and put his hands behind his back. He felt sweat itch in his scalp despite shivering.

John looked about the room. It was mostly bare with whitewashed stone walls and a naked wood planked floor. To the right side stood a black pot-bellied stove that smoked. The round metal chimney rose up the wall then turned ninety degrees to run along just below the ceiling, over his head and pass through the wall into the next office. John could feel the heat radiating from the stove. In front of him stood a plain wooden desk littered with ledgers, papers, ink well, a couple of pens and a blotter.

The Colonel blotted the letter, pulled it to one side and looked up at John. For a few seconds he seemed to be studying him. John wandered if he recognized him. There was no real reason why he should have; he was just another body in the ranks. He'd never done anything to distinguish himself.

"So you're John Martin?" the Colonel inquired.

"Sir." replied John.

"It has come to my attention that you have been seeing a girl by the name of Janetta Rundel."

"Yes, sir," he replied, feeling a little more at ease since there was no law against that.

"Would it surprise you to know she works in my house?"

Was this a trap question John wondered? If he said 'no' he'd surely be caught lying and if he said 'yes' would he be laying himself open for some criticism? He crossed his fingers.

"Yes sir, I mean I know she does, sir."

"What are your intentions towards Miss Rundel?"

"Intentions, sir?"

"Do you intend to marry the girl," the Colonel sounded a little rattled at his slowness to comprehend the question.

"I doubt she'd av me, sir."

"Have you asked her?"

"Yes, sir."

"Has she said yes?"

"Not yet, sir."

"I presume you do know she's pregnant?"

John couldn't believe his ears. He wasn't expecting this.

"Nn no sir, I don't."

"Well that puts a different complexion on things, doesn't it, Martin?"

"Yes, sir," replied John, trying to take it all in.

"I suggest you do the right thing and ask her again. Can't have my men taking advantage of my personal staff and not taking responsibility, can we?"

"No, sir."

"Right that's settled then. Report back to me when you've had her reply."

"Sir," replied John.

"Dismissed, Bombardier Martin."

John saluted, spun around to face the door and marched out of the office. When he'd gone the Colonel sat back in his chair, lit a cigar and pondered this deception. There was no proof John was the father. There was more likelihood that it was going to be his child, but he couldn't marry her. John would make a more suitable husband. Janetta's admission to being pregnant hadn't gone well. He had become suddenly very angry. It was bad enough finding out that she had another lover, but then to be told that he was the father of her child was too much. How could he be sure it was his? He had lost his temper and reduced Janetta to tears, telling her that he would have to think about what to do with her. He hadn't been kind and now regretted it.

He decided to settle twenty guineas on Janetta as a wedding present. It was a tidy sum but he could easily afford it and it eased his conscience.

****

John sat by the fire in the snug and waited for Janetta to arrive. She was late, but it gave him time to have a drink and relax a little before she joined him. During the last couple of days, he had given a lot of thought to marrying Janetta and being a father. He'd get a little extra pay for being married but it wouldn't be much. On the other hand, he'd have the most beautiful wife in the regiment. Her pregnancy had been a shock. He'd only rogered her once, and it was just his luck that she had become pregnant. Still, being a dad wouldn't be so bad; he quite fancied the idea.

As he sat staring into the fire he hadn't noticed Janetta approaching him.

"Allo John," she said quite cheerily. "Got a gin for me av ya?"

"Allo Jan. Yeh 'ere you are."

Janetta took her cloak off and sat down opposite him. She cupped her hands around the gin glass as if it would give her warmth, and took a big mouthful, "God I needed that!" she gasped.

"I've been thinking, Jan," announced John.

"Blimey! Don't 'urt yaself will ya!" grinned Janetta.

"No listen Jan," stammered John, not wishing her to be flippant. "About wot I asked ya before. Ow about us getting hitched then, what d'ya fink?"

Janetta looked up at him startled, "Blimey! You are serious, ain't ya?"

"Yeh cors I am, I love ya Jan. You love me don't ya?"

"Yeh, I does John, ya know I does, but…"

"But wot?"

"But!" she couldn't finish the sentence. She'd lose him if he thought she was pregnant. She didn't want him to think he was pushed into a corner. On the other hand marrying John would give her respectable support for her and her child. But what if he ever discovered he might not be the father?

"I know yer with child Jan, it's all right, 'onest."

"You know…how?"

"The Colonel told me a couple of days back."

"Oh!" was all Janetta could think to say. They sat in silence for a minute or so. "What exactly did he tell ya then?"

"Said he knew you were seeing me and that you had got with child. He reckoned I should do the honourable thing, and marry ya, and I agree of course."

He hadn't told John about their affair. Janetta suddenly felt very angry. He was deliberately removing himself from all responsibility. He was engineering this wedding to get himself off the hook. She looked up at John who sat waiting expectantly for her reply.

"Right, I will marry ya John, I will," she said in a very business like manner, "but first ya gotta know somefing, an ya ain't going to like it John, but you an' I might profit from this I reckon."

"What are ya talking about, Jan? What won't I like?"

"Well first off John, I do luvs ya and I do want ta marry ya."

"Good."

"But ya may not be the farva John."

"What?"

"The Colonel's had me John, I had to go to him, see, an get spanked an groped and bedded."

"Jan!" stammered John, not believing his ears.

"I neva wanted to John…neva…I had to see, or I'd a lost me position."

John sat silent, his mouth open, and stared at her as if he had seen a ghost.

"But I luvs you, John... 'onest!" She leant forward and stroked the side of his cheek. She was taking a big gamble here. She could lose him? "If ya still luvs me we could do well out o' this I reckon, John."

She lowered her head and looked up into his eyes. She felt him soften as he looked at her. He'd had a shock but he was besotted with her and was beginning to not care about the Colonel. After all he was going to have her in his bed from now on. She knew it even before he did.

"Yeh sure I luvs ya!" whispered John. He was slowly recovering from the news and was beginning to focus once more on her two beautiful blue eyes and soft voice. What was she saying?

"Listen my sweet," she whispered across the table, "if we're careful we can make 'im pay for what he's done to me."

"How's that then?" asked John, still a little slow to understand what she was saying.

"Well...it would be mighty embarrassing if it got known, wot he liked to do to his maids at night wouldn't it?"

John nodded, "It would, wouldn't it?"

"So I fink he would be very grateful to you fer keeping quiet, and me fer agreeing to marry ya."

John wasn't happy about the idea of blackmailing his regimental colonel, but she was right. Why shouldn't he pay?

It was agreed then. They would marry and the Colonel would be made to see how grateful he should be.

They spent a pleasant couple of hours together drinking and cuddling on a bench by the fire. Janetta began to feel quite content with the idea of marrying John. Her dreams of becoming a lady of a big house were fading fast and she resolved to make the best of the new opportunity.

At five in the evening she threw her cloak about her shoulders, and arm in arm with John, left the inn to return to the Colonel's house.

After they had left a young man stood up from a seat in the corner a few feet away from where John and Janetta had been sitting. He left some coins on the table and walked towards the door. Seeing him leave, the barmaid called out to him.

"Good night, Mr Faversham."

CHAPTER 6

Plots and Death
1876

Faversham returned to the house in a pensive mood. He walked with his head down looking at his snow-covered boots and replaying in his mind the conversation he had overheard. He had expected that after his announcement about Janetta seeing John Martin, she would be expelled from the house, or at the very least dropped like a hot potato by the Colonel. He hadn't foreseen the possibility of her becoming pregnant; and he certainly never imagined that she would scheme to extort money from the Colonel. He had to think carefully about his next move.

One option would be to simply expose their plan to the Colonel, but that would do nothing to gain Janetta's favour. Above all, he wanted to have her in his bed and informing on her would not achieve that end. Rescue, after her fall from grace now seemed to be a hopeless course. She would obviously turn to Martin after being rejected by the Colonel, unless of course Martin wasn't available. Perhaps if Martin died "*maybe I could kill him*" he thought. However, this option would still alienate him from Jan's affections. Besides, he couldn't really see himself as a murderer.

No, there had to be a better way.

Faversham could not get his head around the problem. "Think, damn you, think!" he said to himself as he trudged aimlessly through the snow. With his head down, and absorbed by his problem he didn't notice that he had walked through the open gate of a cemetery. Before him stretched row upon row of white-topped grave markers, in a white field, with an endless-haze shrouded horizon. Only one set of footprints preceded him, and he pensively followed them, stepping in each footprint. The prints were small and close together, making it uncomfortable for him to shorten his stride. They were the prints of a woman. Gradually the prints veered off to the side of the path and entered one of the silent rows. He followed, and quickly found himself approaching an elderly woman holding a small and rather pathetic posy of flowers and brushing snow away to expose a half-buried vase.

He stopped and watched her. Feeling his presence she looked up at him.

"They'll die in this cold," he said.

"They'll die anyway ducky!" she replied, "but it's the thought that counts. He'll like 'em!"

"Your husband?"

"Close enough! Fucking bastard he was, an no mistake!"

"Doesn't sound as if you loved him, but you must have done," said Faversham gesturing to the flowers.

"Didn't love 'im at first, but he grew on me in time." She looked affectionately at the stone, "I wanted to marry someone else, see, but me parents said I 'ad to marry 'im, so the bastard got me, didn't he."

She turned to look at him.

"You got a young lady then?"

Faversham just shook his head.

She studied him for a moment, "Won't 'ave ya eh!" she said. He could feel her eyes going right to his soul. "Well if ya want her you'd better get her before you lose her, see."

Faversham gave a little courtesy smile. "Good day to you," he said and turned away from her.

"She may not see it now, but she'll luv ya in the end."

He stopped and turned back to look at the old woman.

"Is that guaranteed? Can you be sure of such a course?"

"Nufink's sure ducky!" The old lady winked at him and returned to arranging her flowers. Perhaps she's right, he thought, perhaps Jan would accept him if he made it clear to her that she would be better off to marry him, rather than a common soldier. Perhaps in time she would even learn to love him.

His mood softened. He would try a new approach. He would woo and seduce her and maybe then she would see him more favourably.

It was a better plan, but he wasn't convinced she would have him. What if she really loved Martin? He slowly developed a backup plan and the more he thought about it, the more his mood improved, and he entered the house feeling much lighter.

****

Two days later Colonel Wentworth arrived home a few minutes early and immediately asked Faversham to send Miss Rundel to him. Faversham hung the Colonel's cloak up and returned to the kitchen where Janetta was helping Ethel Atkin prepare the evening meal.

"You're wanted in the library, Miss Rundel."

"Wot now?" asked Janetta in surprise.

"Yes now!" replied Faversham as he brushed some dust off a bottle of wine.

Ethel raised her eyes and tutted. These visits to the Colonel were becoming much too frequent and she felt put out not knowing all the details. Janetta went upstairs to the library.

"What's going on with her, Faversham?" asked Ethel. She didn't like Faversham, but she guessed he knew more about what was going on than she did.

Faversham put the wine bottle down and started polishing a decanter.

"There's trouble brewing Mrs A," he said, "Gone and got herself pregnant hasn't she."

"No!"

"Yes Mrs A and..." he leaned towards her and lowered his voice, "it's by no means sure if the Colonel's the father."

"Silly girl!" sighed Ethel. She wasn't shocked. It was almost inevitable, but she liked Janetta and wouldn't have wished it on her.

"Silly girl is right Mrs A, she'll be on the street, and you see if I'm not right! She's a hussy Mrs A a hussy!" He spat the last words with a sneer.

Ethel ignored his venomous attack on Janetta. She actually felt quite sorry for her. For all her misgivings, Janetta was a very likable girl, and Ethel was saddened to think that she might be heading for ruin.

Janetta entered the library. Colonel Wentworth seemed in a good mood.

"Ah! Jan my dear come in and sit down," he waved her to a chair. This was unusually familiar treatment and she felt uneasy sitting down with him this early in the evening when she was still working as his maid. He sensed her discomfort. "Never mind anybody else, sit down. To hell with them, I'm sure they all know anyway."

"I haven't told them," replied Janetta truthfully.

"No need, they're not stupid, I'm sure they've both known for a very long time."

"Yes, sir," she hung her head trying as much as possible to appear to be a fragile helpless woman. "*A few tears would do about now*," she thought, unfortunately she couldn't produce any.

"Now Jan," he spoke softly, "do you have any news for me?"

"Yes, sir," she kept her head down but raised her eyes to look at him, "John asked me to marry 'im alright."

"And what did you say?"

"Said I would, but I don't know what we'll live on, sir. Don't think I could manage on a soldier's pay, wot with the baby and not workin'."

"Well I think I can help you there, Jan."

"Sir?" she brightened up.

"I thought I'd give you a wedding present of, say…ten guineas!"

Janetta couldn't believe her ears. It was a very generous amount. For a moment she forgot herself and leapt out of her chair and threw her arms around his shoulders.

"Oh sir you're so good to me," she squealed, as she kissed him all over his cheeks. Tears flooded from her eyes and for the first time in her life she actually felt a genuine affection for a man. Nobody had ever been that kind to her and she was quite overcome with gratitude.

"There, there," laughed the Colonel, who was enjoying the moment immensely, "it's the very least I could do. It's you who have given me so much pleasure. I'm going to really miss you."

Janetta sniffed and smiled at him.

"Now when's the happy day going to be?"

He looked at her beaming, tear-streaked face and wanted to hold onto her as tightly as he could. He hadn't had any idea until now just how much he loved her. Now that it was over, he wanted to cry like a baby and beg her to stay, but it could never work, and he knew he had no choice but to end it.

****

On the following Friday morning, John was called to the Colonel's office. When he entered he found the Colonel standing by the window gazing out at the parade ground. A squad was marching up and down in the slush to the screams of the Sergeant Major; Colonel Wentworth followed them with his eyes and tutted. John snapped to attention in front of the Colonel's desk and tried to remember what he had rehearsed. He was nervous and only too aware of what a risky business he was about to embark upon.

At first the Colonel ignored him and continued watching the squad on the parade ground, but shortly he turned and looked at John for a second, and then returned again to watch the ragged performance outside.

"Some men never seem to learn, Martin! It's like herding cats! Look at them for Christ sake!" This last statement was not meant to be taken literally, and John remained where he stood.

"You wanted to see me, sir?"

"New recruits, Martin," replied the Colonel, gesturing to the squad. "Appearance, if nothing else you see. You should at least look like a bloody soldier."

"Yes, sir!"

There followed another pause and then…

"I understand you've asked the girl to marry you."

"Yes, sir!"

"Well, I presume she accepted your offer!"

He knows damn well she did, thought John, "Yes, sir, she did!"

"Good, that's settled then!"

"Begging your pardon, Colonel sir," John was about to push his luck.

The Colonel still stared out of the window, "What is it man?"

"Well, sir, I've been thinking about a potential problem we might have, sir."

"We? Martin."

"Yes, sir, well… you more than we, sir."

Colonel Wentworth turned slowly round to face Martin; "I have a problem, Martin? And what would that be?" The Colonel's voice shrouded a threat.

"With respect, sir, you hold a position of high rank and considerable respect, not only in the regiment, sir, but also in the town."

The Colonel took a few steps further into the room and stood immediately behind his desk. His boots made a heavy footfall on the wooden floorboards and sounded hollow in the spartan room. He glared straight into John's eyes, but said nothing for a moment. He didn't have to. His soul-piercing look was enough to tell John he was on very thin ice. Then he broke the silence.

"What of it?" he replied with studied calmness.

"Well, sir, it would be a terrible thing if the regiment, a-a-and the town even, were to find out that you had an enlisted man's wife as your mistress…sir."

He'd said it. It was too late to go back. He wanted to remark on how the Colonel took pleasure in spanking his maids, but decided to hold that bombshell in reserve. Now he waited for the thunderbolt to hit him.

There followed a frightening silence. Colonel Wentworth stared at him without showing any sign of recognition that he had understood what he had said. The door opened breaking the silence, and the adjutant came in with some papers. The Colonel switched his gaze at the intruder and erupted.

"Get the fuck out of here!" he screamed.

"Yes, sir," the adjutant replied and hastily retreated the way he'd come, closing the door behind him.

The Colonel's gaze returned to Martin who stood his ground and waited for a tirade of fury to hit him. Colonel Wentworth bent forward and placing his knuckles on the desk, leaned his weight on them.

"Now I wouldn't have thought you the venal type, Martin?"

"Venal, sir?" John didn't know the word.

"Are you blackmailing me, Martin?" he asked in a calm voice that told John he was summoning all his reserve of energy to control his anger.

"No, sir, I wouldn't dream of such a thing, sir."

"You're a lying bastard Martin, and I could have you horsewhipped!"

Still the Colonel held his fury in check and spoke in almost a whisper. John realized how perilously close he was to being thrown in the brig, or worse, receiving a severe flogging.

"Sir, I just thought that the chances of Jan's baby not being mine were quite high under the circumstances, and I'm sure you would want the best for your son, sir. But on my pay…."

"I think you've said quite enough, Martin, don't you?"

"Sir!"

Colonel Wentworth walked back to the window, but his eyes couldn't focus on the ragged line of men marching passed outside. For the first time in his long career he could not think how to handle this impertinent soldier in his office. If he disciplined him he'd have to explain why and everything would come out; on the other hand if he did nothing he'd live forever at his mercy. Then there was Janetta. He couldn't believe she would do this to him. Perhaps she didn't know what John was proposing.

"I suppose Miss Rundel put you up to this little scheme."

"Oh no, sir," John lied. "She knows nothing about this; and I'd appreciate it, sir, if you didn't say anything to her about it. She really liked you, sir, and she would be none too pleased if she thought I'd spoken to you about this matter. Best kept between us men, sir eh!"

This little piece of fiction seemed to placate the Colonel because he visibly softened before returning his gaze out of the window.

"It's within my power Martin, to make life extremely unpleasant for you, should you ever do, or say, anything that might be deemed embarrassing to your commanding officer." He turned to look at John over his shoulder.

"Sir!"

"If I were to give you a wedding present, strictly because you're marrying my employee, you understand, I should expect that to be an end to the matter."

"Absolutely sir. Very kind of you sir."

"Shall we say …five guineas then!"

John remained silent. Colonel Wentworth turned and stared at him and one eyebrow lifted slightly.

"Perhaps ten would be better," he offered in a rather sarcastic tone.

Still John didn't move or respond.

"You're pushing your luck, Bombardier Martin."

Still silence. A small bead of sweat formed on John's scalp.

"I thought, sir," he began after a minute or so, "I thought, that with Jan having to give up work during her confinement, it might cost quite a bit to raise the kid, sir. Perhaps we might manage on say fifteen sir!"

"Fifteen!" Wentworth nearly choked. It wasn't the amount that angered him, but the sheer nerve of the man. He came within an inch of losing his temper and ordering John to be publicly flogged but he took a deep breath and forced himself to calm down; it was for Janetta after all. Or was it?

"I'll give you fifteen on one condition, Martin," he hissed.

"Thank you, sir, very generous!"

"One condition damn it, that you marry the girl as soon as possible; and on the understanding, between us, that if you ever mistreat her, or leave her and run off with the money, I'll hunt you down like a dog. Do I make myself clear?"

"Perfectly clear, sir, but you won't have any cause for dissatisfaction with me, sir, I'll be a good husband and father, sir!"

"You'd better be, Martin. You'd bloody well better be!"

****

Janetta hastened along the path leading to the Citadel. Her boots were new, but not particularly waterproof, and her feet soon became damp as she waded through the melting snow and slush puddles. Little rivulets ran down gullies in the ice and trees dripped as the temperature warmed. A sea mist rolled in from *The Sound* and Janetta shivered more from the damp than the cold. She would meet John as he came from the front gate. Together they planned an evening in a small tavern not far from the wharf. She was apprehensive as to how John had made out with the Colonel; she knew he was a kindly man and wouldn't be vindictive towards John. At least she hoped as much.

She made a right turn before reaching the end of the street and entered an alleyway that led between two factory buildings and came out on the sea front, some quarter mile from the Citadel. She came this way often, but always in daylight. It was a dirty alley full of badly maintained outhouses that perpetually overflowed effluence onto the path. Industrial waste and dog faeces lay about in haphazard piles to be carefully avoided as you walked, and dark shadows concealed possible lairs for thugs and thieves.

The afternoon had already begun its passage into evening, and the winter gloom hastened the loss of light. Janetta felt nervous and walked as determinedly as possible through the alley. When she was less then ten yards from the far end, a dark figure stepped into the alley from the street ahead and stood blocking her way. She continued walking towards him, determined to show no fear. The man was silhouetted against the gray light of *The Sound* and so it wasn't until she was almost right in front of him that she realized who it was.

"Hallo, Jan." It was Faversham. Janetta stopped in her tracks and stared at him in disbelief.

"Where the bleed'n 'ell d'ya come from?" she said.

"You didn't know I knew your route did you?" He stepped further into the alley and Janetta instinctively took a step back. In the safety of the house she had no fear of him, but out here she wasn't too sure of herself.

"I knew you were coming this way and I thought I'd just wait for you see!"

"Why?" stammered Janetta.

"You and I have to have a little talk, Jan dear," he took a quick step forward and pinned her to the wall. "It's all about your little plan see. Didn't know I knew about it did you now?" He held on to her arms tightly. His voice softened and he tried to imitate the wooing lover.

"Jan, you must know how I feel about you, and it pains me to see you throw yourself away on *this soldier*." His tone now ending with an air of distain.

Janetta tried to free herself from his grasp but he held her too tightly.

"I know all about you and the Colonel, so does Mrs A, but I could understand that, he's rich after all; but not 'soldier boy'. You'd hate being a soldier's wife."

"It's none of your bleedin' business, is it?" snarled Janetta.

"Ah! But you see I think it could be my dear, because I could offer you much more than Martin. Marry me and you'd still live in a nice house and I won't always be a butler you know. I've got plans to be in business."

"I'd neva marry you Faversham, neva!"

Faversham's voice hardened. "Think carefully about what you say Jan, I can be very forgiving and understanding. Why, I might even allow you to continue to get your little spankings every now and then. I'm sure I could come to a satisfactory arrangement with the Colonel."

"Pig!" she yelled and spat in his face.

"Now Jan I'm trying to be nice and friendly. Don't piss me off!"

"Le' go ya bastard!" hissed Janetta. Faversham gave her a sudden sharp slap across the face and pushed her hard against the wall, banging her head on the brickwork. "I ain't marrying you, an that's final see!" she gasped.

"Shut up, shut up!" he yelled, his voice echoing down the passage. "If you won't marry me perhaps you'll consider another offer."

"Piss off!"

"Shut up and listen girl," he growled, "now you and I are going to come to an arrangement see. I know you're 'setting up' the Colonel, but the thing is, does he know? I suspect not. Don't suppose he'd be too happy to know that you're just a cheap little gold digger. 'Cause he loves you doesn't he?"

"You're hurting my arms," Janetta whimpered.

"So here's what we're going to do, Miss Rundel. You're going to be nice to me, you're going to come to me willing like. You can marry your soldier boy if you must. You can get your money from the Colonel and I expect soldier boy will get his, but I will also get mine so to speak. Do you follow me, girl?"

"No you bastard, we'll give yer nuffing!"

Another sharp slap brought blood from her mouth. "Not 'we', you! You're not listening are you? I don't want your money girl, I want your arse!"

"Fucking bastard," she screamed before being knocked forward over a dustbin. Faversham grabbed the front of her dress and hoisted her back to her feet tearing the dress as he did so.

"First payment now I think," he said as he thrust his hand up the front of her dress and grabbed her by the crotch. Janetta instinctively doubled over to protect herself, and Faversham stepped behind her, pulling her dress over her back. Janetta however, was a fighter. Years of experience with men had taught her how to cope with unwanted advances or attacks, and before Faversham knew what had hit him, her fist came up between his legs and took the wind out of his fight.

"Shit! You bitch!" he screamed as he staggered back holding his groin. She whirled round and grabbed his hair in her left hand and took a great swing at his face with her right sending him sprawling on the ground. She should have run at that moment, but instead she found herself panting for breath and watching Faversham recover from her assault. Before she could think clearly he was on top of her again hitting her for all his worth. She crumpled to the ground blood pouring from her mouth and forehead.

"Bitch, I'll put paid to your little scheme," he yelled as he kicked her in the ribs. But as quickly as his savagery had begun, it stopped. He didn't follow up with another attack, but staggered back against the wall holding his still-aching groin. He wiped the blood off his mouth with his sleeve. Janetta moaned and lifted herself up into a sitting position and lowered her head between her knees as she struggled to recover. Neither of them had the breath to continue fighting, and Faversham, although furious, was having regrets at having brutalized her. The better side of his nature was taking hold of him and he found himself breathlessly murmuring an apology.

"Hope I didn't hurt you too much, Jan. I didn't want to hit you,"

"Fucking bastard," replied Janetta but with no hate in her voice. She partly understood him. They were as bad as one another; both out for themselves, both out for what they could get. "Touch me again and I'll kill ya! So help me!"

At that moment someone entered the alley. It was John. He stopped in his tracks and looked at Janetta on the ground and Faversham leaning against the wall, bent over at the waist, panting. He ran over to Janetta and lifted her to her feet. Then seeing the blood on her face and her torn dress, he turned on Faversham.

"You're dead you bastard!" and he lunged at Faversham ramming his head back against the wall. Faversham brought his arms up fast knocking John's grip from his face and then he smashed his fists down on John's head. John staggered back but recovered quickly and started throwing punch after punch at Faversham's face. Sprays of blood and spittle flew in all directions.

Janetta stepped back into the shadows and out of harm's way, "Don't kill him John, don't kill him!" John couldn't hear her as his anger rose to fever pitch and he pummelled Faversham in the stomach and chest.

Faversham, realizing he didn't stand a chance, threw himself to the floor to evade the blows and rolled across the alley forcing John to come after him. The slush made slippery going and John staggered a little to hold his footing. It was just what Faversham needed to gain his escape. and he thrust one of his legs under John's feet tripping him and causing him to topple forward hitting his head against the wall. He was only momentarily taken off guard, but Faversham was up and running for all his might back down the alley into the black shadows.

John pulled himself to his feet and after briefly turning to Janetta to say he'd be back, ran off down the alley after Faversham.

Faversham slid and stumbled in the slush as he realized that John was right behind him. Panic set in, and he prayed he could make it out of the alley and into the street where he would have the protection of witnesses, before he was caught. John closed the gap and yelled after Faversham, "I'll fucking kill you when I git hold o'ya." Faversham ran on as fast as he could with John right on his heels. They were just yards from the street. Faversham was sure he was going to make it when he felt his coat being pulled from his back. John was right behind him reaching for his collar but could not quite make it. Faversham made an extra spurt to pull away from John's grasp just as he emerged from the mouth of the alley. He succeeded in breaking free but as soon as he entered the street he hit a patch of ice, and losing his footing staggered out into the road in the path of the Portsmouth to Exeter coach.

The lead horse hit him square in the chest and sent him sprawling to the ground. In a second he was under the horse's hooves tumbling like paper in the wind, as the first, and then second horse trampled over him. Then he was hit by the coach, which bounced as it ran over him. The driver pulled back on the brake and the coach skidded to a stop.

John stopped in the mouth of the alley and looked at Faversham's body in the road. There was no point in even checking; he instinctively knew he was dead. He stepped back into the shadows of the alley. He hadn't been seen. The coach driver jumped down from his seat and ran to look at the bloody heap lying in the road. A small group of passers-by gathered round the body. The coachman was in shock and could only stand and repeat, "I never had a chance…he just ran out in front of me! I never had a chance!"

A woman came forward and put her arm around the driver to console him as he suddenly bent forward and vomited into the slush.

John stepped back into the shadows of the alley, then turned and hurried back to where he had left Janetta.

"Come on," he said, "I think we'd better leave here while we can."

"Ya didn't kill 'im did ya John?"

"Didn't hav' to Jan, he got 'it by a coach."

He put his arm around her and together they slipped away into the night.

****

Janetta didn't arrive back at the house until half past eleven that evening. By then the house was usually quiet with everyone having retired, but on this evening the lamps were still lit, and when Janetta entered the back door she found Ethel sitting at the kitchen table sobbing.

Janetta closed the door behind her and went over to put her arm around Ethel.

"What's the matter Mrs A?" she asked

"Oh Jan you'll never guess." Ethel sniffled, "It's Faversham. He's been killed!"

"Killed!" she tried to sound surprised.

Ethel looked up at her and suddenly stopped sniffing.

"What happened to you?" She held Janetta by the chin and turned her face first one way then the other, studying it carefully. "You're all cut and bruised girl. Have you been in a fight?" She stood up and took a step back to get a good look at her. "Look at your dress; it's all wet and muddy! What have you been doing, girl?"

Janetta sank back onto a stool. There was no avoiding this. She couldn't hide her injuries, and besides, it was too much of a coincidence her being in a fight the same night that Faversham died. All she could try to do was keep John out of it.

"Oh Mrs A I've 'ad a terrible night," she sighed. "Faversham is dead ya say? How?"

"Run over by coach on the Citadel Road. We had soldiers round here earlier telling the Colonel. He had to go down to the mortuary to identify him. He's pretty upset, Jan. Asked to see you when you got home. Where have you been girl?"

"At the Swan Mrs A, I needed a drink and Mabel helped clean me up."

"What the hell happened to you?"

"I'll tell you later Mrs A. I'd better go and see the Colonel."

Janetta wearily went upstairs to the library where she found the Colonel sitting in his favourite chair by the fire. He barely glanced up at her but gestured to her to come and sit by him.

"Ah, Jan my dear your back. Come and sit with me I've got some bad news for you."

"Yeh I know, Mrs A told me. It's Faversham."

"Yes he's been killed, poor chap. Run over by the Exeter chaise."

Janetta sat on the floor beside him and rested her head on his knee. It felt strange but somehow right to do so. Their relationship was over now that she was to marry John, yet she still felt real warmth when she was with him. She felt safe, as she did when she was with her father. He placed his hand on her head and began to gently stroke her hair.

"I shall miss Faversham you know Jan. He was a good fellow."

"I'm sorry he's dead but he weren't so good you know," said Janetta.

"What do you mean, Jan?" The Colonel was surprised by this statement and didn't know what to make of it.

"Look I didn't know he'd been killed an' I'm sorry an all, but I can't feel too upset about it 'caus…"

"Because what Jan?"

"'Caus he tried to rape me this evening, that's why!"

"He did what?" flared the Colonel, suddenly becoming very angry as his protective spirit towards Janetta rose quickly to the surface.

"He tried…"

"I'll kill the bastard!" he exclaimed; then realizing the futility of what he'd said he slumped back in his chair. "The bastard!"

“I bumped into him in the town and he wanted me to marry ’im and not John. When I says ‘no’ he gets angry an’ drags me in an alley an’ tries to rape me; but I fought ’im off. We hit one another quite a bit and then he runs off. That was the last I sees of ’im.”

“Oh my poor Jan,” whispered the Colonel as he looked at her face. In the light of the fire he began to see her cuts and bruises. He gently ran his fingers over her wounds before leaning forward to kiss each one in turn.

“Then I suppose he fled in guilt,” he said, “and ran under the wheels of the coach. Poor devil, that’s no way to die!”

Janetta rested her head back on his knee and watched the flames of the fire. After a couple of minutes the Colonel broke the silence.

“Do you have a ‘best dress’ to be married in?”

“I’ll wear my green one.”

“Will you let me buy you a new one, Jan?”

“You’ve been too good to me already.”

“It would make me very happy to do so, Jan.”

She squeezed his hand affectionately and together they sat and watched the fire.

CHAPTER 7

Mrs Martin
1876

The morning of Saturday February 1st was full of dark clouds. Rain fell steadily in a chilly wind. Janetta arose from her bed, reluctant to leave the warm cocoon of her sheets and stepped out onto the cold wooden floor. She could see her own breath in the cold air of the room, but there would be no hiding in the warmth of her bed today. Ethel had already knocked on the door twice and was now standing over her with a cup of tea. Janetta was used to getting up at six every morning to light the fires and help prepare the breakfast; she assumed she'd be allowed to sleep in a bit on this morning as it was her wedding day. Ethel, however, was too excited for her and couldn't wait to get her ready.

"Come on girl, it's your big day today. Up you get now."

Janetta groaned as she sat on the edge of her bed and timidly put her feet down on the cold boards. She threw a shawl about her shoulders, and on tiptoe so as not to put her feet right down on the cold floor, she went to the window.

The wind was blowing the rain hard against the glass and rattling the casement. Janetta shivered.

"It'll clear up, you mark my words," said Ethel. "Now get dressed and come down to the kitchen and I'll do your hair."

"Ta, Mrs A," yawned Janetta as she reached under her counterpane for her bloomers and vest. She always kept them there in the winter so they wouldn't be too cold to put on in the morning. The sound of the rain and the dark gray of the early morning sky gave her no enthusiasm for her big day, and she found herself dreading the whole thing. Her hands were too cold to do up the laces on her boots so she sat on the bed cradling her tea to warm her fingers.

Ethel scurried about in the kitchen preparing breakfast and getting herself in a tizzy over all the things she had to do. She felt as if her own daughter was getting married and she alone was responsible for getting everything just right.

"Oh come on, where is that girl?" she muttered to herself as she fried the Colonel's sausages and potatoes.

Janetta came down the stairs looking as if she'd been at an all night gin party. Her hair was unbrushed and her dress half unbuttoned. She'd been sick and was feeling decidedly fragile.

"I feel dreadful," she announced as she entered the kitchen.

"Morning sickness and wedding nerves, a perfect combination," said Ethel, relieved to find her up at last. "Want some breakfast?"

Janetta screwed up her face, "Christ, no! Got any more tea though?"

"Pity your folks can't come to your wedding," said Ethel as she poured some more hot water into the kettle. "Your side of the church is going to be a bit thin isn't it?"

"Mmm," agreed Janetta who hadn't told Ethel that she'd not invited her parents. It had only been a month since she'd rowed with her mother and this hasty wedding would only serve to justify everything her mother had said. Perhaps she was a slut after all, but she was damned if she was going to give her mother the satisfaction of saying, "I told you so." She had decided to marry, have her baby, settle down and then, when a suitable amount of time had passed, she'd go home to visit and show off her new husband and child.

The only problem was Jane and Thomas. They knew, and were coming to the wedding. Janetta pleaded with them to keep her secret and although much angered by the deception, they reluctantly agreed.

"I hung your dress up last night so there shouldn't be any wrinkles in it," announced Ethel as she poured more tea into Janetta's cup and buttered a slice of bread for her. "Beautiful it is! You're going to look a real picture, that's for sure."

Janetta slurped her tea.

"Bless the Colonel! What a kindness it was for him to buy it for you. Don't know as I know a kinder man."

"Yeah!" agreed Janetta, not wishing to get involved any deeper in the conversation. She half-wondered if Mrs A was being sarcastic since she knew all about their affair; but decided that it wasn't in her nature to be catty and so let it go without comment.

"Well I do believe the rain's stopping," said Ethel as she looked up through the basement window, "sky's not so dark now!"

Janetta pushed her chair back, and with the bread hanging out of her mouth and her tea in her hand, she mumbled that she was going to go and do something with her hair.

"Quite right! Time to get yourself ready! Off you go."

Janetta sauntered back up the stairs, still half asleep.

****

Down at the Citadel, John had also been woken up earlier than usual. Reveille was not for another half an hour, but he was up and wide-awake, pacing up and down between the bunks wishing his stomach would settle down. Sergeant Bennet came into the barrack and grinned from ear to ear.

"Bugger me the handsome groom's all a tizzy," he said. "Can't wait for your orders, eh, lad?"

"No sarg!"

The previous day John had asked Sergeant Bennet to be his best man, and the Sergeant had beamed with pride at having been asked. "Tis an honour you scoundrel," he'd said, "You bloody need me there anyway to sees ya don't make a right bollocks of it, lad!"

John now fished in his pocket for the ring he'd bought Janetta and gave it to the Sergeant.

"You'll need to take care of this for me sarg."

Sergeant Bennet looked at the ring with some surprise. This was no soldier's brass ring, but a real gold band, and John could see in the Sergeant's eyes what he was thinking.

"It was me mother's, sarg. I just had it polished up to look new, like."

"Very nice too lad! Lucky girl your bride!"

John could sense the Sergeant wasn't sold on the story, but he could hardly say the money came from the Colonel. That would have been far too suspect.

"Well come on, lad. Best dress uniform for today. And polished boots so's I can sees me face in them." Then turning to the rest of the sleeping squad, he bellowed, "Come on you bastards out of bed." He slapped his swagger stick across their legs as he walked up the aisle between the beds. "Got a wedding to go to today. Up, up come on, I'm ya reveille this morning, git ya asses out of bed!"

John grinned at the sight of all his mates scrambling to get out of their bunks, rubbing their eyes and moaning about the hour.

John's day had come. He was jubilant if not a little nervous. He was about to become the envy of every soldier in the Raglan barracks, having the prettiest wife in the battalion. He was determined to cherish this day and enjoy every minute of it, as long as the damned rain stopped.

By ten o'clock the rain had stopped. A fine mist continued to cast a depressing haze over the otherwise pretty village church of *St. Luke with St. Andrew* in Stoke Damerel. The trees around the churchyard dripped on the cold tombstones, and there was a heavy scent of damp earth and moss. A small group of people stood under the trees waiting for the bride to arrive, but most had gone inside to shelter from the damp air.

Jane and Thomas Vanson stood by the church gate sharing an umbrella. Thomas looked very smart in his stovepipe hat, but felt distinctly uncomfortable as he always did when dressed up. Jane kept slapping his hands away from his cravat as he fiddled with it.

"Damned thing's choking me, Jannie! You did it up too tight!"

"Oh do stop complaining Tom, you look very smart for a change."

"Wish she'd arrive, I'm getting damned cold out here!" Thomas tried to loosen his cravat again by running his finger round his neck and pulling. Jane tutted at him.

"This Martin fellow's got a damned fine turn out, I must say! Half the bloody army in that church!" Thomas said, pointing at the church.

"I wish Mum and Dad were here," said Jane to nobody in particular. She hardly expected Thomas to be listening to her. "Daddy would be so happy. She was always his favourite you know. He would wish to be here, Tom, it's too much of Janetta not to invite him. That's what it is, too much! Daddy should be giving her away!"

A look of sudden horror crossed her face.

"Who's giving her away Tom, who?"

Thomas shrugged his shoulders and straightened his waistcoat.

"Oh it's too much Tom, it really is," exclaimed Jane, and then seeing the carriage turning into the driveway, "she's 'ere, Tom, at last she's here." She turned to take one last look at Thomas before Janetta arrived and slapped his hands away from his waistcoat, "Oh do stop fiddling, Tom!"

The coach stopped beside the gate, but too close to a heap of wet, steaming horse manure on the road. Jane jumped into action.

"Driver pull up a bit more, we can't have the bride stepping out into that."

The driver looked down at the mess and grunted.

He clicked his tongue and the horses stepped forward a couple of feet.

"That'll do driver, thank you," called Jane and then turning to Thomas, who had been watching the performance with a bemused grin on his face, "Well do something. Help Jan out."

Thomas opened the door and for a second he stopped breathing. Janetta sat poised on the edge of her seat ready to step down. He couldn't remember ever seeing such a beautiful young woman in all his life. Janetta smiled at him and held out her hand as she waited for him to help her down. She was dressed in her new burgundy gown the Colonel had purchased for her. Her hair was styled in small ringlets that peeked out of her ivory colored bonnet and framed her face. Her pale blue eyes sparkled.

"Allo Tommy dear, does I look alright?"

Only her diction, thought Thomas, told you she wasn't a real lady.

"You look absolutely enchanting, sis. Here, let me help you down."

He took her by the arm and assisted her out of the carriage. Jane stepped forward to greet her younger sister.

"Jan, you look absolutely wonderful," she said as she gave her a kiss on her cheek, and then asked, "Jan, who's giving you away?"

Janetta straightened her dress and thought for a second as the question sank in. Her father would have been so proud to walk her down the aisle and for a second, a lump rose in her throat. Thomas reached into the carriage and retrieved her posy of flowers and handed them too her. Janetta thanked him and then grabbed him by the arm.

"Tommy will, won't you love!"

"Oh! Er, I'd be honoured Jan dear, to be sure," Thomas stammered.

Jane gave a disapproving look, but realized that Thomas was the nearest male family member, she sighed, "Yes, well he'll do, I suppose."

"He'll do very nicely!" replied Janetta, and Thomas beamed with pride. Jane groaned under her breath.

Their attention was diverted by the sound of a horse being ridden hard up the lane towards them. They all turned to see a young Royal Artillery officer wrapped in a dark blue cloak, rein in his horse by the church gate. The mount was mud-splattered and sweating from its gallop, and the officer looked as if he was on urgent business. He jumped down and hurried through the gate, excusing himself as he passed Jane and Thomas, but upon seeing Janetta, he stopped briefly, tipped his cap and met Janetta's eyes for a second.

"Good luck to you miss," he said in a soft gentle voice.

Janetta smiled and thanked him, while thinking how handsome he was; almost pretty she thought.

The officer continued on into the church, while Janetta watched him go in silence.

Jane, noting Janetta's gaze, broke the spell, "Butter wouldn't melt in his mouth, would it? Handsome devil though, I'll give him that!"

Ethel Atkin, who had stepped out the other side of the coach assisted by the driver, walked around from the back of the carriage. She too was all dressed up in her Sunday best clothes, but Thomas, rather uncharitably, thought she resembled mutton dressed up as lamb.

"Jane, Tommy," said Janetta; "I'd like you to meet my dear friend, Ethel Atkin."

"Pleased to meet you, I'm sure," said Ethel in the most refined voice she could muster. "Rain's held off at least."

"Yes indeed, very fortunate," replied Jane. "Shall we all go in. I think they're all waiting for us."

Thomas politely tipped his hat at Ethel and then, with Janetta on his arm, started walking proudly up the gravel path to the church.

****

John had been waiting in the church, with his Sergeant beside him, for over half an hour. Janetta wasn't particularly late, rather John had insisted on being very early, much to the amusement of the minister. The church, as Thomas had observed, was filled with soldiers in their best dress blue uniforms. It made an impressive sight. The few civilians were John's family and a handful of Janetta's friends. It was cold and damp in the church and John sat in the first pew idly exhaling and watching his breath dissipate in the frigid air. The Sergeant checked every couple of minutes to be sure he had the ring and looked more nervous than John. John grinned at him.

"Worse than facing enemy fire this, eh Sarg?"

"Not long to go now, lad. You'll be fine!" replied Sergeant Bennet.

"*Yes, but will you be,*" thought John.

The latch on the church door clattered and everybody turned around to see if it was the bride, but an adjutant entered looking rather uncomfortable as he walked up the aisle towards John. When he got to the front he nodded at John, rather formerly acknowledging him, "Martin!"

"Sir," John replied.

The adjutant then stepped up to the sergeant, bent forward and whispered into his ear. Sergeant Bennet looked shocked and said, "Right sir, as soon as we get back sir."

The adjutant nodded again to Martin and walked back down the aisle and out of the church. A murmur ran through the congregation. John, worrying that it might have something to do with Janetta, whispered to Sergeant Bennet, "What's going on Sarg?"

"Nuffink fa you to be concerned with on ya wedding day, lad," whispered the Sergeant, checking his pocket for the ring again.

John felt a sinking feeling in the pit of his stomach. Had the Colonel done something to interfere with the marriage? No! After all, he hadn't stopped the service. Was he regretting what had passed between himself and John? Was he going to arrest him when he got back to the barracks for blackmailing a superior officer? Was the adjutant outside this very minute talking to Janetta?

"Must 'av been pretty serious to bring the adjutant all the way here, sarg!" said John.

The Sergeant grimaced realizing that John was not going to be satisfied until he was assured it had nothing to do with his wedding.

"It's the Colonel lad," whispered the Sergeant.

John worst fears were about to come true. He felt himself break out into a sweat.

"He's had an attack!"

"An attack?" John felt almost relieved.

" 'is 'art lad,"

"Bloody 'ell!"

The church door latch echoed in the stone walls as someone opened the door. Immediately the organist began to play and there was a loud shuffling as everyone got to their feet.

John was about to become a married man.

****

Ethel thought the entire wedding was the most beautiful she'd ever seen. She mopped her nose and dried her eyes on her handkerchief all through the service. She always cried at weddings but this one seemed more special to her. It was as if Janetta was the daughter she'd never had. How beautiful Janetta looked as she stood beside her dashing young soldier boy in his smart blue uniform with its bright red stripe down the leg and shining black boots.

Thomas played his part with dignity and even Jane had to admit that the whole wedding was quite perfect, despite the absence of her mother and father.

For Janetta, the next hour passed in a blur of mumbling sermons and singing of hymns, punctuated by a few moments of clarity when she had to concentrate on repeating her vows. She stood beside John wondering if this was what it was supposed to feel like on your wedding day. She was cold, but didn't feel it. Happy but didn't notice it. Confused and befuddled by everything about her and all the time aware of John looking so handsome beside her.

She'd never seen him in dress uniform before and found herself ignoring the service as she looked at him in amazement. He was so dashing. His blue tunic had a fine red line down the front and a row of gold buttons each with the regimental emblem on them. He wore a white belt and white sash that hung over his right shoulder and went diagonally across his chest. His collar was faced in red and he held his black helmet under his right arm. He was her very own soldier boy.

Her mind wandered to the Colonel. She wondered where he was at that moment and whether he was regretting having let her go. She thought about the beautiful house that could have been hers, and then about the soldiers' wives' cottages next to the barracks. What would she do all day while John was off soldiering? Would she like her new army friends? Then she thought about the money. It was a goodly sum; more than she had ever expected to possess, so for now she was going to be comfortable. Perhaps this marriage was going to be all right after all. Perhaps she could mould John into the type of soldier that would make a good sergeant. Perhaps she wouldn't be a lowly bombardier's wife for too long. She had to show her mother she could make good in the world, and this was her first real opportunity.

The minister announced that they were now 'man and wife', and she found herself being kissed by John and knew that it was done. She was officially Mrs Janetta Martin.

****

After the wedding service, the rice throwing outside the church and the tearful good wishes from Jane and Ethel, they had got into a rented wagon and driven off to the barracks and their new home.

John didn't tell Janetta about the Colonel for fear of spoiling the wedding. Janetta therefore enjoyed her big day and looked forward to settling in and making a new home.

When they arrived at Raglan Barracks, Janetta was surprised to see a large crowd of soldiers milling around outside the gate. Once again they were pelted with rice and Janetta received a great many whistles and several over-enthusiastic kisses. John became the butt of lewd, yet good-natured gibes and after pulling a couple of enlisted men off his wife, gave her a big smile and said, "Welcome to the army luv."

They drove on through the crowd, John with a broad self-satisfied smile on his face, and Janetta giggling at the treatment she had received from the soldiers.

"See, they luvs ya already!" said John as they drove down a small street at the side of the barrack's outer wall.

Before her, Janetta saw a row of small terraced cottages. They were plain red brick and quite small, but ivy covered some of the front wall giving them a slightly quaint appearance that softened their facade. It seemed to her that everyone in the street was standing outside waiting for her to arrive.

"Who are this lot?" asked Janetta.

"Them's your new neighbours, they are," replied John as he brought the carriage to a stop outside number six.

A small crowd of women gathered round to welcome them. John jumped down and held his arms out to lift Janetta out of the wagon.

All the women gathered round and seemed to be speaking at once. All welcoming her and inviting her for tea and complimenting her on how beautiful she looked. Janetta didn't know who to respond to first and was quite overwhelmed by the attention.

"Ladies, ladies," said John, in an attempt to calm them. "Let her get in. You can all meet Janetta in good time. Come on now let us through!"

They reluctantly parted to allow John and Janetta to push through to their new front door. Somebody had already opened it and Janetta wondered who else, other than John, had a key.

John suddenly bent down and swept her off her feet, cradling her in his arms. She gave a little scream of surprise.

"There now!" said John grinning from ear to ear. "Gotta carry me bride over the threshold, ain't I?"

He turned sideways and stepped into the dark hall, being careful not to bang Janetta's head on the doorframe. Once inside he nudged the door shut with his foot and let her stand down. A small cheer and the sound of clapping could be heard outside as the door shut.

John gave her a long kiss before reluctantly turning back towards the door.

"I'll get the bags," he said.

He disappeared back out to the wagon and the crowd of ladies while Janetta looked about her in the hall. Her heart sank into her belly as she studied the interior of the cottage. She wasn't in a hall at all but the front parlour, a very small dark and damp room with virtually no furniture. There was a table in the middle of the room and two rickety old chairs. Against the back wall stood an old and badly chipped sideboard. In front of her was a black fireplace that hadn't been cleaned out. The floor was bare wood.

Janetta's eyes, used to working in the Colonel's house, instinctively scanned the line where the walls met the ceiling and counted the cobwebs that hung in clumps. Dust covered the mantal and some horsehair stuffing was showing through a tear in the seat of one of the chairs.

A staircase ascended to the second floor and a door led through to a kitchen at the back.

Janetta's disappointment was profound. Certainly she'd been raised in a small, overcrowded miner's cottage, but at least it was cosy and respectable. This was depressing to say the least.

A pot clattered in the kitchen and Janetta went through expecting to find a stray cat making a nuisance of itself. Instead she found herself staring at the large rear end of a rather scruffy middle-aged woman who was bending over and rummaging through a cupboard under the sink.

"Who are you?" asked Janetta with some surprise.

The woman stood up and groaned as she held the small of her back. She turned to face Janetta and gave a huge grin exposing her missing front teeth. She ran her hands over her unkempt hair and sniffed.

"Gawd look at me now! What a state I's in! Hoped to get cleaned up a bit before you got 'ere!"

She took a step towards Janetta, seemingly unaware of her horror, and stuck out a grubby hand in greeting.

"I'm Essie dear, short for Esmeralda," she shook Janetta's hand rather too vigorously. Janetta winced as she felt the woman's hot sweaty palm.

"Esmeralda Wicks. Gunner Harry Wicks is my man. Drunken sot he is, but I luvs him… well you got to ain't ya dear?"

"S'pose you 'ave yeh," replied Janetta who was beginning to think she was in some bizarre dream. "Excuse me but what were ya doing?"

Janetta really wanted to ask "*Who the bloody hell are you and why are you in my house*?" but she thought she had better not be rude.

"Lost me bleeding egg whisk…think I may have lent it to her next door," she gestured towards the wall.

"Why would your egg whisk be under my sink?" asked Janetta. There was a slight pause, as realization of what Janetta was thinking slowly dawned on Esmeralda.

"Oh, I sees," she wailed and gave an overly loud laugh, "Didn't tell ya then?"

"Tell me what?"

"We're roomies see! You have the front room and front bedroom and we have the back parlour an' back bedroom. We share the kitchen and the outhouse of course."

"Oh!" said Janetta, unable to hide her disappointment.

"Don't you worry dear, we'll get along just fine. By the way everyone calls me Essie!"

"Right!...Yes well! Essie..."

Janetta heard John coming in with her bags, so she turned and retreated from the kitchen.

John saw the look on her face and came over to her and hugged her. "You've met Essie then?" he asked.

Janetta just nodded her head and sniffed.

"Oh John, this is awful, we've got money."

"Shhh!" hushed John. "Best keep that just between us."

"Yes, but we can afford better than this John."

"I know luv, but in the army it's best if you keep your privates to yerself. I'm only a bombardier and this is all I'm supposed to be able to afford. These are army married quarters. They'll do fine for a while. Besides, we won't be here very long."

"Won't be 'ere long? Where we going then?" Janetta perked up. Anywhere would be better than this.

"India I think, we're being posted."

"India!" Janetta shrieked. "You ain't leaving me here I 'ope!"

"No 'course I ain't. You'd like to see India wouldn't ya?"

"Blimey yeh, John! Ain't never travelled further than Plymouth."

"Good I'll arrange your ticket then," said John as Esmeralda came through from the kitchen.

"Clean forgot to congratulate ya both. What a day it's been eh? You two luv birds getting' hitched and then the poor Colonel."

Janetta's eyes widened with fright, "What about the Colonel?"

"Lord didn't they tells ya? The whole regiment knows dearie, he 'ad an 'art attack this morning."

"Oh God," exclaimed Janetta, "is 'e...?"

"No 'e ain't dead dearie, but they say 'e's pretty poorly, not expected to last."

Janetta turned pale, and for a second or two she swayed as if she was about to faint.

"I didn't want to tell you 'til after the wedding," said John supporting her by her shoulders.

"Oh God, I got a see 'im, John I gotta," she wailed and pulling free of his grasp she fled the house, tears streaming down her face.

"Gawd! What av I said," exclaimed Esmeralda, holding her hand to her mouth.

"It's alright Essie," John reassured her. "I'd better go with her!"

John ran out of the house to find Janetta on the buggy seat gathering the reins into her fingers. Tears streaked her face and the group of women in the street watched in amazement as John jumped up onto the buggy just in time before Janetta vigorously slapped the reins on the horses back.

"Gee-up," she yelled, and the mare took off at a gallop so that John, who had barely had time to seat himself, had to hang on for his life. John made a couple of attempts at taking the reins from her, but she slapped his hands away and pushed the mare harder, so he resigned himself to being a terrified passenger.

It didn't take long to get to the Colonel's house. John had never been there before and was surprised at how big it was. Outside were a collection of buggies and horses tethered to the black iron railings outside the front door. Janetta reined in the mare stopping her too quickly, her hooves skidding slightly on the damp cobblestones. She jumped down and ran to the front door. John sat breathlessly recovering his wits before getting down and tying the mare to the railings. Janetta had already gone in.

She wasn't used to coming through the front door but today she gave it no thought. Still in her wedding gown, her hair neatly curled in delicate ringlets, she looked more like a lady than a servant so nobody tried to stop her. The hall and front room were full of officers looking particularly grim and speaking in low tones.

Janetta looked about her as if expecting to see the Colonel chatting amongst his guests. For a second she even expected to see Faversham serving drinks on a silver tray.

The officers all looked in her direction when she came in. It was apparent that several of them were struck by her uncommon beauty but did their best to conceal their admiration because of the graveness of the gathering. Janetta didn't notice them.

"Janetta dear," it was Ethel coming down the stairs. She had been crying. "He's up here. He'd like to see you."

Janetta ran up the stairs taking two steps at a time, and Ethel almost chastised her for not behaving in a lady-like manner, but let it go because of her distress.

Janetta entered the Colonel's room. The curtains were drawn so that the room was dark and stuffy. Six or seven officers gathered about the bed. Janetta peered into the gloom waiting for her eyes to adjust to the dark. The Colonel was lying on the bed in his uniform, but the tunic and shirt were undone. He still had his boots on. He turned his head to look at her and a smile crossed his face. He waved a hand towards the door, "leave us gentlemen, please," he said in a weak voice. "Jan, open the damned curtains. Let me look at you."

She crossed to the window as the officers filed out onto the landing, and threw the curtains back allowing the sun to brighten the room.

"That's better! Never could understand why people think you should die in the dark. Come here, girl."

Janetta walked over to him and sat on the side of his bed.

"Oh Jan, how lovely you are in that dress. I'm glad you're here, because I wanted to say how very sorry I am that I didn't marry you."

"Shhh," whispered Janetta.

"No it's alright, Jan. I feel better for saying it while I can." He frowned and stiffened slightly as if fighting a spasm of pain. Janetta squeezed his hand.

"But it wouldn't do ya see, they would have made you feel unwelcome, they would have been horrid to you."

"It's alright, really it is."

Janetta couldn't believe the heaviness she felt inside. When she worked for him, she thought he was a pathetic old man with kinky sexual practices whom she could manipulate into marrying her for his money. Later she had no compunction to extort money out of him. Yet now she saw a kind, quiet, introspective man who really had loved her in his own clumsy way, and she felt a terrible loss and guilt.

"If I had married you Jan, you would have been a rich woman but scorned and shunned by society. It's better this way. John's a resourceful man. You'll do well together."

Janetta wondered what he meant by resourceful. Was he referring to John's blackmail? Did he know that they had conspired together?

"I'm sorry," Janetta wept, "I'm so sorry, I did… no I do love you and I don't want you to leave me," Janetta sobbed.

The door opened and the doctor came in. He placed a hand on Janetta's shoulder and asked her to leave. "He needs to rest my dear," he said in a rather condescending tone.

"I'll see you again, Jan, I'll see you again," the Colonel whispered.

Janetta leaned forward and kissed him on his lips, before standing up and allowing herself to be lead out of the room by the doctor.

Outside, John was still waiting by the buggy. He hadn't gone in. He felt uncomfortable in the presence of so many officers and besides he recognized that this was part of Jan's life that she had to conclude on her own. He also felt a little afraid of facing the Colonel again after having blackmailed him.

Ethel and Janetta came out of the front door together. Ethel had her arm about Janetta's shoulder and Janetta looked utterly dejected. They passed a couple of words on the step before Janetta walked back towards the buggy. Ethel waved at John and gave him a sympathetic smile.

Janetta sat back in the buggy and waited while John released the reins from the railings and got up beside her.

"Take me home, John," she said wearily as she laid her head on his shoulders and quietly wept.

CHAPTER 8

Posting
1876

Janetta's introduction to the life of a soldier's wife did not start smoothly. She wasn't sure what she had expected. She knew her lifestyle would decline considerably from having lived in the colonel's house; but she wasn't prepared for the upheaval that awaited her.

Settling in was makeshift to say the least and Janetta wondered if it was even worth unpacking her clothes since they may be off at any moment. She decided that even if it was only two days, it was still worth hanging up her dresses to let the creases fall out. The bedroom had one small wardrobe that was hardly big enough to hang her wedding dress. When she opened it she discovered it was full of mice.

She screamed and collapsed onto the bed. She wasn't afraid of mice, there had been plenty in the Colonel's house, but she wasn't expecting to see a dozen or more scurrying around in the bottom of her closet.

Esmeralda was just outside on the landing, and hearing Janetta scream she came into the room and immediately started stamping her foot on the mice that were trapped in the corners of the cupboard.

"Bleedin' things," she said. "We'll soon get rid of them for yers! Not scared of a couple of bloody mice are we dear?"

"N-no," stammered Janetta trying to pull herself together. She could see that Esmeralda thought she was a weakling. "I'll be fine Essie."

"You'll soon get used to the place dear, don't you fret none! Best air it out some eh!"

Esmeralda went to the window and tried to open the casement. It seemed stuck, so she braced herself and pulled harder. "Come on you bleeder," she spat through her clenched jaws as she strained. Janetta couldn't help noticing the size of her arms as her muscles tightened against the reluctant window. Finally it gave way and she was able to jerk it up.

"I'll get me man to put some axle grease on it, that'll do the trick!" she said, then gave a great sniff and spat out of the window. Janetta winced and turned away in disgust.

****

A couple of days drifted into a week and a week into two and still the orders to move out didn't come through.

"Typical bloody army!" John moaned as he lit a taper in the fire and brought it up to his face to rekindle the tobacco in his pipe. "Still bloody 'ere."

In the second week the Colonel died and Janetta sank into a depression. It wasn't that she really missed him so much, rather his death signalled the end of a chapter in her life. There was no going back now. She was trying to come to terms with her new lifestyle and that was proving hard to do.

Esmeralda came into the front parlour with a couple of tin mugs of very weak tea. "Er ya go dearie," she said as she handed one to Janetta.

"Ta!" said Janetta in a very unenthusiastic tone as she looked at the dirty smears on the rim of the mug.

Esmeralda sniffed and left the room, and John looked at Janetta with irritation in his eyes.

"Christ Jan, why can't you be civil to Esmeralda, she's got a kind heart."

"Well…!" Jan said dismissively, but couldn't finish the sentence.

Since moving in, Janetta and Esmeralda had come to a kind of frosty understanding. Janetta was appalled by Esmeralda's lack of personal hygiene and didn't make any effort to hide her repulsion, and Esmeralda considered Janetta to be a "stuck up little madam who's no better than she ought to be!" as she told her husband. However, both women tolerated one another and struggled to be civil for the sake of domestic harmony. During the day, they tried to stay out of one another's way, but in the evening when the men came home the tension between them was palpable.

Janetta didn't see much of Essie's husband, Harry, although she liked him better than Essie. He arrived home each evening with John after a day at the battery and he'd usually say, "Evening" as he passed through to the back room and then, "good night," when he and Essie went up to bed. That was about all that Harry ever said. Janetta and John would lie in bed some nights and smile at one another as they listened to Harry and Essie making love. The knocks and creaking of the bed could be heard easily through the thin dividing wall, and Essie was very vocal in her passion.

Although entertaining, it actually bothered Janetta quite a bit to think that some nights Harry and Essie laid awake listening to them and it stopped her from giving John the full benefit of her appetite. A fact that didn't go unnoticed by John.

"You've been as miserable as sin all week," said John, who had been feeling frustrated at the situation and helpless to do anything about it.

"Shit! Look around ya for Christ sake! Look at it!" Janetta screamed in a sudden fit of pique, "It's a bleed'n dump and we shouldn't be 'ere. We can afford much better than this if we're staying, or a ticket to India if we ain't, but I didn't marry ya to sit around in this crap 'ole. So do sumfin about it or I will, and believe me you won't like the outcome of that!"

John was taken by surprise by this sudden outburst and stared at her in astonishment.

He had married the most beautiful woman he had ever seen. He was intoxicated by her long dark hair and petite trim figure and congratulated himself on marrying a woman with an energetic and sensuous libido, despite the fact that he hadn't seen much of it lately. He worshipped her and found himself wanting to cry with sheer delight every time he laid in her arms, then suddenly he was broad-sided by her vicious outpouring of venom. The fire in her eyes changed from lust to blind anger and for a second or two he actually feared her.

"What the fuck do you expect me to do? I'm in the army and the army tells me when I can move and when I can stay. And as far as anybody is concerned we ain't got no money."

"Oh who the 'ell cares anyway," spat Janetta.

“I think,” said John, half whispering through his clenched teeth as he leaned forward in his chair and stared straight into Janetta’s eyes, “that you have forgotten ’ow we got it and who we got it from. So keep ya bleed’n mouth shut.”

John’s anger quieted Janetta and she scowled as she sipped her tea and stared into the blackened and cracked tile fireplace.

This was not what she expected when she married John. She visualized her new house, not grand, but quite respectable, and she imagined herself playing hostess to the other wives in her own parlour, serving them tea in nice china with white doilies and delicate sandwiches. She dreamed of attending social dances with the regiment and dancing with all the soldiers in their smart uniforms. She saw herself having servants about her bungalow in India and John rising through the ranks and becoming an officer, although in truth she knew the chances of that happening were extremely slim unless he purchased a commission. She had pictured herself moving up in the world, but still they sat in front of a pokey fire in a small, damp room, in an old, dark house that they shared with a scruffy and unhygienic tenant.

This was not what she expected at all.

****

Four weeks after the Colonel’s death, on Janetta’s washing day when the house was covered in damp sheets and assorted undergarments airing on a wooden clothes horse and the backs of chairs, a set of bony knuckles tapped on the front door.

Esmeralda opened it to find a short slender gentleman in a dark suit standing on the doorstep. He was almost completely bald but for a thin strip of long, greasy and graying hair that circled the back of his head. A pair of thin wire-rimmed spectacles perched on his nose. Under his arm was a small portable writing table.

“Good day to you, Miss Rundel,” he beamed, and pulling a small card from his waistcoat pocket, he thrust it at Esmeralda. “I’m Joshua Heartley of Ficks, Ficks and Heartley, solicitors of law.”

“Well Mr ’eartley,” cut in Esmeralda, “I’m not Miss Rundel and Miss Rundel ain’t Miss Rundel neither, and that’s a fact!”

“Oh!” exclaimed Mr Heartley.

"But you'd better come in!" She opened the door to its fullest extent and turned away from the visitor to call out to Janetta, who was in the kitchen ironing. "It's a gentleman for you dear!" she called. "A Mr 'earthrug!". Esmerelda chuckled to herself; pleased with her little joke.

"Heartley!...Joshua Heartley, Miss Rundel, at your service." His voice tailing away as Janetta entered the front room and he no longer had to shout.

He stepped further into the room looking for a chair not covered by laundry. Janetta pulled a pair of bloomers off one, and the gentleman smiled appreciatively and sat down.

"Our company is handling the estate of Colonel Wentworth, Miss Rundel."

"I'm Mrs Martin now!" interrupted Janetta, who remained standing causing Mr Heartley to nervously stand up again. "Sit down do, Mr Heartley."

He smiled, nodded his head and sat down again.

Esmeralda, full of curiosity, remain standing by the door.

"The Colonel left a very extensive will, in which he describes in detail how he wished his estate to be divided... and I'm happy to inform you that you are particularly mentioned."

He paused at this point as if expecting Janetta to respond with some exclamation of excitement; when she remained silent and stony faced he seemed, for a second or two, to be disappointed.

Esmeralda moved a little further into the room.

Mr Heartley cleared his throat and pressed on.

"Well he has left you, Mrs Martin, the princely sum of ten pounds," he stressed the amount as if to emphasize how fortunate she was.

Esmeralda gave a little gasp of excitement but hushed immediately as Janetta glared at her.

"Well, thank you for telling me," she said, showing no sign of surprise or gratitude.

"There was...one other item," said Mr Heartley rather apologetically. Janetta raised an eyebrow but otherwise remained as silent as before. "He also bequeathed to you his fob watch and chain; that in itself was quite valuable I'm led to believe,...however, I'm sorry to have to inform you Mrs Martin, that the watch in question is nowhere to be found among his possessions. Er, if it should turn up, it will of course be passed on to you."

Janetta gave a slight smile and a gentle nod of her head to indicate she understood.

"May I inquire what you would like us to do about the ten pounds Mrs Martin? Do you have a bank in which we may deposit the amount?"

"No, I don't," said Janetta, "I'll just take the cash thank you!"

"Oh! Well!" exclaimed Mr Heartley nervously, "It's a great deal of money Mrs Martin, but if you insist."

He laid his writing desk on Janetta's table, opened the lid and took out a bundle of papers tied together with a ribbon, a pen and a bottle of ink. After examining a couple of the papers, he laid one down on the lid of the desk and smoothed it out with the back of his hand.

"Now, Mrs Martin, this document is a receipt that says that I have given you the sum of ten pounds." He dipped the pen into the ink and handed it to Janetta. "You may make your mark just there, if you please."

Janetta lent forward and carefully scratched an x beside her name taking care not to blot the ink. Mr Heartley seemed pleased and beamed his approval. He pulled from his wallet a large, crisp, bank note folded it in half and handed it to Janetta, who took it from him and slipped it into her apron pocket.

Esmeralda let out a long low whistle.

****

For three long months the regiment waited for their orders. Nobody seemed bothered by it, except Janetta. John was used to the ways of the army and took it in stride despite Janetta's restlessness, but her anger simmered, and she became sullen and uncommunicative.

Her despair was lifted when the orders came through that the regiment was finally moving on May 5th; then shattered once again when they heard that John's battery, the Fifth, stationed in Devonport wasn't going with them. Apparently, there were supposed to be two ships, but for some unexplained reason there was only one, and it could not accommodate the entire regiment. The Fifth Battery would have to wait until the ship returned, and India was not the destination after all.

Janetta took this as a personal slight and tore into John. How dare they put her through this kind of humiliation. Didn't they know how much she longed to leave this hovel? Hadn't John pleaded their case with the brigadier?

"Damn the bloody army," she swore, "damn them and damn you for putting me through this, and damn Esmeralda for being such a..." She stopped short in her rant. It really wasn't Esmeralda's fault. She really was a kind-hearted woman, for all her coarse and common faults.

John was out of his depth with Janetta's mood. He was a trained soldier. He could stand the pounding of guns. He understood the monotonous tedium of the army's daily routine. He tolerated the sergeant major's screams of abuse on the parade ground, that was all part of his world. Despite her beauty Janetta's nature was becoming increasingly volatile. Rather than coming home to face her, John preferred to take on extra duties at work. He was beginning to find out that his beloved Venus was no angel, no esoteric goddess from the dreams of men. His wife was a woman of the earth, a being of flesh and blood and fiery passion; a woman just as capable of rage as loving with passion and sweet feminine seduction. He knew of course that Janetta was not all sweetness and light, for it had been her who instigated the blackmailing of the Colonel, clearly not the act of an angel, but he had been intoxicated with her and blind to her darker side.

John slowly began to fear her as the seeds of doubt were germinating within him. His love was being sorely tested, and he prayed for the new posting as a diversion for Janetta.

****

On the morning of the fifteenth a light drizzle fell. It had been a beautiful spring, but on this day, the sky was heavy with cloud and a dampness in the air that chilled the bones.

Janetta, wrapped in her best shawl, hastened along the coast road towards the *Master Attendance Jetty* where a three-masted clipper lay moored.

There were soldiers and wagons everywhere on the jetty and overflowing into the street. Groups of men stood guarding their kit bags. Clusters of army wives and lovers hung about in animated conversation. Outside the gates a dozen whores assembled to say a well-practised and tearful goodbye to customers, before new ones arrived on the next tide. The bustling atmosphere created a sense of organized chaos.

Janetta, feeling sorry for herself, had decided to see the regiment off. She didn't know why. Perhaps it would make her feel closer to the day she would leave her horrid little house. Perhaps she wanted to wallow in her depression, to feel left behind and have a damn good cry. Perhaps she just needed to get out of the house and away from Esmeralda for a few hours.

Whatever the reason, she pushed her way through the crowds until she found herself a relatively quiet spot between two warehouses. Here she could be alone, away from the gibes and whistles of the soldiers, yet still see everything that was going on.

The ship was only about thirty feet away from her and she found herself staring at it with fascination. It was the first time she'd ever been so close to a ship of such size. There had been plenty of small fishing boats in Tywardreath harbour but never a seagoing sailing ship. She was amazed at how small it looked. Surely, she thought, it couldn't accommodate all those men, wagons, horses and supplies.

Cranes creaked under the load of wagons as they were lifted into the hold. Horses were led up a gangplank and waited to be hoisted into the hatch. Soldiers hung around in untidy groups on the dock, impatient to board.

The aroma of the jetty was overpowering and Janetta walked a few steps closer to the edge to look down into the water. It wasn't the clean clear water of Tywardreath, but a brown, slime-covered soup in which floated an assortment of garbage and a dead cat. Her nostrils were assaulted by the smell of seaweed, mud, tar and horse manure.

Janetta looked at the name, *Assistance*, painted across the stern in yellow letters nearly a foot high. An apt name, she thought, for a troop transport.

"Ugly beast isn't she?"

An officer, who had just walked up to her, suddenly broke Janetta's musing. The sun came out from behind a cloud and Janetta had to squint when she looked up at him. He was silhouetted against the sky, but Janetta had the impression he was very handsome.

"Yes it is," she found herself saying as an automatic response. Then focusing her thoughts, "I'm disappointed that it isn't a steamship. I would like to have gone on a steamship."

The officer chuckled and stepped to one side so that Janetta didn't have to squint into the sun.

"Yes that would have been most agreeable, but you know the army, if it still floats, it'll do."

Janetta smiled at his mock military wisdom, then, seeing him clearly for the first time, recognized him as the young lieutenant who had rushed past her, outside the church on her wedding day. She noticed then how handsome he was and now she thought, he was actually quite pretty. His hair was so perfectly blonde, she wandered if it had been dyed and the waves were exactly correct for the fashion. He stood before her as if posing for a painting, immaculately dressed and looking like he had just spent several minutes fussing in front of a mirror.

"I remember you," she said laying her hand on his arm in perhaps a too familiar manner.

"Mrs Martin," he said formally with a slight nod of his head, and then softening his voice, "it's wonderful to see you again."

"Likewise," she replied, drifting into her most refined voice. "Tell me Lieutenant, where are you going?"

"Nowhere at present. I'm awaiting my orders just like your husband. But it won't be anywhere exotic I know that much."

He stepped closer and bent forward bringing his face closer to hers, and pointing down the jetty.

"See those men there."

Janetta nodded.

"They're with the First and Second Batteries from Forts Staddon, Bovisand and the Citadel and they're going to Dover. To the left of those wagons," he directed his finger at another group. "Those are the Fourth Battery from Ball Point going as far as Woolwich, and the Third – where are the Third?" He looked up and down the jetty but couldn't see them. He shrugged his shoulders. "Well anyway, they're from Fort Picklecomb and are going to Shorncliff, but where we're going is anybody's guess."

"So why are you here, Lieutenant?"

"Came to deliver a dispatch to Brigadier Vachell of the First. Thought I'd hang around a bit though and see them off."

"Me too," said Janetta wistfully.

They stood there for a few minutes watching the commotion around the ship and engaged in occasional small talk. Janetta found that she felt very comfortable with this young Lieutenant. Obviously from a higher station in society, he spoke beautifully and conducted himself in a most gentlemanly manner, so Janetta worked particularly hard at properly pronouncing her words. Her time with the Colonel had taught her well. She had learned many of the refinements of a middle class lady, how to hold her cutlery, how to walk without slouching, how not to use short form words, and most of all, not to use profane language in mixed company. It didn't come naturally. She was always conscious of sounding stiff and practised and knew she would always have her Cornish accent, but if she could just stop herself from sounding common, she might be able to mix in better society.

The Lieutenant didn't seem to notice her stiffness although he undoubtedly knew she was putting on airs for his benefit. He really didn't mind. It was pleasant to be in the company of the most beautiful woman in the regiment. Somehow, her beauty overshadowed her lack of breeding. She wouldn't do in society of course, but there was nothing wrong with befriending her, and he felt proud and quite cocky at being seen standing with her. He knew that at least three quarters of the men on the jetty felt envious of him, wishing they could be with her instead.

"Lieutenant," said Janetta breaking a momentary silence.

"Ma'am?"

"We have been standing here very pleasantly chatting for over ten minutes, and you still haven't introduced yourself to me. I do think it most unfair of you to have this advantage over me."

"Oh ma'am, I do apologize," replied the Lieutenant, with some embarrassment. "I'm Lieutenant Bird ma'am, Timothy Bird, at your service."

"Well Lieutenant Timothy Bird," Janetta teased, "I think it's very gallant of you to spend your morning keeping me company on this very smelly jetty, but I must ask you to do something if you wish to remain talking to me."

The Lieutenant became a little uncomfortable, unable to tell how serious she was being.

"But of course ma'am, what is it?"

"You must stop calling me ma'am. Makes me feel like an old woman." Lieutenant Bird relaxed and grinned at her.

"I do apologize, ma - Janetta," he said bowing slightly before her.

Janetta giggled and slapped him on the arm, "that's much better Lieutenant."

They stood in silence and watched the hubbub of activity for a couple more minutes. The Lieutenant, for all his assured countenance, actually found himself tongue-tied, and a couple of times he took a deep breath and opened his mouth to say something and then refrained.

Finally he blurted out, "Your husband's a very lucky man, Janetta!" No sooner had the words left his mouth he felt a fool. He had crossed that thin line between innocent social chitchat and opening his heart. He paused and held his breath, waiting to see what Janetta's reaction would be.

She didn't look at him but continued watching the sailors toiling on deck.

"Thank you, Lieutenant, I think he is!"

Lieutenant Bird stifled a laugh, "You're teasing me again!"

Janetta turned to look up into his face and smiled, "Just a little, because you're very sweet, dearie."

"*Damn*", she thought, she had slipped; a lady wouldn't use a term like 'dearie'. The Lieutenant didn't notice however, or at least he didn't show it. He was too besotted with her to worry about the way she spoke.

They were interrupted by the approach of another officer. Lieutenant Bird instinctively stepped back from Janetta to create a respectable distance between them, but the gesture did not go unnoticed by the officer, who gave Bird a severe look of disapproval. As he approached he barely acknowledged Janetta, giving her just the hint of a nod of greeting and turning his attention to Lieutenant Bird.

"Lieutenant you shouldn't be here. You're supposed to be on your way back to Devonport, man!"

The officer was at least two inches taller than Lieutenant Bird and had a face pockmarked by smallpox, greasy shoulder length hair and badly discoloured teeth. He gave a withering glare at Bird, which spoke volumes of his dislike.

"Yes sir, I was just leaving."

"Then see you are, Lieutenant. See you are gone from here!"

He looked at Janetta with disdain, turned and marched away.

"I don't think I like him, Lieutenant," said Janetta as she watched him go. "What a frightening man 'e is!"

"There aren't many who do like Major Bernard Cope. He's a most disagreeable man. A good soldier I'm told, but he doesn't like me I'm afraid. I'm not tough enough for him d'ya see."

Janetta placed a soothing hand on his arm.

"I've never seen action you see. He has." Nodding towards the now distant figure of Major Cope. "Don't know how I'd stay the course in a real fight. Not a brave man really. Don't even like it much when they fire the blessed guns." He gave an embarrassed laugh. "And me in the Royal Artillery!"

Janetta found his confession quite compelling and his sad, puppy dog eyes made her want to cuddle him.

"Well I fink you'd do wonderfully," she whispered to him and gave his arm a slight squeeze, while kicking herself for speaking carelessly.

The Lieutenant made an effort to shrug off the effects left behind by the major.

"Your all kindness, Janetta. Now I really must be off. I hope we meet again."

"I expect we'll be sailing together, Lieutenant," replied Janetta in cheerful voice. "Good day to you."

Lieutenant Bird gave a brief bow, turned and walked off down the jetty looking every bit a professional soldier, and feeling on top of the world at having made such a stunningly beautiful friend.

Janetta watched him leave and sighed to herself. She wasn't a wicked woman, was she, for feeling so happy after spending time with a handsome young Lieutenant? There was no harm in it. No law that said a married woman couldn't talk to another man. It was the almost imperceptible feeling of excitement that seemed wrong. It was a feeling she hadn't even felt on her wedding day. She cast her mind back to the day she allowed John to seduce her on the dining table of the alehouse. She'd felt it that day that nervous anticipation of meeting a man that would inevitably lead to sex. It was that venture into the shadows of morality that excited her and made her body ache with desire. That was it! That was the old feeling she hadn't felt for a long time. Certainly never with the Colonel and rarely with John since that first time. This wasn't just sex, she was well used to that, this was a more intense feeling that scared her.

The earlier drizzle had stopped and now it started to rain, a few large drops fell from the leaden sky and bounced on the cobbles. A chilly damp breeze blew off *The Sound.* The stench of seaweed and putrid mud filled Janetta's nostrils as she pulled her collar up over her neck and turned away from the sea. It was time to return home, to her dark little house and Esmeralda's insipid tea.

****

John's battery finally got its orders to move out on May 13th. They were to sail on the 15th, so Janetta packed her trunk and placed it in the hall ready for the move.

Essie laughed at her. "Can't get out of 'ere fast enough eh!"

Janetta winced with embarrassment, not wishing to appear as though it was Esmeralda she was glad to be leaving.

"Still," continued Essie, ignoring Janetta's discomfort, "can't say as I'd be sorry to leave this dump. Always glad to see some place new, I am! Gotta be better then this eh?"

For a second Janetta was stunned, only slowly comprehending what Essie had said. She was leaving with them. Essie was not being left behind. "*Oh God,*" thought Janetta, "*I don't believe it!*"

Janetta nodded her agreement with Essie and on a pretence of having forgotten something, excused herself and went upstairs to her room. Once inside she closed the door and flopped onto the bed with a constricted chest and clenched fists. She gave a couple of sharp kicks of frustration on the bed's foot board, and fought back tears as she stared at the familiar cracks on the yellow stained ceiling.

How could she not have realized Essie and Harry would be coming with them? She assumed she would not only be escaping her dingy little house, but also Essie. She had been so wrapped up in her own desire to get out, it simply had not occurred to her. It was obvious really. Harry and John were in the same battery, so why wouldn't they be travelling together? "Stupid cow!" she said to herself. "Stupid, stupid, stupid!"

Venting her frustration she thrashed about on the bed, kicking her legs and thumping her fists on the mattress. With her eyes tightly closed and teeth clenched, she gave a muffled scream and spat a string of profanities at the ceiling.

When the maelstrom had passed, she was surprised at how much better she felt. She felt relieved by the little outburst of violence. She lay there panting for a minute or two, composing herself before sitting up and smoothing her hair down with the palms of her hands. Then she took a deep breath and prepared to return back downstairs.

"You alright dearie? Lot of banging up there!" said Essie when Janetta reappeared in the kitchen.

"Yeh fine," lied Janetta, "just trying to get something out from under the bed. Heavier than I thought!"

"'Urt yourself moving heavy furniture. Should 'ave ask me, I'd 'ave 'elped ya!"

"Yeh, thanks. Didn't think," responded Janetta, wishing Essie would drop the subject.

"Had a cuss'in who put her back out good an' proper lugging furniture. She was never right after that!" continued Essie as she stoked the fire in the boiler to get some water hot.

"*Oh for Christ's sake, shut up*", thought Janetta, then in an effort to change the subject she asked Essie, "Can I help you with dinner tonight."

Essie straightened up and looked at her with some surprise. She had always cooked the evening meal. Being a good ten years older than Janetta and having lived in the house for some time, she had just continued cooking for all four of them. She had got used to working in the kitchen alone and had never asked for help because she enjoyed cooking, despite not being too accomplished at it. She also suspected that Janetta had never cooked anything in her life.

Janetta, on the other hand, had not offered because she couldn't bear the thought of sharing the kitchen with Essie, preferring instead to stay out of her way.

"Of course ya can ducky!" she said. "Rabbit tonight. Do ya want to skin it for me dearie?" Essie pointed to a headless rabbit lying on the table. "*That'll test her metal,*" thought Essie, "*we'll see how the little madam copes with that.*"

"Fine," said Janetta, and went to the drawer, pulled out a knife and tested its edge across her thumb. Satisfied that it would do the job, she cut off the two front feet, made incisions around the hock joints, slid the blade between the hocks and across the lower part of the body.

Essie watched her with admiration of her technique. Janetta worked fast cutting off the tail then, holding the rabbit by its back legs, she pulled the skin down and forward over the body, turning the pelt inside out. She laid the smooth pink carcass on the table and gave Essie a triumphant look. She knew she had been tested and was determined to prove she was strong enough for such work. Essie didn't know Janetta had been brought up in a poor miner's cottage and had been taught how to cook and skin rabbits by her mother when she was a child.

Essie grinned at Janetta, fully aware that she had lost that round. "Nicely done, dearie! Well you don't need me, obviously! I'll leave ya to it then shall I?" and she turned and left the kitchen perhaps a little too hurriedly. Janetta watched her go and allowed herself a little self-satisfied smirk.

"Cow!" she said under her breath, turning away from the retreating Essie to look for a large pot.

That evening the four of them sat around the table in the front room and ate Janetta's rabbit stew in appreciative silence. Essie had to admit to herself that the stew was much better than anything she'd ever made. The sight of Harry and John heartily digging into second helpings and mopping their plates with bread, made it quite clear that they thought so too. Janetta ate in polite silence and enjoyed Essie's defeat.

Essie may have been bested by Janetta but she wasn't a spiteful woman and she happily reassessed her opinion of Janetta. She still felt Janetta was a little madam thinking herself above everyone else, but at least she now knew Janetta had domestic talents and should make John a good wife. Essie privately worried about John. She liked him and felt he deserved to have a good wife. She did, however, secretly believe that John had fallen in love with Janetta's obvious beauty while being blind to her many flaws.

She was concerned about the fact that Janetta – the wife of a mere bombardier – was too concerned about her wardrobe and toilétte. Janetta always seemed obsessed with her appearance rather than the housework, and there was disturbing gossip going about among the neighbours concerning her past.

"Our last meal together in this house," said Janetta.

"Barring breakfast," interrupted Harry.

"And tomorrow we'll be onboard the *Assistance* and out on the ocean," continued Janetta.

John looked up from the last wiping of gravy off his plate.

"The *Assistance*?" he asked, his eyes fixed on Janetta so that she couldn't side step the question.

"Yes," replied Janetta as nonchalantly as she could, realizing that she was the only one who knew the name of the ship. "Not a very pretty ship!"

"How do you know that?" pressed John. Essie and Harry sat quiet not wishing to get between a husband and wife during what promised to be an embarrassing discussion.

"Oh I went for a walk," Janetta replied in a girlish voice, while making little circles in her gravy with the tip of her knife. "I went to see the first lot off. I was curious."

"Bloody long walk!" replied John testily.

"It was a nice day!" She hadn't looked him in the eye but continued to stare into her plate.

"No it weren't, we had gunnery practice and it bloody rained!" snapped John.

"Just a little, John dear, it was nothing. Besides I enjoy a good walk."

"Who d'ya go with?"

"Just me, dearest. On me own."

"You're telling me you walked all the way down to the harbour, in the rain, alone, and just by chance you saw the Regiment leaving, and thought you'd go and wave them goodbye!" John was getting redder in the face and Essie and Harry fidgeted.

Janetta, realizing that playing the sweet innocent wasn't working, also started to get angry. "Yeh so wot! I was fed up sitting around the 'ouse and decided to go out. Is there a problem?"

"Yeh!" John raised his voice. "Soldiers can't be trusted around women and you go and flaunt y'self about the dock like a common 'ussy!"

Janetta slammed her knife down on the table. "Oh, a comm'n 'ussy I am now, am I?" she yelled, scraping her chair back and storming out of the room.

There was a quiet pause then John reclined back in his chair and took his clay pipe out of his jacket pocket. "Goddamned shit!" he said to nobody in particular.

Essie stood up and started stacking the plates.

"I'll get on with the dishes then!" she said in a subdued voice.

"Yeh, I'd better start packing," said Harry. John was left alone with his pipe and his ill humour.

****

The following morning was bright and sunny with wisps of cloud streaking a pale blue sky. The river *Tamar* changed from brown to green with a gentle swell. Small white caps appeared on some of the waves and then flickered out as if too shy to be seen. Seagulls circled overhead with their ceaseless screeching. The gray sails filled with wind, and the rigging creaked with the gentle strain.

Janetta stood by the starboard rail, her dark hair blowing across her face. She looked radiant in the morning sun and had a contented smile on her lips. She arched her head back, closed her eyes and felt the warmth of the sun on her face. She held the hair from her face with one hand, steadied herself against the rail with the other and drifted into a world of sublime happiness. She soaked up every glorious feeling of the moment. The warmth on her face, the wind in her hair, her dress blowing about her legs and the smell of the salt sea was as perfect as it could be.

She was awakened from her reverie by a sudden knock against the side of the ship as a wave broke and foamed into white mist. Janetta, squinting against the wind, looked back from where they had come and saw the *Master Attendance* jetty with its gray stone warehouses slipping further into the distance as the *Assistance* headed out into St John's Lake towards *The Sound.* St John's Lake wasn't a lake at all, but a wide expanse of water where the River Tamar opened out before funnelling through the half-mile wide narrows, guarded by the Citadel. Beyond the Citadel ships entered *The Sound* and ultimately the English Channel.

"I haven't seen you look so happy in weeks."

It was John, who had suddenly joined her by the rail. Janetta looked at him with a warm contented smile, linked her arm in his and leant her head against his shoulder. The argument from last night was forgotten and their new adventure was beginning.

"I am happy," she said. "We're leaving at last. Goodbye Plymouth and hello to the open ocean and new horizons."

John chuckled at her dramatization.

"We're only going to Dover!"

"Yeh, but I ain't never been on a ship, nor to Dover. It's a wonderful adventure John! As far as I know, Dover could be the other side of the world."

John laughed at her and put his arm around her. Here was the beautiful, happy, girlish Janetta he had fallen in love with, and he put aside all the anger and frustration he'd felt for her over the last two months. He thought instead of their new home, their impending baby and of his bride, the most beautiful woman in the regiment.

"Ain't never been nowhere accept Plymouth and Tywardreath, John. Never done nothin'!" She paused then looked up into John's eyes. "Now the Colonel's dead, we can use some of that money to get a better house in Dover, can't we luv?"

How could he refuse her now, as she melted him with those dark eyes and gave his arm a gentle squeeze? He had his Janetta back.

"Yeh alright! New beginnings eh!"

"Thank you John, it'll be wonderful you see. We'll make a beautiful home John, just for you, me and the baby."

"But we still 'ave to be careful luv. After all a lowly bombardier can't afford much. Tongues will wag!"

"I know! I know!" she teased, "I can be discreet!"

"*But can she?"* John wondered, and then dismissed the thought to enjoy watching the seagulls swoop and dive about them.

CHAPTER 9

Cope's Venture

Janetta looked aft towards the poop deck and noticed the Captain talking with two officers. One was Lieutenant Bird and the other was the disagreeable Major Cope. The Captain noticed her looking in his direction and excusing himself walked over to them. John kept his arm about Janetta's waist but otherwise pulled away from her to greet the Captain.

Captain Summers was a scruffy, bearded man in his forties wearing a dark blue double-breasted jacket and small peaked cap of the same colour. As he approached them he tipped his cap and held Janetta's eye ignoring John.

"Ma'am it's a pleasure to have you aboard!" he said with a slight grin on the side of his weathered mouth.

"Captain!" replied Janetta in acknowledgement of his approach, and held her hand out to him.

Captain Summers took her hand and raised it to his mouth as if to kiss it. Janetta noticed the calluses and signs of arthritis in his knuckles.

"May I name my husband, John Martin?" said Janetta.

The Captain released her hand and swivelling slightly at the waist to face John, gave him an almost imperceptible nod of recognition.

"I do hope you enjoy the voyage, madam," he continued, addressing Janetta directly. "Have you been to sea before?"

"Lord no!" said Janetta feeling as excited as a schoolgirl, "It's wonderful isn't it? Not rough at all!"

The captain gave a laugh.

"Rough!" he croaked. "My, we're not even out of the River Tamar yet, ma'am. It'll pick up some when we're clear of the Citadel. But don't you mind none, the weather will prove to be quite fine I think!"

The Major and Lieutenant wandered over to join the conversation.

"Ma'am," said Lieutenant Bird; "I presume you must be Mrs Martin."

Janetta was about to protest that he *"knew very well who she was"*, but then realized he was being discreet in front of John. She smiled and bowed slightly to acknowledge him. Lieutenant Bird then looked straight at John with a broad boyish grin, "Martin, are you looking forward to your new posting?"

"Yes, sir," was all John could find to say. He liked the Lieutenant but was feeling his inferiority of rank in front of two officers and the captain.

"That's the man!" said the Lieutenant cheerily.

Major Cope stood slightly back from the group saying nothing. He treated John as if he wasn't there but never took his eyes off Janetta, who felt uncomfortable under his gaze.

"Tell me, Captain," continued Lieutenant Bird. "Have you been at sea all your life?"

"I 'ave that, sir," replied the Captain, obviously enjoying the Lieutenant's company, "all my life. Born to the salt sea you might say. Me grandfather fought the Frogs and Dons at Trafalgar, sir. Served in Admiral Collingwood's squadron he did. Said it was the best day of his life, sir."

The Captain broke off his story and looked forward, frowning.

"Mr. Harwood," he yelled aft to his first officer, "not so close to the buoys if you please!"

"Aye sir," called back an officer on the poop deck, and then to the sailor at the wheel. "Two points to port helmsman."

Satisfied with the course correction the Captain returned to his attention to his passengers.

"Yes sir! Born to the sea I am!"

"And a jolly fine life it must be," agreed the Lieutenant with much affability.

Major Cope still said nothing but continued to look Janetta up and down. John pulled her closer to him to reinforce the fact that she belonged to him. Major Cope silently sneered at John.

"Well, I hope you enjoy your voyage," said the Captain, raising his forefinger to his temple and stepping back from the group. The Lieutenant nodded pleasantly to John and Janetta and walked down the deck with the Captain. Major Cope joined them but took no leave of the Martins.

John visibly relaxed when they had all left.

"What a very nice man that Lieutenant is," said Janetta, "and how thoroughly unpleasant is that Major Cope."

"Yeh," said John not hiding the repulsion he felt. "Right nasty bit of shit 'e is. Really enjoys flogging 'e does. Sadistic bastard!"

Janetta shuddered as if somebody had just walked over her grave.

The three men walked down the deck towards the bow, acknowledging whoever they past.

"That Mrs Martin is a damned fine woman," said the Captain, "think I'll invite her to dine with us tonight. What do you think? Eh?"

Lieutenant Bird didn't say anything. Certainly he'd like to have her company but didn't feel comfortable with the tone of the Captain's voice.

"Won't do!" said Major Cope. "If you invite her you have to invite him as well."

"Fine I'll invite Martin as well."

"He's an enlisted man. He can't dine in the officers' mess!" growled the major.

The captain stopped and turned to look at the Major.

"This is my ship," he snapped. "I dine with whoever I bloody well choose." Then looking from the Major to the Lieutenant, "What do you say, Lieutenant?"

"I reluctantly have to agree with the Major sir. Think of how Martin will feel. He'll be most uncomfortable, I assure you."

"Wouldn't invite your crew to dine with you, would you?" added Major Cope.

"Hmm!" The Captain pursed his lips, "S'pose your right. Pity! Damned fine woman!"

*****

John and Janetta leaned against the rail and watched the ocean gurgle past the hull. Every couple of minutes, Janetta glanced forward to watch the Captain, and the two officers continue their rounds chatting with other passengers. John seemed more at ease now that the officers had left them in peace; he was content to be hypnotized by the waves running past the ship. Janetta brushed her hair out of her face, held it back at the neck and squinted into the sunset.

"'Tis going to be a fine day tomorrow," she announced, noticing the reddening horizon.

"Mm," replied John dreamily.

John had been leaning on the rail staring into the water for several minutes. When he stood upright he momentarily lost his equilibrium and stumbled slightly. He steadied himself by grabbing hold of a stay doing his best to act as though nothing had happened. Janetta didn't notice as she watched the shoreline drift by.

"Think I'll go below and make the hammocks up. Don't want to be fumbling about in the dark, do we." said John.

"I'll stay here a bit I think, John, it's awful down there. It stinks! I think I'd rather sleep up here."

John chuckled. "Don't think the Captain would approve of that some'ow."

Below decks the space was divided into a series of sleeping quarters according to rank. The Captain had the nicest cabin right at the stern, but John hadn't been allowed to see that. Ships' officers and passengers of rank had smaller wood panelled cabins, no more than six feet by eight feet only containing a trunk and wooden cot attached to the wall.

Lesser officers had a space on the main lower deck no more than six feet square and had walls of hung sail canvas designed to give a minimum of privacy. They slept in a hammock slung from iron hooks in the upper deck beams. The enlisted men all slept in hammocks in one large communal deck surrounded by their kitbags and night buckets.

Toilets on board were of the naval variety. There was a bucket supplied for urination. For defecating the men were expected to go forward to the bow of the ship, climb over the forward rail and squat over the ocean in the nets that were hung either side of the bowsprit. For a nimble man this posed no great difficulty, but for a woman in long skirts it proved somewhat dangerous and so ladies were encouraged to defecate in the urinal buckets.

The whole ship below decks stank of sweat, urine, tar and an assortment of other noxious smells wafting up through the deck boards from the hull below the waterline.

Janetta had almost retched when they first came on board and she held a handkerchief over her face as she descended the stairs to the lower deck. "You'll get used to the smell, miss," remarked a sailor kindly, while carrying her bag. "We don't notice it after a while but I know for you folks it's pretty bad. Best stay on deck if the weather's fine."

Occasionally a rat would scamper across the floor and disappear behind some bulwark or ladder, but nobody seemed to take any notice. "Don't mind them little buggers," one of the sailors had said, "they're with us all the time, they are! Been all over the world those little critters 'ave!" He laughed with a toothless grin and went about his business.

So Janetta decided she would stay up in the fresh air as long as she could, and enjoy every moment of it.

"I'll go down then, and make everything as comfortable as possible," said John, turning to leave the rail.

Janetta reached up to his face and gave him a small peck on his cheek, "I shan't be long," she replied.

She watched John walk back down the deck toward the hatch. The ship heaved slightly, causing John to skip sideways on one leg before recovering his balance. She giggled at John's obvious lack of sea legs.

John had no sooner disappeared down the hatch, than Janetta heard the sound of army boots on a teak deck right behind her. She turned to discover Major Cope standing behind her with his hands folded behind his back and a smile on his pockmarked face that gave Janetta the shivers.

"Mrs Martin, we didn't have a chance to talk last time we were together." He had a clear, distinctly aristocratic voice, and spoke slowly as if weighing each word before saying it. His manner was cold, but he sounded as if he were trying hard to soften that impression. He was smoking a clay pipe and was having difficulty keeping it lit in the sea breeze, so he sucked hard on it to encourage an ember to catch.

"It seemed to me, Major, that you had every opportunity to talk to me when we were named by the Captain; as I recall, you stood back from us and said nuffin." She forgot herself for a second and allowed her natural way of speaking to leak through. The Major wasn't fooled by her refined accent. It was artlessly performed, but he let it slide past him.

"You are correct to chastise me, Mrs Martin, but you see I only wished to speak with you when we were in private. I have a pressing matter to discuss with you, and you only. This does not include your husband." He paused as if uncertain of this last point. "At least...not at present."

"Well, Major, you have my undivided attention now. What is it?"

"Not here, Mrs Martin. An open deck is a very public place and sailors have very good ears, so I'm told."

Janetta began to sense that the Major was bent on some mischief. She couldn't think what it could be since she hardly knew the man. She was sure John had no business with him because he hated him, so what was he up to?

"What do you suggest then?" asked Janetta suspiciously.

"Come to my cabin at say eleven thirty. That should give everybody time to finish dinner and settle down. Mine is the third door on the port side. You know which is port do you?"

Janetta nodded that she did.

"A lady, and a married lady at that, would hardly enter a gentleman's cabin in the middle of the night without a very convincing reason, Major. I have my reputation to think off!"

Major Cope scoffed at her comment. "Madam you flatter yourself and you will be there!" He strongly emphasized the 'will'. "I knew Colonel Wentworth ma'am, knew him well. You'll be there!"

Major Cope didn't even take his leave of her, but walked on down the deck stopping a couple of times to rekindle his pipe.

So that was it! But what was the connection between the Colonel and the Major that could involve her? Was the Colonel's history and money going to haunt them again? The more she thought about it, the angrier she became and a wave of nausea swept through her. She would attend this meeting and find out exactly what this odious Major knew, and then she'd decide what to do about it.

****

Dinner below decks was more than Janetta could stomach, but she forced down some cold cuts of ham and some pickled beetroot followed by a glass of ale. After dinner the men played cards and smoked their pipes. Janetta retreated up on deck again to fill her lungs with fresh air. She was surprised to discover that during the last couple of hours the wind had died down and they had hardly made any progress out of the Lake. The City of Plymouth was a sea of twinkling lights off the port side and a few lamps could be seen glowing in the hamlets of Penhale and Innswork about a mile off on the starboard side.

The first officer of the watch strolled along the deck to meet her.

"Good evening, ma'am. Still evening isn't it?"

"Yes," replied Janetta. "Can't we go any faster?"

"Not without the wind ma'am. We could of course signal for a tug, and they'll come and tow us out, but the Captain doesn't like to do that see. He's a stubborn old sea dog he is, and he don't like the stinkpots."

"Stinkpots?" she interrupted.

"Steam vessels ma'am. Reckons they ain't proper ships, see ma'am, and he ain't going to give them the satisfaction of towing him out."

Janetta was amused by this first officer's description of the Captain.

"The only danger spot is the narrows under the Citadel," he continued. "If there's not enough wind we could drift helpless like, onto them rocks."

"Oh!" exclaimed Janetta, putting her hand on her heart, "I trust there will be enough wind Mr. er…"

"Goodman, miss. Oh yes, miss there'll be enough. As soon as we enter the narrows we'll pick up the breeze off the *Sound*, see. At the moment we're sheltered by the land."

Janetta visibly relaxed.

"Don't you worry none, ma'am the Captain's done this a hundred times before."

Goodman tipped his hat and turned to go back to his post by the helm.

"What time is it, Mr Goodman?" she asked.

"Four bells, ma'am," then paused before making the correction, "Ten o'clock ma'am sorry."

"Thank you kindly Mr Goodman," she replied.

She had over an hour to wait for her rendezvous with the odious Major Cope, but it was a beautiful night and she enjoyed being in the fresh sea air. When the ship's bell struck six she prepared herself to meet the Major.

If it was dark on deck it was worse going down the steep steps to the lower deck. There was a glow from a lamp hanging on the wall in the lower corridor, but Janetta still had to hold onto the rope rail and feel with her feet for the next step. At the bottom of the stairs she saw a narrow corridor, in the centre of the ship, heading towards the stern where she knew the Captain's cabin must be.

The corridor consisted of panelled walls painted white and each cabin door had a polished brass handle. There was nobody about but she could hear muffled voices coming from a couple of the cabins indicating that some of the officers were still awake.

She arrived at the Major's door and gave it a very delicate and almost imperceptible tap with her knuckle. To her surprise the door immediately opened and Major Cope thrust his head out to look up and down the corridor. Satisfied that she was alone, he grabbed her by the arm and quickly pulled her into the small cabin. There was barely room for both of them to stand. Against one wall was a cot with its blanket dishevelled and in the very small space at the side was the Major's personal chest. His uniform jacket hung on the wall and his boots stood at attention behind the door.

Because of the space they were forced to stand in front of one another, so close that one might take it they were about to kiss. Janetta could smell rum on the Major's breath, and mixed with his body odour and the smell of his feet, the overpowering stench was enough to force Janetta into stifling a gag.

"Sit down, Mrs Martin," Cope said as he dragged her towards the bed onto which she collapsed in a heap. The Major opened the lid of his trunk to vent yet another noxious odour into the room, this time the smell of unwashed laundry. He moved a few items from one side to another until he had found what he had been looking for. He took out a small bundle wrapped in white linen, then looked at Janetta and grinned before closing the lid and sitting on it.

He fondled the little bundle for a few seconds before beginning his interrogation.

****

John wasn't happy. Janetta had come to him in some distress while he was making up their hammock. She had told him that the Major wanted her to go to his cabin late in the evening to discuss a matter of some delicacy. She couldn't imagine what this delicate matter might be. John thought of two possibilities. Either he wanted to 'roger' her or he knew about their arrangement with the Colonel.

"He was on the Colonel's staff ya know," he'd said to Janetta, but he couldn't believe the Colonel would have confided in a man like Cope. John bridled at the very idea of his wife being alone in Major Cope's cabin, but she had calmed him down and told him it would be alright.

"Don't worry I can 'andle him. I've coped with tougher sods than 'im before," she'd said, but he'd felt uneasy ever since she'd gone. Every fibre of his body told him to crash into the Major's cabin and rescue her.

While doing his rounds below deck, Lieutenant Bird had seen John white-knuckled and red-faced, pacing up and down in his little cubicle.

"Are you alright Martin?" he asked with some concern.

"Yes, sir," snapped John trying not to be rude to a superior officer.

"You're not you know!" said Bird in a kindly voice that soothed John a little.

"That bastard, begging your pardon, sir, has my Jan."

"What bastard? Where is she man?"

"Major bleed'n Cope sir. In his cabin sir."

"Unchaperoned?"

"Sir," John growled.

"Good God! This won't do. Won't do at all!"

"Trouble is, sir, enlisted men aren't allowed in the officers' cabins, sir, else I would have gotten her out."

"Quite!" The Lieutenant frowned seeing what was coming next, "It's up to me then. I'll have to get her out, Martin."

"I'd be much obliged to you, sir if you could," replied John.

The Lieutenant nodded and turned as if to leave, then hesitated. He detested Major Cope; he was the worst sort of army bully and

Lieutenant Bird knew he was woefully incapable of standing up to him. He wasn't exactly a coward, but he much preferred to avoid trouble and had often wondered what would happen if he were to see action. Would he disgrace himself? He shuddered to think. It wasn't as if he had the rank to order Cope. All he could do was walk in on them and find an excuse why Janetta was required elsewhere. Perhaps Cope would let her go passively so as not to be embarrassed. On the other hand if there were two of them they might convince Cope not to put up an argument because there were witnesses. He turned back to face Martin.

"I think it might be better if we both go. Two of us should be able to take the Major don't you think?"

John grinned as if to say, 'just let me at him'.

"We'll do this in a gentlemanly manner I think Martin, don't you?"

John grunted his assent and followed the Lieutenant aft.

****

Major Cope sat opposite Janetta so that their knees kept bumping, and he grinned, exposing his blackened teeth.

"My father," he began in a calm but cold voice, "is Lord Tallis of Norfolk. Don't suppose you've heard of him have you my dear?"

Janetta shook her head.

"Bloody rich he was. Had estates all over the place. But he gambled you see and wasn't very good at it. Lost half his estates, abandoned my dear mama." Janetta thought she detected a wavering in his voice as if he were about to cry, but then he looked her straight in the eye and recovered. "And frittered away the rest of my, and my brother's inheritance."

"What's this to me?" asked Janetta defiantly.

"I'm coming to that my beauty, patience now."

He looked down at the small package in his hands and let his fingers caress the linen.

"Since there was precious little left for me to inherit, he purchased me a commission in the army and since he was a good friend with Colonel Wentworth I was seconded to his staff. God rest his soul!"

"I see," said Janetta.

"Doubt it," snorted Cope. "Lots of people have wondered about you Mrs Martin. Quite the mystery lady, aren't you?"

"Don't see why?"

"Well now, let's face some facts shall we! You're undoubtedly the most beautiful woman in Plymouth. I'd like to say 'in all Devon', but don't want it going to your sweet head."

His voice was now taking on an edge of bitterness and Janetta started getting worried about where this was going. The walls and door were very thin and she reckoned a good scream would soon have everybody running to her aid if she needed help.

"Nobody can quite figure out how come a cracker like you has ended up with a numbskull like Martin." Janetta didn't rise to his bait, so he pressed on. "'Cause everybody knows you're no lady, brought up in a mining family I understand, but it is puzzling how you manage to mix so well with some of your betters and how Martin has been able to pay for all these nice clothes you wear. Quite a conundrum!"

"A what?" Janetta asked.

Major Cope looked at her and grinned. "A conundrum, my pretty one, is a riddle. You're a riddle!... Or are you?"

Once again he caressed the linen package on his lap.

"It was a real shame when the Colonel died. Everybody liked the Colonel. He was a gentleman! Wouldn't you agree, Mrs Martin?"

Janetta nodded her agreement.

"A man of valour on the battlefield and honour off it. A true gentleman who treated his fellow man with courtesy and the ladies with the respect they deserve. Wouldn't you say that was true, Mrs Martin?"

Janetta was beginning to tire of this game. She knew what he was doing, and if he thought she was going to be an easy mark, he had another think coming.

"Get to the point, Major," said Janetta, not bothering to hide her impatience.

"I was at the Colonel's house after his attack. I saw you there. Ran upstairs all flustered you did as if he was your dying father. But he weren't were he; you were his maid."

Janetta fidgeted.

"What, I wonder made you so terribly upset when your employer died? I would be astonished if my maid or batman acted like that when I died!"

He began to slowly unravel the linen parcel on his lap.

"After the Colonel died, I, along with Lieutenant Bird, were asked to clean up his desk, arrange for any regimental papers he may have had in his possession to be returned, and generally put his military affairs in order."

He opened the package to reveal two small books.

"Having no next of kin, one or two of his personal items were going to be thrown out, but I said to Lieutenant Bird that some of this stuff was very interesting and ought to be preserved. Don't you agree Mrs Martin?"

"I'm sure Lieutenant Bird didn't share your view on the matter."

Major Cope chuckled to himself.

"Dearie me, Mrs. Martin! How rightly you know Lieutenant Bird. He's much more of a gentleman than I am, I can assure you."

He held up the smaller of the two books. It was only about three inches wide by four inches deep and had a blue cover. She recognized it immediately as the Colonel's signalling book he used in the dining room. Major Cope opened the book and giving Janetta a glance, began to read from it.

"Jan 4th – dinner fifteen minutes late – gave girl 20 spanks.

Jan 10th – spilt soup – 10 smacks

Jan 15th – Girl was cheeky –"

Here Major Cope gave a sly grin at Janetta before continuing.

"*Smacked girl's buttocks 'til they were red.* – Shall I go on Mrs Martin?"

Janetta stared at the ceiling as if she were totally bored by the whole revelation, so the Major put the small book down and picked up the larger one.

"I'm sure you'll find this book far more interesting," he said, smirking. "It's the Colonel's personal diary. Very interesting stuff this, Mrs Martin."

Janetta said nothing but was beginning to get really nervous. She had no idea what the diary was going to tell, but if Major Cope thought it was good, then it had to be bad.

"December 22nd 1875," he read. *"Have to go to tiresome Regimental Christmas Ball. Wanted to spend Christmas with J. Will propose to her as soon as I return*".

Cope looked up at Janetta and grinned. He enjoyed making Janetta squirm.

Jan 3- Seen sense at last but don't know how to tell J

Jan 6 – J pregnant by Martin – severe blow!!!

He emphasized the words '*severe blow*' to mock her in her moment of discomfort.

Jan 8 – should have married J, too late now. J was the only one that made me happy. Will give J wedding present of 10 guineas and buy her wedding dress.

Jan 15 – That little shit Martin blackmailed me. Gave him 15 guineas for J's sake. Hope he treats her well."

Major Cope closed the book, and looked at Janetta.

"There's more," he said, "but I don't think we need dwell on it do you?"

Janetta shook her head in silence. She was shaken but still defiant.

"Well now," continued Cope. "Whoever would have thought it!" he gave a couple of clicks with his tongue. "Martin a blackmailer. How'd he know about your spankings I wonder? Oh of course, yes, you must have told him. So you were in on it! Of course you're a blackmailing gang. Poor Colonel didn't stand a chance did he?"

The Major stood up and paced about in the little room.

"So what we have here, is a Colonel getting his jollies by spanking his maid. She gets 'with child' and no husband. Colonel won't marry her so she and her lover blackmail him out of nearly a fifteen guineas. And here you are dressing and acting like little Lady Muck. Don't seem right somehow does it my dear?"

"How we got our money is private between the Colonel and us."

"Not any more it ain't," chided Cope.

"What do you want then, Major," said Janetta with no sound of respect in her voice for his rank.

"Well I've been thinking about that," said Cope running his fingers along his moustache and twirling the end.

"Fifteen guineas is not a lot of money to me but it is to you. Would you agree? You wouldn't want me to do anything that would jeopardize your money. So what do you have that I might want as payment for my complicity?"

Janetta began to see where this was leading. So, she was to become his whore was she? She almost felt sorry for the Major because he was now meeting her on her own ground. She knew just how to handle this little shit.

"As I see it," said Major Cope, leaning in toward Janetta so that they were almost nose to nose and she could smell his stale breath, "we have a couple of options to consider."

"Fuck off, Cope!" said Janetta in a half whisper. The Major grinned.

"Firstly, you could pay me, say, three guineas."

"Three guineas," Janetta gasped. "That'll be the fuckin' day."

"And I won't say a word," interjected Cope as he grabbed Janetta by the cheeks, squeezing her mouth, "but if you choose that option and don't pay up, I can make life really difficult for your hubby. We'll call this option one," he said and started shaking her face back and forth in time with his words. "So many rules to obey in the army and most of them are flogging offences."

Janetta shook herself free of his hand. "You snake," she spat.

"Or there's option two," he lowered his voice and stared straight into her eyes. "Perhaps you don't have to pay me a penny, after all you're in need of it more than I am, and I don't really want to see Bombardier Martin being flogged."

"*Ere we go*," thought Janetta, "*so bleedin' obvious!*"

"Because all you have to do is come to me say…oh, I don't know, let's not be too greedy…say once a month. Come to me and get a damn good rogering, eh! What do you say to that? I bet you may even enjoy it."

Janetta jumped to her feet and hit him with a clenched fist full in the mouth. Major Cope was taken completely by surprise and found himself floundering about on the trunk as he hit his head on the back wall. Janetta almost got to the door before Cope was on top of her, pinning her to the wall.

"Now that really wasn't very nice was it? But I can overlook a little feistiness."

He grabbed her right breast and squeezed it hard enough to make her wince.

"The offer still stands my dear, you just think about it!"

A knock came on the door and it immediately opened. Lieutenant Bird and John Martin stood blocking the exit. Major Cope stepped back from Janetta.

"Ah Lieutenant!" he said trying to appear calm and collected. He ignored John.

"Sorry to barge in," said Lieutenant Bird jovially, yet forcefully, "we were looking for Mrs Martin, and indeed it seems we've found her."

He offered Janetta his arm, which she took.

Cope gave Lieutenant Bird a malevolent look but did nothing to stop him. He had said all he wanted to say and now had no reason to detain her any longer.

"Thank you Major, good night to you," said the Lieutenant with a forced smile on his face as he closed the door behind Janetta, leaving the major in his room nursing his sore mouth.

John, Lieutenant Bird and Janetta went back along the corridor, but when they came to the companionway Janetta stopped.

"Do you mind if I take some air," she asked.

"Not at all dear lady," replied Lieutenant Bird. "Best go with her Martin, 'tis not safe on deck in the dark."

"Yes, sir I will. Good night to you, sir."

"Goodnight Martin," Bird gave a slight bow to Janetta, "Ma'am," and turned to walk back to his cabin.

"Oh, sir," said John calling him back.

The Lieutenant stopped and spun around on his heels in a playful manner.

"Yes Martin?" he said with a broad smile.

"Thank you again for your help, sir."

"Think nothin' of it Martin, it was my pleasure don't you know."

In truth Bird was mightily pleased with himself. He had scored a double triumph in the last couple of minutes. He had rescued Janetta without making Martin look bad, and he had stood up to Cope without any outer signs of nervousness or getting into a scrap. It had been masterfully pulled off and he went to his bunk feeling like a new man.

Janetta started to climb the steep stairway. It wasn't easy in the half dark and in a long dress. She needed both hands to pull herself up by the rope banisters, which left no hand free to hitch up the front of her skirt. She kept stepping on the front hem of her dress. John came up behind her and hands on her waist helped steady her so that she could let go the rope with one hand. Half way up the steps the ship leaned slightly to one side and there was an audible creaking in the timbers. Janetta froze, wondering what had happened.

"It's all right Jan, we've just picked up some wind. We must be coming out into *The Sound.*"

At the top of the stairs, Janetta and John stepped out onto the dark deck and the evening air hit them. The ship was eerily black. A collection of barely recognizable shapes silhouetted against the night. They walked carefully up the slight slope of the deck to the weather rail where they stopped and leaned their backs against the gunwale. Slowly their eyes adjusted to the dark and Janetta could make out two figures at the stern of the vessel. One would have been the helmsman, the other the officer of the watch. Neither of them moved. The sails above their heads occasionally flapped if the wind veered behind them and the rigging creaked as it took the strain of the wind. The black, unseen ocean beyond the gunwales slopped and gurgled as it ran past the hull.

John and Janetta stood huddled against the night air shivering slightly with the damp sea breeze. They watched the dark coastline slowly slide past. To starboard they could just make out the silhouettes of houses in the village of Cremyll and one small lamp flickering in the dark. On the port side, the town of Plymouth spread along the shoreline with a multitude of dim lights showing from its taverns and lodgings, and on the port quarter loomed the great solid mass of the Citadel walls that guarded the harbour entrance.

Outlined against the darkening sky, Janetta could see the crenellations along the top of the wall from which great plumes of flame would spurt their death at any enemy ship that tried to enter the naval yards. How vulnerable she felt exposed under the eye of the guns and how small and fragile their ship seemed. For a few moments she really understood her husband's job. She wrapped her arms about herself and shivered.

John removed his tunic and placed it around her shoulders.

"Things look black John."

"Yes there's very little moon tonight," replied John, glancing up at the sky.

Janetta tutted and frowned at him – annoyed that he wasn't keeping up with her thoughts.

"Cope!" she exclaimed testily.

"He didn't do anything to you, did he? I'll kill him if he did!"

"No I'm fine, but we've got a real problem John. He knows everything. He has the Colonel's diary and pocket book. The Colonel wrote everything down, John, everything!"

She buried her head in his shoulder, her anger turning to sobs of frustration. John tried not to shiver.

"What are we going to do? We've got to get the books back, but he'll still know, won't he?" she sobbed.

John didn't reply at first, his thoughts were spinning. He knew this problem wouldn't go away and that Cope wouldn't let it go.

Janetta pressed herself into his chest as if begging for protection and he knew that at this moment he was totally under her spell. She was his goddess and Cope's target; the anger seethed inside him and he knew he'd walk off the edge of the world for her and damn the consequences.

"First we get the books back, then I'll deal with Cope," he said. "Did you see where he keeps the books?"

"Yeh, in 'is chest wrapped in white linen."

"Good, now all we've got to do is get him out of his cabin so that one of us could nip in and grab the books. Was the trunk locked?"

"Don't think so."

"Good." John was thinking hard. What he needed was an excuse to get Cope out of bed and up on deck.

Just then the companionway door opened letting a shaft of light illuminate the deck and a figure emerged from below. John couldn't believe his eyes, it was Major Cope. He was playing right into their hands.

The Major stepped out onto the deck. John and Janetta froze. They were only a matter of a few feet away from him but he didn't see them. He was intent on lighting a pipe, and having done so he turned towards the leeward side of the ship and strolled forward until he disappeared behind a skiff lashed to the roof of the centre deckhouse.

"This is our chance," whispered John. "Come on."

They walked back towards the companionway. As Janetta started down the stairs, John wandered whether the helmsman and officer on watch had seen them. They were a hundred and fifty feet back and just black silhouettes to John's eyes, but these were trained seamen and he felt they must be used to seeing in the dark. He decided to test them so he turned and waved at them. Sure enough the officer acknowledged his wave.

"Goodnight to you," John called out.

"Goodnight, sir," came the reply.

"*Fuck*," thought John. He didn't want a witness, but at least the officer had seen them go down below leaving Major Cope on deck alone.

Janetta reached the bottom of the stairs and John followed right behind her. They started to walk quietly down the central passage that led between the officer's cabins. It was dimly lit by two oil lamps screwed to the wood panel walls. They could hear laughing coming from one of the cabins, probably a card game in progress but nobody heard them as they crept past.

Janetta stopped at one of the doors and very gently tried the handle. It opened and she slowly peered into the small cabin.

"This is it," she whispered.

They entered the cabin and were pleased to discover that the Major had conveniently left the lamp burning so that they didn't have to grope about in the dark.

Janetta turned to John. "I can find the books. You go and keep an eye out for Cope."

"Right," replied John and he stepped back out into the corridor. He realized that even if Janetta found the books the Major would continue to haunt them. John feared the Major's power to make both Janetta's and his own life miserable – unbearable even.

He looked up and down the passage and began to form a plan. The passage ran aft towards the stern cabins and forward under the skiff. He wondered if there was a second companionway to the deck at the forward end. If there was, he could get back on deck without being seen by the helmsman because the skiff would block their view. Cope could return the way he went out, in which case John would miss him if he went forward, but he decided it was worth the risk to find out.

He went forward, looking back over his shoulder to see if Cope was returning behind him. At the end of the passage he turned a corner to find – as he had hoped – a second set of stairs going up to the deck.

At the foot of the stairs was another lamp that would light up the deck when he opened the door, so he blew it out. Now in darkness he climbed the stairs and very quietly opened the door and looked out. Cope was only fifteen feet away from him leaning on the rail and puffing on his pipe.

John knew that when he emerged from the stairs the skiff would hide him from the officer on watch, but there was nothing preventing Cope from seeing him if he should turn around. He would have to rely on stealth and a great deal of luck.

He stepped out onto the deck making sure he didn't let go of the door, which he knew would slam shut behind him, because of the tilt of the ship. He closed the door gently but it still made a click as it its latch engaged and John froze.

Cope suddenly stood up straight, but only to get his flint out of his pocket and re-light his pipe. John breathed a sigh of relief when Cope resumed his position, leaning his elbows on the rail.

John wasn't really sure how to proceed at this point. He had to cross the open deck to reach Cope and by doing so would be seen by the officer on watch or the helmsman. He also didn't want to kill him by leaving any obvious signs of murder. Somehow he had to get Cope quietly overboard without killing him first so that it looked like an accident. He could sneak up behind him and throttle him into unconsciousness but he'd be seen and there would be an inevitable struggle. He decided on a very risky procedure, which would either work well or be a complet disaster.

Cope was leaning on the rail with his weight on his right leg, which was extended straight and stiffly backwards. His left leg was bent at the knee with his left foot supported on the toe under his right ankle. This gave John his idea.

He went down on his hands and knees so that he wouldn't stand out against the background. He very quietly and slowly crept in the shadows towards the Major until he could reach out and touch his ankles. All he had to do now was grab his ankles and give one enormous pull and Cope would fall flat on his face where John could throttle him before he made a sound. An incredibly risky manoeuvre and one that he wasn't sure he could pull off, but it was now or never.

John steadied himself to support the pull and then reached forward with both hands for the Major's ankles.

****

Janetta opened the Major's trunk lid and was repulsed by the smell of old dirty laundry. It was so bad that she didn't want to put her hands into it, but she had to find the linen bundle.

"Filthy bastard!" she whispered to herself as she pulled shirts and britches aside to dig deeper into his trunk. She began to panic as she removed more and more of the Majors belongings without finding the books. Finally she'd reached the bottom and her hand found a gentleman's gold watch and chain. She picked it up more out of curiosity than anything. She looked at the time, a quarter past four, it had stopped, and then without knowing why, she opened the back where she found an inscription. When she saw it, she was shocked. She sat there for a moment or two rereading the inscription over and over.

"*My dearest Janetta. No hour passes without my love. F.W.*"

"Shit," she spat, "what's the bastard doing with this?"

She slid the watch into her pocket and continued searching for the books. She doubted he had them with him when he came up on deck, so where the hell were they? She began putting everything back in roughly the same order she'd taken them out, and as she did so she examined each piece to make sure the books weren't concealed in pockets. There was no sign of the linen package. She closed the trunk lid, sat on it and slapped her leg rather too hard out of frustration.

"Shit, shit," she whispered to herself.

There was a sudden loud bang as a cabin door burst open and several voices could be heard down the passage.

"Come on it's too early to turn in," said one voice.

"No, sorry I'm tired, besides I've lost too much tonight," said another.

"Sod you then. C'mon let's get Copey, he'll play a few hands with us," said a third.

"Shit!" exclaimed Janetta again and she dived for the door and threw the small latch bolt. There was too much light in the cabin so she turned the wick down extremely low so that it gave practically no light at all, and then waited. Almost immediately someone hammered on the door.

"Come on Cope, wakey wakey, you're needed at the card table," said a drunken voice outside the door.

Janetta froze her heart pounding.

"Oh let him sleep," said the second voice, "he's a sore loser anyway. I'd rather not play with him."

"Fine! As you wish," said the drunken voice. "Nighty night Major Cope." A small tapping sounded on the door.

"Oh do come on. Stop being an ass. Let's play on," said the voice of reason, and the three officers retreated back down the passage and closed their cabin door.

"Oh God!" exclaimed Janetta. Her heart was beating so fast that she had to sit down for a minute so she flopped on the bed and sat on a lump. She felt under her bottom and discovered something hard concealed under the blankets. She stood up and raised the wick in the lamp again. Throwing the blankets off the bed she uncovered the linen package containing the two books.

"Thank Christ!" she said to herself clutching the books to her breast.

****

John couldn't believe how easy it had been. Especially since Cope was considerably heavier than himself. He'd taken a deep breath, grabbed his ankles and jerked backwards as hard as he possibly could. The Major had been taken completely by surprise. His feet had been pulled out from under him and he'd collapsed like a house of cards, hitting his chin on the rail, knocking him senseless.

It was all over in a matter of two seconds and the Major hadn't made a sound except a low thud as he hit the deck.

John lay over his legs and looked back at the two seamen on the poop deck. Had they seen Cope suddenly disappear from the rail or heard the thud? Apparently not as they both continued their duties undisturbed.

John lay on top of Cope for several seconds getting his breath and not daring to move. Now he had rendered him unconscious, he had to get him overboard and he wondered how he was going to achieve that. John raised his head and looked towards the bow of the ship. He couldn't stand up to heave Cope over the rail because he'd be seen. He could only do it if he was obscured from view by the skiff and that meant going forward to the bow. He'd have to drag Cope nearly fifty feet on his hands and knees, which would take forever. On the other hand, if he dragged him the few feet to the companionway he'd be sheltered from view and he could then pick him up unseen.

John backed up off Cope's legs, keeping low on his hands and knees, then tugged at Cope's ankles again and dragged him backwards about twelve inches. This was going to be hard work. He crawled back a couple of steps and dragged Cope again, then again, and again, each time a few inches or so. He was amazed how heavy Cope was but eventually he managed to get him in front of the skiff and out of view.

He sat Cope up and leaned him against the companionway doors. Now all he had to do was pick him up and carry him to the rail at the bow. He put one of Cope's arms over his shoulder. The stench of body odour nearly overpowered him. "Filthy bastard," he muttered to himself. He got his right arm under Cope's legs and tried to lean backwards to get Cope laying forward over his shoulder. It took a bit of doing but he managed to get him in position. Then he tried to stand up but couldn't do it. Cope was just too heavy and the strain on John's back was too much to take. He had to find a better way to get him on his shoulder without having to bend forward.

He sat down for a moment to think about his problem. If it hadn't been for the two sailors he could have grabbed Cope's legs and heaved him straight over the rail, but he would have been seen and Cope would have cried out. So instead he was left with the task of carrying him fifty feet to the bow, and he wasn't sure he had the strength to do it.

The enormity of what he had done slowly dawned on him, and he began to feel a sense of panic. He was in the process of committing murder. His heart pounded, and although there was a chill in the night air, he ran with sweat. His throat was dry and he longed for a cool ale. It was not too late to back out. Cope didn't know it was him. If he left now, Cope would regain consciousness and never know what had happened to him. On the other hand John would never have a better opportunity than now, and being at sea meant accidents could happen.

He sat with his back on the companionway door and slowly an idea came to him. He opened the door and backed down the first few steps. Then grabbing Cope's ankles once more, he pulled him towards the opening until his legs were dangling down the stairs. He then reached forward and took Cope's arms pulling him into an upright sitting position. Steadying himself, he pulled Cope forward until he was in danger of tumbling head first down the stairs, but instead he fell straight over John's shoulder while John was still in an upright standing position. It was easy! John could now take his weight without any problem and he carried him up out of the stairs, taking care not to let the door slam behind him.

Cope was still heavy, but he was manageable now and John began his journey forward making sure to always keep the skiff between himself and the helmsman. It wasn't that easy in the dark because there were obstacles on the deck to step over or go around.

He was only ten feet from the bow when the ship was hit by a sudden squall and the vessel groaned and heeled over to port. John, taken completely by surprise, found himself staggering down the sloping deck towards the port rail. Under the weight of his load, he fell to his knees and dropped Cope, who collapsed onto the deck, his head hitting the teak with a terrible thud.

John lay on his back staring up at the black masts and tons of dark canvas ballooning out as they filled with wind, and listened to the straining of the rigging. He sensed the ship turning to head up into the wind. A voice rang out in the dark.

"Mr Thomson what's happening!"

John recognized the Captains voice. "*Fuck*," he thought, "*I'll be spotted for sure!*"

"Sorry sir!" replied the Officer of the watch, "My fault entirely sir. Should have seen that coming!"

"Rounded the point have we?"

"Yes sir."

"How many times have I warned you about that Mr Thomson?"

"I know sir I'm terrible sorry sir. I wasn't paying attention sir. I should have seen it coming by the speed of the clouds sir."

"All right Mr Thomson. Head up another point or two I think don't you, for the comfort of our passengers. Don't want to scare the shit out of the townies do we now. So take it gently."

"Yes sir, No sir! I mean I'm sorry sir."

"Mr Thomson!"

"Yes sir."

"Stop flogging yourself man, yer doing fine!"

"Yes sir. Thank you sir!"

"Ya can't read the sea in the dark, Mr. Thomson, so keep yer eyes on the sky."

"Yes sir."

"Right, well, the ship's in good hands Mr Thomson. I'm going back to bed. Good night to ya."

"Good night and thank you sir."

The aft companionway door clicked shut and there was silence once more. John gave a long exhale and laid his head back on the deck with relief.

Cope gave a low moan as he began to regain consciousness, which reminded John of his task. He wasn't going to be able to get Cope back on his shoulder, so he lifted him under his armpits and dragged him backwards the last few feet to the bow.

He leaned Cope against the rail and took another breather. Cope flopped against his chest and began to groan a bit louder. He was slowly gaining consciousness and if John didn't get him overboard soon he'd have a real problem. He grabbed Cope's head and banged it hard against the rail and he went quiet again. It made a thud but he didn't think it could be heard so far back.

John lifted him up as high as he could then turned him and allowed him to bend forward over the rail. It wasn't easy. Cope was a dead weight, but he somehow found the strength he needed. Cope's head and arms dangled down against the outside of the hull. Then John wrapped his arms around Cope's waist and heaved him over some more. Cope began to moan as he became conscious and dimly aware of his upside down position. One more heave, thought John and I'm finished. He bent down wrapped his arms about Cope's knees and after taking one last look over his shoulder to be sure he wasn't being watched, he stood up, allowing Cope to slide down the outside of the hull. He released his hold and Cope dropped, entering the water with barely a sound, and was gone into the black sea.

John sat down, leaned his back against the rail and gave a great sigh of relief. The deed was done and he felt surprisingly good about it. There was no way of linking him with Cope's disappearance.

He made his way back to the companionway and when he reached the bottom of the stairs he re-lit the lamp in the passage. The only thing left to do now was return to Janetta in their cabin, but he couldn't go back on deck, he would have to risk passing through the officer's quarters again. He peered round the corner and looked down the passage. Nobody was about and it sounded as if the card game was still in progress, so he slipped back down the passage and made his way to his own cabin.

Inside, Janetta was already in the hammock, reading the Colonel's diary.

"Where 'ave you got to?" she whispered.

"I've been taking care of Major bloody Cope," replied John, keeping his voice very low so as not to be overheard.

"What 'ave yer done, John?" asked Janetta.

"He won't bother us any more my love. You can sleep well tonight."

John kissed her, snuggled in beside her, and slept a fitful sleep.

CHAPTER 10

Dover

The next morning was as perfect an early summer morning as you could wish for. The sun shone brightly in a pale blue sky streaked with fine wisps of white cloud, and the sea, usually brown or green, now shimmered a deep blue. The *Assistance* sailed on an easterly heading up the English Channel before a gentle following breeze. Her canvas filled and pulled against the yards and gentle foam gurgled below the stern and left a small phosphorescent trail in her wake. Squawking gulls dipped and soared over the vessel while John and Janetta sat on the deck, leaning against the hatch cover, their faces raised to the warmth of the sun.

It was such a beautiful morning that after breakfast virtually everybody was up on deck enjoying the sun and the sea air. Soldiers of all ranks sat on deck and smoked their pipes. Some engaged in conversation, but for the most part everybody just dozed and soaked up the sun's warmth and enjoyed their short holiday.

Esmeralda walked round the deck passing a few pleasantries with whomever she met, and stopped for a couple of minutes to talk with Janetta before continuing her round of socializing. Captain Summers also paced the deck and chatted jovially with anybody he met.

It was a scene full of peace and serenity and deception. John and Janetta were not at peace on this beautiful morning. After John had told her what he had done, she had been greatly relieved, but now she sat and brooded. She thought of the child she carried in her womb and about their future. She saw John on the gallows and herself bringing up a child without his income. She thought about the Colonel and wondered again whom the father really was, as if it mattered at this point. She was glad to be rid of Major Cope but worried about what consequences would follow. She found that she thought only of herself and her own small part in the murder. She was so absorbed in her own concerns that she barely thought of John and what he must be feeling. After all, she thought, he was a soldier and trained to kill. What was it to him to rid the world of a snake? But she had the future of her child to consider and the child's future was dependent on her security.

John felt sick to the stomach, and his bowels had turned to liquid. He'd had a restless night's sleep and couldn't face his breakfast. He'd never killed a man before and he had never thought himself capable of killing in cold blood. Firing an artillery piece at an enemy ship could shatter, kill and maim scores of men, but that was war. This was personal. As the events of the previous evening went through his mind he tried to convince himself that he hadn't murdered Cope. After all he was still alive when he had lowered him over the side. All John had done was to knock him unconscious and then throw him overboard. Perhaps Cope had swum ashore and was now drying his clothes in front of some tavern fire. That thought didn't make him feel any better because he knew Cope was barely conscious when he entered the water, and that he would have drowned before he knew where he was. No, John had blood on his hands and somehow he had to come to terms with the fact. He had killed for Janetta and now he must find the strength to live with the memory, and most importantly to appear innocent when the investigation began.

"Well, Mr Martin you do look peaky!" It was the Captain who now stood towering over John and blocking out the sun. John squinted at the dark silhouetted figure in front of him and tried to shield his eyes from the sun with his hands.

"Good morning Captain, Just a little wobbly, I'll be fine," replied John trying to be as civil as possible.

"Funny thing, 'sea sickness', some people can be made as sick as a dog by the slightest movement of the ship and yet be fine in a maelstrom."

John wished the Captain wasn't quite so enthusiastic about the subject. It wasn't helping John's stomach.

The Captain was suddenly diverted from his train of thought by something off the starboard side. John raised himself up a little higher to see over the gunwale. It was a steam ship passing in the opposite direction. It was much larger than the *Assistance*, and quite new by the look of her paintwork. The ship's iron hull towered above the deck of the *Assistance* and her two masts looked too small to be of any real use, although the presence of a yardarm suggested that she could carry sails. Two tall funnels protruded from her deck belching a long horizontal trail of black smoke. As it passed them, John got a sudden brief whiff of coal smoke.

"Damn stink pots," growled the Captain to nobody in particular, then picking up his tone, "Well I suppose that's the way of the future. Won't be many of us left soon."

He turned his attention back to John.

"If you need a draught to settle your stomach, just talk to the first officer."

"I'll be fine, but thank you," said John as pleasantly as he could.

The Captain tipped his hat to Janetta, "Ma'am," he said, taking his leave of her and walking on up the deck.

Curiously, Major Cope wasn't missed until mid-afternoon. John couldn't believe that nothing had been said all day about the whereabouts of the Major, and it perversely annoyed him. An officer had been murdered and nobody seemed to care. The fact was, that nobody liked the Major and if he wasn't in sight, he was happily out of mind.

The peace was only disturbed when the Brigadier needed Cope for something and went about the ship asking if anybody had seen him. Nobody had, and soon the officers undertook a general search. The enlisted men were not troubled too much by the search party. Occasionally they were asked if they had seen the Major, and when they said "no," they were left alone.

By the early evening it was evident that Major Cope wasn't on board and the Brigadier decided to hold a public enquiry on the main deck the following morning. For John and Janetta this meant another night of worry. The wait became intolerable for John, and Janetta had to calm him down and go over their story more than once. They both agreed that they had nothing to fear, because there was no reason for anybody to link them with the Major's disappearance.

After breakfast on the following morning the entire Battery convened on the main deck for an impromptu hearing. The proceedings consisted of a list of witness sightings of the Major in chronological order throughout the afternoon and early evening.

Lieutenant Bird had testified that he had seen Major Cope in his cabin in the early evening but didn't go into details about rescuing Janetta, for which she was very thankful. She had been prepared to testify that Lieutenant Bird had rescued her from Cope's clutches after he had tried to seduce her. It was stretching the truth but she didn't wish to mention the blackmail, thereby giving John and her a motive for murder. All in all, Lieutenant Birds' silence on the matter saved them a lot of explaining.

The officer of the watch, Mr Thomson, came forward to testify that he had seen Major Cope come on deck for a smoke after dark. He also mentioned in passing that John and Janetta Martin were also on deck at that time. John was called to give evidence. He was nervous but knew he was safe in his testimony and that some of his nervousness would be ignored as natural, because of giving evidence in front of the officers and the entire Battery.

John told his story and Janetta silently prayed and mentally coached him. "They had come on deck for some fresh air as Janetta was feeling a little faint in the closeness down below," John said and Janetta thought that was a nice touch about her feeling faint. He went on to describe how they had seen the Major come on deck, light his pipe and go to lean over the port rail. After a few minutes they had retired to bed leaving the Major still on deck.

Mr Thomson confirmed John's story and remembered saying goodnight to them as they went below. He also remembered seeing the Major smoking his pipe at the rail after the Martins had retired to bed, but he couldn't remember seeing him after the ship was hit by the squall.

The Captain also testified that he came on deck when the ship heeled unexpectedly as a result of being hit by a small squall as they came around the headland but didn't see the Major on deck.

A couple of officers gave evidence that they went to Cope's cabin later that evening to ask him to play cards. They described how they had banged on his door but got no reply. They assumed he was asleep but agreed it was more likely he was not in his cabin.

Finally the Brigadier brought down a verdict of 'Accidental Death,' and listed him as 'missing at sea, presumed dead'. Major Cope had been leaning on the rail when the ship heeled over in a squall throwing him off balance and he went overboard.

Case closed. John and Janetta looked at one another and gave a deep sigh of relief. It was over, and off the port bow could be seen the white cliffs of Dover.

****

As with all sailors, the entire company remained on deck to view the coastline as they got closer in shore. The sun made the white cliffs glow in the afternoon light. Janetta marvelled at such a sight. The cliffs stretched for several miles in each direction and rose and fell in gentle switchbacks that followed the contour of the land. On the very top was a paper-thin layer of bright green; the green that comes from England's lush climate.

In a natural cleft in the cliffs nestled the town of Dover, and as they came closer, they could make out individual houses climbing up the steep hill at the back of the town. Overlooking Dover, on top of the cliffs stood the gray, majestic walls of Dover Castle, the Battalion's new home. Janetta couldn't keep her eyes off the great stronghold on the cliffs. For five hundred years it had stood on guard at the gateway to England and she stared in awe of its power and sheer immensity. It seemed to grow right out of the very ground upon which it stood – anchored, immovable, impenetrable.

The *Assistance* moored up at the Admiralty Pier in Dover harbour in the late afternoon of the twenty-second of May. It had been a pleasant voyage for everyone on board except the Martins, but now they were eagerly anticipating having their feet firmly planted on solid ground again. There was agitation on the deck, as the men had to wait their orders before going down the gangplank. They stood with their packs on their backs and grumbled about the wait. The senior officers were the first to step ashore and everybody waited impatiently as they chatted with dock officials. Then the ladies were allowed to go ashore and Janetta gave John's hand a gentle squeeze before leaving him to join the ladies. It would be a couple of hours before she would see him again.

The ladies, all sat in wagons with their baggage, left the harbour in a stately column to begin their journey up the steep hill to the castle and their new quarters. As they drove off the pier Janetta looked back and saw the men still standing onboard waiting to be allowed off. As they proceeded up the hill, Janetta's stomach felt a little queasy. The road seemed to gently heave up and down like the swell on the ocean, and she found the sensation made her feel quite unsettled.

"You'll soon get your land legs back," observed Esmeralda who had climbed up onto the wagon beside Janetta.

"Didn't feel sick on the ship so why does I feel it now?" moaned Janetta. Esmeralda just laughed.

Janetta was pleasantly surprised when she saw the married quarters. They consisted of a large and very long stone building, two storeys high, with rows of doors and windows facing into a courtyard. Each unit was self contained and she was pleased to discover that they didn't have to share with anyone else. She felt particularly satisfied when she discovered that Esmeralda was at the far end to her and her next door neighbours were to be Sergeant Welland and his wife Betsy whom Janetta rather liked.

She dragged their trunk into the front door and then gave herself a quick tour of the apartment. The rooms were quite small and the stone walls were about eighteen inches thick. The upper floor contained a bedroom, which went the full depth of the block with a window both ends. Janetta stood by the back bedroom window and looked out over the top of the outer bailey curtain wall to the ocean. She imagined how very cold it would get in the winter when the wind came in off the sea and hit the back of the building. She ran her hands gently over the wooden window frames, feeling for drafts. She detected none, but then it was a calm day and she didn't doubt for one moment that the chill air would whistle through the frame in the winter.

In the main room was a fireplace that had one or two inadequate logs piled up in it, and in the back kitchen was a large black iron stove that hadn't been left too clean by the previous occupants. All in all, she thought it would do very nicely.

At first their stay in Dover was uneventful but John wasn't the same. He gradually became distant from her and his mood grew more sullen. He had never been much of a drinker but he now began drinking more heavily. Although he was not religious, his Welsh chapel upbringing had kept his drinking habits strictly moderate, but now he was taking to staying out later drinking with his friends in the tavern. Twice he had been put on a charge for being drunk while on duty and his commanding officer had even talked privately with Janetta trying to ascertain the reason for his change of attitude.

Their stay in Dover should have been a happier time but Janetta couldn't help feeling that fate was dealing her a bad hand. In August she gave birth to a son whom they named Robert, but he didn't survive more than a couple of days and Janetta sank into a depression that lasted all through Christmas.

Christmas came and went and John and Janetta drifted into a routine of married indifference.

April 1877

It was much lighter now in the evenings, and Janetta stood at the foot of their bed and stared at the goose feather mattress and pillows as if looking upon the grave. Tears welled up in her eyes but they were tears of frustration and anger. She was at the end of her tether and about to explode; now she would have one more attempt at putting things right.

Her hands began to pull fitfully at her laces as if she couldn't get her dress off fast enough, or perhaps she wanted to get it off before she changed her mind. She let the dress drop in a heap on the floor and stepped out of it. It was still quite early in the evening and John was downstairs in the kitchen eating his evening meal. As she undid her chemise and slipped it off her arms Janetta prayed, that on this evening, they would not be disturbed by neighbours or friends.

She paused for a moment as if questioning what she was doing. She'd played games before; manipulating men was an easy sport for her, but this felt oddly wrong. She felt uneasy about an untried approach and strangely uncertain of the outcome, but still she gathered her resolve and allowed her bloomers to drop about her ankles.

She stood at the foot of the bed in her nakedness and felt vulnerable and alone. "*Why,*" she thought, "*does nakedness make you feel lonely?*" There was a mirror standing in the corner of the room and she turned and studied herself in the glass. She swivelled away from it and looked over her shoulder at the reflection of her back. Yes, she was still very beautiful. She knew only too well that she only had to give the nod and half the regiment would fight over her. So tonight she would fight; and she'd fight with the best weapon she had, her body.

A cool breeze blew off the ocean and the stone walls chilled the room. She felt goose bumps crawl up her arms, so she threw a shawl round her shoulders and went silently downstairs.

****

John had slipped into a steadily deeper depression as his guilt over the murder of Major Cope slowly consumed him. It began in such a subtle manner that Janetta hardly noticed it at first. John would be quieter than usual, which she put down to the fatigue of his work. Then he gradually lost interest in her and the bed became a place of slow rejection. Janetta took his lack of interest in her very hard. She was a naturally tactile woman, who demanded physical attention and John's excuses for going straight to sleep became increasingly irksome to her. She'd lost her son and now it seemed she was losing her husband.

Janetta's frustration had been building for some time and she had actually accused John of having affairs, which she knew he wasn't having, and which only served to start a series of rows. John became more distant and increasingly incapable of talking to her but tonight she resolved to push him into declaring his feelings for her, one way or another.

She slipped quietly down the stairs and walked barefoot into the kitchen. John sat drinking a tankard of ale, and paid her no attention. He sat with his elbows on the table and his head hung down between his hands. His fingers combed through his hair in a posture of despair. Janetta walked slowly around the table and stopped almost beside him. John didn't look up. She allowed the shawl to drop to the floor exposing her nakedness. He took no notice of her.

"John," she said in a most seductive tone, "look at me, John."

He sat motionless, head hung down, deaf to her.

In a sudden and almost violent move that jolted John out of his stupor, she slammed her right foot up onto the tabletop, spilling his tankard and thrusting her belly right in front of his face.

John sat back, startled. He studied her for a few seconds; his eyes fixed, unseeing, upon her belly, confused and dazed. "*This,*" thought Janetta, "*would surely shake him into action.*" This was no subtle feminine hint that a man could – and most likely would miss – this was a flagrant demand.

"Well!" she said as warmly as she could.

John remained stubbornly silent.

"Well?" she asked again a little louder.

Still he didn't respond, but let his eyes slowly wonder away to the far side of the room as if she didn't exist.

She grabbed his head and slammed his face into her belly. "Well!" she demanded, her voice becoming more aggressive. "What are you going to do? Are you going to be a man and take me, or sit there getting drunk all night?"

John forcefully pulled his face away and glared at her. His cold eyes were full of loathing. They made her suddenly shiver with fear.

"Cover yourself up, for god's sake!" he growled. "What do you think you are? A bloody whore!"

Janetta lowered her leg and backed away from him. Her tactic hadn't worked. For the first time in her life she discovered that her body couldn't always conquer a man's mind and supply every need. She picked up the shawl and clutched it in front of herself as if a stranger had just entered the room.

"You're my husband, you shit! And you can't even look at me any more. Wot the 'ell's the matter with ya any'ow?" In her despair she drifted back into her naturally common speech. Her years of pretence at being a lady were forgotten.

John's face turned red with sheer rage as he screamed at her.

"I blackmailed my commanding officer 'cause of you."

He stood up and slammed his knuckles on the table, "and now I've killed for ya! What's next eh? What will ya want me to do next?"

Janetta, so stunned by this outburst, couldn't speak for a moment. She backed away from him shaking her head and trying not to cry.

"I swear you must be a witch," he continued as his violent outburst subsided. "So goddamned beautiful, yet so fucking dangerous. I could swing because of you!"

He collapsed back into his chair. "They say the devil shows himself in beautiful form to tempt us into sin."

"John?" she whimpered, not believing what she was hearing.

"Evil, that's what you are!" he spat. "I'll be condemned to hell and you'll survive just nicely, you will!"

"John, for god's sake you're scaring me! I'm not evil…John," she pleaded.

"Cope'll haunt me, he'll follow me to the gibbet and laugh as I swing." John was becoming hysterical. He was trembling and sweating and Janetta, partly to shut him up in case they were overheard, punched him in the face.

"Shut up," she yelled into his startled face. "You're not going to hang, and Cope was a worm, he deserved to die." She was recovering quickly from the shock of John's wrath and was now coming back into the fight.

"Murder's a sin. I'll go to 'ell I knows I will!" John trembled, his eyes glancing feverishly from side to side as if he were looking for a ghost.

"Shut up," she growled at him, teeth clenched and eyes on fire, "pull y'self together."

John whimpered and shook violently as he drifted into a private hell. He clasped his hands together and thrust his knuckles into his mouth trying to stifle a scream.

"Attennnn…shun!" Janetta screamed into his face, and John gave a mighty shake, his eyes bugging white as his consciousness suddenly snapped into focus and he jumped to his feet.

"It's alright! It's alright!" she said, calming him.

Janetta stooped down beside his leg, caressed his arm and looked up into his horrified face and spoke softly to him.

"There's something you don't know. Something I didn't tell ya," John's face twitched in spasms of fear as he stared about the room. Sweat ran in rivulets down his forehead but he was listening.

"That night on the ship, Cope didn't just want our money, John, he wanted me." She pounded her chest with her fist to give herself emphasis. She paused to see what effect this had on John. He didn't seem to take it in, so she continued.

"He wanted me to go to 'im on a regular basis. He wanted to 'roger' me, John… he wanted to fuck me every month as his prize for keeping quiet… but I wouldn't 'ave that, cause I'm your woman, John, and I'd never be 'is."

John's eyes began to focus on her. "Cope deserved to die John, 'cause he was wicked and you were defending my 'onour. That's wot ya was doing John luv. You won't go to 'ell for defending your wife's 'onour."

John's shivering subsided and he slowly became calmer as her words came into focus in his mind.

"Cope'll still haunt me," he whispered.

"Cope won't 'aunt ya John, because he didn't see ya, did he? He didn't know who killed him, so he can't haunt ya can he?"

A couple of seconds passed as this revelation sank into John's tormented mind. "*She's right*," he thought, "*I hadn't thought of that*."

"No," he said softly. "He didn't see me. He had no idea what hit him." A smile slowly crept across John's strained face. "He can't get me can he?" he said.

"No my sweet he can't get ya," agreed Janetta.

John looked down at her and tears welled up in his eyes. "I'm not going to hell then?"

"No luv."

"And you don't think I'll swing?"

"No, ya won't swing, John. The court said he died accidentally when he fell overboard. It's all over. You can relax and forget it."

John leaned forward and buried his head in her hair and she caressed him as he gently wept on her shoulder.

The winter past into spring and an uneasy truce developed between them.

CHAPTER 11

The Storm
1878

It was one of those nights when all living creatures retreat to their burrows to find warmth and shelter. A night when animals crouched and huddled together in an attempt to keep dry; when men everywhere sat before their fires with the shutters closed, warming their hands and their hearts on mulled ales. Fishermen pulled their boats up high on the beaches and ships stood out to sea as far from the coast as possible. The cold gray sea came into the shore, foaming at the crests and hurled itself against the harbour wall sending great plumes of spray into the calmer waters inside. All the ships at the jetty chafed at their moorings and the harbour workers huddled around their fires hoping they wouldn't need to go out to secure any line that had thrashed itself loose.

The glistening streets of Dover were deserted, swept by the wind and dashed by the pounding rain. Trees came down and blocked the roads and leaves and small branches blew about the town like rice at a wedding. The wind howled as it funnelled through alleys, slamming garden gates and scattering rubbish. Inn signs squeaked as they shook from side to side, as if trying to escape their hinges.

It was barely past eight thirty in the evening yet everywhere was as dark as midnight and as cold as the heart of winter.

At the Bull Inn the fire spattered and smoked. The bar was devoid of its usual throng of clientele and the landlord sat at a table in the corner with a mug of chocolate and a sullen expression that hid his usually cheerful countenance. He sat with his elbows on the table and stared morosely into the fire. Only one other person sat quietly in the bar, alone with her own thoughts, a glass of wine and a jug of hot water. She sat by the great fire, her white stockinged feet spread out before the hearth. Occasionally a clap of thunder disturbed her thinking and the wind blew down the chimney sending smoke into the bar stinging her eyes.

Neither of them spoke. They had said all there was to say about the foul weather, and now they just sat and waited. They both stared into the fire and listened to the window casements creaking and the wind winding up outside. Then after a slight pause it would fall with a heavy blow against the inn, making pictures shudder against the wall and the flames in the fire lay flat against the logs before flickering back to life.

The door flew open and the bar filled with a blast of freezing air, as three cloaked soldiers entered. The last one pressed his body weight against the door to push it shut. They all gasped, shivered and shook their cloaks leaving small puddles on the wooden floor.

The innkeeper looked up expectantly. Customers and company had arrived to relieve the tedium and add coins to his purse.

"Gentleman," he welcomed them, making no attempt to disguise his enthusiasm for new custom, "take off your coats and dry yourself before the fire. What a night, sirs, What a night! Come, sirs, sit yourselves down while I get you some brandy."

The three soldiers pulled chairs closer to the hearth, shivered and held out their hands for warming by the fire. The young woman looked at them with a slight smile on her face. They were so concerned about getting warm that they hadn't taken any notice of her. She knew them well enough since they were all from the castle and she had spent many a night drinking with them in this bar.

"Gentlemen!" she announced, "didn't think to see anyone tonight."

They all focused on her and great smiles spread across their wet faces.

"Jan…Mrs Martin," said Freddie Longhurst correcting himself. "How wonderful to see ya. But what ya doing 'ere on a night like this?"

"I'd been into town t'look round the shops and I got caught by the storm. Thought I'd wait it out in 'ere."

"Well we're certainly glad you're here," said Anthony Walls, a corporal with a reputation for enjoying his drink, "t'night is looking bett'r already!"

Janetta smiled at the compliment.

"But we can't stay," interjected Sergeant Wilkins, "we have to get straight back to barracks, lads. Just stopped in for a quick drink to warm us and then up the bloody hill again in this wind."

"Pity!" teased Janetta, "we could have made a night of it. Oh well!"

"Another night, ma'am," replied the sergeant, and the other two looked most disappointed.

"Perhaps we could escort you back to barracks, ma'am," offered the sergeant. "Three strong soldiers should be able to stop you from being blown away, ma'am!" he said with a broad smile and the other two laughed at the thought of holding her down in the wind.

"That's very kind of you, Sergeant," laughed Janetta.

She was about to take them up on their offer when the door burst open again and Lieutenant Bird rushed in and shook the rain off his cloak.

"...But I was thinking of staying 'ere the night." The innkeeper's ears pricked up at the possibility of some extra custom. "You could do me the service, however, of stopping by and telling John not to worry and I'll be home in time to make 'is breakfast."

"Certainly, ma'am, it'll be my pleasure." The sergeant turned his attention to the landlord. "Mind you give Mrs Martin a clean room with no bugs."

"Always the one to give gammon, ain't ya?" replied the landlord.

"You'll 'ear from me if there's bugs!" The Sergeant chided.

"I runs a clean 'ouse and Mrs Martin knows it, so she does."

The Sergeant turned and winked at Janetta and then addressing his two companions, "Com'on lads drink up. We'll 'ave to be getting back t' castle".

The Lieutenant walked toward the fire, acknowledged the Sergeant and his men and gave a stiff bow to Janetta. The stiffness was more from cold and wet than formality, yet it served to show a public respect for a married woman.

"Mrs Martin it's a pleasure to see you."

Janetta bowed her head in a gesture that suggested mere politeness.

Lieutenant Bird, having paid his respects retired to the far side of the room and ordered a jug of wine.

The Sergeant and the two soldiers sat quietly chatting to Janetta for a couple of minutes, and then, feeling the pressure of having an officer watching them, they said their good-byes.

They bundled themselves up in their greatcoats and with heads bent forward ventured once more into the howling night.

The fire spattered and the flames almost flickered out as the door opened. Janetta gave a shiver and wrapped her shawl tighter about her shoulders and stared into the fire.

The innkeeper came over to the Lieutenant's table with the wine and placed it before him.

"You're not too good for business tonight, Lieutenant. You're frightening off my clientele."

Lieutenant Bird made an exaggerated performance of looking all about the room before replying, "What customers?"

The innkeeper just grinned, shook his head and motioned with his thumb towards the fire; "She's await'n for ya!"

"Thank you Mr McNeal," replied the Lieutenant in a tone that implied it was none of his business. He picked up the wine bottle and scraping his chair back, stood up and walked across the bar to where Janetta sat huddled by the fire. At first she ignored him and remained staring into the flames. The Lieutenant sat down in the chair recently vacated by the sergeant, and placed his bottle on the side table.

"Sorry, I couldn't get away," he said in a low voice.

Janetta turned her head slowly towards him. "Thought you weren't coming."

She wasn't angry but she had been waiting over an hour and was about to give up on him and return to the castle with the Sergeant.

"I do beg your pardon Jan, but I couldn't get away. Damned officers' dinners, they don't like it if you cut out early!"

"Well, Lieutenant you're here now and I'm very grateful."

"You don't have to call me lieutenant in private," he said, leaning forward and looking kindly at her. "Call me Timothy,"

Janetta smiled and nodded in appreciation, "That's very kind of you…Timothy."

"So!" he said sitting back in his chair and taking a cigar out of his jacket pocket. "What did you want to speak to me about?" He struck his flint and held it up to his cigar and puffed hard 'til the end glowed.

****

The Sergeant and his two men struggled up the castle hill against the torrent of rain. By the time they got to the top they were breathless, cold and wet through. A warm fire and bed seemed very inviting.

They walked through the main gate and headed towards the barrack block. It was easier going now in the shelter of the walls but the rain still came down hard. The Sergeant stopped half way across the courtyard, remembering Janetta's message for her husband.

"You two carry on," he said "I'm going over to tell Martin where his wife is."

The other two nodded and hurried on to their beds. Sergeant Wilkins turned away from his companions and walked across to the Martin's quarters. He stood before their front door and rapped his knuckles against it. There was a groan from inside and a minute later the door opened and John Martin appeared leaning against the doorframe to support himself. It was obvious that he had been drinking. His shirt was undone and out of his trousers and his eyes struggled to focus on his visitor.

"Oo's zat?" he slurred in a malevolent voice.

"Sergeant Wilkins, Martin."

John vaguely aware that he should be smarter in front of a sergeant, tried to stand up straighter, and in doing so, swayed as if standing on the deck of a ship.

"Can I come in? It's bloody wet out here!" said the Sergeant, fully aware that he had the authority to enter, but wishing to remain civil. John staggered to one side to allow the Sergeant to squeeze past him.

"I just came to tell you that Mrs Martin is staying at the Bull tonight because of the storm. Not to worry, she'll be back early in the morning."

John took a second to comprehend what he had been told. After a few contortions of his face as he struggled to form his thoughts, he waggled a limp finger at the Sergeant and said, "Suppose she's entertaining half the bloody regiment down there!"

"God no!" exclaimed Sergeant Wilkins, seeing where John's thoughts were heading. "Everybody's in the castle. There's only Lieutenant Bird down there."

As the words escaped his mouth he regretted letting them go. John's already red face took on a frightening countenance.

"Lieutenant bloody Bird!" he exclaimed. "Lieutenant high and mighty bloody Bird's with her! I'll show 'im! I'll teach that bastard whose wom'n she is!"

John staggered back into the parlour and picked up his tunic. He turned round and around as he struggled to get his arm in a constantly retreating sleeve. "God dammed bloody Bird!" he spat as he spun about the room until the spinning got the better of his head and he collapsed onto the floor.

Sergeant Wilkins breathed a sigh of relief when he saw John pass out on the floor.

"That's better Martin!" he said to the barely conscious heap on the floor. "You sleep it off." He left the Martins' quarters and ventured back out into the rain. He got across the courtyard and was about to enter his own quarters when he heard a door slam behind him. He turned around to see the distant shadowy figure of John, half dressed, staggering across the compound heading for the main gate.

"Goddam the man!" he said under his breath, and then went inside to get dried off. He put his coat over the back of a chair to dry out in front of the fire and opened a bottle of brandy. It had been a miserable night out and he was so glad to be in the warm again. With a chunk of bread and a large slice of cheese on a pewter plate he flopped exhausted into a second chair and tugged off his boots.

"Damn stupid man!" he said to the empty room. He really liked Janetta and although he had assumed for some time that her friendship with Lieutenant Bird was more than met the eye, he didn't think any worse of her for it. Indeed he and most of the regiment envied Lieutenant Bird for his "friendship" with her. If they were having an affair he didn't want Janetta to get into trouble over it; especially since he didn't think much of John Martin.

"He's a drunken oaf who doesn't deserve a beautiful woman like her!" he muttered. "Oh, damn the man, he's gone down to make trouble, I can smell it!"

He sat before his fire, eating his supper, sipping his brandy and listening to the wind howl outside. He was getting warm and comfortable and all the time he thought of Martin staggering down the hill in a drunken state, on his way to do mischief at the Bull.

"She's his wife," he mumbled, "what's it to me if the Lieutenant gets beaten up by a jealous husband?" But it wouldn't do. Sergeant Wilkins had always been on the best of terms with the Lieutenant and the last thing he wanted was for him to get hurt or killed, or for that matter to see Janetta get beaten by her drunkard husband.

"Can't understand Martin," he said to himself, "used to be a good man. Gets himself a beautiful wife and goes to pieces."

He swallowed the last of the brandy, "Damn the fellow! Damn! Damn! Damn!"

Sergeant Wilkins pulled his boots back on, then his wet coat and headed back out into the night.

****

Janetta and Lieutenant Bird had been sitting in front of the fire in quiet conversation for more than an hour. She had told the Lieutenant about how John's behaviour had been getting steadily worse. How he had become abusive and even struck her on occasions, and how he was drunk more than he was sober. Lieutenant Bird listened to her very intently. Nothing she was telling him came as a surprise, since the whole battalion had watched John's steady decline over the last few months. His commanding officer had expressed concern over John's ability to perform his duties and John had been put on a charge on more than one occasion for drunkenness. All John's comrades and even some of the officers had turned a blind eye to his faults because they all liked Janetta, but his behaviour couldn't go unpunished for much longer. John was becoming an embarrassment.

Lieutenant Bird listened to Janetta and watched her eyes water slightly as she poured out her heart to him, and all he could think about was how close the bedrooms were and how beautiful Janetta was. This was the chance of a lifetime; a stormy night, alone in an inn without her husband and nobody to see them. The innkeeper would say nothing; he'd seen this many times before and besides, he was more interested in the custom.

Bird watched her lips moving as she talked about her loneliness and he hardly heard her at all. He already knew the situation Janetta was in.

He just wanted to lean in towards her and kiss her captivating lips. He was besotted with her, but as a gentleman, he hesitated. Was he taking advantage of her? Perhaps she'd melt into his arms and let her passion flood over him, then again, perhaps she'd pull away, offended by his advances and accuse him of taking advantage of her vulnerability. He doubted how vulnerable she really was and knew she could work a man's heart as easily as dough on a kitchen table, but was he willing to take the risk?

Janetta seemed to be oblivious to his heart and desires and simply blathered on about her bore of a husband. So Timothy Bird decided to sit back and allow her the time to purge herself of all her marital anxiety, while he listened as intently and as compassionately as he could between momentary lapses into lustful wishes.

And so they sat together before the fire, their feet stretched out before them to warm before the grate and the wine and hot water were replenished. The rain continued to hammer relentlessly at the windows. Janetta exhausted herself talking about her husband and became more pensive. Lieutenant Bird, under the influence of the warm fire and wine, became drowsy as he slumped in his chair.

They sat together in silence for several minutes and stared into the fire. They both felt content in one another's company, and the Lieutenant had resigned himself to the belief that he should just allow Janetta to decide whether she wished his company for the rest of the night.

They were both feeling relaxed and mellow when the door burst open and a wet and bedraggled John Martin staggered in and fought to close it behind him.

Janetta and Lieutenant Bird both turned their heads to see who had entered. They were so surprised that they jumped to their feet and gaped at him in astonishment. He stood inside the door and scowled at them, rain trickling down his face and neck.

"Very pretty!" slurred John. He had sobered up considerably on his cold walk down the hill but he was still intoxicated, and agitated by his anger. He had spent the time it took him to come down the hill rehearsing everything he would say and do, if he caught her with another man. Even murder had entered his tortured mind, but now that he saw his wife standing awkwardly beside Lieutenant Bird he was dumbfounded. He had always liked Lieutenant Bird. Of all the officers, he was the only one he really trusted. He may be a 'gentleman' but he treated the men under his command with civility and respect. He was the last man in the regiment he suspected of wife stealing. Perhaps it was that trust he had in the Lieutenant that made him feel so much more than just jealous – he had been betrayed.

"John?" Janetta whimpered in her shock.

"Martin, you look wet through man. Come and warm yourself."

The Lieutenant was doing his utmost to appear as though absolutely nothing was wrong.

"Don't 'John' me! I know what's going on 'ere." John was addressing Janetta in a sneering tone. He ignored Bird for the moment. He may have been furious but he also knew he was in the presence of a superior officer, so he held his tongue as long as he could and strode across the bar towards them, leaving wet, muddy marks on the floorboards, his face and eyes red and twisted in rage.

"Martin, this is not the way it looks!" protested the Lieutenant. John still ignored him and turned on Janetta.

Janetta found herself shivering with fear. She had seen John drunk and violent before, but tonight he had a wildness in his eyes that turned her cold. John grabbed her by the arm and pulled her hard away from the fire.

"Com'n ya bitch! Your com'n 'ome where ya belong!"

"Martin let her go, that's an order!" snapped Lieutenant Bird in as strong a manner as he could manage while flustered.

"Hah! That's an order is it?" John turned ferociously on Bird and he took a step backwards as John advanced toward him. "Goin' to pull rank on me are ya? This is private business between me an me wife."

Seeing Lieutenant Bird starting to wilt under John's advance, Janetta stepped between them, "Now John you've got it all wrong," she protested.

"Out a me way whore," John snapped and before Janetta could react, the back of John's hand had come across her face, sending her sprawling on the floor.

Lieutenant Bird was appalled at seeing her bloodied and prostrate on the floor and immediately went to help her up.

"No ya don't," snarled John, dragging the Lieutenant back and throwing him against the table. "You'll keep ya 'ands off my wife."

Lieutenant Bird gripped the table to stop himself from rolling off it and falling to the floor. He looked at John, half expecting him to land a couple of punches while he was caught off balance, but John was just glaring at him as if frozen to the spot. Janetta rolled herself onto her back on the floor and propped herself up on her elbows in an effort to see what was happening. The innkeeper hearing the commotion had now entered the bar from the back room and the three of them remained motionless for a few short seconds as they stared at John.

The expression on John's face had turned Janetta cold. His wild stare had changed to one of puzzlement, almost astonishment. His eyes, bulging out of their sockets, stared into space and beads of perspiration glistened on his forehead; it was as if he had been paralyzed by the sight of some hideous demon. He swayed gently to and fro, his lips quivering as he tried to mouth some unheard plea to the unseen visitor and dribble ran from the corner of his mouth. His pleas gone unheard, the spectre overwhelmed him. He gave a twitching spasm, folded his arms in front of his chest to contain an inner explosion and gasping, he crumpled into a heap on the floor.

Lieutenant Bird dropped to his knees beside him and struggled to loosen his tunic. The colour had drained from John's face and his breathing was laboured but he was still alive. Janetta let out a weakened scream and hastily crawled across the floor to cradle John's head in her arms.

"Don't die, John, don't die on me," she whimpered.

"We need a physician quickly," yelled the Lieutenant to the innkeeper. "Is there one near by?"

"Yes, sir, as it 'appens there's one right across the street, sir. Directly opposite sir," replied Mr McNeal as he bent over John with a look on his face that implied this was very bad for business.

"Well hurry, man! Fetch him!" said the Lieutenant frustrated by his hesitation.

"Oh! You'll be wishing me to go then will you sir?" said Mr McNeal somewhat put out at the thought of leaving his bar.

"Indeed I do, sir! Hurry yourself!"

"You'll be looking after the bar then will you? While I'm out there knocking up the doctor," enquired Mr McNeal.

The Lieutenant gave Mr McNeal a withering look, which left no doubt concerning his resolve in the matter; and so he backed off the subject without further argument.

It seemed an eternity until Mr McNeal returned with a short, stout gentleman with very thin hair, carrying a black medical bag.

The doctor barely acknowledged either Lieutenant Bird or Janetta, who still clung to John's shoulders and nestled his head against her breast.

"Let me see now, young lady," he said as he bent over John.

Lieutenant Bird helped Janetta up off the floor and led her away to her chair before the fire.

"He's in good hands, Jan. We must just wait and hope," he said to her in gentle tones.

Janetta sat down, tears streaking her cheeks and her knuckles going white as she gripped the chair arm too tightly. She didn't say anything but kept her eyes on John, who laboured to breathe while the doctor looked him over.

Lieutenant Bird couldn't help noticing how, after all she'd told him about John's abuse towards her, now that he lay on the floor in peril of his life, she sat in a state of distress over his wellbeing. *"Is this love?"* he thought to himself as he looked at her. *"Would she stay by his side and nurse him and support him, despite his brutish faults."*

He found a new admiration for Janetta in those moments of crisis. He knew she was an outrageous flirt, that she aspired to be more than she was, that she was beautiful, at times manipulative with men and above all, completely adorable; now he saw how she could be genuinely loving and loyal to her husband. She was a complicated woman, this Janetta Martin who had captured his heart so easily.

"Do you have a bed to spare?" inquired the doctor to Mr McNeal.

Mr McNeal hesitated. He suddenly found himself being manoeuvered into offering a bed to a dying man who could not, in all likelihood, afford to pay for it.

"I'll pay for the room," snarled Lieutenant Bird who read the innkeeper's mind.

"Oh! Indeed I have a room," replied Mr McNeal recovering quickly, "a very accommodating room with clean sheets freshly put on."

"Then help us carry him up," said the doctor as he pulled John into the sitting position.

Mr McNeal and the Lieutenant stepped forward to help lift John off the floor.They grasped his arms and legs and proceeded to carry him upstairs. Janetta followed in a state of bewilderment. She had not expected anything like this. John was young and strong. How could he die this way? She trembled as she wiped the tears from her face and followed up the stairs.

"Mind his head there!" said the doctor as they negotiated a narrow bend in the stairs. John's head flopped from side to side as he was manhandled to the bedroom. His breathing was shallow and laboured.

"Young lady," the doctor addressed Janetta firmly, "squeeze past us, if you would and get the door."

The two men stopped on the landing, groaning and going red in the face while they waited for Janetta to brush past them and go to the bedroom door. Inside, the room was spartan, but clean enough and the three rather unceremoniously dropped John on the bed. The overweight doctor sat down on a wooden chair beside the bed and gasped as he tried to regain his breath. Mr McNeal puffed out his cheeks and gave a long exhale. "E wasn't light was he, fer such a scrawny one?"

"Dead weight!" said Lieutenant Bird between heavy breaths.

Janetta winced, and Bird realizing what he had said, became suddenly very contrite.

"Oh I do beg your pardon Mrs Martin," he stammered, "I wasn't thinking."

Mr McNeal hid a sneer behind his hand as the Lieutenant addressed her formally.

"*Oo's he bloody foolin'!*" he thought, "*bleedin' hypocrite!*"

"Is he alright doctor? Will he live?" whimpered Janetta.

The doctor, still not yet fully recovered from the trip up the stairs, pursed his lips as if annoyed at being asked to look at his patient. He leant forward and lifted his frame off the chair, then sat again on the edge of the bed. His examination of John seemed almost cursory. He listened to his heart, 'hummed' and 'hahed' a few times, tutted a couple of times and then stood up, looked at Janetta and asked, "Are you his wife?"

Janetta nodded meekly.

"He'll do I expect!" he said in an offhand manner, "if he survives the night, he'll live!"

He then turned to the Lieutenant and taking him by the arm, led him towards the door and away from Janetta's hearing.

"His soldiering days are over, Lieutenant. He'll have to take life very easy from now on," he said in very low tones.

"But he will live?" asked the lieutenant.

"For the short term, yes, he should. But long term..." here he pursed his lips again and shook his head just enough for Lieutenant Bird to see, but not Janetta, "I very much doubt it, Lieutenant, very much doubt it indeed!"

CHAPTER 12

Homecoming
February 1st 1880

Corporal William Rayner sat on the gun carriage, with the reins loosely running through his fingers and talked calmly to the horses. “Steady my beauties, steady.” The lead mare pawed the cobblestones with her hoof and nodded her head excitedly. They tugged gently at the carriage rocking it back and forth an inch or two. They had been standing too long and wanted to move but his voice soothed them.

He sat behind his team looking slightly scruffy. He wasn’t a handsome man. His face was weathered and gaunt, with high cheekbones and angular jaw. His tunic hung on his thin frame as if it was two sizes too big for him. Only his eyes betrayed his hard countenance, for they sparkled the palest blue, showed great kindness and made women go weak at the knees. Will, however, was no womanizer. He was shy and uncomfortable around women and was only really happy when tending to his horses.

All about the quayside was the hum of hundreds of voices and the familiar controlled chaos of a regiment on the move. Men led horses down the gangplanks of ships moored against the wharf, and gun carriages and wagons were lifted out of hulls by block and tackle suspended from the yardarms. The horses looked thin and many glistened with lathered sweat, a sure sign of anxiety. Others were listless, droopy and fretful. A couple of horses refused to come down the gangplank, being unsettled by the noise and confusion on the dock. Their handlers spoke soothingly to them and coaxed them forward.

Will looked anxiously at the poor animals and did his best to prevent his team from being spooked. This was a team of fresh mares sent out from the barracks to bring back the guns and supply wagons. The regiment’s horses would have to convalesce before being put back to work.

The Sixth Battalion of the Royal Artillery had arrived home. The docks at Dover were crowded with soldiers setting foot on English soil for the first time, after ten years in India and weeks at sea.

It had rained hard all morning, giving rise to a multitude of wisecracks about 'bloody English weather'; now it just drizzled, and Will sat on his carriage and shivered. He'd forgotten how cold the rain could be in England, and how it soaked through your heavy woollen uniform and chilled you to the bone. When it rained in Secunderabad, it came down in torrents and was a welcome, if short, reprieve from the oppressive Indian heat. Then, the sun beat down again and everything steamed and smelled of cow dung. In England the dampness hung in the air as an almost invisible mist that clung oppressively to your soul. He thought about Kalpana, his *bibbi* he'd left behind in India and found himself missing her more than he ever thought he would. He wandered what she was doing right at that moment back in Secunderabad. She'd probably found another English soldier to comfort her, but Will preferred to believe she was missing him too.

Will looked about the docks and tried to take in all the sights he had remembered from when he was a lad so many years before. Nothing much had changed. Dover still looked gray and forbidding in the rain. Up on the cliffs he could see the gray stone walls of Dover Castle and the harbour swarmed with a multitude of small craft going about their business in the gloom. The gray-green sea heaved beyond the harbour wall and Will felt mightily glad to have his feet on firm ground again.

It smelled different too. He had become accustomed to the smells of India, and had marvelled at how you could smell the country ten miles out to sea. India was full of the aromas of blossoms, spices and the ubiquitous cow dung.

But the Dover air was quite different. His nostrils were full of the odours of horse sweat and dung that lay in heaps about the streets, but this was such a common smell that it went unnoticed. Beyond that was an air of sulphurous smoke, damp moss-covered brick work, salt wind, sewage and human perspiration. It all invaded his nostrils and thrilled him. He was home again.

Sergeant Major Horrocks broke his meditation with a shrill, barked order, "Fall in you bastards! On the double!" Hundreds of boots clattered on the cobbles as men jostled into rank four abreast, and straightened their alignment. "Simmons!" screamed the Sergeant Major. "Where the bloody 'ells your rifle? Don't think you need it now your 'ome?"

Simmons nervously glanced at his shoulder where his rifle should be, "Yes, sir!"

"Well! Where the bloody 'ell is it?" screamed Horrocks.

Simmons eyes flicked over to where he'd been waiting at the dockside and saw his rifle lying on a wooden crate.

"Well it won't come on its own will it lad?"

"No sir" replied Simmons.

"Well fall out Simmons. On the double you 'orrible bastard"

Simmons ran out of line to retrieve his weapon from the edge of the wharf.

"Come on! You think the regiment's going to wait all day for ya?" Horrocks was red in the face as he bellowed across the wharf.

Will glanced back over his shoulder and smirked to himself at seeing Simmons running back in line as he struggled to sling his rifle over his shoulder.

"What are you looking at, Rayner? Eyes front!" said Horrocks, the edge taken off his voice somewhat.

Down the line other sergeants were repeating the order to 'fall in', and other brigades formed themselves into marching ranks. The boot scuffling gradually subsided and for a few minutes a strange silence fell upon the quayside.

Will's team of six horses, their coats glistening in the rain, began to anticipate the order to 'move out'.

"Steady, whoa, steady," said Will softly, calming the team, and they snorted and shifted their weight.

Will instinctively straightened his back in preparation for the move. He tugged the wrinkles out off his sleeves and adjusted his chinstrap in a last minute effort to look his best. He felt uncomfortable in his full uniform yet proud to be wearing it, and wanted to look like a soldier as they paraded through the town. There would be a march of some eight miles along the Folkstone road to Sandgate, and then a further three to the north until they came to their overnight stop at Shorncliffe Barracks.

There would be a day or two at Shorncliffe and then the journey across Kent to the Regiment's home barracks at Woolwich. Many of the town's folk would be waiting with great anticipation for the Regiment's return, especially the tradesmen and young women. But others, Will knew, would be apprehensive about it. The local men would have competition for their women and in the streets at night may be scenes of drunken fights. Many of Will's Battalion were eagerly looking forward to tasting English ale again and sampling English girls.

"Companyyyy forrrrw'd". Will heard the command from a couple of hundred yards forward of his position, and his team agitated to move again. From his elevation on the gun carriage he could see the troops ahead of him starting to move forward at a walk, in broken step, and turn the corner at the end of a warehouse. When the ranks in front had moved off, Horrocks gave the command "Forward". Will gently rippled the reins and clicked his tongue and the team moved forward at a walk. The brigade walked along the quay and then turned left into the road leading towards the quay's gate. At the entrance the column halted and the ranks all closed up into neat files behind the high wooden gates that led out into the town.

There were a few frustrating moments while the column waited for the back ranks to catch up, and the team fidgeted.

Finally the gates were swung open and a voice from the front of the line bellowed "By the left, quick march". The drums of the regimental band began beating out a marching roll. The whole Regiment seemed to respond like an enormous centipede, and a thousand pairs of boots beat out a rhythm on the cobblestones.

Will felt proud as he passed under the gated arch, driving his team and pulling behind a shiny black cannon with its brass work polished until it reflected like a mirror. This was one of those rare moments when the drudgery of soldiering was made worthwhile. He'd come a long way since the days when he worked as a collier, carrying sacks of coal to people's houses. It was a hard, dirty life, and although he was under age, he'd manage to escape it by talking his way into the army. It wasn't hard; the army wasn't really particular who they took, and if you looked old enough and were reasonably fit you were in. His mother had cried of course, but his father, despite his protests, seemed rather proud of his boy's wish to become a soldier. "It'll make a man of ya lad," he'd said.

Now he was coming home, handsome and smart in his blue uniform and in command of six beautiful horses pulling a magnificent gun. He felt as though it was his own personal gun and made an extra effort to look tough and commanding.

Outside the gate the street was lined with a thin yet respectable crowd who had come out to cheer them along their way. The rain had stopped and the sun struggled to peer out from behind the clouds.

The horses' hooves clattered, the iron wheels of the gun carriage rattled on the cobbles and the army of boots pounded rhythmically on the road. Will's heart soared.

The column moved along the street between rows of shops, and hundreds of carts and wagons of all descriptions. Will, keeping his head forward at all times, glanced side to side taking in all the sights he'd missed during the last ten years. There were so many people in civilian clothes. He'd lived for so long surrounded by military uniforms and Indian saris and ohotis that he'd forgotten what it was like to be in England. English clerks and tradesmen had worn civies in India but they were few. He noticed how the fashions had changed a bit too, and how drab everyone looked. He suddenly found himself missing the kaleidoscope of colours of an Indian street.

The regimental band started playing as they turned into the high street and a few bystanders began to applaud.

As he approached the corner, Will gave a gentle pull on the reins to guide the lead mare around, but it was hardly necessary as the team instinctively followed the ranks ahead of them.

A young woman standing in the crowd on the bend, suddenly caught his eye. For a second he forgot himself and turned his head to look at her. He could feel Horrocks' eyes on him, and imagined the sergeant major hissing under his breath, *"eyes front Rayner"*.

Somehow Will didn't care about Horrocks, the dark-haired beauty, half hidden by other bystanders in front of her, fascinated him.

No sooner had he seen her, than he was past, and couldn't crane his neck any further round without getting an earful later from an irate Horrocks.

It began to rain again, but he hardly noticed. He was almost unaware of the rest of the parade. His mind was occupied by the vision of this beautiful woman with the long hair, smooth skin and blue eyes. He was sure she had looked right at him as he rode past, or at least he imagined she had. It's ridiculous, he thought, he'll never see her again, yet he couldn't get her face out of his mind.

The band played on and the regiment moved on up the hill as they climbed away from the sea, and soon they'd be back in Shorncliffe Barracks after so many years.

CHAPTER 13

The "Puddler"
May 1880

Janetta walked along the path that meandered between the river and an open meadow where a small herd of cows grazed contentedly. It was a bright sunny spring day and insects buzzed about in the hedgerows and birds sang in the trees. It was the kind of day that made you feel alive but Janetta sauntered along the path not noticing the fine weather or the birds' songs. She was depressed and could not concentrate on life with anything approaching her usual enthusiasm.

As beautiful as the countryside was she simply couldn't believe she was there. For the last couple of years she had been living in the small village of Morriston in South Wales – miles from her family and the regiment. She was living with John and his parents in a dingy little cottage. They were dour and dirty people, who barely tolerated her.

John had become increasingly bitter towards her over the Major Cope affair. He couldn't forgive her for involving him in murder, or for her friendship with the Lieutenant. Every time she spoke to another man, it confirmed in his mind that she was a harlot. To add to her depressing life, the family and half the village were teetotal and strict chapel. This didn't come as any surprise to her since Tywardreath, where she had grown up, was also mostly chapel, but in the years with the regiment she had grown fond of her glass of gin and regimental functions.

After John's heart attack in Dover he was invalided out of the army and had returned to his family in Wales. His mother and father had nursed him back to health despite the fact that they could barely afford to feed themselves.

Janetta did the only thing she could to help, and that was to take in laundry from the neighbours. She had given the last of the Colonel's money to John's family so now the few extra shillings helped pay for her keep, but she hated every minute of the job. She couldn't see herself as a cleaner of other people's dirty clothes when she had worked so hard to improve her situation.

"No," she thought as she ambled along the path, *"I had married John because he was handsome and because it got me into the regiment. But it was a big mistake!"*

Her only chance to get out of the gutter was to become the mistress of an officer, and to gain as much of his wealth as she could. "But how am I going to do that stuck out here in this God-forsaken land," she muttered to herself.

She even cursed herself for having been so noble as to stay by her husband's side; even through the abuse and hatred he heaped upon her. "I should have stayed in Dover," she grumbled.

Her dark thoughts were interrupted by the sound of voices. She had arrived at the canal with John's lunch, a tin can of hot tea and a hunk of cheese and bread wrapped up in a napkin. Gangs of labourers were busily digging in the mud and a large steam hammer pounded stakes into the sidewalls of the trench. The din of construction had suddenly replaced the tranquility of the countryside. Men dug and hammered, the pile driver thumped and hissed steam. The workmen sang and shouted to one another above the noise of the hammer.

As Janetta approached a whistle blew and everything stopped for the lunch break. She walked along the bank past sweating, mud covered men who looked up at her as she drew near. Their eyes and teeth shone white as their grubby faces smiled at her.

"Allo Jan luv!" said one and, "ave ya bought me any lunch, Jan?" cried out another.

Every day she came with John's lunch and every day she walked past this gang of wisecracking workers, and every day she enjoyed every minute of the attention.

"I'll bring ya a fick 'ear! Cheeky!" retorted Janetta. This was no place to put on the airs and graces. The men laughed good-naturedly.

"Wot ya brought Johnny boy today, Jan? Somfin sweet I'll be bound!" called out a large burly man in corduroy trousers and tattered leather jacket, who stood knee deep in muddy brown water.

"I always have somthin' sweet, Charlie Davis, but you ain't getting' any!" called back Janetta with a broad grin on her face. "Now where's my Johnny got 'imself to, eh?"

“He’s furver up luv, puddlin’,” replied young Tommy Evans who was sitting on the edge of the bank almost in front of her.

Puddling was applying clay to the bottom and sides of the canal to make it watertight in loose or porous soil, and John had found himself a job as a “puddler”.

Janetta walked on up the bank past more mud-splattered men and more friendly gibes, looking for John. She was just passing the steam hammer when Harry Morgan climbed out of the ditch and stood blocking her way. Harry was a young man in his early thirties with a great, unkempt mop of dark hair, a swarthy complexion, bright eyes and an oversized ego. He was well known locally as a ladies man and all the girls in the village had been the target of his affections at one time or another. He stood on the path, tall and straight-backed with his hands on his hips, grinning from ear to ear.

“Now Jan my luv, you’ll start rumours if ya persist in visiting me every day like this,” he said as she approached him. There was a titter of uncertain laughter amongst the men. They all adored Janetta but feared Harry and his uncertain temper.

“Now I aint got time to banter with you, Harry,” she replied as she attempted to walk past him.

Janetta was quite capable of looking after herself where men were concerned, but Harry Morgan bothered her. He was too full of himself. Too cocksure that every woman would be honoured to have his affection; if it was affection. She also knew that when Harry teased her, he meant it.

Harry stepped to the side to block her way.

“Don’t be in such an ’urry,” he said in a soft velvety voice designed to relax her. “You can give Johnny lad ’is lunch when you’ve paid to pass this way.”

“Oh I see yoos own the path now does ya?” retorted Janetta.

“Just a small toll my dear, nuffin more,” then turning to his fellow workers in the ditch, “wot does ya think, lads? A small kiss for payment. Not much to ask is it?”

There was even less enthusiastic laughter from the workers as they sensed coming unpleasantness.

“You’ll get nuthin from me, Harry Morgan,” retorted Janetta in a stern voice. “Now outa me way!”

She attempted to walk right through him in the expectation that he would back off, but he grabbed her by the arms and stood his ground.

"Now Jan luv, you've always fancied me, ya knows yoo 'ave. Just one kiss. Ain't much to ask?"

She tried to pull free of him but he pulled her too him and gave her a muddy faced kiss full on the lips.

"Oi! That's enough 'arry!" yelled one of the workers and suddenly there were half a dozen men surrounding them trying to pull Janetta free.

John had been sitting by his wheelbarrow of clay about fifty yards further down the trench when he heard the commotion. He decided to go and investigate when one of the men ran up the bank calling to him.

"Johnny come on, Harry's got Jan. Come on!"

They ran along the bank to where the scuffle was taking place. At first John couldn't see his wife, but when he got closer he saw that Harry held Janetta in front of him by having one arm around her waist, while he threw punches at anybody who tried to get Janetta away from him.

John saw red. He suspected that his wife was really enjoying the attention but for the sake of appearances he had to defend her. Besides he hated show-offs like Harry Morgan and his years in the army had taught him to stand up for himself. He threw himself at Harry, punching him from behind and forcing him to drop Janetta and defend himself. Harry, under the pressure of so many punches cast Janetta aside and she tumbled over the edge of the bank and fell eight feet into the stinking mud on the canal bottom. She landed face down in the ooze and as she turned herself over in order to breathe she succeeded in rolling herself in the mud and becoming almost unrecognizable.

The crowd that had gathered on the bank split into two. Some jumped down into the trench to rescue Janetta while the others stayed on the bank and tried to separate John and Harry who were throwing punch after punch at one another, but mostly hitting air, as they ducked and weaved to avoid the blows.

John finally managed to connect one of his punches full on Harry's nose, which sent him sprawling on the path. John, breathless, could hardly carry on the fight so bent forward and supported his weight by bracing his hands against his knees. Harry remained on the ground holding his nose.

"You fucking bastard Morgan!" wheezed John, "I'll teach you to mess with my wife!"

He started to walk forward as if to continue the fight when he stopped, his eyes widened his body underwent a terrible spasm and he gripped his arms across his chest and fell to the ground.

For a second nobody moved but then one of the workmen dropped to his knees beside John and turned him over. John's face was pale and his eyes stared lifelessly at the sky. He was dead.

In the canal trench, Janetta fought in the slime to struggle to her feet aided by a couple of men. She wiped the mud from her eyes and mouth and stood there for a second or two bewildered and not quite sure what had happened.

"Come on lassie we'll get you up top again," said an elderly gray haired man with a kind face. He helped her slipping and sliding to firmer ground and finally to a ramp leading up to the path.

Janetta gasped and tried to laugh at the state she was in.

"Oh God!" she said, "where the 'ell's John's lunch?"

"Somewhere in the mud I don't doubt," said her elderly supporter, "but don't reckon 'e'll want it after it's been in the mud, do you?"

Janetta laughed weakly as she struggled up the ramp, her dress feeling twice as heavy under the weight of the mud. Her hair was thickly matted with the stinking muck.

When she reached the top she was met by a large group of downcast looking faces that stood aside as she walked past them.

"Sorry Jan!" said one of the young lads who met her without his usual smile. She thought he was referring to her tumble in the mud and laughed it off.

"It's nothing really, I'm fine!" she replied and walked on through the men until she came to where John lay across the path.

"John wot are ya doing? Git up fer God's sake and 'elp me 'ome!" she said hardly looking at him.

Her elderly rescuer came to her side and took her arm.

"He's gone my dear," he said in a low voice. "I'm very sorry."

Janetta didn't immediately understand until she looked at John again and saw his eyes staring, unseeing, towards the sky.

"Wot?" she whispered.

"He 'ad an 'eart attack. Died real sudden like." He turned to one of the men, "Jimmy close 'is eyes will ya!"

Jim knelt down beside John and closed his eyes with his fingers, trying his best not to get mud on his already dirty face.

Janetta felt her legs giving out under her and the elderly man caught and supported her.

"John," she said, "John, get up I've brought your lunch," she dropped to her knees beside him and tried to raise him by his shirt.

"John, John," she yelled louder and louder as if to wake him.

"'E's gone luv, let him be now. I'll take you 'ome and the lads will bring 'im along."

The gray haired labourer helped her to her feet and guided her away from her husband.

Janetta didn't resist leaving him. With her mind in a turmoil, and mud dripping down her neck, she walked slowly back down the path. Harry Morgan had stood up and was once more in her path. She stopped in front of him and looked him straight in the eye. He began to lose his nerve as he looked at Jan's face and a tear rolled down his cheek.

"Sorry, Jan," he whispered before stepping aside, with his head lowered and his hands fidgeting with his cap in front of his body.

John was lifted up by four workers and carried behind Janetta and her elderly supporter to his parents' house.

John's mother was outside her front door chatting with a neighbour when the procession of labourers came down the road. At first she only saw Janetta who was covered from head to toe in thick clotted mud.

"Lord 'ave mercy what 'appened to you my girl?" she exclaimed, and then not waiting for an answer, looking past Janetta at the rest of the men. When she caught sight of John's body hanging limp in their arms she went as pale as a ghost.

Mrs Martin let out such a howl that she made Janetta start. She then rushed past her and threw her arms about John's neck and body and burst into uncontrollable fits of tears. The procession carried John, hindered by his mother's grief and hugging, into the house and laid him out on the kitchen table.

Janetta was inadvertently left outside and found herself standing almost alone in the road. She felt numb, tired, deserted and suddenly very dirty. She turned away from the small group of people that had gathered outside the house and walked towards the pump that stood in the street just a few yards down the road.

She cranked the handle a couple of times and when the water flowed, she thrust her head under it. It was freezing cold but she didn't care. All she knew was that she had to get the mud out of her hair and off her face. As she scrubbed at her hair and watched the muddy water running down unto the cobbles, she felt a great weight lifting from her. She felt as though the water was washing away everything that oppressed her. As she was freed from the mud so she was freed of her husband, of this foreign village and of her cold parents-in-law.

She straightened up. Water ran down the front of her dress. She wiped water from her eyes and saw the little crowd of onlookers, watching her in amazement.

She didn't give a damn any more, but she thought that for the sake of John's parents, she'd better play the part of the grieving widow. So she summoned up an appropriate expression of grief and made her way into the house to take her place as principal mourner.

PART THREE

CHAPTER 14

Swansea
1883

Janetta stared at herself in the mirror for several minutes. Her face was clean, bright and free of blemishes and she considered herself lucky that at the age of twenty-seven she was still extremely attractive, despite not wearing any rouge. Her long black hair was pulled straight back, tight against her scalp and twisted into a bun at the back. She wore a plain, yet smart, brown cotton dress and a white starched apron. A small lace ruff protruded from the top of her neckline and around each sleeve at the wrist. She looked quite presentable despite her modest dress and hairstyle.

Then a slight frown crept across her forehead and she leaned in closer to the glass to study her hairline. Sure enough, she hadn't been mistaken, there were a few gray hairs appearing at her temples. She tutted and tried to pull a couple out. She was not pleased to have gray hairs, although it was not unusual at her age. She had always been proud of her dark hair and didn't appreciate any sign that the years may be passing her by.

She was startled by a sound behind her and she glanced over her shoulder in the mirror and saw the reflection of a young man.

His head was tilted to one side and his shoulder hunched upward as if trying to meet his cheek. He had dark greasy hair that hadn't seen a comb in days and it stuck out in all directions. His eyes had wildness in them and his pockmarked face sprouted a considerable collection of black heads. His nose ran and his head jerked about in uncontrolled spasms.

"You're bootiful," he slurred in a half whisper.

"Oh it's you, John! You startled me!" said Janetta.

The young man took a step closer to Janetta and she felt his hand suddenly cup her buttock.

"You're bootiful," he slurred again.

Janetta spun around and knocked his hand away. She found herself looking up into John's grinning face. His teeth were dark yellow and crooked and his breath stale. John Lewis was thirty-one years old, but she found herself staring into the eyes of a child.

"I've told you before not to do that," she snapped. Then jabbing her finger towards his face, "I'll tell Mrs. Brant if you don't stop it."

The grin left his face as he fixated on her accusing finger and Janetta thought he was on the point of crying so she softened her tone.

"Now John, I've got work to do and I'm sure you've got something better to do, haven't you?"

John's eyes lit up with excitement at something he'd remembered.

"Walk Mitsy in the park," he said. Mitsy was the family terrier and John's job was to walk her daily.

"It's pissing with rain, John, you'll 'ave t' wait 'til it stops! Now come on wipe yer nose!"

John raised his arm.

"Not on yer sleeve, use yer 'anky."

He pulled a dirty gray handkerchief from his pocket and blew into it within inches of her face. She winced and tried to turn her head away as he made loud blowing sounds.

"That's bett'r!" she said, trying to be as encouraging as she could.

"Mitsy likes her walkies," said John excitedly and left the room, closing the door behind him.

Janetta turned back to the mirror and gave her hair one last prod into position. She sensed the door quietly open again and turning towards it, saw John's face peer around the door.

"You're bootiful!" he slurred once more and then his face disappeared and the door clicked shut again.

Janetta smiled at the closed door. "Poor sod!" she said under her breath.

A strong gust of wind rattled the casement window and the rain slashed harder against the panes. She turned and looked across the room towards the window. It was quite a well-appointed room; tastefully furnished with a deep pink chaise-lounge in front of the fireplace. The fireplace consisted of a large, dark, ornate wooden surround in which was mounted the mirror Janetta had been scrutinizing herself in. A black marbled clock stood on the mantal and ticked loudly. Maroon flocked wallpaper with a large floral pattern adorned the walls and the windows were framed with red velvet curtains. In front of the window stood a low dark oak table with a white linen cover that supported a large brass pot, out of which grew an aspidistra that almost blotted out the light from the window. A three-foot high china dog sat sentry by the door.

Today the room was quite dark as the leaden sky refused to allow any sunshine in.

Janetta crossed the room and holding aside a couple of aspidistra leaves, looked out at the sodden street. The rain beat against the windowpanes and ran in rivers down the glass. She groaned as she peered out at a heavy sky, sombre houses and gray glistening street. It was an entirely damp world. She shivered and a tear ran down her cheek.

What had happened to her? What had become of her dream to be a lady? What was she doing in this town and in this job? Was she crying for her husband or for herself? She didn't know any of the answers. She wasn't sure she really wanted to know. She wasn't sure she wanted to face the fact that she was crying for herself rather than the loss of her husband. She only knew she felt lonely and deserted in a strange house, in a strange town; after five long years she was right back where she had started – a domestic servant in somebody else's house.

To complicate matters she now had a new experience to come to terms with. She had found herself a new lover, but in a love that both repelled and fascinated her. A love she knew must be ended; yet couldn't quite let go of. Perhaps it was this love that held her together, in what seemed to be her lowest hour. Somehow, when she was in her lover's arms she no longer cared about anything. She had a warm body to snuggle into, a comfortable bed in a beautifully furnished bedroom, and no worries about what the future would hold. The world could go hang itself; what did she care?

But she did care. She knew it mustn't last and she desperately wanted to get out of Swansea and return to the regiment. For all its drawbacks and hardships, the regiment had become home to Janetta and she enjoyed being amongst the soldiers; the centre of attraction everywhere she went. She had become a military wife with all that it meant. The hardships, the barrack life, and the low pay were all compensated by the sense of family and regimental loyalty. How she missed the camaraderie of the soldiers' wives, the hard drinking nights and the companionship of so many men. Oh, the men; the handsome, glorious soldiers who used to hang around her and make her feel so beautiful. Where were they all now?

A couple of organ chords interrupted her rapid decline into self-pity, and as she watched the rain bounce on the cobbles of St. Helen's Road, the house filled with the sounds of Bach.

Janetta wasn't musically inclined. Most of the music she had ever heard was from street barrel organs or fiddlers in pubs and fairgrounds. She was partial to having a singalong in the pub after a few gins, but nothing moved her as much as the sound of Mr Brant playing Bach on the organ in the back room.

She hadn't known it was Bach of course. One day, filled with curiosity, she had abandoned her chores and gone into the back room to stand and listened and watch as William Brant practised at the keyboard. He didn't mind the interruption and had asked her, in his refined London accent, if she liked the music of Johann Sebastian Bach, and wasn't it the finest music in the world? She'd never heard of Johann Sebastian Bach, but didn't admit to the fact. She simply agreed it was indeed the finest music in the world and, after a couple of minutes, went back to her work.

Mr. Brant was her employer, or rather his wife Charlotte was. William Brant was only forty-two but was prematurely bald except for a great fleece of untrimmed and graying hair around the sides and back of his head. With his wire-rimmed glasses and red face he was not considered a handsome man, but he had a certain presence that made him appear very distinguished. He was an organist by profession and frequently gave recitals all over South Wales. Being used to performing in public had given him an air of confidence but he was far from being vain about his talent. In fact he was the most amiable of men.

There were three other people in the house, apart from Charlotte Brant. One was a young man named William Pearce who worked as a general servant and lived in perpetual hope that Janetta might actually like him; then there was the simpleton John Lewis whom the Brants cared for and the third was Ellen Barry, Charlotte's sister.

Janetta never understood why Ellen lived with the Brants. She had obviously been married once to a Mr Barry and had been left with an income, which allowed her to live with the Brants as a paying guest. In her position as a servant, Janetta had never inquired into Ellen's past; it was not her place to do so. Yet she had always liked Ellen, and for some reason, Ellen had taken to her, despite the seventeen years difference between them and their difference in social standing. Charlotte Brant thought Ellen was far too familiar with the domestic staff, and with Janetta in particular; but with the exception of a few disapproving looks, she said nothing.

Janetta looked down at the glistening street and saw John Lewis leave the house with the dog. He pulled his jacket collar up against the rain, which was now easing off, and skipped like a child towards Victoria Park. John was another mystery to Janetta. The Brants had given him a home, but as far as she could tell he was not a relative.

The door to the front room opened and startled Janetta. She quickly started rearranging the leaves of the aspidistra in case it was Mrs Brant, but it was Ellen and Janetta relaxed, turning her head away to the window again.

Ellen approached Janetta without saying a word. She stood just behind her and placed her hand gently on Janetta's shoulder. It was a gesture of familiarity that would have been shocking to an outsider.

"What a miserable day!" she said in a half whisper.

Janetta could smell Ellen's perfume and longed to be able to wear it. She could never afford it of course; not the good perfume anyway. She occasionally purchased lavender water; John used to like that, but now she felt like the poor relation standing next to Ellen. She looked down at her drab brown dress and white apron and then turned to see Ellen's beautiful sea blue gown with its delicate lace and a string of pearls around her neck. They were not expensive pearls, Janetta was sure of that, but Ellen wore them well. She wondered if she would ever be as grand as Ellen.

Ellen looked at Janetta's face with its silvery trails running down her cheeks left behind by her tears, and thought how beautiful she was. She raised her hand and with the lightest touch of her fingers, brushed aside a tear.

"It's been raining inside as well as out I see," she said. "Can I help?"

Janetta shook her head, and as she did so, found her cheeks being clasped between Ellen's hands and her face being drawn towards Ellen's lips. She didn't resist. She welcomed Ellen's warmth and gentleness. She was drawn forward slowly and deliberately until their lips touched ever so lightly; Janetta wanted to cry out in protest, but found herself pressing forward into Ellen's soft, sweet smelling cheeks. There was no beard or stubble to rasp against her face, just the velvety smooth touch of warm skin, and Janetta clung to her as if she was a child again, nestling in her mother's arms.

The clouds parted and for a moment the sun shone through the window and felt warm against the side of their cheeks as they kissed. They both recognized a magical moment and turned their heads simultaneously towards the window and smiled. How wonderful the world seemed when the sun shone and you felt safe in someone's arms.

Janetta turned back to Ellen, looked into her bright blue eyes and found herself whispering, "I love you."

"Do you?" replied Ellen with some surprise. "Do you really?"

Janetta didn't respond immediately as she was slowly realizing what she had just said. She felt such a fool. She didn't love Ellen at all. She had said it as a response to the beauty of the moment. She enjoyed their moments together so much, but she didn't love her. At least she didn't think she did.

"You shouldn't you know! I'm sure I'll end up hurting you! Besides you're not really in love with me. We both like men don't we, and one day I'm sure we'll both fall head over heels in love with some handsome gentleman."

"I expect you're right," whispered Janetta.

"In the meantime we've been good for one another, haven't we?"

Janetta nodded, somewhat relieved that Ellen hadn't taken her declaration of love too seriously.

Ellen, still with her arms about her, stared past Janetta's shoulder and out of the window. A smile slowly spread across her face.

"Well now, the sun comes out and brings handsome surprises with it."

Janetta, puzzled by Ellen's flippancy, turned to look out of the window again and couldn't believe her eyes.

****

Lieutenant Bird had spent all morning trying to find the Brants' house. It hadn't been easy. He had arrived in Swansea on the morning train, not having the faintest idea where he might find the Brants' residence. He had eventually gone to the postmaster's office and inquired there after the Brant family and had been given no less than eight different addresses. He had no option but to purchase a street map and walk from house to house until he found the right one. This he would have happily done, because he enjoyed walking, but since it was pouring with rain, he had hired a hansom cab to drive him around the town.

When he arrived at the sixth address, he asked the cab to wait as he had done each time before, and approached the front steps of the house. The rain had eased off somewhat but he still felt the chill of the day and pulled his cloak tighter as he took the steps two at a time and pulled the handle of the doorbell.

He heard the bell ring deep in the house and a wave of apprehension passed through his stomach. All the other houses he had visited looked an unlikely address, but this one was a real possibility. What on earth was he doing here? He had come to Swansea on Regimental business, but all he could think about was the lady he'd met at a ball some two months before.

What a beauty she was. He had danced with her, laughed and whispered sweet nothings with her, and eventually slept with her, in one night of bliss. One exquisite night, in which he had forgotten his betrothal to Lady Dawlish, whom he barely knew. One night he couldn't forget, and here he was looking for her in a strange town on a wet and dismal day, when he should have been on business. What on earth would he say to her?

****

Ellen struggled to contain her excitement when she saw Lieutenant Bird below in the street. She gently pulled away from Janetta.

"We have a guest by the look of it," she said softly and as nonchalantly as possible, so as not to give away the fact that she recognized the caller. "Visit me tonight?"

Janetta absently nodded but continued staring incredulously at the soldier on the doorstep.

Ellen left Janetta and walked back to the door, but before leaving she paused and turned back to Janetta, who still stood behind the aspidistra looking down into the street.

"Don't forget. I'll be waiting."

"Yeh!" replied Janetta without taking her eyes off the visitor on the doorstep.

Ellen crossed the hall at the same time as Pearce was coming up from below stairs.

"If it's for me, I'll be in the drawing room," said Ellen as casually as she could contrive.

"Very good, ma'am," replied Pearce as he reached the front door.

Lieutenant Bird was just about to pull the bell chain a second time when the door was opened.

"Goodday to you, sir," said Pearce in a well-practised haughty voice.

For a second, Lieutenant Bird found himself speechless, until Pearce raised one eyebrow, which suggested certain suspicion on his part.

"Does a Mrs Barry live here?" said the Lieutenant in a tone strong enough to intimidate the strongest willed domestic.

"Yes sir," replied Pearce, "Who should I say is calling?"

Bird stepped into the hall and shook off his cape, allowing Pearce to take it. "Lieutenant Bird." he replied.

"Yes, sir, if you'll wait here, sir."

Pearce entered the parlour and announced Lieutenant Bird who was already walking in behind him. Pearce gave him a disapproving look as he walked past him into the room.

"Mrs Barry," he said rather formally; then when he heard Pearce close the door behind him, he mellowed his tone to one of intimate familiarity. "Ellen, it's wonderful to see you again."

Ellen beamed at him and gestured towards a chair.

****

Janetta, still in shock from seeing the Lieutenant, tried to concentrate on her housework. She aimlessly flicked a feather duster over the furniture and wondered how she could get to speak with him. He was a ghost from her past and a very welcome one at that; but she didn't have to ponder the problem for too long as the door opened and Charlotte Brant entered.

"Ah! There you are Martin," she said as if she'd been hunting for her all over the house.

"Ma'am," responded Janetta.

"Mrs Barry has a guest in the parlour. Take them some tea would you."

"Ma'am," Janetta gave a slight bow of the head and left the room.

She almost ran down to the kitchen and scurried about putting cups, saucers and plates on a tray while she anxiously waited for the kettle to boil.

She sliced some of Charlotte's favourite fruitcake and poured the steaming water into the teapot. A few minutes later she arrived outside the parlour door.

For a second or two she stood there in the hall with the tray balanced on one arm, almost afraid to enter the room. It had been a long time since she last saw the Lieutenant and she wasn't proud of being seen in her current position. She thought of all the years she'd struggled to be a lady and here she was again, a domestic servant in a middle class house, in a gray town; she suddenly felt quite ashamed of herself.

If she was to get out of this house, however, she had to make contact; so she took a deep breath, tapped on the door, held her head up high and entered the room.

At first Lieutenant Bird didn't recognize her. He was oblivious to her, as he would naturally have been to any domestic servant. When she bent down to pour the tea, however, her face was on a closer level to his, so that he could see her easily without taking the effort to look up at her.

The effect on him was one of utter surprise and confusion. For a second he forgot where he was, and finding himself in the presence of Mrs Martin he immediately stood up, as would be expected of a gentleman in the presence of a lady, not a maid.

Ellen was startled by his sudden rise and looked at him with some alarm. Janetta paid no attention to him but continued to pour the tea as if nothing had happened. Ellen noted the stunned look on his face as he gaped at Janetta with his mouth open.

Janetta, having finished laying out the tea things, took a couple of steps back from the side table.

"Thank you, Martin," said Ellen in a formal yet quite proper manner.

Janetta gave a perfunctory curtsy; she glanced momentarily right into the Lieutenant's eyes and left the room.

Ellen watched her leave and then turned her gaze back to Lieutenant Bird, who was still standing and staring at the closed door.

"Pretty wasn't she!" observed Ellen.

"Hmm," replied Bird whilst still in a dream.

"You know a lady could take this personally!" said Ellen with a small grin, trying to gain the Lieutenant's attention.

The Lieutenant suddenly came back to the present and sat down.

"Oh! I do beg your pardon Ellen. I do indeed!" he stammered.

"Well our maid certainly seems to have made an impression on you, Lieutenant," teased Ellen.

"It was such a shock seeing her again, that's all," said the Lieutenant, still looking past Ellen at the closed door as if expecting Janetta to re-enter at any moment.

"Seeing her again?" Ellen stressed the 'again'.

"I used to know her, you see."

"In the biblical sense I presume," Ellen chided.

Lieutenant Bird appeared shocked at the suggestion.

"Mrs . ..er Ellen," he corrected himself, "I do assure you…"

"Took advantage of your host's maid, while staying for the weekend, I shouldn't wonder!" she interrupted.

Lieutenant Bird looked at her as if he couldn't quite believe what she had said. He decided she was baiting him and chose to ignore her dig.

"It's been a couple of years now. She wasn't a maid when I knew her."

"What was she? Pray do tell, Lieutenant you have me quite fascinated."

Ellen's tone suggested that she resented this sudden interest in the maid, when he had come to visit her, but couldn't resist hearing the details.

Bird took a sip of his tea, sat back in the chair and let his mind wander back to the days in Dover. Several seconds passed in silence.

"Lieutenant, I do believe you're no longer with me. Would you like to share your thoughts?"

Bird was beginning to find Ellen's manner rather irritating. He had considered her to be one of the handsomest women he'd ever met, and had eagerly looked forward to finding her; however now that he had seen Janetta again he found he had almost completely lost interest in Ellen and craved meeting with Janetta again.

Ellen was clearly put out at being upstaged by a domestic, and was trying her best to be civil, while at the same time finding out as much about Janetta's past as she could.

"She was married to one of my men. Bombardier John Martin. A fine soldier."

"And what was the wife of 'one of your men' to you, Lieutenant? I sense a little indiscretion on your part, I think!"

She was fishing and they both knew it, but she had to draw him out somehow.

"She was the most popular woman in the regiment…Ellen. Everybody liked her. She was…" he paused, unable to finish the statement without giving away his feelings for her.

"Yes, Lieutenant, she was…"

"She was…very much appreciated by the whole regiment for her wit, her dash, her hospitality!"

"My goodness! Are you sure you're talking about our maid?"

"I am, I assure you," he replied as he replaced his empty teacup on the table. "How long has she been here?"

"A couple of years now," replied Ellen coldly.

"And you knew nothing about where she came from?"

"I take little interest in the domestics, Lieutenant," she lied, "they're nothing to me."

Bird felt the visit was becoming tense. What should have been a happy reunion between them had turned into a session of revelations concerning her domestic servant. It wasn't flattering to Ellen to spend so much time discussing Janetta, but he did feel she was just a little too annoyed and wondered what the cause was.

"Well!" he said preparing to stand up, "I suppose I should be getting along."

"You've only just arrived, Lieutenant. I'll see more of you I hope?" she said, turning on the charm in an attempt to repair any breach that had opened between them over Janetta. She stood up in front of him and casually brushed some imaginary dirt off his blue tunic; a familiar gesture designed to turn his attention back to her.

"I fear I must return to my regiment tomorrow. There's a train at eight fifteen I understand." He was trying his best to be friendly and attentive while at the same time firm about his leaving. "I just thought it would be nice to look you up since I was in town."

"Yes, well, now you know where I am you must 'look me up' again, Lieutenant." She was also trying to be civil, but her voice took on a formal tone that implied she knew she wouldn't see him again, now that he had found Janetta.

****

Janetta had retreated to the drawing room again where she could keep up the pretence of continuing her housework, while at the same time keeping an ear on the hall. Presently she heard the parlour door open and Pearce came into the hall to help the Lieutenant with his cloak. Charlotte had followed the Lieutenant out into the hall and was passing farewell pleasantries with him as he put on his cloak.

Janetta came out of the drawing room and without looking at Bird, passed across the hall towards the drawing room.

"I'll clear away the tea things, ma'am," she said as she passed Ellen.

Ellen gave her a severe look that said she fully understood Janetta's timing, but quickly turned back to the Lieutenant, who, having seen Janetta, took the opportunity to pass her a message.

"I've decided to stay at the Crown tonight," he said to Ellen as he adjusted his cap, "I understand it's a reasonably comfortable hotel."

"*Very clever*," thought Ellen, "*Janetta couldn't avoid hearing that*."

"Well perhaps you'll find some good company there," she said. "Goodbye, Lieutenant Bird."

"Goodbye, Mrs Barry. It was a pleasure seeing you again." And he turned and walked out into the rain.

Pearce retreated down to the kitchen and Ellen went back into the parlour where Janetta was stacking the cups and plates onto the tray. She didn't say anything to Janetta at first, but stood close behind her in silence for several seconds. Janetta lifted the tray as if to leave.

"So you knew Lieutenant Bird!"

Janetta said nothing.

"He remembers you. Remembers you quite well!"

"It was a long time ago," replied Janetta. "Didn't think he'd recognize me."

Ellen laughed.

"Oh! I'm quite sure you did."

There was another long, uncomfortable pause.

"Excuse me, ma'am, I must clear away these things."

"Was he your lover?"

Janetta paused before turning to face Ellen, "No, he never was."

"But you wished he had've been."

"I was married and Lieutenant Bird was a friend and a gentleman, ma'am. Nothing more," replied Janetta rather formally.

This answer seemed to satisfy Ellen. Janetta turned away towards the door but Ellen caught her arm to hold her back. She lowered her voice to a half whisper.

"I'll be waiting for you tonight, Jan." There was a slightly threatening edge to her voice, "Don't be too late, will you?"

"No," Janetta replied in a whisper, and left the room with the tea tray.

****

Janetta walked unhurried down the hall with the tray and into the kitchen. Pearce sat at the kitchen table drinking a mug of tea. She placed the tray on the table and grabbing her coat from the hook behind the door she said, "Be a luv and cover for me, I have to go out in a 'urry like."

"Wot ya mean, go out. Ya can't just go out! Wot if Mrs B. wants ya?" replied Pearce.

"You'll think a somefing," replied Janetta as she bent forward and gave him a gentle kiss on the cheek. "I won't be long. Promise!"

Pearce, upon receiving the kiss and smelling her hair as she came close to his face, found his objections melting away.

"Yeh alright, Jan, but don't be long for Christ's sake!"

"You're a luv!" said Janetta, and picking up Pearce's umbrella that stood in the umbrella stand behind the door, she left the kitchen and ventured out into the rain.

She wasn't sure which way Lieutenant Bird had gone, but she knew where the Crown was and decided to make her way there in the hope that was his destination. It was raining quite hard and coupled with her anxiousness to talk with Lieutenant Bird, she found herself walking very fast. Before long she broke into a run and ignoring all her better judgment of feminine behaviour she hitched up the front of her dress and sprinted as if her life depended upon it.

Because of the rain there were not too many people about, yet several times she found herself running out into the muddy road to get around pedestrians blocking her way. She could almost feel their looks of disbelief as she ran past them dodging horses, dogs and soggy dung in the road. Her bonnet had come off and was hanging on her back by a thin cord that cut into the front of her neck, and her umbrella, still unopened, was securely grasped in her right hand as if she was a night watchman holding his cudgel.

She turned into Francis Street and then decided to cut through Victoria Park, thereby considerably reducing the distance to the Crown. For some reason Francis Street seemed unusually busy with wagons, carriages and cattle being herded along to market.

She ran off the curb and skipped nimbly between the vehicles and the piles of damp steaming manure that decorated the road every few feet, until she arrived unscathed at the other side of the street close by the park gate.

Here she stopped and sat on a low brick wall for a couple of minutes to gather her breath before pressing on. She was surprised at how wonderful she felt after her dash through the streets. She felt totally free and alive and for the first time in ages she didn't give a damn about appearing to be a lady. Her heart pounded in her chest, she perspired in the chill rain, her hair hung wet and lank; she loved every minute of it. Seeing the Lieutenant again had given her drab life renewed hope and she wasn't going to let the opportunity pass her by.

The rain began to fall harder so she opened the umbrella and started off again but at a slower pace than before. After her brief rest she became aware of her fatigue but she was still determined to make good speed through the park.

A couple of hundred yards into the park the heavens opened and the rain came down with such ferocity that she was afraid the umbrella was going to collapse under the impact of the water. The rain bounced off the path, spraying her feet and dress with mud and great gusts of wind threatened to turn her umbrella inside out.

A few yards ahead was a small but welcome gazebo and Janetta ran as fast as she could to take cover under its roof. She ran up the wooden steps and collapsed onto one of the benches inside. Closing the umbrella, she laid her head back against the wooden wall and allowed herself the pleasure of letting out a loud gasp of relief. Closing her eyes, she concentrated on the sound of the rain drumming on the roof and the rivulets of water that ran down her cheeks and neck cooling her overheated body.

What a glorious day this had turned out to be and for a few brief moments she didn't care if she ever saw the Brants' house again. She thought only of the Regiment and Lieutenant Bird.

"Mrs Martin, what an unexpected pleasure!" said a voice in the rain.

Janetta, startled out of her reverie, sat up and stared towards the direction of the voice. There, in the shadows of the gazebo, sat Lieutenant Bird with a broad grin across his face.

"Oh my dear, Mrs Martin, I do hope I didn't startle you!" he said.

"Ah…yes, I didn't expect to see you there," said Janetta, still not believing her eyes, or her luck.

"I thought you took a cab," said Janetta in astonishment at seeing him.

"I did, but decided to walk through the park. I was very surprised to see you earlier. I hoped you had got my message about how to find me!"

"Yes…as you see I am here, Lieutenant."

She almost immediately regretted such a confession of unlady-like haste, but having said as much decided to press on. "I was so pleased to see you and I hoped I could catch you and speak with you before you left."

The Lieutenant smiled and walked over to share her bench.

"I never thought I'd see you again…and to find you here, Swansea of all places. How did you come to be here?"

"John's family lived near here," she panted, still fatigued by her long run. "After his illness he wanted to return home to be near his parents."

The Lieutenant nodded sympathetically.

A man in a bedraggled suit and no topcoat ran past the gazebo with a half drowned dog on the end of a leash, struggling to keep up behind him. The man kept his head down to shelter his face from the rain and his free hand clasped his two jacket collars together under his chin. He was either unaware or disinterested in the shelter of the gazebo, for he ran on into the downpour and quickly disappeared in the curtain of rain.

"And how is he?" inquired Lieutenant Bird after John.

"He died a couple of years back, and I am as you find me, working for the Brants."

"I'm sorry about John. I liked him very much. He was a good man."

The Lieutenant felt uncomfortable about giving such platitudes but he was sincere nonetheless.

"And you, Jan, are you happy?"

"Oh… the Brants treat me well enough, but…" she wasn't sure how to continue. Should she simply throw herself at his feet and beg to be taken away, or should she hold on to some semblance of dignity?

"How can you be happy here Jan?" said the Lieutenant in a low and sympathizing tone. "This is not your home!"

"Oh shit…," said Janetta willingly allowing her guard to drop. "I'm not! I miss the Regiment, Tim."

A silence fell between them for a couple of minutes as each wondered what the other would say. Finally the Lieutenant broke the silence.

"Jan, you know I've always loved you but I am betrothed now to Lady Dawlish."

"Congratulations," replied Janetta with no real enthusiasm.

"But I love you," he repeated.

"But you're spoken for with lady what's-her-name."

"Quite!"

Here was the truth of it. He adored Janetta, but was engaged to someone he hardly knew. Janetta would never make him a good wife because she was penniless. His family would never stand for it. A long silence fell between them. They both sat and stared into the grayness, neither one knowing how best to proceed.

For a few dreadful moments, Janetta wasn't sure whether the Lieutenant wanted her company again. He was obviously happy to see her but that didn't necessarily translate into a renewed friendship. It was better, she thought, to end the suspense now. She had no good hand to play and her wits were her only trump. It was a gamble that had to be taken; she hung her head down, stared into her lap and fiddled with the small blue tassel on the umbrella. She then gave a sniff, groped in her pocket for her handkerchief which she applied to her nose, and after a couple of discreet shudders of the shoulders and in a cracking and pitiful voice whispered, "take me with you."

Lieutenant Bird, seeing Janetta in such a state of agitation, put his arm around her in a consoling manner and begged her not to distress herself. All would be well, he assured her, to which she sobbed more and said how she dreamed to be back home with the Regiment and how she was dying in this drab and lonely town.

"There, there, do not distress yourself so," pleaded the Lieutenant.

Janetta looked up at his face with tears running down her cheeks and sobbed that he was, 'the only true friend she'd ever had'.

"Nonsense, nonsense!" consoled the Lieutenant.

She continued in this vein saying how she would willingly place herself under his protection but never be an encumbrance upon him, as she knew how important it was for a gentleman to honour his engagement.

Lieutenant Bird found himself weakening. Not that he was going to put up any fight against taking her with him, but he needed a couple of minutes to digest the problem.

"Jan, you can come with me to London, if that's what you really want!"

Janetta suppressed her sniffling enough to whimper, "I can? You'll really take me with you?"

"I will, of course I will! I can't promise you anything mind, except that I will do everything in my power to make you comfortable while I'm free to do so. In the meantime you'll be back with the Regiment. What do you say to that?"

Janetta threw her arms round his neck and kissed him several times on the face. He didn't resist, but held on to her petite frame and longed to be able to hold this moment forever.

After a couple of minutes she suddenly pushed herself away from him wide eyed. "My God I've got so much to do."

The Lieutenant laughed at her sudden panic.

"It's alright, Jan dear the train doesn't leave 'til eight thirty in the morning; if you're not there on time I'll wait for you and we'll go on the nine thirty."

"You'll wait for me?" she said as pathetically as she could.

"Of course I will!" he laughed. "How could I go without you?"

She smiled at him, cupped his face in her hands and gently kissed him again, this time on the lips as if she meant it.

They had hardly noticed that the rain had stopped and the late afternoon sun was trying to peer through the clouds. Janetta reluctantly pulled herself away from her soldier and after a couple of sweet goodbyes, she walked slowly back down the gazebo steps.

Without looking back she retraced her path through the park. As she walked water dripped from the trees, birds came out of hiding to sing again and the earth smelled potent. Janetta felt alive and in control again. After months of boredom and servitude she was going to become her own woman again. This time she would make it. With a wealthy Lieutenant on her arm she could 'take the world' and take it, she bloody well would!

That evening was a busy time for Janetta. She cooked and served dinner as usual and after cleaning the dishes and tidying up the kitchen, she went upstairs to speak to Mrs Brant. She found her sitting with her husband in the parlour.

"Yes, what is it, Martin?" enquired Charlotte as Janetta entered the room.

"Sorry to bother you ma'am, but something has come up."

Charlotte shifted slightly in her chair to face Janetta more directly and Mr Brant looked up from behind his evening paper and stared at her over the top of his classes.

"I met an old, and very dear friend of mine this afternoon."

"Really, I didn't know it was your afternoon off!" said Charlotte raising her eyebrows.

"No, ma'am he came here to visit Mrs Barry and we met purely by chance, ma'am."

"I see!"

"Well, he knows how I miss the Regiment, ma'am, and he's returning to Woolwich in the morning and has offered to take me with him."

"Has he indeed!" Charlotte didn't sound impressed by this arrangement.

"He's a very respectable officer ma'am and he's engaged to be married. I'll be quite safe with him I assure you."

"Hmm!" Charlotte pursed her lips suspiciously.

"Anyway, ma'am, I'd like to go with him, so I'm tendering my resignation. Sorry it's such short notice but I don't really have any choice as he's leaving so soon."

Charlotte looked at her husband in the hope that he may have something helpful to say. Mr Brant, uncomfortable about getting involved in staff problems, shrugged his shoulders.

"It seems to me, my dear, that the girl has made up her mind, and the best thing we can do is pay her what we owe and wish her every happiness."

Charlotte wasn't impressed by his contribution but decided not to put up a fight.

****

It was gone midnight when she stepped out of her room in her nightgown and tiptoed down one flight to Ellen's room.

She didn't bother to knock but quietly opened the door and slipped into the room. One oil lamp was left burning on a very low wick that cast a faint golden glow around the room. Ellen was in bed as if asleep. Janetta went to the side of the bed, lifted the sheets and climbed in beside her. Ellen lay on her side facing away from Janetta, so she cuddled up in the spoon position and put her arm over Ellen to caress her breasts. Ellen groaned with appreciation and turned her head in an attempt to face Janetta.

"I'd almost given up on you," she whispered.

"Had things to do. It's been a busy night," replied Janetta, nestling her head in the crop of Ellen's neck. "I'm here to say goodbye."

Ellen suddenly twitched and spun herself around to face Janetta.

"Goodbye! What the hell do you mean, goodbye?"

"SHHHH!" hushed Janetta, putting her fingers against Ellen's lips. "Do you want to raise the whole house?"

Ellen thrust her hand aside and moderating the volume of her voice continued, "What do you mean goodbye?"

"I'm going to London."

"London? When?"

"Tomorrow morning. I'm going with Lieutenant Bird."

Ellen's eyes almost doubled in size and her colour turned an unhealthy shade of scarlet.

"Get out!" she screamed, thrashing her arms and legs at Janetta in an attempt to kick her out of the bed. "Get out you ungrateful bitch!"

"What, for Christ's sake what?" cried Janetta as she fended off Ellen's kicks.

"He came for me, he was mine you bitch!" screamed Ellen as she kicked and mauled Janetta, "and you're stealing him from under my own roof!…Whore!…Harlot!"

Janetta scrambled out of the bed to avoid Ellen's attack, only to find that Ellen was coming after her. She backed towards the door, shielding her face from a barrage of slaps and punches as Ellen vented her rage at her. Janetta quickly found herself on the landing with people appearing at other open bedroom doors. Mr Brant and Charlotte stood and gaped at the scene in their night attire; and Pearce had appeared from his room on the floor above and was leaning over the banister to discover the cause of the commotion.

Ellen continued to scream abuse and beat Janetta with a pillow, forcing her to retreat up the stairs to the floor above. All the while Charlotte tried to restrain Ellen by holding her arms and Mr Brant observed the scene from a safe distance, in a state of complete bewilderment; exclaiming "Dear dear, what is the trouble? Oh my dears this will never do!"

Janetta scrambled up the stairs to her room, bolted the door and hurriedly got dressed. Below she could hear Ellen continuing to scream and cry and voices were raised in an attempt to calm her. Janetta was no longer worried about missing the eight thirty train; her only wish was to flee the house and not face the shame of standing before Charlotte and Mr Brant's accusations of her 'unnatural behaviour'.

She frantically stuffed her belongings into her carpetbag, the tears streaming down her face, more from fright than anger, and tried to do up her bootlaces with trembling fingers.

Her bag packed, herself dressed – although somewhat disheveled – and her coat on, she picked up Charlotte's farewell letter and ventured out onto the landing again. There were still voices coming from Ellen's room. Ellen was crying and Charlotte and Mr Brant were trying to soothe her as Janetta tiptoed passed the door and down the stairs to the hall. She left the letter on the hall table, silently let herself out of the front door and slipped out into the night.

CHAPTER 15

Rescue

She ran as fast as she could under the weight of the carpetbag, more to put distance between herself and the house, than because she was in any great hurry. In the storm that had preceded her flight, she had given no thought to where she would go. It was almost one o'clock in the morning and the streets were dark and empty. At least the rain had stopped, although a chill wind blew off the Bristol Channel.

Her first thought was to go to the Crown, so she made her way back towards Victoria Park, but after a while she thought that a bad idea because it would be all shut up at this hour. She turned around and walked back towards the railway station. She resolved to spend the night on a bench outside the ticket office. At least she wouldn't be late for the eight-thirty train.

As she walked through the town, the wind bit into her coat and the carpet bag got progressively heavier. The thought of a warm bed made her walk slower and slower until she eventually stopped and looked back the way she had come. Perhaps she could get into the Crown after all. She was sure somebody would let her in, and she would be warm and safe for the night.

Having changed her mind for the second time, she started to retrace her steps and walk the mile back to the Crown through the damp, lonely and deserted streets.

As the Town Hall clock struck two, Janetta found herself standing outside the Crown Inn. She was out of breath from her long walk and the carpetbag had cut into her fingers. She was uncomfortably hot inside but her neck, face and ears had become frozen by the night air. She looked up at the Crown. All the windows were dark and silent. The building gave no sign that there was life within. A dog barked way off in the town and as she stood before the black door she could hear the hall clock ticking just a few feet inside. She rested her forehead against the door, gave a quiet prayer that someone would come to let her in and then gave a strong pull on the bell chain.

The ringing of bells inside the house seemed so loud that she feared she'd woken the entire street, but as the bells fell silent, nobody stirred inside. She gave a glance up and down the street as if expecting to see an angry mob, aroused from their beds, coming out of their houses to apprehend the disturber of the peace. Then, satisfied that Swansea still slumbered, she pulled on the chain again, and for a second time the bells rang out to disturb the night.

"Who the bloody 'ell's that, waking up honest folks in the middle of the night!"

Janetta, startled, stepped away from the door and looked up at the window above. An elderly man in a white night shirt was leaning out of the window. His night cap dangled down against the outside of the wall.

"Excuse me, sir," replied Janetta rather timidly at first, "I wonder if I might be put up for the night?"

"No, good night to you!" he replied and started to pull his head inside.

"Oh but sir," called out Janetta in a more anxious tone, "I've come to find Lieutenant Bird."

There was a pause and then the elderly gentleman reappeared at the window.

"Who d'ya say?"

"Lieutenant Bird, sir, I believe he's staying here."

"Can't it wait 'til morning?"

"No, sir, please tell him I'm here. He'll want to see me, sir, I assure you."

The elderly gentleman grunted and disappeared back into the room and the window casement closed.

"Damn!" exclaimed Janetta, but as she was about to pull the chain a third time she saw a faint glow of light through the small glass panels above the door and heard footsteps shuffling through the hall. Two bolts slid aside and a chain rattled behind the door before it was opened and Janetta came face to face with the elderly gentleman. He was short and very stout with a red face and bulbous nose. Janetta thought he looked like a garden gnome in his nightcap and shirt.

Behind him stood his stern faced wife, equally as short, and whose hair was tied in white curling rags.

"Who is it, George? What's she want this time of night?" she demanded.

The elderly gentleman turned to look at his wife over his shoulder.

"I am about to ascertain that, my dearest," he replied in a tone that suggested she should not ask stupid questions.

"No respectable woman walks abroad this time of night. We're a respectable 'ouse we are! You tell 'er go on!" she said, prodding her finger in her husband's back.

"We're a respectable 'ouse we are!" said the gentleman in an unenthusiastic tone, since it was obvious that Janetta had heard what his wife had said.

"Quite right! You tell 'er!" chimed in his wife.

"We don't allow 'professional' ladies in this establishment," he said to Janetta in as cross a voice as he could muster; more for his wife's sake than Janetta's.

"Sir, I assure you I am a respectable lady," replied Janetta who by now had edged her way into the hall.

"Respectable!" exclaimed the wife, prodding her husbands' back again, "did ya 'ear that! Respectable, at this time of night! She must think we're soft!"

The gentleman closed his eyes and bit his lip as his wife's voice pierced the still night.

"Madam," he said when he felt the opportunity to get a word in, "do not distress yourself so. Let me deal with this." He turned back to Janetta.

"Why do ya insist on waking us and our guests at such an hour?"

"Sir, I beg of you to allow me to speak with Lieutenant Bird."

"I bet ya does!" exclaimed the wife who had pushed her husband aside and was now standing between him and Janetta. "Wot's so important as can't wait 'til morning then?"

Janetta, feeling she had a better chance at persuading the gentleman than the wife, continued to address her remarks to him.

"I am a respectable lady, sir, whom circumstances have conspired to leave me without shelter for the night. Lieutenant Bird will vouch for me, sir, I promise you."

"Suppose it won't do no 'arm to tell the gentleman she's 'ere," he said to his wife in a conciliatory tone.

His wife turned to give her husband a disapproving look and tutted loudly, making no effort to hide her displeasure.

"You'd better wait in there," she said to Janetta, waving her hand towards the parlour door. She brushed past her husband and started to go up the stairs, muttering to herself.

"Follow me," said the gentleman.

His wife stopped on the stairs, turned around and hurriedly came back into the hall. She took the lamp away from her husband.

"Follow me," she said to Janetta, then turning to her husband, "and you go and wake up the Lieutenant."

She placed the lamp on a side table and turned up the wick. Janetta followed her into the parlour and dropped the carpetbag on the rug.

Sounds of rapping on a bedroom door could be heard upstairs. Janetta and the landlady stood in silence and listened uncomfortably to the voices from upstairs. In a couple of minutes, footsteps came back down the stairs and the landlord entered the parlour, followed by the Lieutenant in his nightshirt, partly covered by a robe that had been hastily thrown on.

The landlady immediately started moaning about her 'house being respectable and no good would come of this and how sorry she was to have disturbed her guest'.

"Mrs Martin!" exclaimed the Lieutenant with some surprise when he saw Janetta standing in the parlor.

"Mrs!" exclaimed the landlady in a shrill voice. "Mrs! A married woman, visiting a single gentleman at his rooms in the early hours of the morning! I knew no good would come of this, George, I knew it!"

"Mrs Davies," said the elderly landlord, "Calm yourself I'm sure the Lieutenant can explain."

"Can he?" replied Mrs Davies as she dabbed a handkerchief to her eyes and appeared to be overcome with emotion. "Can he?"

"Madam," cut in the Lieutenant in a consoling tone of voice, "Mrs Martin is a widow and her late husband was a long time friend of mine."

"There you see my dear, there's nothing untoward in the matter," said Mr Davies.

"Madam," cut in Janetta, "Lieutenant. I do apologize for this late interruption," she continued addressing the Lieutenant, "Sir, terrible circumstances have arisen that make it impossible for me to go back to St. Helen's Road. I shall explain all the details to you in the morning, but right now I beg of you to shelter me for the night." She turned to address Mr Davies, "I am in no legal trouble I promise you, and no misfortune will fall upon this hotel by my staying here."

"Well now," said Mrs Davies, crossing her hands in front of her and shrugging her shoulders, "If the Lieutenant gentleman vouches for ya, I dare says there's no 'arm in ya staying, but we aint got no empty rooms, and I aint 'aving no widow woman spending the night with a single gentleman under my roof, no matter 'ow respectable they claims to be."

"Ma'am," cut in the Lieutenant, "I'm sure I have no objection to Mrs Martin having my room, and with the kind loan of an extra blanket, I will be very comfortable in this armchair before your parlour fire and I will of course pay you for double occupancy."

Mrs Davies pursed her lips and rocked back and forth on her heels in an effort to come to terms with the new arrangement. Being unable to find any new objection to Janetta staying, she tutted again and turning to her husband, said, "well don't stand there all bleeding night! Get the gentleman a blanket and put some more coal on the fire, it's almost out."

"Yes, my dear," beamed Mr Davies, relieved that he had been spared the agony of having to throw Janetta back onto the street. "I'll find one immediately."

****

Early the next morning, Elsie, the maid, entered the parlour with a bucket of coal and an empty bucket for yesterday's ashes. She put the buckets on the floor and went to the window to throw open the curtains.

A shaft of weak gray morning light filled the room and Elsie returned to the buckets and was about to clean out the fire when she gave a scream and staggered backwards. The Lieutenant woke up with a start and the two of them stared at one another for a few seconds, neither one quite comprehending what was happening.

“Who the ’ell are yoo’s?” gasped Elsie, brandishing the coal tongs.

“Oh, I’m sorry if I frightened you,” he yawned. “I’m the gentleman in number three…or rather I was. Somebody else is in my room now.”

“Well you gave me a fright an’ no mistake. ’Ere, does the governor knows your in ’ere?”

“I assure you he does. He gave me this blanket.”

“Well I don’t know I’m sure,” replied Elsie. “Now you’re in my way ya know! I got t’ do the fire and set breakfast.”

“I wonder if you would do me a kindness?” said the Lieutenant, straightening out his dressing gown that had twisted itself around him in the night.

“Wot?” said Elsie putting her hands on her hips and pursing her lips.

“I wonder if you would go to number three and wake up the young lady who is in my bed, and ask her if I might get my clothes. Or better still, perhaps you could bring them down to me?”

“Blimey! As if I ain’t got enough to do!” complained Elsie as she left the room on her new errand.

She returned in about five minutes and dropped his uniform on a chair.

“There ya’re!” she said in an offhand manner. “Can I get on with the fire now?”

“Indeed you can. You’re very kind,” said the Lieutenant.

Elsie dropped to her knees and dragged the empty bucket up to the fire. She proceeded to rake out the ashes and shovel them into the bucket. Lieutenant Bird watched her rear end waving at him for a few seconds before he came to the conclusion that she was not going to leave the room to allow him to get dressed in private. Since she was engrossed in cleaning out the cinders and seemed oblivious of his position, he decided to get dressed right there behind her.

An hour later the fire was burning brightly, the table was laid for breakfast and Janetta came down looking more refreshed than she had a right to be after her adventures the previous night.

The Lieutenant and Janetta greeted one another warmly and Janetta was introduced to the other guests as, one by one, they appeared at the breakfast table. Lieutenant Bird was itching to hear the story behind Janetta's unexpected arrival in the night. He had to be patient, as the other guests, all of whom seemed enchanted with Janetta, monopolized the breakfast conversation.

Janetta was on top of the world. She felt completely liberated from her servitude in the Brant's house, and was as excited as a schoolgirl at the prospect of starting a new life in London. She was surrounded by half a dozen gentlemen, all of whom gave her their full attention, much to the annoyance of the other two female guests who were trying to get their share of the conversation.

Janetta sparkled at the breakfast table. She outshone the other ladies in her beauty, wit and conversation. She had recovered her refined manner of speaking and Lieutenant Bird looked on in complete admiration, remembering how she had been so admired back in the Regiment.

With breakfast over, the good-byes said, and the bags packed, Janetta and the Lieutenant left the Crown and made their way to the station. They arrived in time for the nine thirty train and after Lieutenant Bird purchased their tickets, they walked onto the platform just as the train was pulling in.

Janetta was fascinated by the giant locomotive in its dark green livery; every part of it sparkling clean and polished, with the words Great Western painted on the side of the tender in gold letters.

When the train stopped, the Lieutenant opened a compartment door and helped Janetta up the step. The compartment was empty and the Lieutenant put his and Janetta's bags on the overhead rack before sitting down opposite her next to the window.

"This is rather exciting," said Janetta, "it's only the third time in my life I've been on a train, ya know."

The Lieutenant gave her a gentle smile and nodded his head.

For a few minutes they sat in silence. Janetta laid her head against the window frame and stared absent-mindedly at the other passengers, who were scurrying up the platform trying to decide which carriage to enter. Lieutenant Bird sat and looked at Janetta. Her hair was not quite as well brushed as it should have been, she was paler than usual and as she tried to stifle a yawn behind the back of her hand, it was obvious that she was in need of an extra couple of hours sleep, but he thought he had never seen her look more beautiful.

"Now!" he said, "you promised to tell me what happened last night."

Janetta sat up and returned her thoughts to the moment.

"Ah yeh, well that was strange that was." She fidgeted slightly to arrange her coat more comfortably under her. "I went to say my good-byes to Ellen last night. Although I was only a servant, the Brants treated me very well and Ellen in particular was very kind to me."

The Lieutenant listened sympathetically.

"She was shocked of course, when I told her I was leaving in such a hurry, but when I mentioned that I was going with you, she threw a fit and started hitting me. She said I had stolen you from her and had betrayed her friendship. She was so violent I fled the house."

The Lieutenant looked grieved.

"Oh dear! I was afraid that was the case. It's all my fault I'm afraid."

Janetta looked at him and feigned surprise.

"I knew Ellen before you see," he said rather sheepishly. "I met her at a ball in Bristol a couple of months ago. We danced together rather more than was appropriate and we both had a little too much champagne and... well...one thing led to another."

The corner of Janetta's mouth turned up into a little grin.

"You didn't *roger* her at a ball did you?" she asked, delighting in his discomfort.

"No!... In the garden...it was dark...nobody saw us!" he found himself getting defensive and couldn't look Janetta in the eye. "I regretted it almost as soon as we had done it."

"Oh come now. You enjoyed every minute of it. Be honest," said Janetta, trying hard not to laugh out loud.

"Yes I enjoyed it! But I knew it was a mistake. She's not my type."

"Doesn't have to be," interrupted Janetta.

"And besides I'm..."

"Engaged to be married," butted in Janetta, who was now having great difficulty holding back her laughter.

"Yes well," he looked up at Janetta's beaming face. "You're laughing at me!" he exclaimed with some surprise and gave her a gentle slap across the knees with his gloves.

"No I'm not, 'onest!" said Janetta stifling her chuckles. "Go on."

The Lieutenant pursed his lips and rolled his eyes as if to acknowledge that he had been seen through.

"Yes, I am engaged to be married. But I had no intention of seeing Ellen again." He lowered his voice almost to a whisper and looked down at his lap as if ashamed. "Then next morning she sent me a note. It was very passionately written. She said she would look forward to my coming to Swansea…I had told her early in the evening that I had business in Swansea and that I would look her up…and she said a great deal more in a very loving manner. I'm afraid she took our tryst very seriously, Jan."

"Then why on earth did you go to her house?"

"Because I thought sufficient time had passed for her to cool down. Besides it would have been rude of me not to see her. I suppose I wanted to be sure she was over me."

"Oh dear! You don't know much about women in love, do ya?" chided Janetta.

The Lieutenant looked embarrassed and hung his head. Janetta stood up and leant across the compartment to kiss him.

"What was that for?" he asked as she sat back in her seat.

"For coming to see Ellen and for being such a dear friend to me," she said in a soft and seductive voice.

Doors slammed shut up and down the length of the train, a whistle blew at the far end of the platform and the engine gave a loud deep roar. After a very short pause the carriage gave a slight lurch and the train began to glide out of the station.

They were on their way to London. For the next ten minutes they both sat in silence and stared out of the window at the passing houses and back gardens. Janetta watched the Lieutenant as he gazed out of the window and it occurred to her that this was the first time they had really been alone together. If she was to cement their relationship she was going to have to do a little prodding. The Lieutenant was far too much a gentleman and much too shy to take the initiative.

She shifted her foot a little so that it rested against his boot. His eyes flickered down at his foot for just a second but he didn't move. She very gently rubbed his foot in such a way that he couldn't ignore it.

He shifted his gaze from the window to Janetta and smiled at her, but otherwise did nothing.

"Damn," she thought, *"have I got to do it all?"*

She smiled back at him and said in her most vulnerable voice, "We have the compartment to ourselves."

"Yes, that's most pleasant," he replied but still did nothing.

Janetta, risking his anger by being so brazen, decided to push him harder. She slowly hitched her dress higher onto her lap so as to expose her ankles and shins. She stopped there to see what reaction it had.

The Lieutenant was now staring down at her ankles and she detected a slight moistening across his forehead. He was becoming aroused but still did nothing.

"There's nobody to disturb us," she said as she lifted her dress a little higher.

Lieutenant Bird wasn't sure what was happening to him. He had adored Janetta ever since that day he met her on the dock at Plymouth. But she was a married woman and from a poor family and he constantly reminded himself that he was promised to be married to Lady Dawlish. Any other officer would not have given any of that a second thought but he was a decent man, a gentleman and believed in treating women with respect, despite his tryst with Ellen. Yet now his head swam and all those objections seemed to fade in the background. Without consciously thinking about it, he found himself dropping onto his knees in front of her and running his hands up her thighs inside her dress.

She didn't object, but instead raised her bottom very slightly off the seat, indicating that he could now pull down her bloomers, which he found himself doing.

"It's no good Jan," he whispered," there's no going back now. I want you too much."

"Good," beamed Janetta as she slid sideways onto the seat pulling him on top of her.

There followed an intense and passionate struggle to remove clothes and get as close to one another as they could. They kissed and frantically fondled one another as if trying to make up for all the lost years during which they had secretly wanted each other. The Lieutenant forgot that he was engaged and went wild with passion. Janetta couldn't believe the change in him and threw her head back and moaned and cried in her passion. It was so wonderful to be loved again; to be wanted and adored. Their lips blended together and Janetta wondered if she'd ever breathe again. Her hands roamed all over his body in a desperate attempt to mentally take in every inch of his warmth. She clung to him and squeezed his chest as he thrust into her and made her eyes roll back in her head. For so long she had been taken by a man who had hate in his eyes and she felt as though she was nothing but a piece of meat to be *rogered*, but not now. Now she had a man in her who really cared and she savoured every second. She made the most of her Lieutenant so that she could play back every movement, every groan and every kiss in her mind when they were apart. This was the love she had been looking for all these years.

Ten miles further down the track and the train began to slow down and the engine blew its whistle.

Lieutenant Bird suddenly raised his head up from Janetta's neck and froze, as if listening for an intruder.

"The next station!" he said.

There followed a mad scramble as they both tried to get dressed again before arriving at the station. Janetta, in her panic, couldn't decide which was the front or back of her bloomers and so threw them into her carpetbag on the overhead rack. The Lieutenant struggled with his britches and fought to tuck in his shirt, while Janetta, with trembling fingers fastened the string of buttons up the front of her dress. As they panicked they bumped one another and got into each other's way. By the time the train approached the station the Lieutenant had his tunic back on and was now on his knees trying to locate his boots that had disappeared under the seats.

The train slowed down as the platform slid past the carriage and eventually came to a stop. Lieutenant Bird and Janetta once again sat opposite one another looking like two innocent passengers, albeit somewhat flushed. Doors opened and slammed shut again up and down the train while Janetta fidgeted slightly to straighten her dress and tucked a strand of stray hair that had come loose from her bun. The Lieutenant tugged down on the waist of his tunic and ran the palm of his hand over his hair.

They both smiled at one another as they shared their secret joke. Their moment of quiet contemplation was broken by the compartment door bursting open. A middle-aged woman of generous proportions wearing an extremely bright blue gown several years out of fashion, grabbed hold of the door frame and grimaced, as she considered entering their compartment.

Both the Lieutenant and Janetta pulled their feet in to allow the lady to pass. She groaned as she mounted the step and then huffed and puffed her way to the far end of the compartment and flopped heavily onto the seat by the far window. She was immediately followed by her very portly husband who had a ruddy face that led one to suppose that he had spent a lifetime enjoying the blessing of a rather excellent claret. His skinny legs supported a rotund stomach and barrel chest covered by a bright green waistcoat and brown topcoat. He too wheezed his way to the far end of the compartment and sat opposite his wife. He spread his legs out either side of his wife's feet and slid his bottom forward in the seat so as to be almost reclining and allowed his corpulent belly to rise up in front of him.

The portly gentleman had left the compartment door open. Lieutenant Bird looked at the door, then at the other gentleman then back at the door again. Janetta grinned at his attempt to drop a subtle hint. Lieutenant Bird looked back at the gentleman and made a croaking sound that suggested he was about to say something. Seeing that the gentleman was ignoring him, he leaned out and pulled the door shut himself.

Janetta started giggling and Lieutenant Bird grinned at her and made a shushing expression with his lips.

"Don't know what we're doing," announced the lady, "never did like trains! Not safe you know! We should have taken the Post Chaise."

"My dear one, calm yourself," replied her husband as he took his cigar out of his mouth and allowed some ash to drop onto the shelf of his belly. "The train is perfectly safe, I assure you!"

"We'd be a lot safer on the coach, you mark my words! Coaches can't come off rails can they?" she exclaimed with some satisfaction.

"No, but the roads are in dismal condition and your bones would be shaken to pieces at a mere ten miles an hour," retorted her husband, "whereas the train is smooth and comfortable at sixty miles per hour. Think of that, my dear. Sixty miles an hour." His voice rose a pitch as he enthused about the speed. "Am I not right, sir?" he continued addressing Lieutenant Bird.

Lieutenant Bird was taken by surprise at being spoken to and stammered, "Oh, yes indeed, sixty miles an hour!"

"There, my dear, the good gentleman agrees with me. Much more comfortable means of conveyance, this!"

Janetta again had to stifle her giggling.

The whistle blew again and once more the train began to move. The lady in blue grumbled to herself and her husband puffed blue clouds of cigar smoke into the compartment.

Janetta and Lieutenant Bird sat quietly smiling at one another; both wishing that they had the compartment to themselves again, but the nearer to London they got, the fuller the train became.

"*Never mind*," thought Janetta, "*I've got my protector now*."

CHAPTER 16

London

Swansea had been a quiet sleepy town that had left Janetta bored and lonely. Plymouth had appealed to her, being larger and much dirtier since it catered to the naval base; but nothing had prepared her for the immensity of London. From the moment they stepped off the train at Paddington station, Janetta's head swam. The station with its high wrought iron ceiling rang with the noise of the steam locomotives, slamming carriage doors, people's voices and the rumbling of metal-wheeled luggage carts up and down the platforms. Porters cried, "mind ya backs now, coming through!" as they hauled their loads through the crowd. Sationmasters blew whistles announcing the departure of trains.

She hung onto the Lieutenant's arm for fear of being separated from him in the crush of people. Outside the station the sun tried its best to shine through a dark haze of smog that hung just above the rooftops, and the noise of the station was replaced by a cacophony of street sounds. The street was jammed with carts and carriages of every description. Horses whinnied at each other as they tried to pick their way through the traffic; pedestrians hurried in all directions as if the entire city was late for an appointment, and vendors of every description sang out their wares on every corner.

Janetta found herself suddenly panicking like a child separated from its mother, and she tightened her grip on Lieutenant Bird's arm.

The Lieutenant led Janetta to the side of the entranceway out of the stream of people. He looked at her with a grin on his face and said, "Well here we are; London! What do you think?"

"Blimey!" was all she could manage to say and he laughed at her again.

"Well let's see," he said, taking his fob watch out of his tunic pocket. "It's gone one. Shall we have lunch?"

Janetta nodded her agreement. She was still overwhelmed by this small corner of the city and couldn't pull her thoughts together. Everywhere there was chaos and something happening that she couldn't miss. She found herself turning her head to the right as a double decker omnibus went past drawn by two horses. The top deck was open to the sky and full of people looking very serious. Then to the left she saw a man with a street organ and a little monkey on a lead that kept grabbing at people as they passed. To the right again a drunk sang to everyone as he sat in a doorway, and an elderly lady swore as she ran out of the path of a beer dray and stepped into a pile of dung.

Janetta tried to take everything in until at last she made herself dizzy with the constant head-turning. She decided to look down at her feet for a couple of minutes. The metropolis was making her head spin.

"Are you alright, Jan love?"

The Lieutenant was looking at her with considerable concern.

"I think lunch would be a good idea," she replied. "I think I need to sit down!"

"A nice cup of tea and some food are required I think," he said and, putting his arm around her waist, he led her down the street a few yards before turning into a doorway.

Janetta hadn't taken notice of where they had gone, but suddenly realized that she was inside the fanciest restaurant she'd ever seen.

It was much quieter inside, although there was still the hum of people's voices and the clatter of cutlery. The restaurant looked enormous to her. The ceiling must have been twelve to fourteen feet high and had beautifully ornate patterns moulded into it. Several wrought iron and brightly painted pillars supported the vast ceiling and everywhere were dining tables with bright white tablecloths.

A very attractive young lady in a clean starched apron and smart little white cap approached them.

"Table for two is it, sir?"

"Please!" said the Lieutenant.

"Follow me if you please," she said with a smile.

Janetta caught Lieutenant Bird's eye with a smirk and she made a slight gesture designed to mock the 'la-di-da' waitress.

"Behave yourself!" he whispered with a smile as he pushed her forward to follow the girl.

They were seated at a table on which stood a three tier silver platter with a variety of fancy cakes. A second girl approached the table with a little notebook in her hand.

"What can I get you today, sir?" she said in a matter of fact manner. Janetta noticed that she wore the same uniform as the girl who showed them in and when she looked around the room she saw that there were several girls all about the same age and all in the same neat clean aprons and little hats.

"A pot of tea for two and..." he stopped and looked at Janetta waiting for her to decide what she wanted. Janetta glanced at the people on the next table who were in the middle of their meal.

"I'll have that," said Janetta, discreetly pointing to the gentleman's plate on the table beside them. Lieutenant Bird and the waitress both looked over to the next table.

"One pork pie," announced the waitress and she scribbled in her little book before looking at the Lieutenant again, "and for the gentleman!"

"I'll have the sausages," he said.

"And one sausages," another notation was entered into the book, "bread and butter with that?"

"Please," nodded the Lieutenant and the girl left them alone.

Janetta and the Lieutenant started laughing although neither knew what about; they were both simply happy to be together.

"Where are we?" asked Janetta, looking at the all the decoration in the restaurant. "Looks bloody expensive! But most of the people seem ordinary folks. How can they afford this place?"

The Lieutenant smiled at Janetta's simpleness and loved her for it. She was of course just a country girl in the big city and he took pride in showing her the world.

"This is a tea room Jan and no, it's not expensive. It just looks it. It's designed to make ordinary people feel, well, extraordinary I suppose."

"Blimey! Bleed'n all right in it!" she said, letting down her guard and speaking in her natural Cornish accent. For a minute or two she felt completely out of place and vulnerable. She was, after all, a common girl and her inexperience of the big city was so obvious to Lieutenant Bird that any pretence of being a lady seemed farcical. She wasn't pulling the wool over his eyes and she knew it. What was the point of all her pretence in this great city? The moment passed and she shook off her insecurity.

"Well I must say I'm quite famished," she said, pulling herself together. She looked at Lieutenant Bird across the table and a frown crept over her forehead. "Where am I going to live when we get to Woolwich?" she asked.

"No problem there!" said Lieutenant Bird as he brushed some crumbs off the tablecloth, "I have a place right outside the barracks. It's rented of course, but you can live there. I'll..." Here he shrugged his shoulders and grimaced slightly, "live in the officers' quarters. I'm sure they could find room for me."

"One pork pie and one sausages." Two plates were laid on the table before them, "I'll be right back with the tea," said the waitress, disappearing back into the maze of tables.

Janetta wasn't sure if the Lieutenant really wanted to live in the officers' quarters or whether he was fishing for her to insist that he stayed with her; the arrival of the food and her grumbling stomach pushed the question aside for the moment.

Refreshed by tea and pork pie, Janetta was eager for them to be on their way. The Lieutenant paid the bill and they ventured out onto the street.

"I think we'll stand a better chance of getting a carriage outside the station," he said, so they walked the few yards back towards the station. "Of course we could take the train as far as Greenwich, it would be quicker, but you'll see more of the city if we go by coach."

A carriage was found and they climbed aboard and made themselves comfortable. The driver was talking to another elderly couple who also appeared to enquire about transportation. After a couple of minutes the driver poked his head into the carriage.

"Begging your pardon, sir, but there's a ol' ma and pops 'ere who are wishing to go to South'ark, and seeing as it's on our way I took the liberty of saying that you wouldn't mind sharing with these 'ere gentle folks, sir."

Lieutenant Bird gave Janetta an apologetic look before replying, "Not at all, sir, we would be pleased of the company."

Janetta gave a slight growl in her throat to show her lack of enthusiasm for the idea.

"Very good, sir," said the coachman before turning to the elderly couple who stood on the pavement with expectant faces. "The gentleman said it would be a pleasure to 'ave yer company, so get aboard my dears, while I puts ya bags on the roof there."

The door opened and an ancient-looking lady pulled herself in while her husband pushed against her posterior. He followed her in and, with some difficulty the two of them settled into reasonably comfortable positions.

"Most um, kind of you, sir and um, um, madam!" said the gentleman once he was settled. "My name is um Stoat, sir, Zachariah Stoat. My card." He handed Lieutenant Bird a crumpled and somewhat dirty card upon, which was written "Stoat and Fox Solicitors, Edgeware Road".

"Stoat and Fox?" said Bird with some amusement.

"Indeed, sir, um unlikely bedfellows wouldn't you think? But, um I assure you, sir that um…Albert Fox is the most affable um…gentleman." The elderly lady cleared her throat. "Oh dear me sir what, um…must you be thinking of, um…me? Pray allow me, um…to name to you, my good lady wife, um um…Minnie Stoat."

Janetta had great difficulty containing her laughter.

"Minnie?" said the Lieutenant, "how pleasant to make your acquaintance ma'am."

Mrs Stoat said nothing but her face lit up with an enormous smile and she nodded enthusiastically to Janetta and the Lieutenant.

The coach jerked slightly as the horses struggled to complete a one hundred and eighty-degree turn in the middle of the road, and having accomplished this, they were off.

They drove down a maze of congested side streets until they came out onto Bayswater Road at Hyde Park. Janetta didn't wish to be rude to their fellow passengers by ignoring their conversation, but she was really far more interested in seeing as much of London as she could, so she opened the window and leaned her head out. The carriage drove around Marble Arch and soon arrived at Hyde Park corner. The Lieutenant did his best to point out places of interest but he didn't know that much himself.

"Used to be the, um…gallows 'ere," said Zachariah. "Used to call it Tyburn. Right 'ere in the middle of the road," he said and Janetta looked hard at where the gallows might have stood.

"Actually, sir, I do believe the Tyburn gibbet was at Marble Arch. We've passed it," said the Lieutenant.

"Indeed your, um,...right sir, I do recollect it to be at Marble Arch".

"Ah! Good!" said Lieutenant Bird changing the subject, "he's turning down Constitution Hill. We'll see the Palace!"

"Indeed we, um...will!" said Zachariah.

Mrs Stoat nodded enthusiastically.

From the palace the coach went down Birdcage Walk, coming out by the Houses of Parliament and Westminster Bridge.

Janetta was disappointed at not being able to see too much of the muddy Thames, because of the wall on the bridge and the congestion of traffic.

"Magnificent city!" bellowed Zachariah with much enthusiasm, "as the bard said, 'when you're tired of London, sir, you're tired of life.'"

"Samuel Johnson, I think!" corrected Lieutenant Bird.

"'Pon my soul sir, I do believe your, um...right! And truthful words, sir, um...truthful words!"

The carriage ambled its way along Lambeth Road in a great convoy of vehicles that ground forward like an army of fattened cattle. When at last they reached a major junction the coach pulled over to the side of the road and the driver jumped down.

"'Ere we are then, St. George's Circle, where you wants to be put down."

"Well, well! Um...it has been pleasant to make your acquaintance, um, but I, um...fear we must now, um part," said Zachariah Stoat, and having shaken hands with the Lieutenant and Janetta he followed his Minnie out of the carriage.

The carriage door slammed shut and there were a few quiet moments while the driver retrieved the Stoats' luggage from the roof.

As the carriage pulled away, the Stoats stood on the pavement and waved goodbye to Janetta who put on a very passable performance of a congenial parting. Once out of sight however she burst into laughter and jumped onto the Lieutenant's lap with her knees astride his legs.

"Alone at last!" she whispered, and he gave her a grin and a couple of clicks of the tongue as if to say *"you're wicked!"*

She reached over and pulled down the blinds on the windows and neither she nor the Lieutenant saw any more sights of London for the next forty-five minutes.

When they opened the blinds again they were on Shooters Hill Road going past Blackheath Common.

"We'll be in Woolwich soon," said the rather ruffled Lieutenant, "I think we should get ourselves tidied up don't you?"

Janetta retreated to her own side of the carriage and grinned at him as she did her dress buttons up. She would soon see her new house and the Regiment's home she had heard so much about over the past few years; a wave of excitement came over her.

CHAPTER 17

The Ghost

For the next few months Janetta was happier than she'd ever been. She settled into the Lieutenant's rented house that, although small, was very cosy and tastefully furnished. He saw to it that there was always food in the house and he gave her a small allowance, sufficient to buy all the little necessities a woman needs. Janetta wanted for nothing.

On the third day after arriving in Woolwich, Timothy took her on a personal tour of the Barracks and she was stunned by the sheer size of the place. There were several three-storey, red-bricked buildings linked together to make one enormous edifice that stretched the entire length of the largest parade ground she'd ever seen. The whole complex stretched over several acres and contained dozens of separate buildings. There were stores, stables, gun carriages, shops and a host of craftsmen such as leather workers and smithies. Janetta felt at home immediately and everywhere they went she could feel soldiers' eyes on her. Timothy Bird positively strutted with pride having her on his arm.

Before long, Janetta received her first invitation to an '*Officers' Guest Night'* and she went to dinner on Lieutenant Bird's arm and lit up the room with her beauty. How grand it all was. She felt intimidated sitting with such refined people at an immaculately polished table and being confronted by the amount of silver cutlery before her. She remembered Timothy's advice before arriving, *"start on the outside and work your way in."* Janetta sat and stared at all the tureens and fine porcelain and reminded herself, *"Come on girl, remember, chew with ya mouth shut; don't swear, speak slowly and precisely and don't drop your aitches."* She needn't have worried; she was a great success and by the time the evening was over there wasn't an officer who didn't find her utterly captivating.

Janetta's first serious hurdle came with an invitation to a Regimental Ball. She could dance, but not in the refined manner that the other ladies did, so she had to take a few lessons. She had three weeks in which to learn half a dozen dances, but she managed it beautifully and nobody noticed her awkwardness. In fact, Lieutenant Bird beamed with admiration as he walked her home. Life was exactly what she had always dreamed it would be and she was deliriously happy.

There was only one thing missing. She wasn't married. The Lieutenant officially lived in the officers' quarters but, two or sometimes three nights a week, he stayed with Janetta. When she lay next to him in bed she felt married and wonderfully content. She felt that she had finally found her true love, but she knew that it wouldn't last.

Lieutenant Bird was a gentleman. He had to marry someone from society and he was promised to a girl half his age. He may not have loved her but she came with a title and considerable fortune so his future was decided for him. Janetta knew that all she could do was savour the moments she had with him and let him go gracefully when the time came. In the meantime, she would cultivate friends amongst the other officers so that she had a fallback plan when Lieutenant Bird inevitably left her.

****

January 1884

A train stood empty at platform six, most of its doors left hanging open by the passengers who had got out. Dozens of travellers walked hurriedly down the platform looking in each compartment, trying to find one that suited them. The station hummed with the sounds of trains' whistles, engines venting steam, baggage trolleys with hard metal wheels rumbling up and down the platforms and a thousand hurried footsteps. Small groups of people stood about on platform five waiting for a train to arrive; some read newspapers others tried to avoid the gaze of their fellow travellers.

Janetta and Lieutenant Bird walked down the platform together in silence. Janetta had her arm linked in his and wore her second best dress and smartest topcoat. She was perhaps a little overdressed for the occasion. Her hair was clean and well brushed and she wore a little rouge. She wanted the Lieutenant to remember her looking her best when they said goodbye.

She felt numb now that the moment had come. She had known for months that she would lose him as soon as his fiancée came of age and now the moment was approaching she didn't know whether to cry or be angry. She hadn't fought him when he had announced his leaving. She hadn't tried to change his mind. What would have been the use? She knew the arrangement. She had lived on borrowed time for ten months and now it was over. She clung to his arm and tried to hold in her mind the memory of how it felt.

They arrived at a compartment that seemed to satisfy the Lieutenant, for he suddenly slung his kit bag into the door and then turned to face her.

"Well…here we are."

"Yes," she replied with a slight cracking in her voice, "here we are!"

They stood in front of one another rather awkwardly for a moment or two, neither one knowing what to say. Janetta stared up the platform as if interested in what someone else was doing, but in reality she was avoiding his eyes. She knew she would cry if she looked directly at him.

The uncomfortable pause was broken when the Lieutenant reached out and pulled her to him. She laid her head against his tunic and threw her arms round his waist.

"I promised myself I wouldn't cry," she croaked as the tears began. It was no good; she couldn't stand to lose him now; not now.

"I know, I know."

A train glided into platform five and there was a loud venting of steam as it came to a stop. People hurried past them and doors slammed shut up and down the train, but Janetta didn't hear any of it.

"You have my address in Plymouth if you need me. I'll write to you as soon as I know what's happening."

"When will you see Lady Dawlish?"

She didn't really want to know but couldn't help asking.

"Oh….I don't know. Next week probably."

They stood in silence for a few seconds hanging on to one another.

"Last time I saw her she was a scruffy little kid. She was all scraggly hair and dirty fingernails. Mischievous little minx she was too!"

"When was that?"

"Oh… seven or eight years ago!"

Janetta laughed.

"Well don't expect to find a dirty little kid this time."

"Hope not!"

Janetta pulled away from him slightly.

"Oh, hoping for something a lot better are you!"

"I'm not hoping for anything. She couldn't possibly be as wonderful as you. You've been the only one in my life Jan. I couldn't love anyone else."

"Why are you going then?" She cursed herself for asking. "*Stupid question,"* she thought.

"You know why!" replied the Lieutenant kindly.

"Well I hope she turns out to be bloody ugly and you'll come running back to me, you bastard!" she said poking him in the ribs.

"Come here," he said as he pulled her back into his arms and began kissing her.

****

A door opened on one of the carriages of the newly-arrived train on platform five and a dirty, badly-stained kitbag was tossed out onto the ground. A large bear of a man followed the bag out onto the platform. Despite his rather shabby appearance he was wearing the uniform of a major of the Royal Artillery. He stepped off the train and bent down to pick up his kit bag. As he did so his eye was caught by a scarlet red stripe on a trouser leg the other side of the platform and looking up, he saw a fellow Artillery officer kissing a woman.

There was something familiar about this officer, but because his head was bent down kissing his girl, he couldn't get a good look at him. The woman's long black hair also struck a chord with him, but again, he couldn't see her, because she had her back to him.

He decided to wait a moment to satisfy his curiosity, but he was too easily seen where he stood, so he walked a few paces down the platform to where there was a tobacco and newspaper kiosk. He stopped just behind the kiosk, dropped his bag, leant against the wall and took a pipe out of his coat pocket. While he struck a match and lit his pipe, he kept his eyes on the kissing couple. It seemed a long passionate kiss and he watched with considerable interest. His eyes only left them for a couple of seconds while he was momentarily diverted by two young ladies walking past him.

The couple pulled apart slightly and he saw the Lieutenant's face. A slight expression of recognition crossed the major's pockmarked face. His eyes half closed and his face darkened, "Lieutenant, fucking Bird," he mumbled under his breath.

****

A shrill whistle blew and some latecomers started running down the platform. Ladies hitched up the front of their skirts and climbed hurriedly into carriages.

"Time to go my sweet," said Lieutenant Bird as he stepped up into the carriage and closed the door behind him. He unhooked the leather strap allowing the window to slide down and then leaned out for one last kiss.

Janetta reached up and standing on tiptoe, kissed him again until the train began to move smoothly out of the station. She walked along a little way to keep up with it, still holding his hands until they were pulled apart. They didn't actually say goodbye, but just looked into one another's eyes as the train gathered speed. The Lieutenant continued waving to her out of the window as the train glided out of the station. Eventually he ducked back into the compartment and Janetta stood there alone, watching the end of the train getting smaller as it left the station and entered the gray daylight outside.

A blue gray cloud of pipe smoke surrounded the major's grizzled face as he watched the train leave. The young woman, still with her back to him, stood and watched until the train was lost to sight.

"How touching!" he growled to himself, and still he waited for her to turn around.

When she did finally turn about, Janetta hung her head down so that he still couldn't see her face properly, but he was sure he'd seen her before. She walked back up the platform towards the exit gate in a distracted manner, but as she came near to him she finally lifted her head.

A broad sardonic grin crept into the corner of his mouth.

"Well, well," he muttered to himself, "what do ya know?"

He tapped his pipe out on the wall of the kiosk and smartly strode across the platform to cut Janetta off. He stopped right in her path so that, as she approached him, she would have to stop or go round him. Either way she couldn't help but see him and when she did, she drew her breath in, her eyes bulged and her mouth hung open with astonishment.

"Hello Mrs Martin," he growled as she stopped dead in her tracks.

Her sad thoughts suddenly interrupted, Janetta stood and stared incredulously up at the major's face. He grimaced at her, exposing his yellow teeth.

"Surprised to see me no doubt!" he said with a sneer.

Janetta tried to talk but the words wouldn't come out,

"It can't be…you're…dead," she stammered.

"Yeh!" he grinned, "I'm a ghost from the past I am. I knew you'd be glad to see me!"

Janetta reeled with repulsion at the apparition of Major Cope standing before her and without thinking, she pushed past him and hurried towards the gate as fast as her legs would allow.

The Major wanted to catch her up but then remembered his kitbag, which was still laying by the kiosk. By the time he had gone back to retrieve it Janetta was at the far end of the platform and going through the barrier.

"Damn!" he muttered but still took off after her.

Janetta rushed through the exit gate, thrusting her platform ticket into the ticket collector's hand. She glanced briefly over her shoulder and when she didn't see the ghost of Major Cope she relaxed a little, but still hurried out of the station.

When she reached the street, she found that it had started to rain quite hard and she didn't have her umbrella. She wasn't even sure where she was going.

"*Home!"* she thought, *"I must get home!"*

Directly in front of the station entrance stood a hansom cab. The driver was already to catch her eye. She ran across the pavement through the rain and opened the cab door.

"Where to, miss?" said the driver.

"Just go!" yelled Janetta as she slammed the door shut behind her. The driver raised his eyes to the sky and tutted before flicking the reigns and moving out into the stream of traffic.

Janetta sat back in the cab and gasped. Then she leaned forward and looked out of the window. As the cab was swallowed up in the London traffic Major Cope came out of the station and stood in the rain looking up and down the street.

Janetta sat back away from the window and breathed a sigh of relief.

The little window in the back of the cab opened and the driver, who was sitting up high behind, called down to her.

"Have ya decided where ya wonna go yet, luv?"

Janetta, still in a state of shock absentmindedly replied, "Woolwich please."

"Woolwich?" laughed the driver; "You don't want me to take ya to Woolwich. It'll cost ya an arm an' a leg dearie! I only does local!"

"I have to get to Woolwich!" said Janetta, looking back to see if the major was still in sight.

The driver, hearing the distress in her voice lowered his head closer to the little window in the back of the cab, "You's ain't from round these parts are ya, luv?"

Janetta made no reply.

"Tell ya what you need, is either the train or the coach. Which'll it be?" She was beginning to feel sick to the stomach, and couldn't concentrate on the conversation.

"Don't care!" she moaned. How could it have been Major Cope? How could it? He was dead. John had thrown him over the side of the ship. It was just a terrible dream. I'll wake up in a moment, she told herself, and it will all have been a bad dream.

"Well I reckons I'll take you to the coach then, shall I?"

Still Janetta didn't respond to him.

"That'll be the best thing then. I'll take you to where the coach stops."

Janetta stared blankly out of the window at all the traffic jamming the street. Horses pulled their loads and defecated on the road. Crowds thronged the pavements. Hawkers sang out their wares and Janetta saw none of it. All she knew was that for the moment, she was safe and her encounter was just a nightmare. She waited to wake up.

Twenty minutes later the driver pulled into a coaching inn and stopped outside the front door. On the other side of the courtyard stood a post chaise and four horses. A small group of people hung about waiting while two coachmen lifted trunks and bags onto the roof.

The cab driver jumped down and opened the little doors in front of Janetta's legs.

"Ere we are then miss!" he said.

Janetta didn't respond. She was now beginning to feel quite faint.

"I'll go and see if this is your coach luv. OK?"

Janetta looked at him glassy-eyed and gave a slight nod.

"Are you's all right luv?" he inquired seeing her pale complexion.

Janetta shook her head; "I feel a little ill."

"All right yoo wait 'ere then."

He walked across the yard to where the corpulent coach driver was supervising two young lads loading tunks onto the roof.

"'Ere mate, ya going to Woolwich?"

"In a couple minutes I is!" replied the driver without taking his eyes off the loading.

"Got room for one more lady?"

"We can squeeze 'er in I reckon."

"She's none to well. You'll look after 'er will ya."

"Not drunk is she? I don't want no drunks puking in me coach an' on me customers."

"No she ain't been at the drink. I fink it's just a woman's thing. You know!"

The coach driver raised his eyes to the sky. "Bring her over then. Be sharp now I'm about to leave."

CHAPTER 18

Will Rayner
March 1884

The pub was ill-lit, smoky, and noisy. The air was pungent with the aroma of the coal fire, spilt beer, and body odour. It was particularly crowded even for a Saturday night. Old men sat at tables playing dominoes. In the corner, an elderly woman with too much rouge played the piano indifferently. The room was packed with soldiers and locals all laughing, chatting and flirting with the girls who frequented the pubs looking for trade. The din of voices and the tinkling of glasses were evidence of a good time being had by all and a healthy trade being done for the evening.

Will Rayner, a bombardier in the Royal Artillery, stood with his mates drinking ale and sharing jokes. They eyed the girls, looking for one to spend the evening with. His friends all boosted one another's courage to talk to the girls, and dared each other to try this girl or that; but Will wasn't interested in whores. He was a shy young man who had a deep respect for women and longed for the day when he could find a nice girl with whom he could settle down and raise a family. His friends teased him for it and tried to get him to chat up a scruffy, straw-haired girl who looked as if she'd slept with half the Regiment, but he wasn't interested.

Will was well liked by his fellow soldiers. He was short, slender and fair-haired. You would not have called him handsome, but he had a rugged face and blues eyes that women found irresistible. His ten years in India had given him a self-assurance that hid his basic reserve and added to his sex appeal. For all this he remained quite shy of women and found it difficult to talk to them.

He was enjoying the evening in his friends' company but his eyes kept going to a young lady sitting all alone in a dark corner of the room, almost hidden by the side of the bar. She looked sad and slightly drunk. Her bedraggled hair hung down over her face but Will could tell that beneath that uncombed curtain was a stunning woman. She captivated him and he wondered how he could approach her.

Alone in her corner, Janetta felt miserable. She sat at her table in the dark green work dress she wore about the house. She hadn't bothered to change into something more presentable before leaving the house. Her dress was wrinkled, sweaty under the arms and the hem spattered with dried mud. Her dark hair hung over her shoulders and face, unwashed and uncombed. She wore no make-up and her eyes were red and puffy as she had been crying. She sat in silent contemplation; a half-pint jug of gin and a half-empty glass was before her on the table. Her chin was supported in her hands; her elbows taking the weight on the table as she wallowed in self-pity.

She hadn't left the house much in the month since the Lieutenant had been posted. She kept herself busy, but she didn't feel very sociable. In fact she felt desperately lonely now that she knew the Lieutenant wouldn't be visiting and to make matters worse she was sure she was pregnant. On top of this, she couldn't get Major Cope out of her mind. She found herself worrying about him most of the time. Just because she saw him in London didn't mean that he was in Woolwich, but then again the chances were very high that he was. Even if he were, she told herself, he didn't know where she lived. She hadn't been to the barracks lately and as long as she stayed away from it she may never run into him again. She couldn't help thinking about John and how he had changed after the murder of Cope. How he had suffered with remorse over what he had done, and it was all for nothing. Cope was alive and well and very close at hand. Janetta shuddered.

"*So it had come to this*," she thought. Ten blissfully happy months with Lieutenant Bird had come to an end. His Penelope Dawlish had finally come of age and he'd left Woolwich to marry her. He had been gone five weeks now and she was dying inside without him. She had never pressured him, nor told him how much she had loved him. She had spent all year playing the dutiful mistress, entertaining his friends, looking glamorous enough to have all the officers buzzing around her at regimental do's; but all the time she knew that the clock was ticking, and sooner, rather than later, she was going to lose him.

How she had loved the parties and balls. She had become the darling of the Regiment. She had acquired a beautiful wardrobe, thanks to the Lieutenant's generosity and had lived the life of a lady despite her plain little house in Ordnance Place. Her 'little house' as she affectionately called it, was still her home, although she had now taken over the responsibility of paying the rent. She had become a laundress and had been very successful at it – if you could call being a laundress successful, for in truth it was the lowest form of employment next to whoring. She had a regular clientele and although everybody in the street knew about her affair with the Lieutenant, nobody gave her a hard time over it. Indeed most of her neighbours secretly envied her and they were all familiar with the hardships of being a Regiment's woman.

The Regiment was full of officers who would be only too pleased to pick her up after the Lieutenant's departure, but nobody had come to call on her. She'd had no invitations to dinner or a dance. Perhaps it was too soon. Perhaps the other officers were hesitant to step in too quickly. Perhaps they were too proud to be seen with a common girl.

What upset her the most was that for all this time the Lieutenant had been her continual lover and they had been so extremely careful not to get her pregnant, since there was no possibility of marriage between them.

He had finally gone, as she knew he would, and now a month later she had missed her period. Her despair was overwhelming and for several evenings she had simply sat in the corner of the bar and drowned her sorrows in gin.

All she could think about was the child growing in her belly and no husband to support her. She was thirty years old and about to become a single mother. What she needed now was a husband and quickly.

****

"I've seen you before, haven't I?"

"Wot?" Janetta raised her eyes from her glass just sufficiently to see a blue artillery uniform standing in front of her table. The uniform piqued her interest, but when she focused, she recognized it to be the uniform of an enlisted man and she made no attempt to hide her disappointment. She lowered her gaze to the glass again.

"I saw you at the Brigadier's dance, didn't I?"

Janetta raised her head again and struggled to pay attention to the man in blue. She was feeling the effects of the gin.

"You wos there, wos ya?" There were no airs and graces from Janetta in this pub. There were no officers to impress. "Don't remember seeing you there."

He was quite a handsome man she thought, even if he wasn't an officer.

"Well I didn't get to go inside. I was a driver, see. I was employed to drive some of the officers' wives to an' from, like."

Janetta made no response.

"But I saw you arrive with Lieutenant Bird. Thought you looked very beautiful."

Janetta gave a derisive little chuckle and then buried her chin back in her hands and poured out the last of the gin.

Will Rayner stood awkwardly fiddling with his cap for a moment or two not knowing whether he should press on with his advances or withdraw in defeat. Since she was ignoring him he decided to withdraw and so turned away from the table.

"Wot d'ya say your name was?" Janetta had raised her chin from her hand again. Will stopped and turned around.

"William," he said rather timidly, "William Rayner."

"William," she replied and paused as if to digest the name. "William Rayner ya say?"

"Yeh!" nodded Will and he slowly stepped back to the table.

"Well Willy!" she said putting too much emphasis on the Willy. "Sit down if ya want."

"William!" corrected Will, "William or Will!"

" 'ow about Bill?"

"Will!" he insisted.

Janetta looked at him as if she couldn't decide which of them was getting the better of this small exchange. "*He really is quite handsome*," she thought, "*for an enlisted man*." She decided not to press her hostility towards this uninvited stranger.

"Sit down… Will," she said, "if yer pleased to?"

Will pulled back the chair opposite her and sat down. Out of the corner of his eye he saw his friends watching him; they made a couple of encouraging, although somewhat lewd gestures toward him. He ignored them, although he secretly felt glad that the prettiest girl in the pub hadn't rejected him. He knew they would be envying him.

"Where are you from?" he asked, "I can't place your accent."

"Tywarrr…reaf." She mumbled.

"Where?"

Realizing that she was slurring her speech, Janetta took a deep breath, concentrated hard on her annunciation and repeated louder and slower, "Tyward…reath."

"Where the 'ells that then?"

"Cornwall," she replied in a tone that implied he shouldn't be so ignorant. Will took no offense.

He changed the subject. "You know Lieutenant Bird."

"Umm," she nodded still looking down at her glass.

"I really liked him. One of the better officers, I'd say."

Janetta lifted her head from her hands and holding her hands out in front of Will said,

"Used to be an officer's lady. Now I do laundry. Look at the state of me 'ands."

"They're 'onest 'ands, they are," replied Will, "There's no shame in doing a 'ard days work."

"Shame!" Janetta almost screamed as she glared at Will with fire in her eyes. "Shame! I never said I was ashamed. I ain't ashamed of nuffin I ain't. And don't you think I am, never!"

Will was startled by her outburst and found himself stammering.

"I…I'm…sorry Miss…"

Will suddenly realized that he didn't know her family name.

"Sorry…I…don't know your…"

Janetta looked around her and saw that several people were staring at her after her outburst. She smiled at Will and lowered her voice, more to reassure the onlookers than to be genuinely friendly towards a soldier who obviously was living in hopes of getting lucky tonight.

"Rundel," replied Janetta, using her maiden name. She wasn't sure why she did that. Perhaps she felt guilty using the name Martin because she no longer thought of herself as a married woman; not even as a grieving widow. John was now a distant memory and she felt pangs of guilt about that.

"Rundel," repeated Will, "Janetta Rundel. Well I'm pleased to make your acquaintance, Miss Rundel."

"Yeh well!" Janetta took the extended hand Will offered her. "Please to meet you I'm sure."

They sat for a minute or two in silence and drank the last of their drinks. Janetta, having swallowed her gin, slapped the glass on the table, sat up straight backed and looked at Will for a long moment. Then she leaned as far across the table as she could without lifting her back side off the chair, stared right in Will's eyes and said, "I'm not a whore Will Rayner, so if your expecting to have my ass tonight you're wasting your time."

For a second or two, Will was left speechless by such a candid statement and found himself feeling a little embarrassed.

"I...I assure you Miss Rundel, it never occurred to me that you were."

"Well good, then I expect you'd like to escort me 'ome, wouldn't ya luv?"

Will was slightly taken aback by her forwardness but recovered quickly when he realized that he wasn't going to have to ask her himself. He nodded his agreement and stood up. Janetta started to pull her shawl about her shoulders and stand up. The gin, having reduced the strength in her legs, caused her to wobble slightly and one side of the shawl dropped off her shoulder. Will instinctively reached forward to help her with it. A couple of "Oo's" came from his friends as they watched Will preparing to leave with the prettiest, although somewhat dishevelled, girl in the pub. Their teasing didn't escape Janetta's notice. She knew only too well the power she had over men and she relished the idea of flaunting it occasionally in public. She decided to help Will impress his friends.

"Ere," she whispered, "let me take your arm."

She linked her arm in his, which steadied her footing and then clung to his side in a display of affection as they pushed their way through the crowd. Will's friends watched in amazement and made a few raucous comments, as they brushed past.

Will felt a warm glow inside and beads of sweat glistened on his forehead. He couldn't believe he was leaving the pub with such a gorgeous woman, and he was conscious of showing off the fact in front of his drinking pals.

When they got out into the cool night air, Will expected Janetta to pull away from him; now that the 'show' was over, but she didn't.

They strolled along the damp, deserted road in silence for several minutes. He had no idea what to say to her; just being with her was enough. In truth he was a little afraid of her and was apprehensive about breaking the magic of the moment. They walked down two streets and finally she steered him into a doorway. He wasn't sure if this was her house or if she had simply found a convenient dark spot to kiss and cuddle.

She leaned her back against the wall of the small porch and pulled him to her. There was no mistaking her intentions, and swept up by the moment, he started to kiss her as passionately as he felt she would allow. She responded by throwing her arms round his neck and almost crushing him.

Their passion quickly got out of control and Will found himself fondling her breasts and buttocks; his hands roved all over her in a feverish attempt to acquaint himself with her whole body. She didn't resist.

Janetta was playing a dangerous game and she knew it. If she allowed him to *'roger'* her she could then say that he had got her pregnant. But would he stand by her? Would he think her a common slut for having sex within half an hour of meeting? Perhaps she'd never see him again, once he'd had her body. What if he did marry her and turned out to be a real bastard?

No, she didn't honestly think that. He was really very sweet, but it was perhaps because of that, she decided not to risk loosing him. Better, she thought, to play him for a little while; to keep him on the end of her line for a week or two. She could afford that time.

She suddenly, but kindly, pulled away from Will's embrace and moved his hands away from her buttocks.

"Not tonight, lover," she whispered, "I fink we need t'get to know one another a bit first." She gave him a small but encouraging peck on the end of his nose. "Now you know where I live, I'll expect yer to come a calling."

"I'd like that, I really would."

"Good, then give us a kiss good night."

He kissed her again, prolonging it as long as he could before she pulled free of him and disappeared into the front door of the house. As the door closed behind her Will looked at the number eight crudely painted on the door. Now all he had to do was make a note of the street name on his way back to the barracks.

To describe him as having a spring in his step when he left, does not do credit to the turmoil in his head. He felt the excitement of a schoolboy after having had his hand up a girl's dress for the first time. He was no innocent. In India he had plenty of *bibis*, many of whom were stunningly beautiful and exotic, but nothing compared to the feeling he had after being with Janetta. She was the most adored woman in the Regiment and many soldiers and officers had longed to try their luck after the Lieutenant had left, but none had dared come forward until now.

"Why me?" he found himself asking out loud to the dark night shadows. "I have nothing! No money, no rank, nothing that could tempt her away from a handsome officer."

Yet there he was, as giddy as a schoolboy, still with the taste of her lips on his mouth, still with the memory of her body in his hands. He would call on her again, and very soon. Nothing was going to pull him away from her now.

****

Over the course of the following two weeks, Will and Janetta saw one another whenever Will could get out of the barracks, which was most evenings. Janetta tempted Will with her kisses and body language but never allowed him to go too far. Neither did she let him know that he couldn't have her. She kept him suspended on the very edge of her passion, while she assessed what sort of man this Will Rayner was. She was already very impressed by him. He was reserved although not weak of character. He was gentle and temperate in his habits; not drinking, smoking or swearing to excess. As enlisted men went, he was a real gentleman.

Janetta was used to gentlemen. The officers were all gentlemen; with the exception of the Colonel and Lieutenant Bird, they were not to be trusted. Oh they'd all like to have her as their mistress, but none of them would ever consider marrying a common working girl from a fishing village.

On the other hand most enlisted men tended to be typical soldiers; only interested in whoring and gambling, but at least they were honest about their lust. The officers wooed with empty promises, but the enlisted men simply groped you and slapped you on the rump and asked if you wanted to be *rogered* in a side alley. Janetta may not have been an innocent virgin, but she still tried to conduct herself in a ladylike manner and succeeded in keeping the men of the regiment in their places.

Will Rayner was different though. She really began to like her skinny little soldier with his puppy dog blue eyes and shy conversation. He was no Don Juan or officer with a private income. He couldn't take her to fancy balls or afford to buy her nice clothes; but he was honest, loving and loyal. Will Rayner was one of nature's gentlemen. In short, he would make a good husband and father; more importantly, his sense of honour would not allow him to abandon her if she should suddenly find herself pregnant.

Janetta decided she would marry Will Rayner.

****

On a bright, clear spring Sunday they went by omnibus to spend the day at Greenwich Park. After a long gray winter, the blue sky and warm sun made the day seem hotter than it really was. They both found it warm work climbing the steep grass-covered hill to see the Royal Observatory. After looking round the building and hearing a guide explain its history they sat on the grass to eat their packed lunch and looked out over the roofs of the Royal Naval College to the great gray River Thames with its forest of ships' masts.

It was a perfect day. They sat eating their sandwiches and staring out over the City of London. A dark haze from thousands of coal fires hung over the rooftops. How fresh the air seemed up on this hill away from the dark city. The sun danced and sparkled on the snaking Thames and Janetta shifted her bottom on the grass to edge closer to Will.

Soon they were hugging and kissing in the grass, not caring if seen by any passers-by. Will soon found himself becoming increasingly amorous as Janetta's lips pecked and probed about his mouth. He couldn't resist fondling her breasts and running his hands up and down the length of her body. Janetta allowed him to explore her contours, unopposed. Her hands never pulled his away from her body, nor did she make any verbal objection. He couldn't believe his good fortune. She was submitting to him; encouraging him, making all the right sounds and movements that said, *"take me, take me now!"* Yet Will suddenly held back.

He raised his head and looked about him. Above him he could see the top half of the Observatory but none of the people on the path at the top of the hill. They were lying below the crest in a very slight hollow. To the left and right of them was nothing but a great expanse of grass. There was a path at the foot of the hill running along in front of the Queen's House but that was several hundred yards away and the people looked very small. In their spot, if they kept low, they would not be seen.

For a few seconds, Will found himself thinking what a great spot this would be for an artillery battery. It had a perfect command of the river, although extremely exposed. The guns would have to be protected by redoubts.

Janetta craned her head to follow Will's gaze up the slope and grinned.

"No one can see us," she whispered, "we're alright!"

Will snapped his attention back to Janetta. "They'll see us if they decided to walk down the hill."

Janetta laughed. "Exciting isn't it?" she teased.

"I must think about your reputation… if somebody should see us."

Janetta felt she was losing him as he lost his resolve. She held his face between her hands and pulled him down to her lips again. She wanted him now, but he had to feel he was seducing her and not the other way round, so she gently squirmed her body under his and caressed his leg with her thighs. That was having the desired effect and soon Will had forgotten how exposed they were and was giving in to his passion.

Before he even realized what was happening Janetta's dress was up around her waist and he was struggling to undo his britches. As he pulled them down he became unaware of anything around them. Nothing else mattered in the world and he held those moments of bliss for as long as he could. He no longer cared if anyone was watching, he was as one with the most beautiful woman he'd ever seen and the world could go hang.

Janetta, her arms about his neck, looked up into the clouds and smiled to the sky. She had her soldier boy.

CHAPTER 19

An Old Enemy

Major Cope had spent the last couple of weeks settling in to his new home at the Woolwich Barracks. He'd found his bearings around the great expanse of buildings, familiarized himself with the daily routine and made a point of knowing which officers were tough and which ones were weak. If there was one thing Major Cope excelled at, it was being able to recognize the officers he should ingratiate himself with and those who had weaknesses he could exploit.

It wasn't long before everybody in the regiment knew who Major Cope was and, depending upon who you were, you either hated him or thought him a damned fine, if somewhat crude, officer.

Yet although this settling in period had kept him busy, he had never lost sight of the fact that he had seen Janetta Martin again and the old excitement he felt for her had bubbled to the surface.

She was never far from his mind and he found himself fantasizing about her more and more. He couldn't quite be rid of the suspicion that she had somehow played a part in his being clobbered and thrown into the sea. He had no evidence of her complicity and indeed couldn't be absolutely sure anyone had done it. All he knew was that his feet had gone out from under him and his head hit something hard. The next thing he knew he was plunging into cold water and gasping for air.

He'd heard all about the enquiry that was held afterwards and the verdict that he had fallen overboard when the ship was hit by a squall. However, something niggled in the back of his mind, and he strongly suspected that somebody had tried to murder him, and nobody had better cause than Janetta.

He was determined to find her again and reopen their last conversation. At the very least, he told himself, he'd get a good *rogering* out of it. He'd have her arse if nothing else. After all, she was just a slag who slept around and now he could have his turn with her. The first problem though, was finding her.

He sat on the edge of his bed and pulled his boots off. The smell of rancid feet filled the small room he shared with Major Sinclair, who immediately screwed up his face and let out an exclamation of disgust.

"God damn it, Cope, don't you ever wash your feet!" he complained.

"Course I do! When I bathe!" Cope replied with a smirk. He was used to other officers' complaints about his hygiene and it didn't bother him in the slightest. He considered personal cleanliness to be irrelevant for a soldier. What was the point of being clean and smelling like a whorehouse when your job is killing? Far too many officers smelled of toilet water and fussed over their finger nails for his liking. "*Call themselves soldiers*", he'd mutter to himself, "*they're just a bunch of pansies*".

"And when did you last see a bath?" Sinclair replied with an undisguised tone of incredulity.

"I had one last…let me see…yeh in February it was."

"Was that this year?"

"Course it bloody was!" said Cope, now getting a little rattled at Sinclair's persistence on the subject.

He laid back on the bed, put his hands behind his head and stared at the cracked and stained ceiling.

"Saw a real beauty at the station when I arrived," he said dreamily.

"Oh yes!" Sinclair was trying to read and was only half listening.

"She was seeing an officer off."

Sinclair made no reply.

"I used to know her too. Her name is Janetta Martin."

"That would have been Lieutenant Bird," said Sinclair without looking up from his book.

A sly grin crossed Cope's mouth. He couldn't believe his luck. He had found someone who knew her.

"You know her then do ya?"

Sinclair, resigned to the fact he wasn't going to be left in peace to read, laid his book down.

"Well I didn't know her as such. Didn't know her name was Martin for a start, but yes, I know her. Most everyone does. She was very popular at parties and balls. She always came with Lieutenant Bird though."

"She was his bit of stuff, was she then?"

Sinclair grimaced at Cope's crude way off expressing himself.

"I never heard anyone refer to her as 'his bit off stuff,'" he replied with distaste. "She's not a whore, Cope!"

"Isn't she now!" Cope muttered, half to himself. Then turning to face Sinclair, "I know more about her than you do I think. She may not sell herself but there're more ways than one to whore!"

Sinclair's ears began to turn red with anger, but he held his temper. He knew better then to get into a fight with Cope.

"Well from what I saw," he said in forced calmness, "she was a very nice lady."

Cope, realizing he was upsetting Sinclair and not having yet got all the information he wanted, mellowed his tone.

"Yes, she is a beautiful lady alright."

Sinclair cleared his throat and irritably reopened his book. He tried to continue reading but found he kept rereading the same sentence without taking it in. In truth, he had also been infatuated with Janetta as indeed were half the officers in the Regiment. But he knew he didn't stand a chance with her. Every officer respected the fact that she was Bird's woman and nobody was sure if, or when, Lieutenant Bird would be coming back to Woolwich. Cope's obvious interest in her made him feel sick to the stomach.

Cope watched him in silence for a couple of minutes to allow Sinclair's tension to mellow. When he felt the air had cleared somewhat he gently reopened the subject.

"Does she live in the barracks then?"

Sinclair dropped the book back on his chest and let out an exasperated sigh.

"No, she doesn't!" he replied irritably. "Only wives live within the barracks, as you well know."

"So Bird had a love nest outside. How cosy!" Cope sneered.

Sinclair didn't rise to the bait, but lifted his book and tried to read again.

"So you don't know where she might be then?"

Sinclair didn't reply.

"Just thought I'd look her up you know. For old times sake."

Sinclair reread the last paragraph.

"Haven't seen her in about five years. I just thought it would be nice to chat over old times."

"Try down by the Academy," Sinclair mumbled. He wasn't keen on helping Cope locate Janetta but he was getting tired of the conversation.

"The Academy?" replied Cope in a light tone that implied he hadn't really been listening. "She lives down there does she?"

"Somewhere near there, yes."

Sinclair made a third attempt at digesting the last paragraph in his book.

"Hmm! Right!" said Cope, as if he didn't care.

****

The sun was quite hot as Will walked along the edge of the parade ground on his way to the stables. It was a slow day as military routines went. He'd looked after nearly all his duties for the day and had decided to go and enjoy a little quiet time with the horses. Will had been a driver for most of his army life and had a natural affinity with the horses; when he felt the need, he would go and spend some time at the stables.

He turned into the stable yard, his boots making a loud clatter on the cobbles. His nostrils were suddenly filled with the familiar smell of horse manure. Several of the gates were open and some of the mares had their heads out sniffing the fresh cool air.

He walked into the largest stable where there were perhaps fifty horse stalls, half of which were occupied. He was looking for Frank Tibbs, the stable master to say hello, but he couldn't see him anywhere. He stopped in the middle of the stable and called out for Tibbs.

"Hello, Frank!" His voice echoed through the stables, but there was no reply.

One of the horses gave a snort, which attracted Will's attention. He walked over to the animal and put his hand out to stroke its cheek.

"Well you're a handsome girl, aren't you!" he said in a gentle voice. He rubbed the horse's nose and spoke to it quietly and softly.

The mare nodded its head and as Will stepped a little closer it nestled it's head against him, and he could feel that he'd made contact.

"Ah! You're a beauty an' no mistake, eh!"

As Will patted and stroked the horse it moved its feet from side to side in the stall and he thought he detected an odd movement in its hindquarters.

"Are you all right, lass, let's take a look at you?"

Will undid the latch and led the mare out of the stall. He stopped in the middle of the main corridor and ran his hands over the animal's neck and sides. The horse stood contented, waiting to be stroked. As his hand ran down the side of the horse's abdomen he came across a large sore area where spurs had dug in. It was much larger and rawer than should ever have been expected. The mare sidestepped away from his hand, as it approached the sore area.

"Whoa! Steady girl," he said as he looked at it more closely. "What son of a bitch has done this to you then, eh?"

He then walked the mare round in a circle and watched the hind leg. She was dragging it very slightly. Will doubted that there was any serious injury, but it was bothering her nonetheless.

"Hello, Will," came a voice behind him that he recognized as Frank Tibbs. "Thought it was you I 'eard a callin." Tibbs walked up to Will and stopped and leaned his elbow up on the horse's rump. "Beautiful animal that. She's the best-natured mare I've ever come across, she is!"

"Frank," Will nodded in greeting. "Someone's been riding her a bit hard though, don't you think?"

Frank grimaced. "Yeh! Right bastard he is too. Pushes her way too hard. Have you seen her sides?"

Will nodded as he patted the mare's neck.

"I've been given a salve to put on it by the vet, but it never get's a chance to heal."

"What about her hind leg?" asked Will.

"Hit a wall while jumping it. 'T was much too high for *Cannonade*. She should never have been taken over it."

"Cannonade?"

Tibbs chuckled. "Yeh, stupid name for her! She's too gentle to be called *Cannonade*." Tibbs ran his hand down her leg. "She had a nasty bruise but it's almost gone now. Still bothers her though!"

"She should rest it," said Will.

"You try telling Cope that," replied Frank, casting his head over his shoulder to indicate an officer walking through the gate.

"Who?" asked Will, but before Frank could reply he was interrupted.

"Hey, you there!" the officer bellowed, his voice echoing off the walls of the stable quadrangle and unsteadying the mare.

"Whoa, girl, " said Will softly to the mare.

"What do you think you're doing? Why's my mare out of her box?" Cope demanded.

"Just checking her sore leg, sir," said Will.

"What's wrong with her leg?" Cope growled.

"She's dragging it a bit, sir. I'm sure it's hurting her, sir. It should be rested."

"Rubbish man. A good run is what she needs. Loosen her right up."

"I wouldn't advise it, sir. Best to let her rest for a few days."

Major Cope looked hard at Will. His eyes narrowed, a slight smile crossed his mouth and in a controlled quiet voice that gave Will a cold chill down his spine, he said, "The mare is fine. I'm taking her out for a run, so saddle her up, lad."

The smile on the Major's face was so full of threat that for a second Will wasn't sure what he was dealing with. He hesitated but decided to press his point.

"With respect, Major, the mare should rest that leg."

"What's your name soldier?" There was still this sickly smile on his face.

"Rayner, sir!"

"Well Rayner, when I want your advice on horse care I'll bloody well ask for it. Now, you'll put the damned saddle on if you know what's good for you."

"I'll get it," said Frank, turning to the stall where the tackle hung.

"No you won't," snapped Major Cope, his voice now taking on a tone of less-disguised threat. Frank stopped in his tracks. "Well?" continued the Major, staring straight into Will's eyes.

"I'll get it," said Will over his shoulder to Frank.

"I knew you'd see it my way." A broad smile crossed Cope's pockmarked face as Will went to retrieve the saddle. He carried it over to the mare and threw it over her back. As he buckled the harnesses Will noticed the Major's boots.

"I see your wearing those star spurs, sir." said Will, goading Cope, "nasty things those, sir. Those sores on her side won't heal as long as you keep using them, sir."

"I'll wear whatever fucking spurs I like, Rayner, and I don't need no poxie bombardier to tell me how to treat my horse."

"Just concerned for the mare, sir," replied Will in as polite a manner as possible.

He'd barely finished attaching the bridle when Cope snatched the reins out of his hands.

"Out of my way, Rayner."

He mounted the mare and gathered the reins, but before moving out of the yard he leaned down, so that his head was closer to Will's.

"I don't like smart arse bombardiers. I'll remember you, Rayner. You see if I don't!"

Major Cope straightened up in the saddle and walked the mare out of the stables, leaving Frank and Will standing alone in the yard in silence. Frank puffed his cheeks out.

"So that was Major Cope," said Will in a rather matter-of-fact manner.

"Nasty piece of shit he is!" said Frank, "You shouldn't goad him like that, you know."

"I hate bastards who mistreat their animals, besides, what's he going to do?"

"Make your life bloody miserable if he gets a chance, that's what!" replied Frank as he took hold of a pitchfork and walked off towards a dung pile.

****

It had been a week since Major Cope had spoken to Sinclair about Janetta and this was his first opportunity to ride over to the Military Academy. It was only half a mile from the barracks and since it was a nice day he took his mare for a canter across the five hundred yards of Barracks Field, over Ha Ha Road that dissected the green and on to Woolwich Common Road.

Beside the Academy were streets of tenement houses and Cope wondered how he was to find which one Janetta lived in. He galloped off the field and crossed the road. On one of the corners stood the Red Lion Alehouse and he decided to ask the publican. If she lived nearby, perhaps she'd be known in the pub.

He tied his mare to a post outside the front door and went inside. He walked into the familiar fog of pipe smoke and the smell of stale beer. The floor was liberally sprinkled with sawdust and the room was badly lit; the sunlight barely filtered through the two front windows, which looked as if they had never been cleaned. There were about a dozen men in the bar, mostly locals and by the look of them Cope guessed they were road labourers. They all looked up at him when he walked in as if surprised to see an officer in this pub. Cope ignored them and walked up to the bar.

The publican stood behind the bar wiping a tankard with a disgustingly soiled cloth. He was a slight man in his fifties with long whiskers down the sides of his cheeks and very thin gray hair. He eyed Cope with suspicion.

"What'll it be?" he asked.

Cope threw a shilling on the bar, but when the publican went to pick it up, he slammed his hand down on it.

"Information!" he said in a soft velvety voice and his usual half smile on his lips, which told you he was dangerous.

"Well?"

"I'm looking for a woman,"

The publican's eyes flashed about the room as if checking his clientele. Satisfied that they were in good company he visibly relaxed and leaned across the counter, drawing closer to Cope.

"You've come to the right place, my dear sir," he whispered.

"A particular woman," Cope clarified through clenched teeth. "One by the name of Janetta Martin."

The publican face went pale and he cleared his throat and straightened up again.

"Don't know no Janetta Martin!" he said and went back to drying the tankard.

"She's about thirty, long dark hair, very pretty and she lives close by." He took his hand off the shilling and slowly pushed it forward with his finger.

The publican looked at the shilling, cleared his throat again and in a loud commanding voice he addressed the entire bar.

"Does anybody 'ere knows a Janetta Martin? Young, long dark hair and very sightly!"

A murmur went through the room.

"Yeh!"

The Major turned to see where the voice had come from. An unshaven man sat silhouetted against the grimy windows.

"I know 'er but I don't fink 'er name is Martin. Hangs out in Ordnance Place."

"And where," said Cope, "is Ordnance Place?"

"Two streets over," replied the shadowy figure, pointing towards the side wall of the bar.

Cope picked up his shilling, much to the annoyance of the publican and walked back towards the door. As he opened it, he flicked the coin towards his informant, who caught it in mid-air and slid it into his pocket.

It wasn't hard to find Ordnance Place. He was only a couple of streets away. He found it to be a small road, lined with two-storey, terraced houses. They were small, but comfortable looking and apparently well kept. They were most likely, he thought, residences for married soldiers. There were few people about. One or two women were out in front of their houses scrubbing the front step or cleaning the windows. Half a dozen children ran up the street chasing a ball and a tinker walked from door to door, selling ribbons and bunches of lucky heather.

He sat on his horse at the end of the street and wondered which of these people he should ask about Janetta. The ball bounced down the gutter, pursued by one of the scruffy boys and Cope was just about to call out, "hey lad!" when his eye was caught by one of the front doors opening on the other side of the street. A young woman stepped out carrying two enormous bundles, one in each hand. She closed the door behind her and walked off up the street.

"My god," muttered Cope to himself, "it's her."

He watched her walk up the street a little before he said, "walk on" to *Cannonade* and started walking the mare slowly up the street.

Janetta hadn't gone more than three houses before she stopped and banged on a front door. A portly woman opened the door and

Janetta handed one of her bundles to her. She waited while the woman fished in her apron for some coins to give to Janetta. Janetta pocketed the money, passed a couple of pleasantries with the woman and then walked on down the street.

Cope slowly followed, being sure to stay well back so that he wouldn't be too easily noticed, although that wasn't easy since he was the only horse rider in the street.

After a few houses Janetta stopped and tapped her knuckles on another door. Once again she handed her bundle to the occupant and received payment. This time though she didn't stay and chat, but said goodbye and started walking back the way she had come.

Major Cope remained seated on his horse as he watched her coming towards him. Surprisingly she didn't notice him until she was almost opposite, at which point she stopped suddenly and stared at him in astonishment. After a brief second or two she lowered her eyes to the pavement and walked on.

The Major pulled gently on the reins, turning the mare's head to face Janetta and walked her across the road to cut Janetta off. Janetta slowed her pace as she realized the Major was blocking her path. He dismounted and stood on the pavement in front of her, a broad grin on his face. He raised a finger to his temple in greeting.

"Good day, Mrs Martin. We meet again I see!"

"What do you want, Cope?" replied Janetta in a less than enthusiastic manner.

"Nothing at all I assure you. I was passing the end of the street when I saw you come out of your house. That's Mrs Martin, I said to myself, I'm sure it is."

"So you followed me down the street!" she said with a slight nod to indicate that she was ahead of him. She stood with her hand on her hip in a pose of defiance and stared at him.

"Just to be sure it was you before I said 'good day'."

Major Cope was doing his very best to act the pleasant gentleman but had never been able to pull it off. The more he tried the more he appeared to be a grovelling toad.

"I see," she replied. "Well good day to you! Now if you'll excuse me I have work to do."

"Laundering is no work for a beautiful lady like you. Times must be hard!" he said with a grin.

Janetta said nothing but stood squinting up at him with the sun in her eyes and a defiant look on her face.

"With Lieutenant Bird gone," he continued, "I suppose you have no income; nobody to support you. No protector!"

"I'm doing just fine, thank you," she replied quietly, trying not to lose her temper.

"I'm sure you are, my dear!"

"I'm NOT your dear!"

Cope ignored her interruption.

"I merely wish to point out that a lady such as yourself, having had the..." he thought hard about getting the word right, "protection of a colonel, a bombardier *and* a lieutenant, should be able to secure a better position than that of a...washerwoman."

Janetta felt the back of her neck becoming prickly as the anger rose up inside. How dare he bring up the Colonel again after all these years? What business had it ever been of his, who she slept with? His only interest was blackmail and even that wouldn't work now. It was all in the past and nobody gave a damn anyway. She wasn't in society any more and didn't foresee a day when she would ever be at a regimental ball again, so he had no hold over her. Cope could go fuck himself.

"As I said, I'm fine," snarled Janetta through clenched teeth.

At that moment three other scruffy looking women who also carried bundles, came across the road towards them. One called out to Janetta as she approached, "'allo Jan luv, who's your soldier boy then?" The other two giggled.

Janetta winced at the thought of Cope being her 'soldier boy' but was glad of the interruption. Cope looked up at the women and grimaced; he wasn't going to be able to finish what he had come to say. He looked back at Janetta and lowering his voice so that only she could hear, he half-whispered, "You deserve better and I can give it." Then looking back to the three women who had now joined them, he tipped his cap to them, and smiled broadly, "Good day to you, ladies." All three smiled enthusiastically and with no regard for modest behaviour, openly prepared to flirt with Major Cope.

Cope, however, had no intention of getting into a flirting match with a cluster of washerwomen and so nodded to Janetta and remounted *Cannonade*.

"Your not orff are yers luvvy?" said one of the three, who Cope thought, would have been quite comely once, "stay an' 'ave a little chat why don't yer?"

"I'm afraid I must take my leave, ladies. Good day to you all," and he turned his mare's head away from them and rode slowly up the street, not looking back.

CHAPTER 20

Theft

The following week was not a good one for either Will or Janetta. The weather had turned unseasonably cold and rainy, which deepened Janetta's already low mood. She hadn't seen Will for several days, and she was missing Timothy Bird. Meeting up with Cope again had also left her feeling angry and a little scared. She had spent the last couple of years putting the memories of Cope out of her mind. His return had not only shocked her, but had brought back all the memories of the night of murder, John's mental decline and untimely death. She found herself consumed with anger. Her chest became constricted and her whole body ached with tension.

Then on Wednesday her period started.

The realization that she wasn't pregnant had left her feeling quite depressed. Under normal circumstances she should have felt a great relief at not being pregnant, since she was unmarried. She had however, become used to the idea. Deep down she was proud to be carrying Timothy's child, but it was also a very useful means of encouraging Will to marry her in the belief that it was his.

She had been on the verge of telling him she was pregnant, and was looking forward to an early wedding, but now she had no leverage. She would have to rely on her charm and manipulative skills to get him to the altar and this left her feeling exhausted.

With a kitchen full of other people's soiled linen and the rain running in rivers down the windows, Janetta felt alone and apprehensive about the future. She no longer felt beautiful and in her funk she let herself go – not bothering to brush her hair or even have a decent wash. She was beginning to feel deeply depressed and no longer had the desire to leave the house.

Will's week hadn't been much better. His run-in with Cope at the stables had far-reaching consequences. No matter what he did or where he went, Cope was always there to snipe at him or find reasons to give him some extra dirty job.

To make matters worse his own commanding officer seemed to do nothing to get Cope off his back. Whenever Major Reynolds inquired why Will was doing whatever it was he was doing, Will would say, "orders of Major Cope, sir," and Reynolds would simply raise one eyebrow and say, "I see…well carry on."

On Tuesday Major Cope had Will greasing a gun carriage just because he was having a quiet smoke break. On Wednesday he didn't see Cope approaching and failed to salute quick enough, so Cope had him whitewashing some stones that lined the path to the officers' mess.

Every day Will found that Major Cope accused him of some trivial offence, and he was becoming really fed up with the situation. But he had been in the army long enough to know that you just had to take the abuse and ride it out. Sooner or later either he or Major Cope would get posted and the problem would solve itself. Will knew that complaining would get him nowhere. Major Cope was a superior officer and he was acting within his rights.

What angered Will the most, however, was that every evening when he arranged for leave to go outside the barracks to visit Janetta, Cope would catch him before he left and get him doing something.

Will was becoming dejected about not being able to see Janetta and he swore that nothing would stop him on the weekend. In anticipation of seeing her, he sent a message to her saying that he would visit on Saturday evening.

****

On Saturday afternoon, Major Cope rode out of the barracks in the rain and made his way across the green towards Janetta's house. He had decided not to be put off this time, but would be sure to have his audience with Janetta. He arrived at Ordnance Place in the rain and tied his mare to a post at the curb. He rapped his knuckles against the peeling paint on the front door and listened as a pair of feet walked down the bare boards of the front room towards the door. A latch drew back and the door opened.

At first Janetta's expression was welcoming but when she saw who it was on her doorstep, the smile left her face and she attempted to slam the door shut again. Major Cope stuck his boot in the door to prevent it closing.

"Mrs Martin," he said, kindly but forcefully, "we really do need to talk."

Janetta hesitated before slowly opening the door a little way and staring at Major Cope through the opening.

"I don't think we have anything to say to one another," she said, with a sharp edge.

"I think we do!" Cope insisted, "I just need five minutes of your time, that's all, and I'm getting rather wet out here."

Janetta eyed him scornfully for a second or two and then, against her better judgment, she opened the door. Major Cope stepped inside, removed his cape and shook the rain off it.

"Ah! That's better!" he said as he walked across the room and stood with his back to the fire to warm himself. A whistle started blowing in the kitchen and Janetta half-turned towards the sound but didn't move.

A smile crossed Major Cope's face, "The kettle's boiling I hear. Good, I could murder a cup of tea."

Janetta clucked her tongue under her breath.

"You'd better sit down then," she said coldly before turning and leaving the room.

Cope looked about the room as he waited. It was a modest room containing a few pieces of furniture that looked as if they were once fairly good quality. There was a red velvet chaise lounge but the velvet had worn badly where people had sat. A writing bureau stood in the corner and heavy maroon curtains with gold tassels hung at the window. The room was clean but rather masculine and Cope wondered whether it was Bird's old house.

He turned to face the fire so that he could dry the front of his trousers. The fireplace was a dark wooden structure with a few modest carved ornamental pillars and built-in mirrors. The mantel was covered with a white linen cloth that hung down a few inches over the edge and finished with a delicate lace fringe. The 'woman's touch', Cope thought. On the mantel stood a clock, a small wooden elephant and a brightly coloured vase with nothing in it.

His eye was attracted to the clock by a small chain that was draped over a wooden finial on its top. Cope took the chain and ran it through his fingers. Most of the chain was hidden behind the clock and when he pulled on it, he was surprised to find a man's fob watch on the end. He looked at it for a moment or two trying to decide whether or not he recognized it. He opened the back and there was the inscription to Janetta.

A sardonic grin curled his lips. He recognized the watch he had taken from the Colonel's room. He had kept it in his trunk and nobody knew he had it, so how had it come to be in her possession?

It now made sense to him. Janetta had indeed been involved in his apparent murder and had subsequently ransacked his belongings for the books and found the watch. So she knew. No wonder she didn't want to have anything to do with him. She was guilty of plotting his murder and here was the evidence.

Sounds of clattering teacups came from the kitchen. He quickly slid the watch into his pocket and turned his back once more to the fire before Janetta returned with the tray.

She laid the tray on a side table and sat down on the chaise.

"Mrs Martin," he began in a soft fatherly voice, "...how is your husband, by the way?" He guessed John Martin was out of the picture because he had seen her kissing Lieutenant Bird at the station.

"Dead!" said Janetta curtly.

"I'm sorry to hear it!" He did his best to sound sympathetic. "I know you've had a long and...respectable...association with the Regiment."

Janetta looked at him with suspicion.

"There was the Colonel of course..."

Janetta glared at him with such ferocity that he couldn't help noticing and so he moved on quickly.

"...Then your husband, Lieutenant Bird and now, alas, you're on your own."

Janetta took a breath to interrupt him, but he didn't give her the chance.

"Many of the officers in the mess have talked about how they miss you and wish you were back amongst them. If you would like to return to the company of regimental society, I can make it possible."

"I'm not alone," protested Janetta.

“Oh!” replied Cope feigning surprise, assuming she was referring to Bird. “I wasn’t aware Lieutenant Bird was coming back.”

“He’s not! I’m with Will Rayner now, so you don’t need to worry about me.”

“Will Rayner!” Cope exclaimed with some surprise. “Another bloody bombardier. Oh, you can do much better than that, my dear.”

Janetta jumped to her feet, overwhelmed by rage.

“And I suppose you’re referring to yourself,” she hissed at him.

Her fury had little effect on him. Indeed it excited him, and convinced he could overcome her wild behaviour with a show of masculine dominance, he grabbed her by the arms and pulled her tightly to him and kissed her hard.

Janetta gave out a muffled squeal as she found herself smothered by his stubbly face. She struggled to pull herself free of him, her face red with fury.

“I wouldn’t come to you if you were the last piece of slime in the pond!” she spat.

Cope felt his face reddening. He didn’t care if she called him names, but her repulsion made him angry.

“Who do think you are? Missy!” he replied in his most dangerous whisper. “You’re no better than a whore. Do you think you’re too good for me?”

Janetta pulled free of his grasp and turned towards the door.

“Will’s twice the man you are, Cope!” It was intended to be her parting shot as she showed him the door, but Cope reached out and grabbed her, pulling her back to him. He didn’t know what he was intending to do. He hadn’t planned any strategy; his temper was now taking over. There was no intention of committing rape, as he didn’t fancy facing a court martial, and he was sure she wouldn’t hesitate to accuse him. Yet, in his rage, he found his hands grabbing for her and finding her breasts. Janetta let out a yell and spun round to face him, thereby forcing his hands away from her bosom. He closed his arms about her and tried to kiss her again and as he did so he felt Janetta’s knee come up into his groin.

He gave a sharp inhale as he felt that wave of pain, that all men dread sweep through his groin and spread through his abdomen. His knees buckled and he sank to the floor, his hands between his thighs gripped tight by his legs as he swooned in agony.

Before he had a chance to recover, Janetta had grabbed his greasy hair in her fist and was pulling him mercilessly towards the door. He let out a yell as he felt his hair being yanked from his skull, and his left hand grabbed Janetta's wrist as if to pull her off his hair. It was a futile attempt because pulling her wrist only hurt his scalp more. Unable to stand up from the pain in his testicles, he was forced to hobble after her like an ape.

Janetta paused only long enough to open the front door before pulling him out into the street, where he collapsed in a heap on the pavement. She then grabbed his cloak off the peg and tossed it out into the rain with him and then slammed the door shut.

"Bitch!" he moaned. "Bloody bitch!" He took a few deep breaths fighting the impulse to vomit, and then the pain suddenly faded away leaving him with a wet and clammy groin. He picked himself up, still sweating and feeling as if he should walk bow- legged.

"Rayner!" he hissed through his clenched teeth. "So she fancies that bastard does she!"

He picked up his cloak and carefully remounted his mare. He was going to have to find a way of getting rid of Rayner, and as he slowly walked *Cannonade* up the road an idea began to form in his mind.

****

By Tuesday the weather had cleared up. The parade ground was covered in large puddles and the surrounding grass was soft and waterlogged. The sun now tried to shine as if it really was summer and by the afternoon the puddles were beginning to steam.

Major Cope, his uniform neatly pressed and his boots shining, strode across the compound. The clatter of his boots echoed off the barrack walls, his swagger stick was tucked under his left armpit and his right arm swung in a determined marching fashion. He looked every bit the perfect soldier. His chin was high, his shoulders back and his demeanour one of self-assured composure.

He entered the administration block and clumped his rhythmic way down the corridor. His boots made such a din on the tiled floor that you could have heard him coming a mile off and yet nobody seemed to take any notice, it was after all a familiar sound.

He stopped outside the anteroom that led through to the Brigadier's office. He had no idea why he had been summoned and felt a little apprehensive about the interview. He stopped in front of the adjutant's desk, cleared his throat and announced himself.

The adjutant who had been feverishly writing in a ledger, looked up from his task, obviously displeased at being interrupted in mid-sentence.

"Ah! Yes, Major Cope! The Brigadier is waiting for you."

He stood up, walked out from behind his desk and opened the door to the Brigadier's office. Major Cope noticed that he didn't knock first. After a brief interlude he came out again.

"You may go straight in."

Major Cope walked through the door with his swagger stick and cap in his left hand leaving his right hand free for a smart salute as he stamped to attention in front of the Brigadier's desk. The Brigadier winced at the sound of his boots stamping.

"Yes, yes Major. Stand at ease."

Brigadier Hanson was an elderly man with tight curly hair and large, silver gray whiskers down his cheeks. Cope noticed his fingernails had been polished and just a hint of a sneer crossed his mouth. He hated soldiers who pampered themselves like dandies.

The Brigadier looked frail, although his eyes were bright and his voice was strong and firm, giving Cope the impression he had a sharp, lively mind. He sat back in his chair and surveyed Cope for a moment or two before leaning forward again and picking up a piece of folded paper.

"If there's one thing I really dislike, Major, it's having to deal with civilian's complaints about men in my Regiment."

Cope's eyebrows narrowed themselves into a frown. "Sir?"

"I've had a complaint from a Mrs Martin," the Brigadier's spoke slowly as if he was trying to compose his thoughts, "she said that you visited her and made improper suggestions to her and acted in a most ungentlemanly manner!"

Cope raised his eyebrows and looked as shocked and surprised as he could manage.

"Sir, I…I don't understand."

"Do you know this lady, Major?"

"Well…yes sir! But she's not the kind of woman you can rely on sir. She's a bit of a…well you know, sir." Cope was squirming and he knew he wasn't doing too well.

"I know this lady very well, Major," cut in the Brigadier, "and she seemed a very good sort to me. Friend of Lieutenant Bird I believe and the Lieutenant wouldn't have anything to do with a lady who was…'unreliable' was it?"

"Sir, I just meant that she is prone to exaggeration. I didn't mean to imply…"

"Quite Major!"

Cope gave up trying to protest and went quiet.

"Do you deny visiting her, Major?"

"No sir! We had old business to discuss sir. Business that went back to the Plymouth days under Colonel Wentworth, sir. And… and… she was totally unreasonable in her refusal to talk to me, sir. She…attacked me, sir and threw me out of her house. Now that wasn't the act of a lady was it, sir?"

The Brigadier sat with a slight smile on his face.

"She attacked you, Major? A big fellow like you! And then she threw you out of her house? She sounds quite formidable!"

Cope felt as though the Brigadier was now beginning to have sympathy for him, and seeing the smile on his face, was encouraged to play the victim.

"Sir," he said, glancing furtively over his shoulder for fear of being overheard, "She kneed me in the nuts, sir!"

The Brigadier started to laugh and Cope relaxed in the belief he had won the Brigadier's sympathy. His hopes quickly faded though as the smile suddenly dropped from the Brigadier's face.

"And what, I wonder, did you say to Mrs Martin to cause her to react in that way, Major?" His voice had now become icy and Cope found himself on the defensive again.

"Nothing, sir!" The Brigadier stared at him so that Cope felt obliged to speak further. "Well I merely asked if I could be her…protector, now that the Lieutenant had left town. What's wrong with that, sir? That's not such a serious matter for her to complain about, is it, sir? …I mean if that's all she can complain about…" Cope knew he was rambling and almost welcomed the Brigadier's interruption.

"Ah! But it's not, Major!" He unfolded a piece of regimental stationery that he had been revolving in his fingers throughout the interview, and began to read his adjutant's notes.

"The day after Major Cope's visit," he frowned at the handwriting, "I noticed that my gold fob watch, that had been hanging on the mantel clock, was now missing. Since Major Cope has been my only visitor, I must assume that he had taken it…she goes on to request that we search your kit and retrieve the watch, because it has great sentimental value."

Cope stood in front of the Brigadier's desk with his mouth hanging open. He'd half-expected this, but he had to play the innocent. He shook his head in a show of stunned disbelief and his lips moved as if to protest, but only gurgling sounds came out. The Brigadier sat and patiently waited.

Finally Cope found the right moment to blurt out his innocence.

"Sir, I would never steal from a woman, sir! The very thought is abhorrent to me."

"I'm relieved to hear it, Major," said the Brigadier in an unconvincing manner. "Unfortunately in a case such as this I cannot ignore it."

"But, sir, I wasn't her only visitor! That's ridiculous! I know for a fact that she's been seeing Bombardier Rayner."

"She says you had been her only visitor since she last saw the watch, Major!"

"She would say that, wouldn't she? She's got it in for me, sir. I guarantee Rayner's got it."

The Brigadier pursed his lips. A deep frown crossed his forehead.

"Then I have no choice. I will have to search both your kits."

Cope silently breathed an inner sigh of relief.

"You can search my kit, sir, you'll find nothing."

"Horrocks!" yelled the Brigadier. The door opened and the adjutant came in. The Brigadier didn't wait for any formalities from Horrocks.

"Horrocks, ask Major McCreedy to join us in Major Cope's quarters."

"Yes, sir!" snapped the adjutant and the door closed behind him.

Ten minutes later they were all assembled outside Cope's quarters.

Cope opened the door and led the way in. The Brigadier stood by the door while Majors McCreedy and Horrocks started politely, turning over Cope's belongings. His bedding was turned upside down and his kitbag emptied on top of the mattress. His spare boots were shaken out and the room was searched for hiding places. There was no sign of the watch and throughout the performance Cope watched stoically.

"Very well!" said the Brigadier as the two searchers came to the end of their hunt. "This has given me no pleasure, Major Cope, but I'm relieved to find nothing."

"Thank you, sir," Cope replied in a soft almost humble manner. "And Rayner, sir?"

The Brigadier looked annoyed that he had to be reminded of his second search.

"Yes, yes! We're on our way, Major."

When they arrived at the barrack block where Will bunked, Will was standing outside talking to Frank Tibbs, who had been walking a mare about the grounds. As the Brigadier and the two Majors approached, Will and Frank stood to attention and saluted. The Brigadier hardly seemed to notice but walked right past them and snapped, "Rayner! Follow me!" as he went by.

Will and Frank exchanged looks of concern before Will fell in behind the party and went inside the block.

"Which is your bunk, Rayner?" said the Brigadier coldly.

"Third on the left, sir." replied Will.

The Brigadier gave a nod to Major McCreedy who went to the bunk and began his search.

"We've had a complaint, Rayner,"

"Sir?" replied Will as he watched in horror while his kit was turned out.

"There's been a watch stolen from Mrs Martin, Rayner. Do you know anything about it?"

Will looked at the Brigadier in astonishment. He'd never stolen anything in his life and the idea that Janetta could have accused him of it left him utterly bewildered.

"No," he said shaking his head, "no I don't!"

"Sir!" Major McCreedy stood up holding a gold fob watch dangling on a chain from his fingers.

Will couldn't believe his eyes.

"Tha…that's not mine," he stammered.

The Brigadier gave him a withering look of disappointment then took the watch from McCreedy. He opened the back and read the inscription.

"It's Mrs Martin's alright! Well! What do you have to say about this Rayner?"

"Sir, I swear! I had nothing to do with it! Somebody must have planted it on me, sir!… I wouldn't steal from my own girlfriend, sir!"

Brigadier Hanson stared down at the unhappy pile that was once Will's clean and tidy kit and let out a low, private moan.

"Bombardier Rayner, I'm arresting you for the theft of this pocket watch."

The Brigadier desperately wanted to believe Will. He'd known Rayner when they were out in India as had Major Horrocks. He knew him to be a steady and reliable soldier, if somewhat lacking in ambition. He also had a deep mistrust of Cope. Deep inside he knew Cope had stolen the watch and planted it on Rayner, but couldn't ignore the evidence. He had to see it through no matter how distasteful the affair was to him.

"I'm sorry Rayner!" then turning to McCreedy he gave a slight jerk of the head to indicate that Rayner should be taken out.

"Come with me, Rayner," said McCreedy, not unkindly.

Will, in a state of shock, followed Major McCreedy out of the barracks. As he passed Cope he thought he could see just a hint of gloating on his dark face, and wondered how it was that Cope was involved in this set up.

Major Cope followed Will out of the barrack block leaving the Brigadier alone with the adjutant. Brigadier Hanson turned slowly to Major Horrocks, and in a quiet voice said, "Horrocks, go and inform Mrs Martin that we have found her watch and that we have arrested Bombardier Rayner. Oh and Horrocks, take careful note of how she reacts, something's not right here!"

"Yes, sir!" said Horrocks before he too left the barracks.

CHAPTER 21

Court Martial

Janetta sat in her chair in front of the fire and stared into the flames. It had been unseasonably cold over the last couple of days and so she had lit the fire. It was pleasant watching the flames flicker on the coals and the warm glow comforted her. Sitting there reminded her of her childhood in Tywardreath when the family would huddle in front of the fire and drink hot tea, bread on long-handled brass forks toasting in the flames. But as pleasant as those memories were, they could not block out the distress she felt.

Her past, having returned so rudely to haunt her, and her realization that she wasn't pregnant had left her feeling alone and depressed. Added to this, her chequered past was now having serious repercussions on Will's career and that was bothering her a great deal. Her first husband had suffered because of her and she wasn't going to let it happen again. As she watched the flames, she pondered over the men who had come to their deaths because of her. There had been Faversham, trampled to death by a horse; Cope, clubbed, thrown overboard and left to drown in the sea, not that she cared about him, and John, who had died of a bad heart but whose death had been hastened by remorse. The only men who had been kind to her were the Colonel, Lieutenant Bird and now Will Rayner. She'd lost the first two and she was damned if she was going to lose Will.

Janetta remained staring into the flames and wondered about her options. Lieutenant Bird must give evidence on Will's behalf. He knew about Cope's blackmailing efforts and could give character references, but he was so far away and would he be willing to get involved?

The afternoon had turned to early evening, the light fading quickly because of the rain clouds.

Janetta went over to the Lieutenant's desk to light a lamp. The wick gave a little hiss as the flame took hold of the mantel, and as she replaced the glass chimney a pool of light made the corner of the room glow. She went into the kitchen and filled the kettle with water from a jug and placed it on the range. When she went back into the front room the pen and ink were the first things she looked at.

How she wished that she had learned to read and write.

****

Early next morning, Janetta hurried to the railway station. She'd had only one thing on her mind all night and she had slept badly. She had to get a letter to Timothy Bird.

Outside the station she found the usual collection of hawkers and vendors in their usual spots on the pavement. Hot potatoes, meat pies, lavender, lace, bread and a host of other salesman crowded and jostled for space in front of the station entrance. But Janetta was looking for a specific service and she soon found it.

Sitting quietly in a row against the wall were three men and one woman. They sat behind small portable writing desks and looked expectantly at each person who walked past.

Janetta was immediately drawn towards a middle-aged man who stood out from the others. He looked like a "*toff*" who had fallen on hard times. He wore an expensive gray suit and bright blue waistcoat and cravat that were now shabby and smeared with stains. One pocket in the jacket was half torn off and the satin lapels were dull and covered in ash and small burn holes from a badly-lit pipe. His shoes, that once sparkled and gleamed, were now gray and coming apart at the seams.

He looked up at her. His dark brown eyes sparkled and a bright smile engulfed his unshaven cheeks. His battered top hat was perched jauntily on one side of his head, and as he raised his head to look at her, she feared it might actually fall off.

"And how may I be of service to you, my dear?" he asked in a soft, refined voice.

Three sheets of paper hung from the front of his desk displaying samples of his penmanship. Janetta studied them carefully. The letters were all perfectly formed and the lines evenly spaced. Here and there he had included a flourish above or below a letter that gave the document an impressive and official look. Janetta could not read too much of it but thought they were the most beautiful letters she had ever seen.

"How much?" she asked.

"Well let's see," he said, "do you want me to write an official letter, legal perhaps? Or is it a friendly greeting letter?"

Janetta thought for a moment. It was about a legal problem but it wasn't to a lawyer.

"It's to a friend," she replied.

"Long or short?"

"Oh short I think…yes quite short."

"Well then, how about tupence?"

Janetta nodded her agreement and the man indicated that she should sit on a small stool in front of his desk. She arranged herself comfortably on the stool and looked at the other scriveners to her left and right. They paid no attention to her. A professional courtesy between them prevented them from eavesdropping on people's private letters as they were dictated. Satisfied with her choice, she relaxed a little.

The gentleman reached into a portfolio and lifted out a clean sheet of white paper and placed it on a blotter on his desk. He dipped his pen into a small inkwell and gently wiped the nip against the side of the jar to remove excess ink. Then he sat and waited for her to begin with his hand perched above the paper.

The sight of his hands momentarily diverted Janetta. He wore brown knitted gloves with no fingers. They were strangely at odds with his suit. They were the one piece of clothing he wore that was not original. These were the gloves of a poor street vendor not a wealthy man. They were working gloves and told of his hours sitting out in all weathers freezing. His white, ink-stained fingers protruded from the gloves and looked weathered and cold.

"To whom am I addressing this letter?" he asked patiently.

"To Lieutenant Timothy Bird, The Regiment of Royal Artillery, Portsmouth," she replied.

"Portsmouth is a big town with many batteries. Can you be more specific?"

Janetta was surprised he knew that but then realized that he was in a military town and probably wrote many letters for soldiers.

"No, I don't really know where he is," she said.

"Oh well I'm sure it'll find him. So what do you want to say?"

What was she to say? How did you write a letter? She didn't want to appear to be so ignorant. She had trained herself to speak well and could always dress up and act as a lady, but she knew her literacy would quickly demonstrate her lack of education. The date, yes she would start with the date.

"10th September 1884" she said.

The man smiled as if amused by her beginning. He neatly wrote the date at the top of the page and then looked up at her, waiting for the next line.

"Dear Timothy," she continued.

What if someone else should read the letter? Perhaps Lady Dawlish would be in the room when he received it and would not be too pleased to see a familiar letter from another woman. She reached her hand out to stop him writing.

"No…Dear Lieutenant Bird,"

That's better, she thought. Keep it formal; it's regimental business. This should be a letter from a woman writing on behalf of a soldier in his command.

"I am writing to inform you that Bombardier William Rayner has been charged with stealing…"

"Wait!" he said as he caught up with her words. He finished getting it down. "Right, go on."

"With stealing," Janetta continued, "my watch, but I know for a fact that it was taken by Major Cope."

"By Major Cope," the scrivener's voice went higher to interrupt her as he wrote. "Yes? Carry on."

"Major Cope has been harassing me in the most unpleasant manner for a couple of weeks in an attempt to reopen the 'old issue' that you will remember."

He finished writing and read back to her what he had put down on paper. That's pretty good, she thought, nobody would know what it was about from that. If pressed, Timothy could simply say it was regimental business and leave it at that. The part about her being harassed by Cope, however, was sure to be enough to bring him back.

Janetta indicated to him that there was more. He refilled his pen.

"I will give evidence myself but feel that your help would be so much more valuable. Please come back and help us."

"Ha hum," he coughed to interrupt her again. "Back… and…help…us," he read as he formed the letters.

Janetta pressed on.

"Bombardier Rayner's career depends upon it and Major Cope should not be allowed to get away with this. Yours truly, Janetta Martin."

Janetta felt the letter to be almost too formal, but she was sure that Timothy would read between the lines and come rushing back.

The scrivener blotted the ink, folded the letter and addressed it to the Lieutenant.

"A most interesting letter, my dear," he said as he handed it to her, "That'll be tupence if you please. I hope everything goes well for you."

With any luck, she thought, he'll be back here in two days and then our problems will be solved. She still felt nervous but at least she had set the ball rolling that would make everything right again.

****

Black storm clouds slid across a slate sea and white caps danced upon the waves in *The Sound*. The leaves rattled in the trees as the branches bent before the wind and slashing rain bounced on the stone battlements of Fort Picklecomb.

Fort Picklecomb wasn't a large place. It was just one of a series of gun emplacements guarding the approaches to Portsmouth harbour against enemy ships. Its battery of guns pointed out into *The Sound* with their great barrels mounted on wooden trucks. These could be turned by means of a single half-circle rail cemented into the battlement. Today was particularly noisy in Fort Picklecomb. It was gunnery practice and the crews were being timed as they loaded the great barrels, aiming at floating targets in *The Sound* and firing. Officers screamed commands at the crews and men hurried at the double to reload; their faces were bent away from the driving wind and their woollen uniforms were heavy with rain.

Lieutenant Bird sat in his office and winced every time a gun fired. He was a good soldier, but had never got used to the ear-shattering blast of an artillery piece. The noise had been relentless for over half an hour and his head was beginning to split. He looked out of the rain-streaked window and watched the gun crews on the wall. Normally the guns would be engulfed in great clouds of smoke but the wind blew so hard that the smoke was driven away over the fort in a matter of seconds. The crews looked soaked to the skin. It was the foulest weather to be out on the ramparts but ideal for gunnery practice. It meant that the crews had to learn to work as a team when there was rain or sleet in their faces, and that they had to compensate for the wind when aiming the guns.

The door opened and a corporal came in from the adjoining office carrying a handful of letters.

"The post, Lieutenant," he said rather casually as he dropped a couple of letters onto the table.

"Thank you, Hawkins."

He picked up the letters and studied the writing on the front. One was an official army dispatch but he knew what it contained so he threw it to one side. The other was more intriguing. He didn't recognize the hand so he opened it immediately. He studied the letter for several minutes, reading and rereading it in an effort to comprehend what Janetta was telling him.

Major Cope was dead. He was drowned in *The Sound* several years before. He knew the 'old issue' referred to Cope's attempting to blackmail Janetta over her affair with Colonel Wentworth, but he couldn't believe Cope had come back from the dead.

"How is Bombardier Rayner involved?" he said aloud.

He found himself feeling oddly jealous of Rayner. He had no right to, he knew that, but he still had strong feelings for Janetta and found it hard to think of her being involved with another man. Perhaps he was just a bystander who came to her aid when Cope was bothering her, he thought. Then again perhaps he was much closer than that. After all Janetta was a beautiful woman. Other soldiers were bound to want to have her. He remembered Bombardier Rayner. He was a good man. He'd help him if he could, if only for Janetta's sake.

Lieutenant Bird had tried to put Janetta out of his mind. He missed her terribly but he had a family duty to honour the promise to marry Lady Dawlish. He could understand why; she had far more money than he did, but their first meeting had been a great disappointment to him. Lady Dawlish had grown up to be a skinny, petulant creature. She was spoilt, bad-tempered and had a disagreeable habit of talking to the servants in a condescending manner. Compared to her, Janetta was a goddess and this letter, although very formal and completely lacking in any warmth or regard for their past affection, brought back intense longing. He decided he would go to her immediately, but to do so he had to acquire permission from the garrison commander.

He threw his cape round his shoulders and ventured out into the rain. The guns hammered on and even in the wind and rain, the air was full of the smell of cordite. He lowered his head against the wind, pulled his cloak tight about him and walked as fast as he could across the courtyard. A gunnery sergeant screamed at one crew who had badly missed their target while another crew worked feverishly to reload a short-barrelled howitzer. The gun loaded and primed, the crew knelt in firing position and the gunner pulled the firing line.

Lieutenant Bird was only yards from the commander's office when the howitzer exploded. With a brilliant flash and deafening roar the howitzer's barrel split into several shards of hot flying metal. The blast lifted the gun crew high into the air. Their bodies torn and bloody, were thrown about the battlements like rag dolls. Chunks of black barrel flew through the air making an eerie whirring sound before bouncing off the stone walls of the officers' quarters and skidding across the cobblestones. Small chunks of metal fell from the sky and clattered about the courtyard. Part of a man's arm crashed through the window of the adjutant's office.

Lieutenant Bird had no time to be aware of what was happening. A sharp pain went through his ears as the blast overwhelmed him and something hit his back as he was lifted off his feet and flung to the far side of the courtyard. The last thing he remembered was the wall of the storehouse coming straight at him.

There followed a terrible quiet. For a few seconds the wind stopped and the rain fell gently and quietly. The storm seemed to hold its breath in shock. Then the wind suddenly howled again and the rain slashed the ramparts even harder than before. Very slowly the other gun crews began to stand up, dazed and bewildered. They looked around the battery in stunned disbelief. The last of the smoke from the explosion was being blown over the wall. The remains of the gun had blown off its shattered truck. The howitzer crew were scattered in a thirty-foot radius around the broken gun. Some looked strangely untouched while others were terribly mangled with limbs blown off. None of them moved. One man was cut into three pieces, his body parts thrown against the wall of the adjutant's office, and across the courtyard lay the body of Lieutenant Bird, face down in a pool of blood.

****

Will's trial was over in almost indecent haste and the outcome was, sadly, predictable.

Janetta had arrived at the barracks on the afternoon of the 24th September 1884 to meet with Lieutenant Smyth, who had been given the task of defending Will. After a short discussion it was quite apparent that the Lieutenant was neither optimistic about Will's chances of acquittal nor enthusiastic about defending him. The evidence was clear and it was his word against that of an officer. Janetta informed him that Lieutenant Bird would be coming to give evidence and pleaded with him to try and get a postponement until he arrived.

"Brigadier Hicks has come in from the Third to sit as an outsider, and therefore impartial judge," said Lieutenant Smyth with some discomfort. "He has made it quite clear that he wants to get it over with as quickly as possible, because he has a dinner engagement in town that he cannot miss."

"*Great!*" thought Janetta. "*He don't give a shit about Will, only about his dinner!*"

The trial began at three that afternoon, and Janetta had to wait fretfully in the corridor until called to give evidence. After about twenty minutes the door opened and an orderly asked her to come in.

The court was surprisingly small. She had imagined something far grander. The room was about twenty feet wide by thirty long and had whitewashed walls. Along one side were three large windows, which made the room very bright and airy. At one end was a long plain table behind which sat the three judges. In the middle she recognized Brigadier Hanson; to his left was the very elderly Brigadier Hicks who had a particularly sour expression and to his right sat another, much younger officer she didn't know.

Either side of the empty chair was a desk facing inwards. Behind one sat Lieutenant Smyth with Will in his best uniform beside him. Will looked very smart but had the countenance of one who knew he was condemned and couldn't understand why he had to sit through this farce. Behind the other desk sat an officer Janetta presumed was the prosecuting officer.

To the back of the room was a couple of rows of chairs but they were mostly empty. Only Major Cope sat there looking extremely smart, confident and, Janetta thought, rather smug.

"Come in, Mrs Martin, and take a seat," said Brigadier Hanson, directing her to the lone chair in the middle of the room. "You understand that this is a court of law and that you must tell the truth and nothing but the truth."

"I do!" she replied nervously.

The prosecuting officer stood up and approached her with the fob watch in his hand.

"Mrs Martin, is this your watch?" He held it out to her. Janetta turned the watch over to reveal the engraved back.

"Yes sir, it is."

"And you reported it stolen?"

"Yes."

"In fact you reported that Major Cope had stolen it, didn't you?"

"Yes sir, he did!"

"Why are you so sure, Mrs Martin?"

"Because he was in my house, uninvited, and after he'd left I discovered the watch missing."

"Would it surprise you to know, Mrs Martin, that when Major Cope gave evidence he swore he'd never seen the watch before?"

"No!"

"No! Mrs Martin and why is that?"

"Because I know Major Cope, sir. He'd sell his own mother to save his skin."

"Oh so you don't like Major Cope, Mrs Martin! But you do like Bombardier Rayner?"

"Yes!"

"Perhaps you like him enough to lie for him, Mrs Martin?"

Janetta flushed with anger and jumped to her feet.

"I don't have to lie for him, he's innocent and Major Cope is a snake and a liar!"

"Mrs Martin!" yelled Brigadier Hicks over her outburst. "Major Cope is not on trial here. Please be seated and answer the questions calmly."

Janetta reluctantly sat down after glaring at Cope, who sat motionless with a slight smirk on his lips. The prosecuting officer paced the floor in front of the judges.

"Mrs Martin…when was the last time you saw Bombardier Rayner?"

Janetta shrugged.

"A week… maybe two."

"Did he come to your house?"

"I suppose he did," she could see where this line of questioning was going.

"And can you positively swear…now you're under oath, Mrs Martin… that you can remember seeing the watch after Bombardier Rayner's visit."

"*The bastard!*" Janetta thought. The truth was, she couldn't swear to that. The watch was tucked behind the clock and she couldn't remember when she had seen it last. The whole idea that Will had taken it was ridiculous. Was she to deliberately lie under oath to save Will? Her mind raced. If she lied was there any conceivable way they could prove it? She took the chance.

"Yes! The watch was there all right."

"Really, Mrs Martin? Then how did it come to be the in Bombardier's possession?"

"I dunno!" Janetta was becoming anxious and her carefully controlled diction was beginning to fall apart. "Bu' he didn't do it!" Then addressing the judges directly, "Lieutenant Bird is coming here to give evidence, sir. He knows the truth!" This was stretching things a bit, she knew, because Timothy couldn't possibly know the truth being in Plymouth; he did know Cope however.

"Mrs Martin," cut in Brigadier Hicks again sounding somewhat impatient with her. "We cannot accept evidence from somebody who is not here."

"Then can you postpone the trial until he gets here?" pleaded Janetta.

Brigadier Hicks turned red in the face, "certainly not young lady! Besides the evidence speaks for itself. The stolen item was found in his belongings. We're wasting valuable time on this case in my opinion." He turned to the other two judges and conferred with them for a few seconds.

Brigadier Hanson looked pained when he addressed the court.

"Thank you, Mrs Martin."

Janetta stood up and went to sit down on one of the chairs at the back, taking good care not to sit too close to Major Cope.

"The court will now take a short recess," continued Hanson.

The three judges stood up and walked out of the room. Everybody else relaxed except Janetta and Will. Will took the opportunity to catch Janetta's eye and he gave her an appreciative smile. Major Cope's smugness became insufferable and Janetta fought back the temptation to go over to him and plant her knee in his groin again.

It seemed no more than two minutes before the three judges returned and took their seats again. They all looked very grim. Brigadier Hanson, looking distinctly uncomfortable, looked hard at Will who stood beside Smyth.

"Bombardier Rayner, you have been found guilty of theft as charged. You will receive," he paused as if debating within himself the merit of the punishment, "fifty lashes and be reduced to the rank of private."

Brigadier Hicks looked at Hanson with disgust; he had obviously voted for a much heavier punishment.

Janetta gave a little cry of dismay. It wasn't possible. The government had abolished the 'cat' back in '81, yet the army was still using it. The punishment wasn't legal, but what went on behind the barrack walls was out of sight to the public and the army had always put great store in the corrective power of flogging.

Will was led away. He glanced back at Janetta as he went, but she had no opportunity to speak to him. Major Cope stood up and walked passed Janetta on his way out.

"Dear, oh dear!" he said quietly as he passed her. "Such a pity! But if you will get involved with these enlisted men!"

"Go to 'ell, Cope!" she spat.

Out in the corridor the small group was disbanding. Brigadier Hicks strode passed her on his way to his dinner engagement and

Cope, Smyth and the prosecuting officer were all walking away together in animated discussion. Only Brigadier Hanson remained in the corridor.

"Oh, Mrs Martin," he said calling her back as she started to leave the building. She stopped and allowed the Brigadier to catch her up.

"Brigadier Hicks will be leaving in the morning, and I see no hurry in carrying out the sentence. Rayner can sit it out in the cells for a few days."

Then he looked her straight in the eye, and as if changing the subject completely, he continued, "It would be good to see Lieutenant Bird again, would it not Mrs Martin? Good day to you!"

He strode off across the parade ground towards the officers' mess, leaving Janetta feeling stunned and a little bewildered.

CHAPTER 22

Rescue

That afternoon Janetta was allowed to see Will in his cell. The guard surprised her by being an unexpectedly kind man. He was heavily built and very muscular with a scarred, battered face, the undoubted result of numerous brawls, and a moustache that drooped down both sides of his mouth. His eyes told you he was not a man to be trifled with but his voice was soft and reassuring.

"This way, miss. Don't you fret now; we'll look after 'im."

Janetta followed him in the wake of his body odour along a cold, damp corridor. He spoke as he led the way without looking back at her.

"Damn shame if ya ask me. We all knows Rayner didn't do it! Plain as the nose on ya face it is!"

"How do'ya know?" asked Janetta, in the faint hope that he may have new evidence.

"Stands ta reason it does. We knows Rayner. He ain't no thief. You can smell a set-up. An' this smells bad, so it does. But don't you fret none." He stopped and turned to face Janetta, "We'll look after 'im."

"How?" asked Janetta with some scepticism. What could a jailer do?

"A whipping is quite an art, see miss. It's all in the wrist action. You can make it appear as if your really hurting a man without doing too much damage, or you can make the whip cut deep into the back to expose the ribs. It's all in the wrist ya see."

Janetta shuddered at the obvious pleasure he took in relating the fact.

"Nar..." he continued, "we'll give 'im a few gentle strokes, maybe a dozen. Gotta look good mind 'cause it'll be in front of the regiment. And then we'll enter fifty strokes in the book."

"Officers can count you know!" she interrupted.

"It's all right miss," he said tapping the side of his nose with his finger, "I've had my orders. These officers are going to forget 'ow to count." The corner of his moustache twitched into an almost imperceptible smile. "Terrible lack of education amongst the officers there is. Mind you, Cope won't like it if we goes easy! Still wot can 'e do?"

Janetta gave a weak smile as the jailer opened the cell door.

Will was sitting on a cot in his shirtsleeves, his back against the side wall of the cell. He looked like a scolded schoolboy with his head in his hands, but seeing Janetta, he jumped to his feet and threw his arms around her.

"I didn't do it I swear, Jan," he pleaded.

"I know! I know!" whispered Janetta as she placed her fingers against his lips to stop his protests. They hugged one another in silence for a few moments, Will squeezed her just a little too tightly.

"I didn't do it," Will whispered into her ear.

"Yeh I know! It was definitely Cope. You're not to blame and Major Hanson knows it Will."

"Then why am I in here? If he knows I'm innocent why didn't...?" Again Janetta interrupted him.

"There was no evidence to prove Cope did it, but I'm hoping it will be coming Will. Major Hanson is going to hold off with the ..." she couldn't bring herself to say 'whipping', "he's waiting for Lieutenant Bird to come."

A frown crept across Will's forehead as he struggled to comprehend what she was saying.

"Bird? What's 'e got to do with this? And why was Cope harassing you? What's he to you anyways?"

"Will, Will!" Janetta tried to stop his flow of questions, "One question at a time, there's a luv."

Will sat back down on his cot, "Yeh well, I'm not sure what the 'ell's going on 'ere. What's special about this watch anyway?"

"The watch was left to me in somebody's will that's all, and Major Cope stole it before I was able to inherit it."

"How did he know about it?"

Janetta sighed. She really didn't want to go into too much detail.

"Because he knew the deceased and went through his belongings before the lawyers could account for all his possessions."

"Who was the deceased?"

"Colonel Wentworth back in Plymouth. I used to work for him."

"Oh," said Will rather weakly. He wasn't sure he understood but there did seem to be an explanation, so for the time being he accepted what he was being told. "And Lieutenant Bird? Where does he come into all this?"

"He knows Cope. He knows what he's like and he knows the history of the watch. He can convince Major Hanson that it was Cope and not you who stole it."

"Can't prove it though, can 'e? The evidence still points to me."

Janetta couldn't deny that, but she felt confident that Bird's testimony would sway the already believing Hanson.

"I don't think anything Bird could say would change the situation," continued Will.

Janetta didn't know what else to say. They just had to wait for Lieutenant Bird; if he ever came.

"Well look!" she said, "if Bird does fail to convince Hanson, the jailer has assured me that they will go easy on you. Nobody believes your guilty and nobody wants to see you suffer for something you haven't done."

Will snorted and turned his head away from her, "This is the bloody army! Nobody 'goes easy' on anybody! 'Specially with the 'cat'"

Janetta remained silent. Will was in no mood to be optimistic. She sat beside him and gently stroked his upper arm in an attempt to show her solidarity, but it was pitifully little help and Will kept his face turned away from her.

The door opened and the jailer who showed her in coughed to announce his entrance.

"Time, Miss!" he said kindly. "Don't worry we'll look after 'im."

"Go on, you go. I'll be fine," said Will, as he struggled to give her a smile. He still wasn't sure about this watch story she had given him, but for now he would let it go. They hugged and kissed one another before Janetta turned away and followed the jailer back out into the corridor. As the door closed behind her, she glanced back at Will. He was sitting back down on his cot with his head leant back against the brick wall so that he could stare at the ceiling. She gave a little wave with her fingers but he wasn't watching.

****

Janetta fretted over the next few days. She'd visited Will every day but their meetings were increasingly strained. They just talked over the same points; Will morbidly relived the injustice of his situation. Janetta was unable to break his sense of hopelessness and each day she wondered what the point of her visits was. She didn't seem to be helping him much.

She couldn't believe that the army was prepared to flog Will despite that fact that it had been outlawed; she couldn't understand why Lieutenant Bird hadn't come to his rescue. Had he turned his back on her now that he was married? Perhaps he was willing to help her but not her new boyfriend. The only bright side to the whole affair was that Brigadier Hanson seemed unwilling to condemn Will and was delaying the punishment. If only Lieutenant Bird would give some indication of his intentions. She decided to get another letter off to him.

It was heavily overcast that day and although it was only the middle of the afternoon, the room was dark and oppressive, casting a shadow over her mood. She leant on her elbows and propped her chin on her hand. What was she to say in her letter? She was part angry, part concerned over his silence and she wasn't sure what to say to him.

Her contemplation of the letter was disturbed by a knock on the front door. She tutted at the interruption, pushed her chair back, and peered out of the front window. She couldn't believe her eyes for there, on the doorstep, stood Lieutenant Bird. She let out a little girlish scream and ran to the door.

Her fingers fumbled on the latch with excitement as she tried to get the door open. Without a care for what the neighbours may think, she launched herself at Lieutenant Bird, throwing her arms about his neck and kissing his cheek and face. Lieutenant Bird stumbled backwards and gave a harsh moan of pain.

Janetta suddenly let go of him and stepped back in shock. Lieutenant Bird staggered to regain his footing. He leant precariously on a cane and one sleeve of his tunic hung empty; his one arm was tied up in a sling. Under his helmet his head was bandaged.

"My God! What happened to you!" she gasped.

The Lieutenant smiled at her reassuringly, "May I come in?" he asked.

Janetta took him by the arm and helped support him as he limped, stiff-legged, into the house. He dragged his leg to the sofa and grimaced as he sank into it. His eyes widened for a second and he let out a long suppressed gasp as his back nestled into the cushion.

"Ah, that's better!" he said; looking up at Janetta's horrified expression he smiled and asked, "I could murder a cup of tea!"

"Tea? Tea! Yes of course!" stammered Janetta as she backed out of the room, still unable to take her eyes off him.

"What happened to ya? How did'ya get that way?" she called from the kitchen as she spooned tea into the teapot.

"Oh! A gun exploded; but I'm fine, really."

"A gun exploded!" exclaimed Janetta with alarm. "You could have been killed!"

"I was lucky. Several were killed."

Janetta continued to pepper him with questions about his wounds as she made the tea. His answers were, for the most part, short and uninformative and Janetta soon found herself talking with little or no response. When she re-entered the parlour she found him asleep on the sofa.

She placed the tea on a side table and sat in her armchair beside the crackling fire. How peaceful Timothy looked. She watched him with great pleasure and a feeling of relief at seeing him again swept over her. Everything would be all right now that he was back. He would talk to Brigadier Hanson and tomorrow Will would be exonerated.

Lieutenant Bird's mouth had fallen open and gentle snores filled the room. He looked so much at home sprawled out on the sofa with his feet stretched out across the carpet and his head laid back on the cushion. But for the bandages he looked as if he'd never left.

Janetta warmed her hands by clasping the teacup and stared lovingly at her reclining Timothy Bird; her beautiful Lieutenant; her love and her comfort.

Lieutenant Bird gave a sudden loud snore and woke himself up with a jerk. He looked bleary-eyed at Janetta, not quite sure, for a second or two, where he was.

"Oh! I'm sorry!" he said as he pulled himself stiffly up into a sitting position. "I must have dosed off!"

"It's alright. Ya looked so comfortable I didn't want to wake ya. Your tea's still drinkable if you'd like it."

The Lieutenant grimaced as he reached forward to take the cup.

"It's good to be back in this room with you again," he said. "Like old times."

Janetta smiled at his remark but changed the subject.

"How is Lady Dawlish?" she asked.

The Lieutenant's face took on a serious, almost pained look. "She's fine," was all he volunteered on the subject. "But how are you? You look as beautiful as ever."

Janetta smiled and lowered her eyes in feigned embarrassment. "I've been fine too," she replied.

"And what about this Bombardier Rayner?" he asked.

Janetta wasn't sure whether he was asking about his trouble or their relationship. She decided to keep it business.

"Oh yes, I do hope you can help him. He's innocent of the theft. It was that bastard Cope." Her anger and desperation was creeping into her voice and the Lieutenant couldn't help notice it. "Can you talk to Hanson? I know he'll listen to you. Can we go in the morning?"

"It's OK, I've already spoken to him."

Janetta hesitated as she took this in.

"You've spoken to him?"

"Yes."

Janetta leapt out of her chair and landed heavily on the sofa almost on top of him, causing him to wince with pain.

"Oh sorry!" she said realizing what she'd done. "Are you alright?"

He gritted his teeth as the pain went through his ribs but smiled and nodded, "Yes I'm fine. Still have twinges when I move suddenly though."

"Oh you poor thing! My wounded soldier!"

Bird tried to laugh but it caused another painful spasm.

"Well don't keep me in suspense. What did Hanson say?"

"Rayner's off the hook."

Janetta clapped her hands and flopped hard against the back of the sofa, throwing her head back so that she yelled at the ceiling. "Thank God!"

Lieutenant Bird winced again at the jolt.

"Actually," he continued, "it wasn't hard. Hanson had already decided to release Rayner. I just confirmed what he already suspected – that Rayner is an honest man and Cope is a bastard."

"Oh ya are a darling aren't ya?" she said as she leant over and kissed him on the cheek.

"You like Bombardier Rayner, don't you?"

His tone was not accusatory or threatening, yet Janetta thought she detected a hint of jealousy.

"'E's been good to me…yeh I like 'im."

She wanted to continue by telling him that she loved him more, but decided against it. Timothy Bird was married now. It was all too late. Besides she had a good man; a man who would never amount to much but who was kind, gentle and would support her. She was surprised to find that she was becoming quite content with her new man; for the first time in her life, she was prepared to settle down without aspiring to become a lady.

"Are ya 'ungry, Tim?" she asked. Her voice relaxing back into its natural Cornish brogue. There was no need to put on her posh airs with Timothy Bird. He knew her too well and she felt cosy and comfortable with him.

"Umm. Just a bit. Just something light."

"I could do something with eggs. Poached? Scrambled?"

Lieutenant Bird smiled contentedly at Janetta. He felt at home again, and no matter what Janetta's relationship with Rayner was, for now they were together again and it felt reassuring.

"Scrambled would be very nice."

Janetta gave him a little peck on the end of his nose and leapt off the sofa. Lieutenant Bird winced again.

"I'll be right back. Don't go away."

She had almost got as far as the kitchen when she stopped, turned round and asked, "Did Hanson say when he would release Will?"

Lieutenant Bird strained his neck to look over the back of the sofa. "Tomorrow! Not 'til tomorrow… he has to 'fix' the paperwork first!"

Janetta tried her best to make the next question appear unrelated to the first.

"You'll stay tonight I hope?"

"If you'll have me…yes!"

"Good," she said and disappeared into the kitchen.

****

Next morning, Janetta awoke to feel the warmth of the sun on her face. She opened her eyes and squinted in the intense glare coming through the window. She groaned, turned her head away from the light and pulled the sheet over her face. She stretched her arm out to the side, hitting a warm body in the bed.

"Ah! Careful!"

"Oh shit! Sorry!" exclaimed Janetta as she jumped with a start into a new day.

She brushed the hair out of her face, rubbed her sleep-filled eyes and peered through the bright sun that illuminated the room. Beside her, Timothy Bird lay on his back, the sheets pushed down around his waist exposing his chest. White bandages had been wound tightly around his ribs, a reminder of his fragile condition.

"Didn't hurt you, did I?" she asked.

"No I'm fine."

He turned his head to look at Janetta and a self-satisfied smile crept over his face.

"It feels as if I've come home, Jan,"

"How long can ya stay?" she whispered.

The smile left his face.

"I've got to go straight back I'm afraid…I don't want to Jan, but I must get the ten o'clock train. I'd much rather stay here with you."

Janetta gave him an understanding smile and kissed him. Secretly she was relieved to hear him say he was leaving. She loved him dearly and having him in her bed again felt natural and comforting, but Will would probably be released today and he was sure to visit her. The last thing she wanted was to have to explain Timothy's presence in her house.

Her beloved Lieutenant had done his good deed and now it was time for him to leave.

"I'll make some tea," she said as she slipped out of bed and pattered across the cold wooden floor. The Lieutenant watched her leave and looked admiringly at her bare buttocks as she threw on a gown and left the room.

CHAPTER 23

Decisions

Will wasn't released immediately, which greatly relieved Janetta. She didn't like the idea of him languishing in his cell longer than necessary, but Lieutenant Bird missed his morning train and hung around the house well into the afternoon.

It had been wonderful for Janetta seeing her old lover again and she had been genuinely grateful for his help, but she was now anxious that he shouldn't bump into Will in her home. She wasn't sure how understanding Will would be at finding the Lieutenant in her house. The fact that it was actually the Lieutenant's house was even more potentially embarrassing. Every minute of the day was torment for her, as she expected Will to bang on the door at any moment.

Brigadier Hanson had postponed releasing Will until after Major Cope had left the barracks. He had found a convenient excuse for transferring Cope to Ipswich and was glad to be seeing the back of him. Cope however, strongly objected to being transferred before he had witnessed Will's punishment because the prospect of seeing Janetta's boyfriend whipped filled him with a great deal of satisfaction. He didn't give a damn about Bombardier Rayner of course, but it was a wonderful way of getting at that 'stuck-up bitch'. Hanson apologized to him with as much politeness as he could summon, but assured the Major that he was urgently needed in Ipswich and had to leave immediately.

Hanson allowed himself a slight smirk of satisfaction after Cope had left his office. How wonderful it was to be able to pull in old favours when you really needed them. A dispatch to an old friend in command at Ipswich had suddenly produced an urgent need for a major in that barracks.

Will was released at four o'clock in the afternoon after Major Cope had left for the station. His rank was reinstated and a note of complete exoneration made in his record. It was the first time in over ten years of service that Will had detected a genuine desire in a commanding officer to apologize. He walked out of the cellblock and marched smartly across the parade ground with his head held high. All he could think about now was seeing his beloved Janetta. He had done a lot of thinking while in his cell and had come to a serious decision. He would go straight to her house and ask her now, while he had the courage.

For Janetta it was much too close a thing. The Lieutenant said his good-byes at four thirty after she had spent a good part of the afternoon trying to hold her nerves together. Every time she opened her mouth she had to think hard about not sounding too anxious to get rid of him. It was as if every innocent comment came out of her mouth sounding as if she wanted him to leave. "*Either he's thick and doesn't pick up on my edginess*", she thought, "*or he really doesn't care about embarrassing me*". He was simply in no hurry to go.

When they finally stood on her doorstep and said their good-byes, Janetta, for just a couple of minutes, was genuinely sorry to part with her Lieutenant again and she held on to him and kissed him long and hard in full view of the neighbours.

Less than half an hour later Will was knocking on her door and the neighbours were treated to a second show of doorstep passion. Curtains across the street twitched. Some neighbours gave a small smile of admiration while others tutted and raised their eyebrows.

It was good to have Will standing in her doorway. He looked tired yet elated at his newfound freedom.

"Will! You're free! Wot a relief!" said Janetta as she backed into the parlour, pulling him in behind her by his arms.

Will grinned at Janetta's obvious relief and a warm glow came over him. Her parlour was not luxurious, but it was a far cry from a cold tiled prison cell. He unbuttoned his tunic and flopped into the chair, barely cold from when the Lieutenant had been sitting in it.

He gave a long exhale and looked up at Janetta, who had sat beside him on the arm of the chair.

"Well! Put the kettle on, woman!" he said in mock command.

"Bloody 'ell!" exclaimed Janetta. "Not out five minutes and act'n as if ya own the place!"

Will's face transformed itself into a beaming smile.

"Yoooou!" she said, giving him a small punch on the shoulder.

"Ow!" Will grasped his shoulder as if in real pain, "'aven't I suffered enough?"

"Yeh I reckon!" she said as she got off the chair. "A couple of days rest and relaxation, more like!" She disappeared into the kitchen leaving Will grinning in front of the fire.

It felt so good to be free again; to be back sitting by Janetta's grate and watching her through the door to the kitchen. He felt at home and the barrack life that he had become so used to was now becoming tiresome. He'd had enough of army food and army beds. He wanted to settle down in a softer home; a home that contained those small feminine touches such as life-sized china dogs, aspidistras and crocheted antimacassars to keep hair grease off the back of the chairs.

He took out his pipe and contentedly began to take tobacco from his pouch and stuff it into the bowl.

He would talk to her as soon as she re-entered the room. He was surprised how nervous he felt at the prospect of asking her, and he rehearsed his words in his mind.

Janetta came into the parlour with the tea tray. As she approached the table she saw to her horror that Lieutenant Bird's best brown leather gloves were laying in full view on the chaise longue. Had Will seen them? How could he not? And yet he seemed engrossed in lighting his pipe.

She stepped in front of the chaise longue, deliberately blocking Will's view of the gloves, and placed the tray on the table.

"Will you pour?" she said to distract him.

As Will leaned forward to pick up the teapot, Janetta reached behind her and moved the gloves to one side and then shoved a pillow on top of them before sitting down. Will hadn't noticed the subterfuge, being preoccupied with the teapot.

"Jan, I have something to ask you," he said nervously.

Janetta didn't miss his uneasiness, and guessed what was coming. Her heart skipped a beat.

"Jan, sweetheart…I," his hand was shaking and Janetta feared for her best china teapot.

"Come 'ere I'll do that," she said taking the pot from him.

Will was glad to be relieved of the job, but was thrown off stride by the interruption. It now seemed that Janetta no longer listened, but concentrated on pouring the tea. He tried to press on.

"Jan, I was wondering."

"Do you want sugar?"

"Wot?"

"Sugar?"

"Oh, yeh ta! Look, Jan."

"Biscuit?" said Janetta, holding a plate out to him.

"Ta!" said Will and he took one from the plate.

"Jan, I really must talk to you seriously."

"Right! Go on then dear, I'm listening."

"Well, Jan, it's like this."

"Milk?"

Will stopped in mid-sentence and starred at Janetta, "Er...yeh, yeh!"

Janetta continued to pour milk into the tea. He was losing his nerve because of the interruptions and found it difficult to get started again.

"You was saying?" prompted Janetta.

"I...I..." he hesitated.

"Yes?" Janetta found his stuttering attempt at proposal quite amusing but she wasn't going to prolong his agony any further.

"I... was wondering whether or not we should...?"

He took a swallow and felt beads of perspiration forming in his scalp. The words were sticking in his throat and although he desperately wanted to ask her, his mind seemed to be shutting down.

Janetta placed a reassuring hand on his knee.

"Yes?" she asked softly, trying to coax it out of him.

Will took a deep breath.

"I was wondering...whether we shouldn't...ya know..."

"Marry?"

"Live together."

There was a pause. Janetta slowly sat back on the chaise and her face started to flush. Her face registered a mixture of shock and disappointment. Will sensed an impending storm and he too sat back in his chair as if trying to put a little more distance between them.

"Live together?" said Janetta, her face starting to contort.

"Well," said Will weakly in an attempt to smooth the coming storm, "I just thought it would make economic sense to pool our resources."

"Pool our resources!" screamed Janetta, her face now bright red with anger. "I'll give you, 'pool our resources'"

Will clutched his teacup closer to his chest in the hope that she wouldn't hit him while he held her best china.

"You bleedin' bastard," she screamed so that the whole street could hear. "A girl likes to think her bloke would marry 'er." Curtains twitched again.

"I will, Jan, I mean I really do want to, but…"

"But wot!"

"Well I ain't got permission to marry ya yet…"

Janetta stood up threateningly.

"And besides," he pressed on, "don't ya think we should try it first an' see if we're compatible…about the house an' that? Ya know!"

Janetta pointed to the door, tears of rage appearing in the corners of her eyes.

"Get out! Go on… get out!"

Will nervously put his teacup down and backed out of her front door.

"Bloody bastard!" she yelled after him as he retreated down the street. "I ain't a whore ya know."

Janetta noticed several curtains move across the street. Furious, she glared at the windows in the houses opposite.

"Well, what are you all looking at then," she screamed before going inside and slamming the door shut.

Inside, Janetta leant against the door and slid down it until she was sitting on the floor, and there she burst into tears and beat her fists against the floorboards.

It wasn't the idea of living together that angered Janetta; in fact plenty of people lived out of wedlock. It was frowned upon but was so widespread that nobody passed judgment on those who did. What upset her the most was that she was not getting any younger. She was scared of becoming an old maid. She could see herself as a middle-aged woman, still trying to snare some unwary officer into marriage and being scorned and laughed at by all her married neighbours. She needed a protector now, while she still had the looks and body to attract someone.

The Lieutenant, whom she had loved for a couple of years, would never marry her. He had a wife from his own class; a wife he didn't love. Janetta's dream of marrying well had come to nothing. The closest she'd been was to Colonel Wentworth and that had fallen through. No, she had to settle for a lowly soldier; someone of her own class, penniless and without prospects. There were plenty of good men in the Regiment, but she recognized in Will a good soul who would treat her well and take care of her when her looks had faded. So why didn't he ask her to marry him? What was he afraid of?

****

Will did nothing for a week. He made no attempt to contact Janetta for fear of discovering that she no longer wished to see him. He knew she was mad at him but was it permanent? How angry was she? He couldn't tell and was not up to facing her. He lost all interest in what he was doing and moped about the barracks like a lovesick schoolboy.

"For fuck's sake go talk to 'er!" said Steve, a burly Irishman whom Will had recently befriended. They were polishing the reins on a caisson. "No point sulking. She won't come to you ya know! Women don't come apologizing to us men folk. We have to go to them real penitent like. Then you'll be forgiven an' all will be alright. You see!"

"I knows it! But I don't think we should marry just yet and she'll talk me into it…assuming she still wants me."

"Cause she bloody wants ya. She's just doing 'er girly thing. Makin' you feel guilty. Anyway why don't you want to marry the lass?"

"I do…not just yet a while. But I don't want to lose 'er neiver."

"Well then ya betta get ya ass round her 'ouse an' stop pissing about, Will boy. Be firm wi'er an' she'll come round, yer see if she don't."

Will polished the reins harder. He knew Steve was right but hated the prospect of going cap in hand to Janetta.

****

On Friday night Janetta sat at her favourite table in the corner of the King's Head. She kept company with her portly neighbour Patty Cummings. She didn't really enjoy Patty's company very much, she was a silly woman who giggled at the slightest provocation and talked of nothing but local gossip. If there was one talent that Janetta lacked, it was gossip, and conversations with Patty were a trial.

Patty was in full flow describing how Mrs Wood had fallen out with Mrs Peterson over a non-returned milk jug, when Will walked into the bar and stood by the door looking around for Janetta.

Janetta caught her breath.

"And then Mrs Wood called Mrs Peterson a name I'm sure I cannot repeat, and oh my dear, you should 'ave heard the commotion." Patty's high-pitched voice set Janetta's teeth on edge.

"Allo, Jan."

Will stood in front of their table, his uniform freshly cleaned and pressed. His buttons polished, his cap at just the right angle on his head. He was shaved and smarter than Janetta had ever seen him.

"Blimey who's this then?" exclaimed Patty. There was nothing unusual in seeing a soldier in the pub but they were rarely as well turned out and as sober.

Will gave Patty a slight, yet polite nod of recognition before turning his gaze on Janetta.

At first she didn't know what to say to him. All she knew was that he looked so handsome and manly. She felt herself melting before him.

"Jan, I must talk to you."

"Oooo," squeaked Patty, and she began to flush and giggle behind her hand.

"I want to talk to you too," said Janetta.

"Aren't you going to introduce me?" asked Patty as she stared up at Will, starry-eyed.

"Good night, Patty," said Janetta as she stood up to leave.

"Ohhh, It's not fair. Not fair at all," whined Patty.

Will gave her a kindly smile. "Nice ta meet ya," he said as he held out his elbow for Janetta to take.

"Oh," melted Patty, "likewise I'm sure."

Will led Janetta out of the bar, feeling Patty's eyes on his back the whole way.

Out in the street they instinctively walked towards Janetta's house. They had gone several yards in silence before Janetta suddenly stopped, turned to face him and, cutting the air with a short sharp hand gesture, she blurted out, "Look! All right! You can move in. We can do the…living together thing!"

Will didn't say a word, but reached out for Janetta's arms and pulled her forward into a long and passionate kiss. Several people were forced to step off the curb to walk around them, and a coal merchant sitting on his wagon behind a dray, gave a long low whistle.

CHAPTER 24

Janetta
8th December 1886

"What are you doing this afternoon Rayner?" Major Tomlins unenthusiastically addressed Will without looking up from a munitions requisition.

"Drilling my new crew, sir. They're not up to speed yet. Most of em don't know which end of the gun is the dangerous end, sir," replied Will as he stood to attention in front of the Major's desk.

The Major didn't overly impress Will. He was one of the younger officers and he wore his uniform with an air of fashionable indifference. Even his hair was far too long for an officer. He had it styled into a series of waves that looked as if they were lapping at his forehead. But it wasn't just his hair that made Will cringe. It was also his polished fingernails, his habit of wearing his fob chain on the outside of his tunic and his sparkling blue eyes that conveyed cunning as well as charm.

If this wasn't enough to unsettle Will, there was also the fact that Major Tomlins made no attempt to hide his admiration of Janetta; admiration that Will suspected was built more on a foundation of lust than respect.

"Good, they need shaking up!" The Major still hadn't looked up to face Will.

It was unusual to be called in to see Major Tomlin. If anything had to be said, it was usually passed down the ranks to a junior officer to do the telling. A summons usually meant trouble.

Five minutes before, Will had been standing behind one of the training gun emplacements, watching his crew struggle to reload the massive gun in a quicker time than they had achieved before.

Will stood with a stopwatch in his hand and a critical eye on the men who sweated, despite the chill in the air.

"Crawford, you bloody idiot!" he screamed, as the hapless gunner bumped into his comrade and made him drop a dummy shell cradled in his arms, ready to load into the open breach. "You pass the other side, how many times have I got to tell ya!"

"Rayner!"

It was Lieutenant Prescott who had just strolled up beside Will to watch the fiasco. He tried to conceal a smile as he witnessed the two men jostling to pick up the shell and get past one another.

"Got your hands full with this lot eh!" he said, "still if anyone can knock 'em into shape, you can Rayner."

"Do my best, sir, but they've got…" His eye had gone back to the gun crew, "No! No! For fuck's sake, Samuels," he yelled, raising his eyes to the sky, "they've a lot t'learn yet, sir!"

The Lieutenant chuckled under his breath, "they certainly have!"

"Samuels you're an idiot! What are ya?" screamed Will at a scrawny ginger-haired youth who had just tripped over the semi circular track the gun swivelled on when being aimed.

"An idiot, sir. Sorry, sir."

"Can Perkins take over here?" asked Lieutenant Prescott. "You're wanted in Major Tomlin's office."

Will hesitated. What the hell was he wanted for?

"Well can he?" pressed the Lieutenant.

"Er, yes, sir!" replied Will, then turning to Bombardier Perkins."Take over my crew will ya Dick. Try not to let them kill 'emselves."

Perkins, who had been sitting on a caisson shaking his head with amusement at the shambles around the gun, jumped down and strolled over.

"It'll be me pleasure, Will. A right miserable lot we 'ave 'ere and no mistake!"

Will grinned at Perkins as he walked past them and then the smile faded from his face.

"What does the Major want, Lieutenant?"

"I don't know! Go an' find out, man!" his voice had an edge of frustration with the question.

"Sir!" said Will as he did up the top button of his tunic, tugged it down smooth at the waist and turned to march smartly towards the administration block.

****

"That girl of yours, Rayner…Janetta is it?" said Tomlins, reluctantly raising his eyes from the paper in his hand.

"*You know dammed well it is*," thought Will.

"Yes, sir!"

"It appears she's having a baby, Rayner," said Tomlins in a tone that Will found infuriating. The casualness in his voice spoke of a slow, almost bored, realization of the fact that Janetta was pregnant. This was a fact that nobody in the barracks could be unaware of since she had been waddling around for the last couple of months and leaning backwards with her hand on her back, in an attempt to balance the weight of her swollen womb. Perhaps, thought Will, it was a tone of disapproval he detected in the Major's voice. Perhaps he was about to get a lecture on the 'moral responsibility of fatherhood'; a lecture he'd had before and could well do without just now.

"Yes, sir," replied Will without any effort to disguise the fact that he had to humour the Major.

The Major's eyes opened wider and he stared directly at Will as if finally waking up from his boredom of the interview.

"Well, man?"

"Sir?"

"She's having your baby," the Major's voice grew sharply in volume. Will didn't move. "Well get the hell out of here," he yelled, "you're supposed to be with her."

"Oh! I see! Thank you, sir!"

Will's heart started pounding in his chest. Panic was setting in as the realization of what the Major had said dawned on him.

The Major sighed and shook his head.

"Dismissed Rayner."

"Thank you, sir."

Will stamped his right foot, saluted and performed a smart 'about face' before leaving the room. Once outside he broke into a run with no intention of stopping until he had reached Janetta's house on Ordnance Place.

****

Janetta wasn't happy! Months of carrying this child in her belly had long since lost its appeal. Constant back aches, always being drained of energy and fighting every morning to do up her boot laces, had left her with the distinct impression that this young visitor had outstayed its welcome. When her water broke it was a blessed relief. The long wait was over. Now all she had to do was 'drop the kid' and she could get on with her life.

She hadn't wanted to get pregnant. Well, that wasn't quite true. It was a way to ensure her man would marry her, if he didn't suddenly disappear. It was inevitable of course. Sooner or later she was bound to conceive, living with a man full-time, and she felt confident that Will was the sort of man who would stand by her; so far he had done so. She had never been so sure about the steadfastness of all the fancy officers she'd known, with the possible exception of Lieutenant Bird but even he had chosen to marry within his class.

No, all things considered, she wasn't so sorry to have been pregnant, but she had never seen herself as a mother. She never 'billed and cooed' over other people's babies as other women did. Nor did she feel any primeval urges to procreate and mother some small, smelly and constantly demanding child.

She had always been her own woman, independent, and the idea of motherhood had, until now, stood in her way of advancement. What gentleman officer would look twice at a woman with a child? No man wished to play second fiddle to his mistress's baby – especially if it belonged to someone else. No, she'd been better off remaining childless if she'd wanted to catch a good man.

But she had her man now. Not a gallant highbred officer; that dream had long faded. Her man was as common bred as she was, but he was good to her and as far as she could tell he would be constant; she hoped and prayed he would prove loyal.

"Where the 'ell is 'e?" she screamed as another contraction swept through her abdomen and her body went into a spasm.

"*Typical bloody man,"* she thought. He liked planting the seeds alright, but when it comes time to harvest he don't want to know. "*No, this is woman's work, this is*", she thought, "*he's happier down the pub congratulating himself on having successfully duplicated 'imself. He's proved his manhood, now it's up to me to prove my womanhood.*"

"Bastard!" she screamed as the sweat ran into her hair and made it stick to her face. "Fucking bastard! Where the bleed'n 'ell is 'e?"

"'E'll be 'ere soon, luvvy, don't yu fret none now," replied Mrs Nora Hawkins, the midwife.

Janetta couldn't abide Nora Hawkins and wished the regimental doctor would come. Will had asked him to be present when Janetta gave birth. It wasn't usual, but they were friends and Dr Willis liked Janetta.

Nora busied herself with a bowl of lukewarm water and a couple of reasonably clean towels. She was a beanpole of a woman in her mid fifties and her body odour overpowered Janetta's nostrils every time she bent over her to pass encouragement. There was nothing clean about Nora Hawkins. Her face, reported to have once been quite handsome, was now covered with blackheads and her gray hair was unbrushed and matted. Janetta, in a moment between contractions, looked at Nora in disgust. An apron that hadn't been white for some considerable time covered her faded blue dress, and her nicotine-stained fingers ended with cracked and blackened nails.

"Won't be long now, dearie. Are yer wantin' a boy or girl then?"

Janetta didn't feel up to small talk with her unwelcome helper, but found herself mumbling "A girl," in reply.

"Ah, yes!" mused Nora staring absently out of the window. "My first was a girl. Girls are beautiful ain't they?"

****

Will turned the corner and hurried down the street towards the house. Nora was leaning against the window casement as she waited for Janetta's next contraction. She watched Will coming as she remembered her first-born and slowly realized who it was.

"Oh 'es coming dearie, 'es 'ere."

"About bleedin' time an all!" spat Janetta as another contraction started, and she gritted her teeth against the pain.

Will barged through the front door and was surprised to find half the neighbourhood in his front room.

"Go on up, Will!" said the old girl from two doors down, "she's waiting for ya!"

Will took the stairs two at a time and burst into the bedroom.

"Jan luv are you alright?"

"We're doing just fine, ain't we?" said Nora and Janetta gave Will a weak smile of recognition before throwing her head back in her pillow, clenching the mattress in her hands and letting out a scream that terrified him.

He was horrified at the sight of his Janetta being attended by such a scruffy woman, and at her distress. She gritted her teeth and a grimace spread across her reddened face as she groaned and curved her body inwards in an attempt to push downward.

"Christ!" said Will, not knowing what he could do.

"Well it's nice you made it, dearie," then turning to Janetta she raised her voice above her moans and cries, "he's 'ere now luv, alright then ay! Not long now!"

Mrs Hawkins turned her attention back to Will.

"Well you wait downstairs now if ya will!" and she started to forcibly usher him towards the door. Just as Will opened the door Dr Willis entered the room.

"Ah doctor, I'm so glad you made it," said Will.

Dr Willis gave Will an almost indistinguishable nod of recognition. His eyes were upon Nora Hawkins and it was evident from his expression that he found her repugnant.

"I'll take over now if you don't mind, Mrs....?"

Nora drew herself up to her tallest, put her hands on her hips and glared at Dr Willis. "Mrs 'awkins, an' I'm attending 'ere".

For a second it looked as if there might be a stand-off. This was Mrs Hawkins' patch, not the doctor's, but he clearly had seniority of rank being a medical doctor. Dr Willis, unintimidated by Nora Hawkins, looked her straight in the eye as he took a step backward, leaving the path to the door open for her. She hesitated for a second. Janetta's contraction passed and she looked up at the doctor and smiled.

"Thank you for coming," she said in a clear voice. Then shifting her look to Nora. "And thank you, Mrs Hawkins, for seeing me this far."

Nora bristled but knew she was out voted. "Well you're welcome of course, me dear. I'll say goodbye then shall I?"

"Thank you Mrs H." said Will, and she sniffed, grabbed her bag and left the room mumbling to herself.

Dr. Willis remained standing beside the open door and in a softer voice he addressed Will.

"I think it would be better if you waited downstairs, yes?"

Will kissed the air in Janetta's direction. Janetta smiled at him weakly and he left the room.

When Will got back downstairs he was confronted by a dozen questions about how Janetta was doing. Making an excuse that he needed to nip out to the privy, he backed as politely as possible into the kitchen and escaped into the yard behind the house. He was not in the mood to be surrounded by well-meaning neighbours. He felt too nervous to be sociable.

He took his tobacco pouch out of his tunic pocket and rolled himself a cigarette. Will had no idea how long he had paced up and down in the alleyway behind the house, when Dr Willis came out looking for him.

"Ah this is where you've been hiding yourself, Rayner. You have a beautiful baby girl. What are you going to call her?"

"Haven't thought," replied Will excitedly, "and Jan?"

"She's fine. Why don't you go up and see for yourself?"

A broad smile crossed Will's face and he ran past the Doctor and took the stairs two at a time.

In the bedroom Janetta was sitting up with a small bundle in her arms. She looked exhausted, but was smiling at the half dozen or so women around her bed who were admiring the baby.

Janetta saw Will approaching gingerly and gave him a welcoming smile.

"I shall call her," she said "Janetta Louisa."

CHAPTER 25

A Year's Engagement

Much to Janetta's annoyance, Will made no mention of their getting married and they continued living together at number eight Ordnance Place tending their little daughter. Officially, Will still lived in the barracks, but he was able to spend a good deal of time with Janetta and the baby and he soon began to feel quite at home.

Janetta said nothing, but felt a little let down by Will's acceptance that they were living in apparent matrimonial bliss without actually having made it legal.

It wasn't that she really had too much to worry about. Will was a kind and loving man, and he always gave her the greater part of his pay packet, as little as it was, so they had a roof over their head and food on the table. But it wasn't enough.

Christmas came and went almost unnoticed. Janetta didn't feel up to much celebrating. The baby kept her up most nights with the colic, and coping with the growing pile of laundry she took in from the neighbours, guaranteed she got little rest. She was also dragged down by her post-natal depression that was worse than she had expected; she found herself sitting by the fire crying more often than she felt was acceptable. Before long she wasn't sure where normal depression ended and feeling sorry for herself began. Her independence had been severely curtailed, and she felt that 'motherhood' had not got off to a joyous beginning.

It took Janetta a long time to become accustomed to her new lifestyle, but gradually the depression faded and the baby began to sleep longer at night. She still had little time or patience when it came to chatting about babies with her friends and neighbours. Maternal cooing didn't come easily to Janetta and she felt strangely detached from her baby, as though some distant relative had dumped it on her to look after, with no certain arrangement for picking it up again.

Although she loved her little girl, she felt a longing for the old days and wished she could afford to pay someone else to mind the baby while she went to regimental dances. Not that she'd been to so many in the past, but those she had attended seemed to grow in significance in her mind. When she thought about the days with the Colonel and Lieutenant Bird, it seemed as if life had been one long string of elegant balls. It hadn't, of course. How many balls had she actually attended? Four, five, she couldn't remember, but her heart seemed forever yearning for the bright lights, gay uniforms and handsome officers.

She frequently found herself running her hands fondly over her best dress and wondering whether she could even fit into it anymore. She put her hands on her stomach and tried to push it as flat as it had been before her pregnancy, but it stubbornly sagged again when she let go. Will laughed at her and said her 'little pot' was beautiful, but she was not reassured. The best she could hope for now was a half-pint of ale or a gin down at the corner pub with Will and his friends, and she didn't need her best dress for that.

Winter turned to spring and little Janetta grew healthy and strong.

Mrs Thomson, from across the road, now past the point of further breeding, gave Janetta her perambulator. It was black and a little the worse-for-wear, having been used as the primary conveyance for eight children, but it was still serviceable and Janetta was very grateful.

Now, when she went shopping, she could leave the baby in the carriage outside the shop while she went inside, giving her both hands free to squeeze fruit and find change in her purse.

On several occasions, while alone in a shop, she would see a soldier of the regiment who didn't know her. Janetta knew she was still very beautiful, despite her little potbelly that she kept tightly laced in, and was pleasantly flattered when she received smiles, nods and even outright lustful glances from some young man in his deep blue *barathea* cloth jacket.

Many times they introduced themselves to her and offered to carry her bags, that was until they got out onto the street and saw the perambulator. There would then follow a back-pedalling as they wished her 'good day' and beat a hasty retreat.

On such occasions, Janetta would look down at her daughter, breathe a sigh of resignation, and say, "well you did it again, didn't ya."

She doubted these temptations were serious; after all she did love Will. It was gratifying, however, to know she still had the power to move men, and she justified these flirtations by reminding herself that she was still a single woman.

But if she still had this power, why couldn't she get Will to the altar?

****

Christmas 1886 was an improvement over that of '85. Janetta was now feeling much better, her daughter was a year old and sleeping well and there was a festive atmosphere around the house she hadn't felt the year before. Money was in short supply. The laundry Janetta took in paid little and Will was still on a single man's pay, but she managed to put on a good spread for Christmas dinner. She had made a couple of dozen jam tarts, and had saved enough dried fruit over the previous weeks to make a decent Christmas pudding. She'd even managed to secure a goose.

When Will saw it on the dinner table his eyes almost popped out of his head. The goose was big enough to keep them fed for several days. Janetta told him that she had been secretly saving her pennies for weeks to afford the bird, which greatly impressed him. The truth was far less admirable.

Janetta had known that the high street butcher, Mathew Wood, was very fond of her. She remembered how Sam Weald, the red-faced butcher in Plymouth, used to tease her, and was struck by how similar the situation was with Mr Wood. The difference, was that Mathew Wood was a fairly young man, no more than forty she guessed, and he had broad shoulders, waving hair and a smile that could turn her legs to jelly. Janetta quite fancied Mathew and often found herself flirting with him while he weighed out half a dozen sausages or found the best cut of meat within her budget.

She knew that he always gave her a little over the odds in weight or a better cut than she was paying for, but would he do a deal with her for a goose?

It was the week of Christmas and her last chance to secure the bird. On the previous two visits she had dropped big hints about not being able to afford a goose. Mathew had listened to her hints with a kindly smile and reassured her that they could come to an arrangement.

Janetta visited the shop when she knew he would be closing. She didn't leave young Janetta out on the street this time, but wheeled the perambulator into the shop, as if to conceal it from passers by.

"Allo, Mr Wood."

"Miss Rundel," replied Mathew as he closed and locked the door behind her. Janetta had given up calling herself Mrs Martin, preferring to think of herself as a single lady until Will married her. He flipped over the little card that hung in the window telling people that he had closed for the day. "You're my last customer today Miss Rundel, and I'm guessing you've come for a goose."

He removed his bloodstained apron and hung it on a hook behind the door.

"Well I'd love to 'ave one, Mr Wood, but I really can't afford it. Two shillings is a lot of money, Mr Wood, and I don't know how I could pay ya!"

"Well now, I ain't a one for takin' advantage of young women, an' I wouldn't want ya to think ill of me 'cause I likes ya, an' wouldn't want to lose ya friendship…"

Janetta moved closer to him, until their chests were almost touching. Mathew swallowed hard and looked down at her soft eyes.

"…o..or ya custom, Miss Run…" he didn't get a chance to finish the sentence before Janetta's lips were upon his. He froze as if momentarily overcome by the experience.

She pulled away from him very slowly.

"Perhaps I can pay you some other way, Mr Wood," she said in her most seductive voice.

No, she hadn't lost her power. She felt him melting before her. She knew he wanted her more than anything in the world at that moment. The goose was as good as hers.

"It's a bit public 'ere," she said, glancing towards the windows, "what's back there?"

Behind the counter was a door leading into a back room. Mathew, finding his strength and reassured that he was on firm ground, took her by the hand and led her into the little room.

It was a cross between a dimly-lit office and a sitting room. A roll top bureau was covered in papers and accounts; a small table stood against the opposite wall with the remains of his lunch on it. There was only one office chair on castors that she assumed did double duty between the desk and the table. The third wall contained a door that Janetta supposed led to an outhouse and rear alleyway.

Mathew closed the door behind him, and Janetta felt herself being manoeuvered towards the table. He gently turned her around so that she faced the table, then pushed against her back so that she lay face down upon the table, knocking a mug and plate onto the floor in the process. Before she had time to think about what was happening, he grabbed the hair at the back of her head to hold her still and hoisted her skirt above her waist.

For the next few minutes she didn't know whether to laugh, scream or cry. She felt certain she had done all three. It was without doubt the roughest sex she'd ever had. There was no loving, no gentle caressing or sweet words; he was just an animal rutting as hard as he could. It was tantamount to being raped, although Janetta had no illusions about that; she fully consented, even encouraged it and she clawed at him and swore at him if he slowed down. She wanted it hard and fast and as rough as he could provide it, and he didn't disappoint her.

They were both brought to their senses by the sound of young Janetta's crying in the shop. Janetta groaned and rolled her eyes. She reluctantly pushed him off her, and after rearranging her dress went out to see to her daughter. Mathew flopped into his chair by the bureau, panting hard and sweating from head to toe. A broad grin spread across his face as he thought about what had just happened. He couldn't believe his luck. Janetta had given him the best 'rogering' he'd ever had, and he decided she had truly earned the biggest goose he had in the shop.

Janetta was standing with her daughter in her arms, rocking her back and forth when Mathew re-entered the shop. He looked exhausted and dishevelled and Janetta had to give a little laugh when she saw him.

"Now," she said as she gently laid her daughter back down, "how much did you say that goose was?"

"Let it be my Christmas present to you, Miss Rundle," he replied as he removed the biggest bird he had from its hook in the window, "for being such a good customer."

"Mr Wood," she teased, "I hope ya don't give these sort of favours to all ya customers. You'll go out of business!"

"No I assure you I don't, Miss Rundel..." Mathew Wood had suddenly reverted back to his shy, overly-polite self that Janetta found so appealing, "I would never normally do that, I assure you!"

Janetta laughed again.

"Mathew, I'm only kiddin' ya. I know you're a good man. And..." she added holding up the goose, "a generous man."

Mathew smiled at her shyly.

"Now are ya going to open the door an' let me go 'ome?"

****

Will sat across the table from Janetta, his tunic slung over the back of the chair and the top button of his shirt undone. He felt full of the contentment of the Christmas holiday, having spent a couple of hours sharing drinks with their neighbours and singing Christmas songs around their friend's piano.

He hadn't been particularly hungry, but when Janetta had walked in from the kitchen with the cooked goose and laid it on the table along with the potatoes, cabbage, carrots and a Yorkshire pudding, his appetite had quickly returned. The goose had been followed by Christmas pudding and vanilla custard. It was the first time Janetta had made vanilla custard and she was pleased with the result.

Now, with his stomach full to bursting, he undid the top fly buttons of his britches, leaned back in his chair and contentedly rolled himself a cigarette. Janetta sat with their daughter on her lap and pushed her plate to one side to make room for their daughter to play with her wooden blocks.

The blocks were a Christmas present from Will and each one had printed pictures of soldiers glued to each side. Janetta had teased him that it was "a boy's toy" but the baby didn't mind. She grasped the small blocks with her chubby little hands and waved her arms about until the blocks slid from her fingers and went tumbling across the table.

Janetta and Will laughed as they watched their daughter squeal with delight over the brightly coloured blocks, and Will thought he'd never been so content.

Janetta was a little distracted over dinner, but Will didn't seem to notice. The sight of the goose on the table was a constant reminder of her barter with Mathew Woods. She had watched Will stuffing the bird into his mouth and making appreciative grunts in her direction.

She knew she ought to feel guilty, but instead, she felt oddly excited. It was her little secret, her sexual fantasy come true, to have hard, passionate, even violent sex with somebody who meant nothing to her. It was the sinning that excited her; the knowledge that what she had done would cause scandal in the street if it got out. Would she ever let it happen again? She didn't know. She didn't think so, yet her heart skipped a beat when she remembered that little back room and the sound of Mathew's panting as he pounded against her buttocks.

She had watched closely as Will ate the goose with obvious enjoyment. She'd had the sex and Will had the goose, and a small voice in her head began to rebuke her.

"How could you have done that behind Will's back?"

"Because I am still single and free to do so," she told herself.

"But Will is the father of your child."

"Yes, and a father who won't marry me."

"Do you intend to keep flirting and getting laid until Will finds out and leaves you?"

Janetta stopped the uninvited voice in her head and stared at Will. After a few puffs of his cigarette, Will felt her eyes on him.

"Wot?" he asked, "aren't you enjoying the goose?" He pointed at her half empty plate.

"Yeh it's fine!" she replied, "I was just finking."

She could lose him, and he was a good man. The sex was all right, not as exciting as with Mathew Wood, but good enough. But was that everything? Will was a good man, a steady man, an honest and true man and a good father. She needed him and for a moment she felt a twinge of panic.

"Marry me!" she heard herself saying.

Will stared at her not quite believing what he had heard. Was she asking him or was it a command?

"Wot?"

"Marry me!"

It definitely sounded like a command and Will wasn't quite sure how to take it, so he decided to make light of it. He stood to attention, clicked his heels, saluted and barked, "Yes Ma'am."

"Sit down! I'm serious Will, won't you marry me?"

This wasn't a demand, there was a pleading tone in her voice and Will flopped back in his chair and let out a long low exhale. There was a moment of silence before Will found his voice again.

"I fink it's usual for the man to ask the woman," he said softly.

"But you haven't asked me 'ave ya?"

"I was waitin' for the right moment."

"The right moment! When would that be?"

The baby threw another block, which hit a teacup.

"I thought, in the spring, when the weather was better."

"So do you want to marry me in the spring?"

"Yeh, Jan, I do. Will you marry me?"

Janetta smiled at him, lowering her head and looking up at him coyly.

"I thought you'd never ask!"

****

April 1886

Will wandered out of the barrack gate and made his way to Ordnance Place. He wasn't happy. It was the third week of April and he had just received some news that not only filled him with dread, but would also spoil their wedding plans. He was on his way to break the news to Janetta and he was wondering if there was any good way to tell her. He doubted there was and thought the only thing he could do was to come straight out with it, and try to downplay the negative side.

He pushed the key into the lock on the front door and let himself in. The baby was whimpering on the settee. He pulled his boots off, unbuttoned his tunic and flopped into a chair by the fire.

Janetta came into the room from the kitchen. She was wiping her hands on a tea towel after having washed some dishes. She could see by Will's demeanour that he was unhappy, but she let him speak in his own time.

"There's a bit of a problem with the wedding, Jan," he began.

"Oh!" Janetta looked a little alarmed.

"We have to bring it forward."

"Oh, why?" Janetta relaxed a bit as the news was not as bad as she feared.

"The Brigade is being posted,"

"Where to?...When?"

"On the 8th of May," Will lent forward in his chair and stared gloomily into the fire.

"Where we going?" Janetta made sure to emphasise the 'we'.

"Ipswich!" he replied with no hint of enthusiasm in his voice.

"Ipswich?" Janetta took a moment to process the name. "Where's that?"

"Suffolk," Will said dismissively.

"Well that's not so bad, is it?"

Will desperately wanted to tell her that Ipswich was where Major Cope had gone, but decided to let it go for the moment.

"No, s'pose not!...We'll have to get married before we go though 'cause I want me mum and dad to be there, an' they won't travel to Suffolk."

Janetta grinned.

"Then I'll just 'ave ta move everyfing up a bit, won't I?"

"Sorry!" said Will, knowing it meant that Janetta would have to reorganize all the arrangements.

CHAPTER 26

Wedding day
May 1887

William Rayner sat on a munitions box chewing on the end of a blade of grass and idly watched a squad of new recruits being drilled on the parade ground. His tunic lay on the ground beside him; his shirt was open at the neck and his sleeves were rolled up above his elbows. He was sweating profusely and small rivulets of perspiration ran down his chest and back. He groaned as he felt his braces pressing his wet shirt against his back.

"Bugger this!" he said, and he pulled his braces down off his shoulders.

A sergeant major barked orders at the recruits and watched critically as they struggled to maintain a straight line while turning left, right and facing about.

Will's arms burned from a full hour of lifting and stacking munitions boxes, so he was taking a five-minute break while there were no officers about to harass him. A broad-shouldered Yorkshireman named Steve Wilks sat beside him, meticulously spreading a pinch of tobacco across a paper and rolling it between his fingers into a cigarette.

"Stevie," Will said, as he followed the marching recruits with his eyes, and thanked God it wasn't him out there, "will ya be me best man tomorrow?"

Stevie ran his tongue along the edge of the paper to stick it together and pinched a couple of stray hairs of tobacco off the end before putting the cigarette in the corner of his lips. "You're going through with it then, are ya?"

"Course I am. Can't let a girl like Janetta slip through me fingers can I?" Will beamed "Besides," he said, lowering his voice and becoming series for a moment, "it's the right thing to do, her being with child an' all!"

Stevie struck a match and lit his cigarette. A thin wisp of blue smoke came out of his nostrils.

"She's a beautiful lass, right enough! You're a lucky sod, Will."

"Well…will ya?"

"Course I bloody will!" said Stevie, "I'd be pissed if yer hadn't asked! You lucky shit!"

Will gave a self-satisfied chuckle and looked down at the ground where he had been kicking a small tuft of grass growing out of a crack in the cobblestones. He idly stabbed at the grass with the tip of his boot and thought about the beautiful Janetta in his bed tomorrow night.

A couple of minutes passed in silence between them. It was Stevie who broke the silence.

"Have yer run into this new major we've got?"

Will shook his head.

"Ugly brute he is, and a right bastard an all."

"No can't say as I've 'ad the pleasure," replied Will.

"'E arrived yesterday. Soon made his presence felt an' all, I can tell ya!"

"Army's full of bastard officers. One, more or less, don't make no difference."

"Yeh well, wait 'til you've seen this one, Will. He's a right shit an' no mistake!"

Their rest was rudely interrupted by a thundering voice behind them, shattering the peace and causing them both to jump out of their skins.

"What the bleedin' 'ell are you two bastards doing of?"

Will and Steve, their hearts pounding, instinctively jumped to their feet and stood to attention. A large bulk of a man in a neatly pressed uniform and gleaming black boots walked round in front of them and leaned forward so that his grizzled face was just inches from Will's.

"Well!" he screamed into Will's face. "Cat got your tongue 'as it?"

Will could smell the Major's stale breath as he spat out the words showering his face in spittle. The Major's dark, sullen eyes glared right into Will's soul as if he was about to commit murder. Will, however, had been in the army too many years to be intimidated by a bullying officer, and his soldier's instinct for survival snapped into play.

"Just taking a five minute break, sir!" he bellowed in reply while making certain he didn't make eye contact with the major by staring into the sky just above his head. "Stacking Anderson's... sir!" He snapped the word 'Sir' in crisp military fashion.

The major recognizing the reaction of a seasoned soldier, who wasn't being intimidated, narrowed his eyes and stared right into Will's soul.

"I know your sort, don't you think I don't, laddie!" he spat before turning his attention to Stevie.

"And who gave you permission to take a break, you skiving little bastard?"

"Nobody, sir!" snapped back Stevie in as soldierly a fashion as Will.

"Then you'll stack munitions until I say you can rest. Think this is a bloody holiday at the beach!"

"No, sir!" replied Stevie.

"I don't like lazy sons of bitches."

The major paced up and down glaring at them both, "think you're bloody smart, taking rests when nobody's watching. I know your sort. Don't you think I don't?"

He stopped and leaned into Will's face again. Will remained stiffly at attention and stared at the major's cap badge.

"When you've finished stacking them," he said in a soft voice that was almost friendly but full of threat, "...neatly mind...you can move the whole bloody lot over the other side of the yard." He pointed across the yard to a storage building some fifty feet away.

"That'll take us all tomorrow, sir!" said Stevie forgetting himself. The major's eyes widened and he turned on Wilks like a vulture pouncing on its prey.

"Shut up!" he screamed into Stevie's face. "You 'orrible bastard you! You can bloody well move em back again the day after as well! Now get on with it! On the double!"

"Sir!" barked Stevie and Will in unison before breaking into a run back to the munitions boxes.

They continued stacking boxes in double time for a minute or two before Will dared glance over his shoulder. The major was walking away towards the main barrack block.

"Shit and bollocks!" said Will relaxing the speed at which he piled boxes. "Who the Christ was that bastard?"

"That was Major bleeding Rawlins," replied Stevie breathing hard from the sudden exertion.

"Shit!"

They both looked at the enormous pile of Anderson boxes. Each box was about three feet long by a foot deep and two feet wide and each end had a rope handle. They must have stacked almost three hundred of them. Fortunately they were empty so they were not so heavy, but the thought of moving them all fifty feet across the yard exhausted them both.

"Can't keep yer mouth shut, can you?" said Will.

"It's your wedding day tomorrow and we have to shift this lot. It ain't fair!"

"I know it ain't fair but when an officer speaks to yer it's 'Yes sir, No sir, Three bloody bags full sir'. "

"I know, I know," said Stevie in a dejected tone.

"Besides, I've 'ad permission to marry from Major Thompson so Major Rawlins can go hang 'imself! I'm getting married and that's it!"

Will looked at Stevie and frowned.

"Look," he said, "I don't want to get you into trouble. You don't have to come with me."

"I'm not letting you get married on yer own. I'll be there and fuck Rawlins and his boxes!" grinned Stevie.

****

On Tuesday morning the 2nd May 1887, Will stood with his best man, Stevie Wilks, in the lobby of the Woolwich Registry Office in the company of a dozen or so of his closest friends from the Regiment. Will's nervousness made him perspire in his newly pressed dress uniform.

His mother and father stood to one side looking uncomfortable in their best clothes; a small group of Will's aunts and uncles hung about talking amongst themselves, their voices echoing in the bare hall.

Janetta hadn't yet arrived and Will was feeling anxious as he paced up and down.

Will's mother, Martha, a rather stout matronly woman, was itching to fuss over her son. She had an overwhelming desire to straighten his tunic or smooth down some wayward hairs on the back of his head. A couple of times she made an attempt to approach him in a motherly fashion but her husband had intervened, "leave the boy be, mother! Don't embarrass him in front of his friends!"

He was right of course; her little boy was a grown man now. After all, he'd been out in India for ten years and had long ceased to be her little boy. She'd half expected him to come home with an Indian girl on his arm and was much relieved when he didn't. She had never met his fiancée and was apprehensive about what sort of girl she'd be.

"Still," she'd said to Will's father while he toiled in his bakery the day before, "William wouldn't get mixed up with any hussy, would he? He's always been a good boy, 'e as!"

Now she was about to meet her daughter-in-law to be, she wasn't so sure. She expressed her worries to her ever-patient husband in no uncertain tones. What if she took an instant dislike to her? What if she was really common?

"We're not exactly royalty ourselves, are we?" he had told her. "We take her as we find her, and be pleased for 'im no matter what!"

"You're right! I know you're right," replied Martha as she sprinkled a little too much flour on his dough pile. Her husband had irritably slapped her hand away from his dough.

"I'm sure she's going to be perfectly lovely. After all my William wouldn't look at any girl who's not fit to bring 'ome, would he?" she fretted.

Her husband, whose name was also William, rolled his eyes to the ceiling and continued kneading the large clump of dough on the counter.

****

Janetta was late. She'd changed dresses three times, finally deciding on the turquoise one that the Lieutenant had bought her as a goodbye present. Marian, her friend and neighbour who was being her maid of honour today, wasn't sure about the choice.

"You really want to get married in the dress your last lover bought you?" she'd asked. "Wouldn't you be happier in the green one?"

"No I don't think I would," replied Janetta. "I think Lieutenant Bird would be honoured to know I picked 'is dress for this occasion. Besides…" Janetta lowered her voice to almost a whisper as she scrutinized herself in the mirror, "my last wedding dress was given to me by my previous lover."

"Wot!" exclaimed Marian, not quite believing what she had heard.

"Nuffin! It's not important!" replied Janetta, brightening up and stepping back from the mirror to get a better overall look at herself. "No this one will do very nicely."

If there was one thing that Janetta knew how to do very well, it was make a grand entrance. When she finally arrived at the registrar's office she was fifteen minutes late, but all fears and anxieties were forgotten the second she walked in.

Everyone in the lobby turned to face her as she came through the front door and an audible gasp of appreciation rippled through the assembled guests.

Will was speechless. He knew he was marrying a beauty, but nothing had prepared him for the angel that walked through the door. Janetta would have stood out as the most beautiful woman at any society ball. She wore her long dark hair pulled up at the back and swept forward into a ball of curls about her forehead and she had a small white flower pinned in one side.

Her bodice fitted her tightly at the waist, emphasizing her hips, and had a row of small pearl buttons up to the neck and a delicate ribbon collar. The long narrow sleeves had high standing shoulder seams and ribbon ruffs at the wrists to match the collar. The dress hung straight down to the floor and had a scalloped hemline. The smooth material of the dress glistened in the light, highlighting the delicate turquoise.

At her waist she carried a small posy of cut flowers in turquoise-gloved hands. She had also paid to have her face professionally made up with good quality cosmetics that she could ill afford, but it was her wedding day after all.

Will walked forward to greet her and to lead the assembly into the wedding hall. He gave her a gentle kiss on the cheek that left him with the taste of rouge on his lips. They looked lovingly into one another's eyes for a second or two then he offered her his arm; but before going in, he guided Janetta over to where his parents were standing.

"Mum…Dad… let me introduce you to my bride, Janetta."

Janetta gave a slight bow of her head as if addressing a noble and said,

"Mrs Rayner, I am so pleased to make your acquaintance, I have heard so much about you I feel part of the family already."

Martha glowed with pride at her son's choice of bride. Janetta then turned her gaze to Mr Rayner and looking him straight in the eye, she shook his hand and whispered with a teasing grin on her face, "Now I know where Will gets his gorgeous eyes from." William Rayner blushed and found himself falling instantly in love with his son's bride.

Martha Rayner was beside herself with relief and admiration; and Will's father found himself jealous of his son and guilty at feeling that way. There was no getting away from the fact that Janetta had won their hearts. The first hurdle was crossed and the second about to be taken. She would become Mrs Rayner.

As the party filed into the wedding hall, Martha took her husband's arm and made no attempt to hide how pleased she was.

"Oh Bill, she's perfect!"

Her husband nodded his agreement.

"She's everything I knew she would be!" continued Martha in full flood of admiration. "She speaks beautifully, don't you think, and so charming!"

Her husband gently tapped her hand, which was on his arm, and smiled with contentment as they walked to their seats.

****

"You bloody idiot, Rayner! You should have come to me first!" snapped Major Reynolds as he stared up at Will from behind his desk.

"You said I could have the day to be married, sir!" Will pleaded as he stood to attention in the Major's office.

"Come off it, man, you've been in the army long enough to know how things work."

The Major was shaking his head with frustration. His voice had a tone of exasperation.

Major Reynolds was a kindly man whom Will regarded with some affection. They'd been in the same unit for some time and had always worked well together. Major Reynolds, although a good officer, had always had a problem with imposing discipline; at least with the men under his command with whom he had always gotten along well. He was considered by his peers to be a good man but a weak officer; too easily befriended by his men and often taken advantage of. He was a fair-minded officer who hated to see men mistreated by other officers, but he also hated to be put in a position where he was forced to make an unpleasant ruling.

"Begging your pardon, sir, but he had no right to…"

"He had every right," bellowed the major as he lost his patience. "He is an officer, and you bloody well know it!"

Will made no further reply, realizing he was on shaky ground.

"And you," said the Major as he turned his gaze on Steve Wilks, "I don't remember giving you permission to leave the barracks."

Stevie remained silent.

"Well!" screamed Major Reynolds, his face reddening as he stood up and leaned forward on the desk.

"I had leave, sir, from Sergeant Harris, sir."

"Hummm!" replied the Major as he flopped back into his chair and leaned the chair back against the wall.

There was a minute of silence during which the Major fiddled with the ends of his moustache and contemplated his next move. Finally he lowered the chair back onto its four legs and picked up a piece of paper from the desk. He studied it for a moment before raising his eyes to Will and Stevie.

"Major Rawlins has filled out an official charge sheet. I can't ignore it!" he said pointedly. "If you had just come to me first, I could have smoothed it over with Major Rawlins… but I can't ignore this!" He waved the piece of paper in the air with a look of disgust.

He lowered his head and studied the paper some more before continuing.

"You've left me no room for manoeuvre here!" He lowered the paper, dipped his quill in the inkbottle and began writing in a charge book.

"I have to enter this in your records! Both of you! For you Rayner I'm going to say 'Married without leave' and you Wilks, 'Absent without leave'. There should of course be an appropriate punishment to go along with this record, but I reckon stacking those munitions boxes again is punishment enough."

"Thank you sir!" said Will. "And Major Rawlins, sir?"

"And Major Rawlins what?" replied the major.

"What will he say, sir, if he thinks you haven't given us sufficient punishment?"

"Major Rawlins left this morning for Dover. I doubt we'll see him again. Dismissed."

"Sir!" snapped Will and Stevie as they saluted, did an about face and marched to the door.

"Oh Rayner!" said the Major just as they were about to live the room. "Congratulations by the way! Who's the lucky girl?"

"Thank you, sir, Janetta Rundel, sir," grinned Will as he closed the door behind him. The Major stared at the closed door in astonishment.

"How the hell did he win that beauty?" he muttered to himself.

CHAPTER 27

Ipswich

On the evening of May 7th. Janetta and Will retired to bed for the first time as husband and wife. Packing for the move and the excitement of the wedding had left them both exhausted and they were asleep almost as soon as their heads had hit the pillows. Janetta had turned onto her side and Will had leaned across and given her a light kiss on her cheek and whispered, “Good night, Mrs Rayner.” She had given an almost inaudible reply before sleep overcame her.

On the morning of the eighth, thirty men of the Sixth Brigade left Woolwich and travelled by train to Ipswich. Janetta travelled separately with a small group of soldiers’ wives and lovers. She was saddened to leave Woolwich and was apprehensive about returning to a small country town.

The journey was pleasant enough, and Janetta found the East Anglian countryside much to her liking. Upon arrival at Ipswich the small group of women found their men gathered outside the main entrance to the station. The baggage was piled up to one side and Will came over to her, peered at his baby daughter snuggly wrapped in a shawl, and gave Janetta a reassuring kiss on the cheek.

“There’ll be some wagons here shortly to take us the rest of the way,” he said, and as if on cue, several large carts drawn by two horses apiece came around the corner and stopped in front of the pile of luggage.

The women and luggage were bundled onto the wagons and began making their way towards their new home. Janetta was starting to feel quite tired as the wagons slowly approached the barrack gates. It had been a long hot day and Will was looking forward to getting his boots off and resting in their new apartment.

Will had fretted about meeting Major Cope again and as his wagon approached the barrack gate his anxiety bubbled to the surface.

The wagon stopped almost right in front of the archway as the small column came to a halt to check in with the guardhouse.

Will took advantage of the stop to jump down and he strolled over to one of the sentries on guard at the gate. He stood beside the sentry but didn't look directly at him.

"Is there a Major Cope stationed 'ere?" he asked.

The sentry didn't move, keeping his head to the front, but his eyes glanced sideways down at the corporal's stripes on Will's right sleeve. He then took a brief look over his shoulder to satisfy himself that his commanding officer wasn't watching before answering Will. For the briefest of moments his face displayed a look of disgust, "Yeh, sir, 'es 'ere alright!"

Will nodded and grunted his thanks and then strolled away from the sentry so as not to attract his officer's attention. He glanced at the last wagon where he could see Janetta sitting with her back to the rail. She was looking forward trying to see what the hold-up was. She had her daughter on her lap and she took her arm and pumped it up and down to wave at her father. Will smiled back but didn't linger.

The officer of the watch seemed satisfied with the driver's orders and waved the convoy through.

Will didn't bother to jump back up onto the wagon, his legs needed stretching anyway and so he walked beside the wagon under the arch and into the barrack compound.

They were met by the brigade commander, Brigadier Phipps, who waited patiently for them to jump down from the wagons and form up in line before him. Half a dozen enlisted men appeared and started leading the empty wagons towards the stables.

Will looked at the Brigadier closely as he slowly paced up the line and spoke a few words to each man. He was younger than he had expected and handsome almost to excess. He spoke with an easy familiarity with the new arrivals, that Will thought showed a possible weakness of command; but when he spoke to Will he was struck by the kindness in his eyes.

Brigadier Phipps took a few steps backward and addressed the small company. Will thought he made a pretty speech. It was short, welcoming and friendly, and everyone thought that this was going to be an easy place to spend a couple of years.

As the small company was dismissed, Brigadier Phipps cast his eyes towards the small group of women and children gathered about the baggage wagon. He was unimpressed by the gathering. They were typical, he thought, of the women who followed soldiers. For the most part they were dowdy, unkempt and with hard lines in their faces. They looked as if they were prostitutes made legitimate by marriage to a soldier, and in all likelihood that's exactly what they were. Not that most of them were married; Phipps knew only too well that the term 'married' often had a broad interpretation in the army. He was about to retire to his office when he noticed a woman with a small child; a woman who stood out from the rest. If it hadn't been for her plain clothes, he would have thought her a lady. She was a real beauty with an air of pride about her and a trim, elegant figure and straight back. She didn't look like a washerwoman or common tart but an educated lady who may have fallen on hard times. *"To what lucky devil does she belong?"* he thought.

His thoughts were interrupted by a harsh grinding voice beside him. It was a voice that had an air of unwarranted familiarity.

"Sir? Today's dispatches are on your desk for signing. Best to be seen to right away, sir."

The Brigadier didn't even acknowledge the officer who had just approached him. He closed his eyes with annoyance at having been interrupted by an officer he detested so much. This officer, all spit and polish, fawned over the Brigadier and did everything by the book. He ran the Brigadier's office so efficiently that half the time Phipps seriously wondered which of them was really in charge. He sighed and nodded his recognition of the major's presence; then turned away, never even looking at the major before walking back towards his office.

The major didn't follow him, but stood and watched the women for a minute, his eyes scanning from one to the other until he spotted the dark-haired beauty that had held the Brigadier's stare. A sardonic grin slowly crept across his face. Major Cope remembered the beauty and he felt his heart thump harder in his chest. He glanced back to where the new men were gathering up their kit and preparing to follow an orderly to their new billets. There was Will Rayner. He hadn't noticed the Major and was starting to follow the orderly in the opposite direction, leaving the women to make their own way.

Cope looked back at Janetta and chuckled to himself.

"Oh my sweet!" he said under his breath, "I'm going to enjoy having you. Oh my, indeed I am! You're in my world now. Yes, you are, you sweet little thing!"

The baggage wagon moved off and Janetta and the other women followed on foot, blissfully unaware that Major Cope was watching them.

****

Their new home reminded Will of the living quarters at Shorncliffe outside Dover. The quarters were situated just outside the barrack wall and consisted of two red brick blocks side by side on the far side of the road. A long white veranda ran the length of each block giving access to the front doors on the second level, and each level contained ten dwellings. They were quite pleasant. Each apartment was clean and airy. There was one communal toilet at the end of the building but each unit had its own running water and gas lighting. Furniture was sparse and basic but otherwise quite adequate.

Janetta was sad at first to leave Woolwich. She loved the hustle and bustle of city life and she worried about how well she would adapt to living once again in a small rural town. But the journey had been very pleasant. Young Janetta had pressed her little face against the carriage window and become excited at the sight of cows and fields. Ipswich appeared to be an agreeable little town and her new apartment pleased her. She was beginning to feel that life in Ipswich was going to be very pleasant indeed.

She spent the rest of the afternoon unpacking their trunks, cleaning the kitchen and meeting her neighbours, who were not shy about popping in to introduce themselves.

****

Brigadier Phipps had returned to his office to take care of the paperwork that Cope had left him. He stood at his office window and watched Major Cope standing in the compound. His feet were steadily planted a foot apart and his hands were clenched behind his back. In the sun his boots gleamed. How he hated Major Cope! He stood for everything that Phipps disliked about the army. Cope was the ultimate "arse licker"; the model soldier; always immaculately dressed when in the barracks, his creases sharp, his boots polished to a high shine and his brass buttons sparkling. He saluted his superior officers with relish and grovelled when around them, ingratiating himself at every turn. As a professional soldier he couldn't be criticized, but when off duty he could be dirty, scruffy and foul mouthed. Phipps detested his hypocrisy and doubted he'd be much use in a battle. He'd known his kind before, all spit and polish but no gumption under fire. Cope, he suspected, was a coward at heart and would be the first to bury his head in a ditch when enemy shells started falling nearby.

Something else irked Brigadier Phipps. Major Cope had two followers. Sergeant Diggins, the regimental bully, twice reprimanded for harsh treatment of his men, and Corporal Hughes, commonly referred to as the "Welsh weasel". Diggins and Hughes, when not seeing to their duties, followed Major Cope around like a pair of lap dogs.

Brigadier Phipps prayed for the day he could get rid of the three, but whenever anything of a serious nature occurred, and it had, there was never any evidence that Cope, Diggins or Hughes had anything to do with it. There were always witnesses willing to attest to the fact that Cope, Diggins and Hughes were nowhere near the scene of the crime.

There had been several incidents that Phipps couldn't clear up.

One soldier had been severely beaten up and, rumour had it, his wife, who hated Major Cope, had slept with him shortly afterwards. Then there were two girls raped in the town by soldiers but the soldiers were never identified. Then there was the matter of the money the three used for gambling. They seemed to have far too much money to lose at cards, and the Brigadier strongly suspected that there was some form of financial extortion going on. It wasn't so uncommon in the army. It was only too easy for an officer to extort money from the rank and file. A superior officer couldn't be argued with and some officers were real bullies. Cope was one of those officers, but proving it was difficult.

Major Cope had wormed his way into a cushy desk job in the Brigadier's office and there was nothing that happened in the camp that he didn't know about. He prepared all the Brigadier's paper work, arranged interviews, heard complaints and organized the Brigadier's social diary. He had almost complete control over the Brigadier's administration and Phipps detested him for it.

Phipps stared at Cope through the window and felt his stomach churn with hatred. He had to be rid of Cope; but how? He needed a damned good reason and he needed allies; he just had to bide his time and wait.

****

Bombardier Michael Shaunessy stood behind his gun crew and watched them as they practised loading and firing the field gun of battery 'A'. He glanced over to his left where the new gun crew from Woolwich was loading the gun of battery 'B'.

The sky was overcast and a light rain fell but the sweet smell of the rain was masked by the familiar stench of cordite. Will stood behind his crew and called out encouragement or rebuke as required.

There was no competition, but gun crews felt an instinctive desire to out-perform their comrades on other guns. The pace increased in both crews.

Michael Shaunessy sauntered over and stood beside Will.

"Now they're a fine bunch of lads to be sure, those Woolwich boys of yours."

Will smiled at him and gave a discrete nod.

"You must be Shaunessy. I'd recognize that accent anywhere. Ulster isn't it?"

"Well Jasus it is! Do you know Ireland then?"

Will shook his head.

"Neh! But I used to know a couple of your countrymen in India. They were good with the horses."

"Oh for sure the Irish know their horses alright!"

There followed an awkward pause when neither man knew what to say to the other. It was Will who broke the silence.

"So is there anything I should know about this place? Is the Brigadier a fair commander?" Will was fishing.

"Oh 'es a fine fella so he is," replied Michael glad to return to conversation. "At least he was until that Major Cope arrived."

"Major Cope?" Will feigned ignorance.

"Focking animal he is, an' no mistake. Ya don't want to be messing with that one." He emphasized the last statement by jabbing his finger at Will's chest.

"What's his problem?" replied Will with forced indifference.

"Well now let me put it to ya this way. If I had a focking pretty wife I'd be a focking worried man in this camp."

"The Major likes women does he?"

"Trouble is the women don't focking like 'im, so 'e has a way of changing their focking minds like."

Shaunessy glanced around to make sure he wasn't being overheard.

"Sweet talker is he?"

"Sweet Jasus he doesn't 'ave to sweet talk the ladies. He just gets his two cronies to beat the focking shit out of their husbands like, and then he promises it won't 'appen again if they agree to lift their skirts for 'im. Right focking shit 'e is an' no mistake."

"And who are these two cronies, Michael?"

"Sergeant focking Diggins and focking Corporal Hughes that's who."

"Why did you say the Brigadier was fine until Cope arrived? Couldn't he just transfer him out of here?"

"You'd think so wouldn't ya now. Ya see it's like this. The focking Major has complete control over the paperwork and the Brigadier can't take a piss without Cope knowing it. He's got the Brigadier by the focking short an' curlies so he has."

"Sounds to me as if the Major needs taking down a peg or two," replied Will. His mind was racing now. He had the most beautiful woman on the base and he knew he didn't stand much of a chance against Cope's two thugs. He was going to have to use some cunning to win the inevitable confrontation. "Are you a good man to have in a brawl, Michael?"

"Jasus, we've only known one another five focking minutes and you're asking me to beat up a focking major."

"If we play our cards right it won't come to that. I've not been straight with ya, Michael. I do know Cope. Him and I, or rather him and my wife, go way back. We both have a score to settle with him and I think it's best done soon, before Cope makes the first move."

“Well any man who is willing to take on the Major is alright in my book, Will. Perhaps we can do the Brigadier a focking favour.”

CHAPTER 28

Copes' Attack

A month had passed since Janetta had arrived in Ipswich and Major Cope was beginning to feel frustrated. No opportunities for seeing her had presented themselves. In fact he had barely seen her at all. His duties kept him in the office most of the time and he rarely ran into Will Rayner. Janetta stayed at home tending to her daughter and her house, and was seldom seen within the barrack walls.

He was sitting at his desk mulling over the problem when Brigadier Phipps stepped out of his office into the anteroom.

The Brigadier handed him a sheet of paper as he scraped his chair back and stood up.

"The reverend's Sunday service," he said absent-mindedly as if he couldn't be bothered with it, "get it printed up and be sure there's a decent attendance this Sunday. There's been too many men skiving off lately! It won't do!"

"Yes, sir!" replied Cope unenthusiastically.

The Brigadier turned to walk away and then checked himself and looked back at Cope.

"Maybe we should send a memorandum to the ladies requesting their presence at Sunday service. It would be nice to see some pretty faces in church for a change. Mrs Rayner would brighten the morning I'm sure!"

He returned to his office not waiting for a response from Cope and closed the door behind him.

Cope looked at the service announcement and thought about the ladies attending. Perhaps Janetta would make an appearance but he doubted that he'd be able to get her alone. Will Rayner would be close by and people would surround them. He couldn't see any advantage to be had here, so he put her to the back of his mind and attended to the pile of paperwork on his desk.

****

Sunday morning was the type of morning that discourages everyone from getting out of bed. The sky was a solid canvas of dark gray, blocking out the sun and casting a chill light over the world. A vertical curtain of rain clattered on the cobbles and ran in small rivers down the gutters. Every few minutes a gust of wind would howl between the buildings and sweep the rain against the barrack windows.

One by one, soldiers ran across the courtyard, heads bowed low and hands clasping their caps to their heads. They were making their way as fast as they could to the small church that stood against the barrack wall. Stamping their feet and shaking themselves, they entered the small porch and jostled one another as they tried to squeeze out of the rain. The fronts of their britches were soaked from the short dash, and they shivered as rain trickled down the back of their necks. The interior of the church was dimly lit and smelled of musty plaster and sodden barathea uniforms. Small puddles formed on the floor around the feet of the congregation and the rain hammered on the slate roof.

The Reverend Holworthy fidgeted at the foot of the pulpit stairs as he waited for everyone to arrive. His hang-jowled face, sleepy eyes and unruly gray hair masked his sharp wit and canny ability to see right through to the soul of his flock. Brigadier Phipps felt immediately guilty whenever he was in the presence of the Reverend and did his best to avoid eye contact. This morning he sat in his usual seat. It was on the front pew but on the far right side of the church where his view of the pulpit was conveniently obscured by an iron pillar. There at least he could avoid the accusing glare of the reverend in full flood of pious indignity at the sins of his congregation.

He turned to look back at the congregation slowly filing in at the door and shuffling along the pews to take their places.

Diggins and Hughes were already settled in their pew on the far left aisle right against the wall, pinned in by six other soldiers. Will Rayner sat four rows in front of them idly thumbing through a prayer book but not reading it. Major Cope entered the church, his uniform glistening with the wet, and rivulets of water running off his greasy hair and down his grizzled face. He stood at the back and surveyed the congregation. He saw Diggins and Hughes hemmed in and Will absorbed in thought. His eyes flickered from woman to woman trying to identify them. Most of their faces were obscured from the back by the frills on the sides of their bonnets, and it took Cope several minutes to determine who they all were.

He gave a disapproving sneer as he glanced at each woman's face. "*What whores,*" he thought, "*dressed up in their Sunday best as if butter wouldn't melt in their mouths. Whores, the lot of 'em.*" He was only too aware of the type of woman who followed the Regiment, seeking protectors. It wasn't an easy life for them but the Regiment supplied a ready source of available men to marry. When the Regiment went overseas and the women followed, those men who did not die a hero's death in some foreign war, probably died from any one of a dozen tropical diseases, such as malaria or dysentery. When one husband died there were many others waiting to take his place. In peacetime, after one or two husbands, the women often didn't bother to re-marry, but lived common law and were accepted as wives. It was the threat of regimental relocation that produced a flood of marriages, for each woman wished to secure her widow's pension.

"*Whores!*" he thought. "*There's only one worth looking for and she's not in church.*" He grinned at the thought of Janetta at home alone, sheltering from the rain. With any luck her neighbours were either in church or doing the same as her and staying in the warmth of their parlours. He turned and elbowed his way against the flow of incoming soldiers until he stood once again in the wind and the rain.

Michael Shaunessy was standing in the porch brushing as much rain as he could from his uniform when Cope shoved him aside and stepped back into the rain. Michael watched him leave the church porch, and hunched against the wind, make his way across the courtyard towards the main gate.

The sight of Cope out in the rain and leaving the base when he should have been in church, struck Michael as very odd and filled him with foreboding. Despite the rain, he decided to follow him. Cope turned left at the gate and Michael ran to catch up and peer round the sentry box. Cope, as he suspected, was heading for the billets on the far side of the street. Michael stopped and wondered what he should do. If he followed Cope to Janetta's apartment he would have to confront him alone and he wasn't at all sure that was a good idea. Better, he thought, to get Will so that there was two of them against one. He also worried about taking on a superior officer but, on balance, decided that it was worth the risk if it meant saving Will's wife from the attentions of an animal like Cope. He turned and ran back to the church as fast as he could.

The door had been closed and he could hear the Reverend Holworthy's voice announcing the first hymn. The door latch made a dreadful clatter as he opened it and he expected to see the entire congregation looking round at him as he entered. To his relief nobody seemed to notice his late arrival. There was a general fidgeting as everyone reach for the hymnbooks and flipped the pages to the right hymn. As usual, the organ struck the first chords before anybody was ready, and the congregation began to sing, weakly at first, as they struggled to find their place.

"The Lord's my shepherd, I'll not want."

Michael walked as discreetly as he could down the centre aisle, his boots squeaking on the wooden floor. He peered down each pew looking for Will. The Reverend looked up from his hymnbook disapprovingly. To Michael's annoyance he found Will right against the wall only four rows from the front. There was no way he could do this discreetly. He pushed his way onto the end of the pew despite there being no room for him. Six men shuffled tighter together until Will was shouldered right against the wall. He didn't notice who had entered the pew and had no desire to know.

Michael tried to look down the pew to attract Will's attention. Will had his head bowed as he read the hymnbook and sang quietly into his own chest.

Michael, frustrated, nudged the man next to him to pass the message down to Will. One by one elbows jostled elbows and heads nodded to the left until at last Will was awoken from his unenthusiastic singing. He listened to the murmurs of the man next to him and bent forward to look back along the pew, puzzled by the interruption.

Michael, having got Will's attention, gesticulated violently that he should get out of the church and follow him.

The disturbance hadn't gone unnoticed and the Reverend glared at them from behind his hymnbook. Brigadier Phipps also glanced over towards them and frowned.

Will was slow to comprehend Michael's sign language and mouthing of his message, and Michael was forced to get louder than he wished.

"Come on," he half-whispered, half shouted down the pew, "it's Cope!" and he jerked his arm towards the center isle.

Will frowned at Michael, "Wot?"

"Ha hmmm!" the Reverend Halsworthy loudly cleared his throat between verses to break up the annoying disturbance.

Michael raised his eyebrows and showed the whites of his eyes to Will in an attempt to display extreme frustration, and throwing caution to the wind hissed through his teeth, "Come on! It's Cope!"

Will spread his arms out to the side and shook his head as if to say "so what?"

The Reverend Halsworthy had enough.

"Gentlemen!" he yelled, bringing the hymn to a stop and silencing the congregation. The organist stopped playing "Is it too much to ask that we have your attention to the service?"

"Sorry, Reverend!" said Michael and instinctively crossed himself causing the most protestant reverend to gape at him in astonishment. Michael turned once more to Will who was becoming agitated at being in the centre of an embarrassing moment. What on earth was possessing Michael to act this way in the middle of the service?

Michael's gaze turned from the Reverend back to Will and ignoring the glare of the officers hissed again.

"Come on! Cope! Ja-net-ta!"

It was the last distinctly-pronounced syllables of his wife's name that jolted Will out of his confused daze.

"Christ!" he exclaimed, giving yet another shock to the Reverend Halsworthy, who hadn't a clue what was causing such an unpleasant interruption to his usually well-ordered service.

Will hurriedly sidestepped his way along the pew in front of the other men, all of who breathed in to let him pass. Before the Reverend or any of the officers understood what was happening, Will and Michael were running down the centre aisle towards the door, their boots thumping hard on the wooden floor.

****

By the time Major Cope had reached the married quarters the rain had begun to ease. A small gap formed in the clouds and the sun attempted to shine through. Still soaked to the skin and his uniform heavy with water, he felt suddenly warmed by the brightening sky and the thought of Janetta at the top of the balcony stairs. He paused at the foot of the stairs and looked back at the barrack gates. No one had followed him. The Regiment was in church with, he hoped, most of the womenfolk. This time he was glad that Diggins and Hughes were not with him. He wasn't in the mood for a gang rape. He thought back to the evening in the *Assistance's* cabin when he had Janetta pinned against the wall with her breast in his hand. They had been interrupted then, but today would be different. Janetta would be alone with her baby and nobody was about to disturb them.

He tugged the front of his tunic down in an attempt to look his best. Did he wish to impress her or was it an automatic reflex to boost his own courage? "A smart soldier is an efficient soldier', he told himself, "a brave soldier; a soldier that attracts the ladies." He smoothed his dank, greasy hair down with the palm of his hand and replaced his forage cap at just the right angle, the strap neatly tucked under his chin.

The wooden stairs creaked as they took his weight. He didn't attempt to hide his presence or be silent in his approach. The sound of soldier's boots on the stairs and veranda were a common occurrence and wouldn't cause any alarm, even on a Sunday morning.

He walked along the balcony looking at the numbers on the doors until he came to number sixteen where he stopped and took a deep breath before rapping on the door.

At first there was silence inside and for one deflating moment he thought she might be out. Then he heard a woman murmur inside and some footsteps approaching the door.

The door opened and Janetta stood before him. He grinned with satisfaction at seeing her, his mouth full of yellow tobacco-stained teeth. For a second Janetta stared at him in stunned disbelief. She couldn't believe her eyes, but her worst fears were confirmed when she heard the rasping voice.

"Allo, my sweet!"

Janetta suddenly slammed the door in Major Cope's face but he was ready for that. His boot shot forward and jammed the door.

He put both hands on the door and pushed it open against Janetta's body weight pressing on the other side. It was almost too easy. Overpowered, Janetta stepped quickly back making him stumble into her front room. She backed away from him in horror.

"What the 'ell are you doing 'ere?" she stammered.

Cope regained his footing and drew himself up to his full height. He closed the door behind him barring her exit.

"Pleased ta see me no doubt eh?" He was grinning from ear to ear and his eyes looked her up and down. She was not in her Sunday 'best', which surprised him. She looked as if she'd been scrubbing the kitchen floor. She wore her brown work dress and white pinny – at least it had been white, her sleeves were rolled up above her elbows and her hair was tied in a tight bun at the back of her head. She had a black smudge on her cheek.

Janetta's mind went into a horrific spin. She suddenly had flashes of Cope's cabin on the *Assistance* and of being presented with the Colonel's diary. She remembered his pleasure at tormenting her with what he knew of her affair and his demands for money to buy his silence. She remembered too his groping hands, stale breath, and her husband's struggle to push him overboard. How this bastard tormented her. Was she never to be rid of him?

She backed away from him until she was standing against the table. Her hand instinctively slid across the tabletop until her fingers felt the blade of a carving knife.

Having closed the door, Major Cope, sauntered casually over to the armchair and sat down. He was in no hurry and had decided to take the soft approach.

"I'm surprised and a little hurt that you appear displeased to see me, Mrs Rayner."

His voice was calm and almost soft. Janetta didn't move. She edged the blade closer with her fingers until she could feel the handle.

"Now, you and I have had a chequered past, have we not? And I think it's about time you dropped your hostility towards me."

Janetta gave a derisive snort. The handle was almost within her grasp.

"Let bygones be bygones eh? Why don't we start again? I'd like to be friends, Mrs Rayner." His tone was smooth and relaxed. Despite her repulsion, Janetta had to admit that he was being quite charming.

It was a good job she knew what a snake he really was. She had no doubt that other women could have fallen under his charming spell, but it wasn't working on her.

"Well now, Major Cope," she replied, without hiding her disgust, "per'aps you might understand me when I tell ya, tha' if yoos were the last man on earth, I'd 'ave no worries about slittin ya bleedin' throat in the night."

The smile dropped from his face and she could see that she had angered him. It was the effect she intended but as she looked into his predatory eyes she had a sudden fear that she shouldn't have provoked him. She had awoken the tiger.

"And I thought we would be getting along really well too!" he replied, straining to keep his composure. "I see now that you're still the little whore you always were." Janetta straighten her back in defiance at such an insult. "And as such I shall treat you as a whore."

"Bastard!" spat Janetta, her hand closing on the handle of the knife behind her skirt.

Cope stood up and took a step towards her.

"Now since you're a little whore, I know you require some business, but I don't pay for the likes of scrubbers like you. I just take 'em if you get my meaning."

"One step closer and I'll kill ya. Ya shit!" Janetta produced the knife and held it out at Cope's chest.

Major Cope looked at the knife and his face relaxed into a broad grin and he burst out laughing. Janetta was perplexed at his reaction. Why was he laughing at her?

"I'm warning ya!" she said, her voice rising and quavering more with rage than fear.

Cope roared with laughter even more, and then in the blink of an eye his face went serious, his hand shot out and caught her wrist. He reached out with his other hand and prised her fingers off the knife handle.

"Bless me, you're a feisty little one aren't you?" he said without the slightest amusement in his voice. Janetta tried to pull her arm away from his grasp, but to no avail. He held her so tightly that the blood flow to her hand was restricted.

"Now my little whore, you have two choices."

"Only two? Ya su'prise me!"

"You can offer yourself to me now or I can arrange for your husband to have an accident every time you refuse me. Your choice, my dear."

Janetta fumed. "So you gutless wonder, yer can't stoop much lower can ya?"

The back of Cope's hand flashed before her and struck her face. She let out a cry, more of shock than pain, as she twisted away from the blow and slumped over the table. Cope was on her in a second and she felt her dress being torn open across her back. He grabbed her shoulders and forced her to roll over. Janetta kept her arms clutched tight against her breast to prevent him from ripping her dress down at the front. Her knees and feet kicked upward at every opportunity, forcing Cope to constantly shift his position to avoid being hurt. She was damned if she was going to make it easy for him.

Cope suddenly backed off and picked up the knife he had discarded on the floor. He grabbed her arm and pulled her upright, shoving the point of the blade at her throat.

"Now I had just about enough of you, my dear," he hissed into her face. She winced at his stale breath. "You're going to be a good little whore and spread your legs for me, or I'm going to spoil that pretty face of yours."

****

Will took the stairs three steps at a time, pumping his arms and panting. His boots thumped on the wooden steps as he raced up to the second floor veranda. Michael followed on his heels. A small group of women had gathered outside their doors to see what the commotion was all about. Will pushed his way past them and threw open the front door to his flat. The door slammed back against the wall and in the shadows of the parlour he could see two figures struggling against the back wall.

The slamming door startled Cope and he swung around to face the intruder. His right arm was over Janetta's right shoulder, his hand tightly gripping her left breast, exposed by her torn dress. In his left hand he held a carving knife pointed at her throat. Janetta was trying to struggle but was prevented by the point of the blade.

Cope squinted at the figure silhouetted against the sky in the doorway and hissed his warning.

"Get out you bastard!"

He had assumed it was one of his cronies come to gawk at his fun, but as his eyes adjusted to the glare of the outside sun he recognized Will Rayner.

Will felt his face flush with rage at the sight of his wife in Cope's grip and his first impulse was to rush into the room and attack Cope, but the sight of the knife at Janetta's throat stopped him. He screamed into the gloom of the room.

"Get the fuck out 'ere!"

The corner of Cope's mouth turned up into a grimace.

"Go and play somewhere else, toad!" he sneered, "This is no place for wet whelps like you!"

Will could barely contain his anger but he was far too wily to get himself trapped in a small room with Cope. He knew his best bet was to lure him away from Janetta and out onto the veranda.

"Get out here you fucking piece of horse shit!"

Cope's grotesque face contorted into a fearsome snarl and Will edged back slightly. Nobody dared speak to Cope that way, not if they wished to live, and coming from that scrawny little runt Rayner was more than Cope could bear. He grunted and threw Janetta violently aside and sent her sprawling on the floor. His eyes half closed, his head strained forward in a malevolent stare, he slowly advanced towards the door.

The sight of this grotesque bear of a man, seething with rage and coming towards the door made Will suddenly have doubts about his own survival, but he was committed now and there was no backing away from this fight.

Will's five foot four inch slender frame was no match against Cope's bulk and his reputation for violence brought sourness to Will's bowels. His best bet was to stay agile and avoid Cope's brick-like fists. He backed away from the doorway, drawing Cope onto the veranda. At least he was away from Janetta. Michael also backed out of the doorway to allow Will to retreat.

"Come on you useless piece of shit!" he heard himself taunting.

"I'm going to tear you apart, Rayner and then I'll take that pretty wife of yours. She'll enjoy that I'm sure." Cope was trying to get Will so mad that he wouldn't think straight. There was nothing Cope liked more than having a nearly hysterical opponent lashing out at him wildly; they made for easy victories. Will wasn't taking the bait; he was too smart for that. He ignored Cope's gibes and concentrated instead on keeping out of trouble and waiting for Cope to make a mistake. Michael and Will were joined by some of their neighbours who had come out of their flats to see what all the noise was about.

"You're going to 'ave to get me first, you ass'ole!"

Cope took a swing at him and Will ducked back so the fist missed his face. Some of the women began to egg Will on and jeer at Cope. This seemed to anger him more. He hated being insulted by women; it reminded him of his mother's constant tongue lashing, never praising, always criticizing.

Michael lunged at Cope's back, grabbing his collar, but Cope swung around and punched him so hard in the face that he was knocked out cold.

Spinning around he took another swing at Will, this time catching him on the mouth and sending him sprawling on the floor.

Will lay face down on the veranda deck and tasted the sweet blood in his mouth. He looked over his shoulder just in time to see Cope pick up an old stool and bring it crashing down. Will rolled to one side and felt the floor shudder as the stool hit it just beside his face.

At this moment, Janetta came out of the flat and started screaming at Cope to distract him, but he was already bringing the stool down a second time, and again Will rolled to the side to avoid it. As the stool hit the floor, Will grabbed it and was able to prevent Cope's third shot. Janetta now joined in the fight and gave Cope a kick in the small of his back. He staggered forward which gave Will the chance to get to his feet.

An elderly lady standing by her front door smacked Cope over the head with a saucepan, it was a cheap pan and the handle bent, but it was enough to distract him. He swung his arm behind him to ward off a second blow and Will took his chance to kick Cope hard in the knee.

Cope let out a small groan as his knee buckled under him. He staggered and Janetta rained blows on his back. Cope shoved her to one side and gritting his teeth, charged at Will.

Will was momentarily taken off guard and brought his hands up to ward off Cope, who was coming for his throat. Will grabbed his arm and ducked to one side, flinging Cope round in a wide arc. Cope, out of control, staggered backwards towards the railing. His arm banged against the iron post supporting the veranda roof and Will heard a sickening, cracking noise. Cope let out a scream of agony and crashed through the railing falling the ten feet to the ground below.

Will, gasping for breath, looked over the edge. Cope was unconscious and his arm was bent backwards, clearly broken.

Janetta put her arm around Will's waist and peered down at Cope lying in a crumpled heap in the dust.

"Serves the bleeder right!" she said, and the old lady with the saucepan laughed and said that she never did like that pan.

Michael sat up groaning and rubbing his jaw.

"Did we beat the focking bastard?" he asked.

****

Brigadier Phipps struggled to contain his laughter. Lieutenant Douglas had brought the news of the fight and Cope's injuries to his office after the service. He stood in front of the Brigadier's desk and looked shocked as the Brigadier struggled to contain his amusement.

"Sir, with respect," he said, "this is a serious matter. A bombardier has attacked a major, sir. Surely we must arrest Rayner."

The Brigadier shook his head and waved a finger at the Lieutenant.

"I don't think so, Douglas. Cope is a shit and from what I understand he more than had it coming. What are his injuries again?"

"A broken arm and possible concussion, sir!" replied Douglas astounded by the Brigadier's lack of concern.

"So he'll be out of action for a while eh?"

"Yes, sir."

"Good!" the Brigadier broke into a laugh, "bloody good!"

Seeing the Lieutenant's expression of disbelief he gave a small cough and forced himself to appear serious.

"No, you're quite right Lieutenant, it's not a laughing matter."

He chuckled to himself again.

"How long does the doctor think it will be before the Major can travel, Douglas?"

"Travel, sir?"

"Yes Douglas, travel."

"A couple of weeks I suppose, sir. I hadn't asked him."

"I understand the Major's never seen India, Douglas. It's a real shame not to see the greatest part of our empire, don't you think?"

"Yes, sir!"

"Find out which brigades will be leaving for that continent in the near future, Douglas. It's time the Major saw a bit of the world. That's all."

"Yes, sir."

The Lieutenant left, not quite sure what had just taken place but the Brigadier was happier than he had seen him in a long time.

PART FOUR

CHAPTER 29

Retirement
Woolwich 1899

Will walked down the courtyard towards the main gate. He felt awed by the immensity of what he had just seen and a spark of excitement filled him. He stopped for a moment to let a horse pulling a cart heavily laden with artillery shells pass in front of him, the iron wheels clattering on the cobbles. He glanced back in wonderment at the buildings around him.

He was standing in the middle of an enormous courtyard almost fifty yards wide and several hundred yards long. The cobbled courtyard had two rows of double storeyed gray stone buildings flanking the east and west sides. Bridging the buildings was a gigantic metal roof supported by iron pillars.

This overwhelming complex was the *Royal Laboratory* and as impressive as it was, it was only a part of the much larger Armoury that covered more than one hundred acres of land on the south bank of the River Thames at Woolwich.

The cart moved on past Will and he continued his walk down the long courtyard; his ears full of the pulsing of machinery and his nostrils thick with smoke and cordite.

He had spent the afternoon being given a guided tour of the *Laboratory*. His head was still swimming with the sound of five hundred lathes. They were powered by drive belts fed from over four thousand feet of overhead shafts, which themselves were driven by two steam engines located at the south east and south west corners.

He knew all about the Woolwich Arsenal of course, what soldier of the Royal Artillery didn't, but seeing it for himself was an extraordinary experience. He'd had no idea how vast the place was and now he was on the verge of working there.

Twenty years he'd been in the army and it was time to retire. The Royal Arsenal was an obvious next step for an artillery soldier and there was plenty of work to be had. He'd been offered the job of labourer. It wasn't much but the pay wasn't too bad at one shilling and sixpence a day. He'd have a secure job and be very close to home, being only a short walk from their flat on the New Road.

Will and Janetta loved Woolwich. Their two years at Ipswich had passed pleasantly enough once Cope had been posted to India. Janetta had given birth to a son they named William and they'd made new friends, but after two years they were posted back to Woolwich and were both very pleased.

Will arrived at the end of the roof that sheltered him from the rain and made his way to the front gate. As he passed under the gate a guard saluted him and he ran across the road dodging a double-decker horse bus and a grocery cart. He kept his head down as he ran through the rain and very nearly bumped into a small two-wheeled cart on the pavement with the words 'Cat Meat' in large yellow letters on the side. The owner of the cart was a scruffy youth with several tears in his jacket, crumpled and baggy trousers and muddy boots with the uppers coming away from the soles.

"Ooy wotch it!" he exclaimed as he grabbed the cart preventing it from being knocked over, "bloody 'ell."

"Sorry, sorry," said Will as he side-stepped around the cart.

He strolled on in the rain contemplating his news of retirement. How would Jan respond? She'd be pleased, he was sure. For some time now she had fretted about how they would survive without his sergeant's pay, so the news of a secure job should put her mind at ease. He'd been very worried about her over the past year. It seemed to Will that she had lost her enthusiasm for life. After giving birth to five children her figure was not what it used to be. She had a little potbelly and sagging breasts, which distressed her, although he thought her as beautiful as ever. Her beautiful black hair, which she still wore long, now had streaks of gray creeping through it and her face and neck were showing the lines of age, but she was still a very handsome woman.

What worried Will the most was her disinterest in the children.

Her joy at motherhood had passed after William was born and now she found herself overwhelmed by noisy, dirty children who were out of control most of the time. As young Jan grew into a teenager she was forced to take over most of the mothering duties, which left Janetta free to do the neighbour's laundry, and to drink. Her drinking was becoming more frequent and when drunk, she flirted outrageously with any man willing to be cornered by her. Most of the neighbours tolerated her behaviour because despite her nightly stupor, she was well liked. It was the men from outside the immediate neighbourhood that Janetta picked on, and they took her to be a common whore and therefore fair game.

All this Will suffered stoically and did his best to support her and encourage her to pay attention to the children. For the most part he was fighting a rear guard action and barely holding his own.

Will walked the last few yards toward his front door feeling tired and footsore. It had been an emotionally exhausting day, albeit exciting, and all he wanted to do was throw off his tunic, drag his feet out of his boots and flop into his favourite chair. A warm cup of tea, a hot meal and a warm bed filled his mind as he pushed the key into the lock on his front door.

As he opened the door the bustle and noise of cartwheels on the cobbles of New Road died away and his ears were assaulted by the sound of tired, cranky children. Little Jane, the baby of the family, was sitting on the floor in front of the burnt-out fire, sucking the tassles on the end of the hearthrug. Seven year old Thomas, always a handful, was doing his best to annoy his younger brother Albert, who was sitting at the table, drawing on the back of a scrap of wallpaper. Thomas mischievously pulled at the paper and grabbed at the pencil with no other reason than to cause Albert to scream and cry all the louder. Janetta, the eldest daughter, now an attractive fourteen-year-old and called May by the family to avoid confusion with her mother, was in the kitchen washing dishes and ignoring the younger ones. There was no sign of the eldest boy, William, or Janetta.

"Tom! Leave your brother alone!" growled Will as he unbuttoned his tunic.

Thomas abandoned his 'brother baiting' and sat petulantly on the floor next to his sister and picked his nose.

"Jan, I'm home!" Will yelled up the stairs.

"She aint in," said May as she came into the room wiping her hands on a tea towel.

"Where is she, luv?" Will asked as he flopped into his chair and began tugging at his boot. It was a question he didn't really have to ask and feared the answer.

"Gone up the *Duke*," said May as she pulled the tassle out of Jane's mouth, "Ach! Nasty! Nasty!"

Jane whimpered her disapproval at the loss of the tassle.

"When d'she go?"

"Couple of hours ago." replied May, and she gave him a look that suggested he shouldn't expect the best.

Will groaned and started pushing his foot back into his boot.

His instinct was to let out a string of profanities but it wasn't in his nature to do so. As a soldier he could swear and cuss with the best of them, but he always held his tongue around women and especially in front of the children. He took a deep breath and bit his lip.

"Feed the little ones will ya? I'll go get 'er."

There was a distinct tone of desperation in his voice. His whole countenance expressed fatigue, frustration and suppressed anger. May wanted to comfort him as he dragged himself out of the chair and began to push his arms back into his tunic, but she didn't know what to say. There was nothing she could say. Nothing that would soothe her father's hurt.

Will buttoned his tunic. He looked at himself in the mirror and drew himself up as tall as he could. He smoothed his ruffled hair with the palm of his hand and tugged down on his tunic to remove the creases. He took a moment to look with pride at his recently earned sergeant's stripes on his arm before taking a deep breath. Chin up, chest out and walk smartly, that was the way. Face the world with fortitude and purpose and do not waiver in the face of adversity.

He gave his tunic one more tug before turning to face the kids.

"Be'ave yourselves, I won't be long."

He walked back out of the door he had entered just five minutes before. It was still raining, and in the growing dark the cobbles were slick and shiny. The lamplighter was outside the house reaching up into the glass lamp with a taper on the end of a pole to light the gas. The gas lamps left small pools of light that reflected on the damp stones. Piles of horse manure slowly disintegrated into soggy heaps of mud in the gutters.

It wasn't far to the *Duke*; just to the end of the street. It was the local pub where all the neighbours met to exchange gossip over a gin at the end of the day. There was usually a small group of people gathered outside the door but tonight the rain had driven them inside. As he approached the door he could hear a piano being played inside, the sounds of laughter and a hum of voices. It was a busy night. He walked into the thick smoke-filled bar and looked round the room for his wife. At first he couldn't see her, and he felt a pang of anxiety wondering where she could be. He strained to look over people's heads or around small groups standing with their drinks in their hands.

He couldn't find her anywhere. Then a shriek of laughter drew his attention to the far corner, where a group of half a dozen young men were seated around a table. They were well-dressed but not gentlemen. They looked as if they were bank clerks or lawyers and by their demeanour it was obvious they'd had far too much to drink. They were all laughing and shouting at one another over their bawdy jokes. In their midst was Janetta, sitting on the lap of a particularly inebriated youth who appeared to have his hand up her dress.

Janetta had her arm round his shoulder and was leaning backwards kissing the man who sat to her right, whilst seemingly oblivious to the hand creeping up her thigh.

They hadn't spotted Will.

Any man, witnessing his wife in such a position, would be filled with an uncontrollable rage. Will, however, pushed his anger deeper into his gut and remained calm as he watched from the far side of the room. He'd seen this all before. It was a pathetically common scene.

For a year now he had watched Janetta slide into a steady decline. She had never made any secret of the fact that she hated housework and cooking. She had raised five children but had never been what you would call 'a natural mother'.

Several times he had witnessed her, alone in the bedroom, holding an old maroon dress to her bosom and admiring herself in the mirror. It was hideously out of fashion and too small for her now, but it had obviously been very expensive when new, far more than he could ever afford. As she gazed at her reflection in the glass, a gentle smile would light up her tired eyes, and for a few brief moments she would be so far away in another time and place that she would be quite oblivious to his presence. Then the spell would fade and she'd fold it neatly in her arms and return it to the trunk.

Her slips into nostalgia became more frequent and Will secretly feared she would eventually lose her grip on reality. The only time she laughed now was when she was drinking, and she was drinking far too frequently. He had become accustomed to his rescue missions in the evenings and more often than not, he found her drunk and flirting with whoever would pay her any attention. Tonight was no different.

He slowly made his way through the crowded bar until he was standing right in front of the table. Janetta didn't see him, continuing to kiss the young man beside her who was no more than eighteen or nineteen years of age. One by one the other men realized he was there and fell silent.

Will was not a large or terrifying man. His five foot four inches and slight build did not give the impression of toughness, but twenty years in the army, and being in command of a gun crew, had taught him how to handle men. He had learned how to stand with presence and how to transform his baby blue eyes into an icy stare, conveying the message that he was definitely not a man to be trifled with.

The young men looked warily at this soldier in his smart blue uniform with sergeant stripes on his arm. They were young and cocky but they understood enough not to cross a sergeant of the artillery. The wandering hand was quickly removed from under Janetta's skirt and the lad's face reddened as he did his best to extricate himself from under Janetta's lap. His squirming broke Janetta's interest in her kissing and she struggled to straighten up on his lap.

Will remained silent yet maintained his cold fixation on the young impressionable faces.

Janetta, realizing that it had gone quiet, turned to look at her companions.

"Wot's a matter wi ya all?" she slurred.

Seeing the look of shock and embarrassment on their faces, she squinted in the direction they were looking and tried to focus on the blue uniform that stood before them. A smile of recognition crossed her sweat-glistened face.

"Ohhh!" she said, her exclamation tailing off musically, "look who's 'ere!"

She struggled to get off her new friend's lap, knocking the table and slopping a couple of ales as she did so.

Will passively watched his wife as she attempted to rise from the table. "*How can a beautiful woman look so ugly in this state*", he thought; and she was still beautiful. The years had taken their toll. She was forty-three now and the lines in her face betrayed her. Her hair was hanging loose round her shoulders, greasy and wet with sweat from her face. Her hands were rough from years of doing laundry and housework and her eyes were tired.

Yet she was still a very handsome woman and Will found himself unable to be truly angry with the young men who now found sport in groping a willing woman. It was common enough for soldiers to get out of hand with other men's wives when in town, either here or abroad, and he knew it meant nothing to them.

Janetta's recent inclination to bawdy and unseemly behavior, however, was beginning to seriously worry him. Was she so discontent with him and their family, that she was willing to make a spectacle of herself in front of all their neighbours? Wasn't she satisfied with the reputation she'd already earned for herself? Was she intent on playing the part to the fullest?

"Well…if it ain't the Sergeant?" she slurred loudly.

People close to them were beginning to abandon their own conversations in favour of watching this drama unfold. Will held his temper and maintained his posture of unflinching command.

"Twenty fucking years…twenty!" she yelled, ignoring Will and addressing her friends who looked very sheepish. "You'd think e'ed 'ave been more than a sergeant by now, wouldn't ya? Twenty fucking years!"

Janetta staggered as her legs gave way under her and she sat back hard on the now vacant lap. The young man groaned under her sudden weight and did his best to push her back up onto her feet.

"Come with me!" said Will in a cold, commanding voice that, for a second, stunned Janetta. He was her Will; her good and loving husband who doted over their children and was always kind and thoughtful towards her. He was her 'puppy dog Will' whom she pushed around and dominated. "Come with me", was all he'd said, but his voice was different now. Now he was addressing his gun crew and it was a tone of voice that couldn't be mocked or ignored. Why did she feel a warm glow in her gut when he spoke to her that way?

Janetta made an extra effort to stand and take a small step forward until her breasts were touching Will's tunic. She looked up at him, smiled a tippled smile and softening her voice, said, "He's my sergeant, my beautiful blue soldier!"

Will looked her straight in the eye, not relaxing his body or softening his eyes. He stood as a rock; his feet were firmly planted eighteen inches apart, toes pointing slightly outwards and his hands clasped behind his back.

Janetta, in a moment of remorse, avoided his gaze by lowering her forehead against his chest and leaned into him.

Will focused once more on the young men. He could feel a score of eyes on him as the bar fell silent. It was as if the crowd was holding its collective breath in anticipation of some violent outcome to this humiliating scene. But Will, as if on parade, was determined to show no weakness. The six young men, who a couple of minutes ago were having the time of their lives with a local trollop, now sat glued to their chairs, frozen in helplessness as they waited for the sergeant's wrath to explode upon them.

Slowly, Will's right arm came up to Janetta's shoulder. She shuddered slightly as his thumb bit into her collarbone. His grip was firm but not hurtful. He slowly pushed her away from him. His eyes met hers again, cold and commanding, and releasing his grip on her shoulder, he pointed with a straight horizontal arm at the door.

Will's eyes immediately reverted to the petrified youths. The message was clear and uncompromising.

A murmur went through the bar. Feet shuffled and skirts rustled as the crowd parted to leave a clear passage between Janetta and the door. She looked up at Will pleadingly as if silently begging him to spare her this humiliating and lonely exit. She felt the eyes of all her neighbours and friends upon her. She knew she was well liked by them, and she knew in her heart that many of them were hurting and embarrassed for her, but tonight she had stepped over the line and most of the sympathy was for her poor husband.

Will's gaze went right over her head and his arm remained as a signpost. There was to be no further communication between them. She lowered her eyes to the ground and fought against the swimming in her head to maintain her balance. It wasn't far to walk. Just a few steps to cross the floor and then she could grab hold of the brass door handle to steady herself. "*Just let me get to the door without staggering too much*", she thought. "*Let me get out of here with a modicum of dignity.*"

She began to walk, slowly at first, feeling the strength in her legs and fighting the sense of being on a ship's deck in a rolling sea. As she passed, she felt the stares of the people but looked at none of them. There were just three more steps to the door.

Will's arm returned behind his back. The youths didn't know whether to watch Janetta leave or focus on the sergeant still in front of them. They feared the sergeant but their hearts went out to Janetta and they almost willed her to make it out of the door without stumbling in front of everyone. Will paid no attention to his wife as she left the bar. He remained fixated on the youths.

Janetta reached the door and grasped the handle. She breathed a sigh of relief at finding something solid to hang on to. She paused for a moment before taking a deep breath and pulling against the spring on the door to open it. It proved too heavy for her in her inebriated condition and an arm in a threadbare tweed jacket came out from nowhere and pulled the door open for her. She barely acknowledged the helping stranger, but gratefully stepped through the door into the cold night air.

The crowd in the bar transferred their attention to Will. Now they expected the fireworks to fly.

Will now skillfully turned his icy stare to a menacing glare. It was a subtle facial change that would hardly be noticed by anyone but those who fell under his eyes, and for those unlucky ones it spelled impending retribution.

The five youths, almost on cue, edged back on their seats as if to put a couple of extra inches between themselves and the sergeant.

Will glared at the nearest lad on his left. He drilled his eyes directly into the hapless lad's soul until he felt him begin to wilt. The lad's lower lip trembled and his eyes watered. Will saw the telltale signs of the lad's willpower breaking. Any moment now he would breakdown in tears and Will felt his power increasing as his dominance grew in intensity. At just the right moment, when he felt sure the lad would pee himself, he decided to spare him and transferred his eyes to the next lad.

One by one he cowed the youths, reducing them to trembling, whimpering children. They felt him mark them forever. Here was a man who could take them any time he pleased and the fear of God swept through their stomachs. The message was clear enough without a single word being spoken. Mess with my wife again and he'd hunt them down. They wouldn't be spared a second time.

The message wasn't lost on any of the other men in the room either. The silence filled them with the horror of the possible consequences of flirting with Janetta. Many of the women smirked behind their hands at seeing grown men cowed before one soldier.

Content that he had achieved the desired effect, Will turned to look at the crowd. His eyes scanned the faces unflinchingly. He was in complete control of the moment and felt no hurry to end the spell.

With his head held high, his chest out and shoulders back, he strode across the bar, his boots echoing on the bare floorboards. He was a military man, a seasoned soldier, a professional killer and a man to be respected.

He left the bar and stepped out into the damp night, where he found his wife down on her haunches, slumped against the wall. The rain glistened on her hair, which now hung limply covering her face. She was quietly whimpering.

Will stood beside her and looked down at the small deceptively fragile looking woman. How pathetic she looked but how so very much he loved her. Despite her drinking, occasional rages and her careless mothering, he was still captivated by her.

She was still admired as one of the handsomest wives in the regiment; the officers no longer hung around her; there was a new generation of beautiful young women upstaging her now. Perhaps that's what depressed Janetta more than anything. Her complaints about the children, the laundry she took in and Will's lowly rank, were all symptoms of her gradual loss of status as the number one beauty in the Regiment. Her pride was hurt and she feared middle age.

He bent down and took hold of her with both hands under her arms and lifted her to her feet. She leaned into him and hung her head against his tunic again. She was a little girl once more, sheltering under the protective arms of her father. She could smell Will's tobacco pouch in his pocket and fancied it was her father's pipe tobacco and that she was back in Tywardreath. Her father would take her home and keep her safe. She'd soon be tucked up in her little bed in the cottage in Chapel Down.

"Come on, let's go 'ome."

Will's voice was strained and tired but not unkind. With his arm around her waist for support, they began a slow, slightly unsteady walk back towards the house.

CHAPTER 30

Sink or Swim

Janetta carried young Jane in her arms as she walked along the dirt path that ran beside the River Thames. May walked beside her, squinting as she raised her face to the sun. It was a beautiful sunny Sunday afternoon. The sky was clear of the smoke that usually bellowed from a sea of chimneys and sunlight glistened on the *Thames*. The great river curved at Woolwich and was about six hundred yards wide on the bend. Even though it was Sunday the river was full of craft going up and down between the city and the sea, and a small steam ferry went back and forth between the north and south bank. There was so much activity and so many people out enjoying the sunshine that the riverbank had a holiday spirit about it.

Thomas and Albert walked ahead, half running, half skipping between the other people taking the air. Thomas was being particularly rambunctious today. He loved to bait his younger brother and Albert, quiet and shy, did his best to stand up to or avoid his brother. Janetta was getting tired. She had spent her whole morning yelling at Tom to behave himself. How she wished she had Will with her to discipline him. Tom was getting out of control and Janetta was beginning to despair.

Thomas was the kind of child who took delight in defying his mother. If Janetta said don't walk in the puddles he obeyed by jumping in them. If he was scolded for throwing clumps of earth at his brother he changed to throwing gravel. He was slowly wearing Janetta down and her ability to control him was slipping further through her fingers.

Thomas now had Albert in a headlock and was running along the path dragging his screaming brother by the neck. Janetta screamed at him but May ran ahead, to separate the boys.

"*Oh!*" thought Janetta, "*for a little peace and a glass of gin.*"

They approached a small jetty that jutted out a couple of hundred feet into the Thames. There was a small sailing craft moored up to one side of it but nobody onboard. The two boys ran down the wooden planked pier to look at the boat.

"Careful!" yelled Janetta after them, but was ignored. Her attention was then distracted from the boys by hearing her name called.

"Mrs Rayner isn't it."

She turned to find herself being addressed by one of two artillery officers, both in their blue dress uniforms. One she recognized immediately as Major Hewitt. Will really liked "old Hewy" as he called him. Major Hewitt was in his fifties, rather stout and very jovial. Janetta had always liked him too.

"Bless my soul it is you, dear Mrs Rayner."

"Major!" replied Janetta with some surprise, "I haven't seen you in ages. How are you keeping?"

May detected an immediate change in her mother's diction. She had suddenly started speaking in a refined voice that she rarely heard these days and which really took her by surprise. There were no clipped words, coarse pronunciation or slang. Her mother spoke in a clear gentile manner that made her stand and stare in astonishment. It didn't go unnoticed by Janetta.

"May dear, your mouth is open! A lady doesn't stare with her mouth open! Goodness me child!" Then she turned and addressed herself to Major Hewitt again. "Children these days Major. Deary me!"

"Your daughter is as beautiful as you, dear lady! Is that not so Pulski?"

"Indeed it is Major," agreed the lieutenant.

Janetta distrusted Lieutenant Pulski and had never liked him. He reminded her very much of Major Tomlins. He was typical of the "idle rich" officers, in that he was more interested in his toilette than in soldiering. Lieutenant Pulski was far too perfect and fastidious to be a soldier.

He was stroking his moustache and looking at May with a glint in his eye and Janetta felt compelled to break his spell.

"Pulski? That's an unusual name, Lieutenant."

The Lieutenant reluctantly switched his attention to Janetta.

"My parents came from Poland, ma'am. But I was born an Englishman, I do assure you."

Tom and Albert, having tired of looking at the boat, moved on to the end of the jetty and gazed through the handrail at the water. The river lapped at the wooden piers beneath them. They leaned over the rail and peered down at the barnacle-encrusted pilings. Seaweed clung to the sides and flowed back and forth under the waves.

"You, Mrs Rayner, have been greatly missed about the barracks. Why don't we see you these days?"

"You're very kind, Major but as you see I have a family and they keep me pretty busy."

Major Hewitt kept looking at Janetta but leaned his head towards the Lieutenant and with a grin said, "Janetta Rayner, Lieutenant, shone brightly in the camp."

"Now, now, Major." Janetta rebuked him coyly.

"Indeed you did dear lady. Half the camp was smitten with you."

Janetta laughed at him. "Major you're a tease and no mistake."

May grinned shyly.

Thomas hadn't forgotten about goading his brother and now that his mother was occupied he took full advantage of the moment.

"Betya can't do this," he said, and immediately climbed up onto the railing. Albert watched him but did nothing. He was half Thomas's size and the climb was far harder for him. Thomas sat astride the railing some fifteen feet above the brown waters and laughed at his younger brother.

"You're a scaredy you is!" he said. "Anybody can do this, look."

He grabbed hold of a small flagpole used to signal the ferry on the opposite bunk and lifted himself into the standing position. He stood proudly on the top rail and looked about him at the view.

"See it's easy! Only 'scaredy custards' can't do this!"

Albert knew he was being taunted and that he'd never hear the last of it if he didn't join his brother on the railing; so he strained to lift his small leg up onto the first railing and pull himself up.

"Now, Mrs Rayner, I would consider it a privilege if you and your husband would join me for dinner one evening," said Major Hewitt. Lieutenant Pulski flinched at the thought but said nothing.

Janetta was taken by surprise. Years ago she would have jumped at the invitation, but years of marriage to Will helped her forget her flippant days as a young woman. She no longer felt beautiful. She was beginning to feel old and tired, trapped by her brood of children and lack of money. Her hair was flecked with gray and her red, chapped hands gave away her profession. She could no longer afford new clothes and her best dress was sadly out of fashion. She was beginning to feel every bit a washerwoman and her identity was eroding away with her confidence. She didn't know how to respond to the Major.

"It's very kind of you, Major…" she said hesitatingly, "but I'm not sure if Will can still fit into his uniform."

The Major looked amused.

"My dear Mrs Rayner an informal get-together of old friends is what I was thinking? Not dinner in the mess. Perhaps we could meet at the *Crown*?"

Lieutenant Pulski smirked behind the hand that continued to fondle his moustache.

"I wouldn't wish to embarrass your Will. Oh my no dear lady! What was I thinking?"

Janetta put the poor Major out of his embarrassment.

"I'll ask him, I'm sure he'd love to talk over old times with you, Major. When things have settled down a bit."

She laid her hand on his arm to reassure him. "He's working very hard right now. But I'm sure he'd be pleased."

The Major's face lit up with the promise of a future friendship with the famous beauty of the Regiment.

"Dear Mrs Rayner!" he said.

"Janetta, please Major," she replied.

"Cum on!" said Tom, "it ain't that 'ard!"

Albert heaved his stomach up onto the top rail, grabbed hold of the flagpole, his little fingers barely able to meet around the pole, and slung his leg over the top rail.

"Nearly made it!" encouraged Tom. "Now stand up!"

Albert bit his lower lip and looked nervously at his brother who towered above him on the railing. He felt his thin legs losing their strength.

"Just hold the bleed'n pole and lift ya'self up! Come on!"

Albert gripped the pole with both hands and lifted his foot up onto the top rail and slowly stood up. He was quite surprised at himself when he was standing. He had made it, and was amazed at the view of the river. He glanced nervously back towards his mother. She seemed so far away and small as he looked down at her. She was standing on the promenade with May and talking to two soldiers.

He looked at the cold river below him and he felt a wave of weakness go through his legs.

"Great, init!" said Tom triumphantly. "It's like standing on the yardarm of a pirate ship. The pirates used to sword fight on the yards."

"Nah they didn't!" said Albert.

"Did too!" retorted Tom. "Like this see." And he started waving his arm about as if he had a cutlass and was fending off great blows from an adversary.

"Stop it you're shaking the pole," said Albert nervously.

Tom's eyes lit up at this. His little brother was scared and he felt the power.

"You're the enemy see," he said to Albert, "and I have to defend the ship."

Tom waved his invisible cutlass about his head and brought his hand down hard on Albert's arm.

"Owww! That 'urt!" whined Albert, and Tom, pleased with his blow did it again. "Stop that!" howled Albert close to tears.

Thomas laughed at his brother and started prodding him from his side of the pole, Albert tried to fend off the pokes and prods and slaps that came at him from both sides.

Janetta's attention was suddenly diverted from Major Hewitt. She heard Albert's shrieks of distress. She looked down the jetty to see her two sons standing up on the railing and Tom slapping Albert.

"Thomas!" she bellowed, "leave your brother be!"

The sudden sound of their mother's voice startled both boys. Tom stopped suddenly and looked at his mother's angry face. Albert was already struggling to hold his balance while defending himself from Tom's attack and now his mother's voice made him turn suddenly and loosen his grip on the pole.

Tom couldn't resist the temptation of getting in one last poke at his brother and punched him on the arm. For Albert there was a second or two where he seemed to be suspended in mid-air and then he found himself plummeting towards the water. The impact stung his face and the sudden cold made him want to inhale, but he instinctively held his breath as the dark waters engulfed him.

Janetta saw her Albert disappear over the edge and heard the deep splash as he hit the water.

"Bertie!" she screamed. She put Jane down, hitched up her skirts, and ran as fast as she could toward the end of the pier, followed by May.

May grabbed Thomas and lifted him down then joined Janetta at the rail staring down into the water. Albert had surfaced and was gasping and frantically flailing his arms about in the water. Janetta was beside herself. She couldn't swim and her favourite son was thrashing about in the water ten feet below her.

May yelled at Albert.

"Bert, listen! Kick your feet and go like this with ya arms," she waved her arms about like a dog digging a whole. "Keep your head up Bert and don't swallow the water."

Miraculously, Albert heard her and kept his wits about him enough to try and follow her directions. He was very close to one of the pilings but couldn't hold on to it because of all the slime and barnacles.

"This way Bertie!" yelled May, pointing to the side of the pier. "Kick ya feet and hands and go that way!"

Albert saw the sense of what she was saying. He needed to go towards the bank and so while keeping his head as far above the wind blown waves as he could, he kicked for all his life and found that he was making good headway towards shallow water.

Satisfied that her child was swimming, Janetta ran back down the jetty and jumped down onto the exposed mud. The tide was going out and the water was already half way down the length of the jetty. She was shocked when she immediately sank up to her shins in the stinking ooze. Her skirts fell about her in the mud and she had to pull them up above her knees in order to drag her feet out of the clinging mud. She staggered forward towards the water and the little head bobbing about amidst the thrashing.

Major Hewitt jumped into the mud behind her. He was overweight and out of shape for a soldier and as his boots sunk into the mud he fell forward onto his chest and had considerable trouble standing up again. Nevertheless he valiantly struggled through the clawing mud. Lieutenant Pulski stood on the promenade with little Jane and watched with a bemused look on his face. He was more entertained by seeing the Major covered in the stinking mud than he was concerned about the boy.

Albert, gasping and half-blinded by the water in his eyes, struggled on, encouraged by May who followed him above on the pier and called out instructions. He was almost to the water's edge now and he could see his mother and the soldier up to their knees in mud struggling to meet him. Suddenly he felt the slimy mud in his fingers and his knees dragged on the bottom. A few more kicks and he knew he would be able to stand up.

Thomas watched from the jetty and didn't say anything. He knew he was going to get into trouble as soon as Albert had been rescued.

Janetta, panting, tears running down her face, her legs and arms covered in the foulest ooze, reached the waters edge just as Albert was finding his feet. She grabbed him by the collar of his jacket and hoisted him up into her arms and sobbed. The Major caught her up and hugged them both. All three of them took a couple of moments to catch their breath and hang onto one another. It didn't feel at all strange to Janetta having the Major hug her. It was a well-meant hug of relief and rejoicing at the boy's safe return. It was the hug that Will would have given them. But in his absence the Major felt very comforting.

When he could find the breath the Major started laughing.

"Well young man, you've learned to swim. Well done!" he stroked Albert's dripping hair. "Well done indeed! Now we'd better get you home and dried off. Eh young man!"

Janetta struggled to laugh through her tears. Major Hewitt put his arm around her and they tried to pull their feet out of the sucking mud. In the couple of minutes while they had stood hugging, they had slowly sunk deeper and deeper into the foul reeking ooze so that they now had to work very hard to get their legs out again. It took them several minutes to struggle back to firm land and, when they reached the promenade, they were completely covered in mud and stank to high heaven. The Major had lost a boot and Janetta had lost both of her shoes but they were happy.

Lieutenant Pulski looked at them in disgust and held a handkerchief to his nose.

“May I escort you home Mrs Rayner?” said the Major and without waiting for a reply he turned to the Lieutenant, “I’ll see you back at the barracks Lieutenant”.

Thomas and May, holding Jane, walked up to their mother. Janetta didn’t look directly at Thomas but saw him out of the corner of her eye, and when he was within range, she slapped him hard on the head and made him yelp.

Albert shivered but looked triumphant.

CHAPTER 31

Crossroads
Thursday June 27 1901

Will stared up at the gray clouds as he was bumped and jostled along the cobbles in one of the small carts used to transport shells from one area to another in the armoury. He was laying flat on his back on the hard wooden boards, his head resting on a jacket to soften the jarring. A great weight pressed on his chest and pains ran down his left arm. He knew he'd had a heart attack and that his life was in peril but somehow it didn't worry him. His mind was full of other things.

"Hang in there, Will, we'll have ya 'ome soon."

The face of James Franklin was looking down at him from his right side. James was his thirty five-year-old friend, work mate and lodger in his house. He liked James who he always called 'Jimmy m'boy'. He considered him to be a good lad, honest and trustworthy.

It had been raining and Will could smell the freshness in the air. It was such a welcome change after the hot stale air inside the armoury. His nostrils were full of the dust, cordite, oil and furnace coal of the works, so that now he felt free again in the clear damp air.

"We've sent ahead for the doc, Will. He'll be waiting for yer at the 'ouse."

Will tried to smile appreciatively at old Frank who was looking down at him from his left side. Frank was an enormous man, a giant among men with huge arms and the strength of three men. It had been Frank who had picked him up like a baby off the floor in the works and laid him in the cart.

Will reckoned there were four of his work mates in the cart with him and one driving the horse.

"*God*", he thought, "*so it will end like this!*"

Eighteen months he'd toiled in the armoury. It hadn't been an easy transition from the army to the factory. It had taken him a long time to get used to the heat, noise and grime of the 'works' and it was hard labour. Most of the time he was pulling small wooden carts loaded with artillery shells from one area to another. They were not armed but very heavy – especially the naval shells – and moving them was back-breaking work.

Will was forty-nine years old and not a big man. The constant heavy work had begun to take a toll on him but he had been happy to be employed.

After twenty-one years in the Regiment, a life of spit and polish, a career topped off with promotion to sergeant, he would end his days on his back on the floor of a dirty wagon. He lay there wearing the filthiest clothes, which in the course of eighteen months had been reduced to rags stiff with grime. There was no point in buying good clothes. He could afford to buy them but the job was so dirty the clothes were ruined in no time.

His hands, once well-manicured and spotless, were now callused and blistered, with dirt pushed so far into the finger nails that it was impossible to wash out.

He was aware of being driven passed groups of workers who had stopped work to see him go by.

"Yu look arfta yuself, Will!"

"See you when you get back, Will. Good luck now."

Will was barely listening. Instead his mind was full of concern for his family. He loved his kids and worried about their future. May was his darling. She was fifteen now and what a beauty she was turning out to be. She was almost as beautiful as her mother, although her features were sharpened somewhat like her father's. His first son, William, now thirteen was working in a costermonger's and doing fine. Thomas was a worry. He was nine and could be a right little bastard. "*If I die,*" Will thought, "*how will Jan cope with him?*"

Then there was young Albert. A smile crept across Will's face as he thought about Albert. He was an adorable five-year-old child. He was skinny, shy and often bullied by Thomas, but so lovable. He would miss Albert. Lastly there was poor Jane. She was only four and, Will suspected, not long for this world. She was pale, thin and sickly, always coughing and crying. What, he wondered, would become of Jane?

He watched the top floors of buildings on the New Road drift by the cart and he was vaguely aware of the cries of the street vendors.

The sides of the cart and the knees of his companions prevented him from seeing much more but he wasn't really interested.

What would become of Janetta? He fretted about her. It wasn't just today that he worried, but every day for the past year. Janetta wasn't coping very well at all. She'd have the income from doing laundry and from their two lodgers but with all those mouths to feed, money would be scarce. Will feared she'd become a drunkard and give up on the kids, but what could he do?

He felt so tired, so very tired and couldn't focus his mind on her any more. He loved her desperately but no longer had the strength to concentrate on her. All he could do was keep her face in his mind as long as he could.

The cart pulled up in front of the house and James jumped down to run and hammer on the door.

"Aw right aw right keep ya 'air on," came Janetta's voice from the other side as she walked towards the door. It swung open.

"Oh!" said Janetta, surprised to see James on her doorstep at this hour of the day.

"Jan, it's Will. He collapsed at work. We've brought him home," he blurted out excitedly.

Janetta looked past him to the cart in the road and the small group of men sitting in it looking down at the floor. She ran out of the house and round to the back of the cart. At first she just stood and stared and then let out a gasp of fright.

"Will! Will!" she screamed as she struggled to climb up onto the boards of the cart. Frank helped pull her up. She swung her backside onto the boards and sat next to Will, hands clasped over her mouth.

Will lay on his back, his face pale under the dirt and his eyes stared unblinking at the sky.

Janetta sat and looked at him in disbelief. She didn't cry or make any sound. She felt numbed by the sight of Will's eyes. Frank put his large podgy fingers on his eyes and lowered the lids. They all sat in the cart motionless and lost for words as the rain began to fall again.

****

The trees creaked and rustled as they swayed against the white clouds that accented a beautifully blue sky. The sun, so warm against her upturned face, made the inside of her eyelids glow red. Starlings chirped in the trees and somewhere close by a bee hummed in the grass. She could smell roses in the air.

It was far too nice a day for death. It was a day to live, a glorious first of July, a day to be glad that you were alive.

"A man is brought up, only to be cut down again."

What was that stupid man saying? What was that voice that droned on a few feet away from her saying, spoiling her moment of tranquility? She couldn't remember the last time she'd stood still and just basked in the heat of the sun. She fancied she was a child again in Tywardreath hearing the waves beating against the rocks, the gulls overhead and the voices of her old school friends playing on the cliffs.

"Earth to earth..."

Janetta was suddenly brought back to the present by the minister's monotonous words. What, she tried to remember, had Dr Cooper written on the death certificate? 'Cardiac arrhythmia. Angina pectoris'. "*Why couldn't he just say he had a heart-attack? Pompous git!*" She made herself smile at that thought.

A small hand tugged at her sleeve. She opened her eyes and squinted in the direction of the minister. He seemed to be waiting for her to do something. A circle of faces all looked expectantly at her. Her son, Thomas, who was standing beside her, clutched at the sleeve of her black dress. She hated black dresses.

She stooped down and picked up a handful of earth and threw it into the hole. It clattered against the lid of the coffin and the minister seemed satisfied and droned on.

"Dust to dust..."

"*Forty nine was too young to die*," Janetta thought, *"he shouldn't have left me so soon."*

The service finally over, the small group that surrounded the grave began to drift away from the hole and wander back down the path towards the gate. Some nodded mournfully at her as they passed.

May, seeing her mother still in a silent, almost absent mood, took Jane and Albert's hands.

"Com'on kids I'll take ya 'ome."

Thomas sauntered off with his hands in his pockets but William lingered by his mother.

"Com'on Will," said May, "leave mum be now." William took a last look at the coffin and turned away.

Janetta was left standing alone staring at the coffin lid,

"What'a yoos doing in there ya silly bugger," she said out loud, and her first tear dribbled down from her eye.

"He's with the Lord now, my dear," said the minister, who still remained at the head of the grave, patiently waiting for Janetta to say her good-byes. She barely acknowledged him.

Sergeant Michael Shaunessy, in his best dress uniform, and with his newly-acquired sergeant's stripes on his sleeve, stood awkwardly a few feet behind her. He waited a couple of minutes before clearing his throat to attract her attention. Janetta gave a very slight glance back to see who was standing behind her. Michael looked nervously at the minister, thinking he should say something.

"Twas a grand service father?" he said at last; then realizing his mistake he quickly tried to correct himself. "Sorry.... Padre.... Your reverence...Oh fock...Sorry," he hurriedly crossed himself.

The vicar stared at the stumbling Irishman and looked amused. "Thanks my son," he said kindly.

Janetta took Michael's arm and broke his embarrassment by asking,

"It was kind o' ya to come, Michael."

"Can I be walk'n ya back Jan?" he replied.

"That ya can," said Janetta unable to resist teasing him by imitating his Irish accent.

She smiled weakly and took a small step back away from the edge of the hole. Michael took her arm to steady her. As they walked away they both had their heads bowed down looking at the gravel and didn't notice a third figure standing a few feet away in the middle of the path.

They walked a few paces, their feet crunching on the shingled path, before they came to the waiting soldier. They stopped and Janetta felt Michael's arm release from hers.

"Sir," he snapped in a very military fashion and he saluted.

Janetta looked up into the kind eyes of Colonel Timothy Bird. He returned the salute and then faced Janetta.

"I'm really sorry, Jan."

Janetta gave a slight nod. "Blimey wot are you doing 'ere?" she blurted out and then, taking a deep breath and pulling herself together. "You have been promoted I see," she said changing her voice to a more refined way of speaking.

Bird looked momentarily gratified that his new rank had been noticed.

"Mmm," he nodded, "May I walk you to the gate Jan?"

Michael Shaunessy took a couple of steps back to allow the Colonel room to stand beside her and offer her his arm. She linked her hand in his arm and gave Michael a quick apologetic glance.

"I was in town on business and heard about Will's death. I had to come…are you alright?"

Janetta nodded. "I'll get by I expect," she said after a short pause putting on a brave tone. They walked on and talked of nothing important. Timothy ached with desire to tell Janetta so many things that filled his heart but held his tongue, for this was an inappropriate time.

They neared the cemetery gate. Janetta also had so much to say to her old friend but felt estranged and awkward with him. He had been the greatest love of her life yet their paths never seemed to cross at the right moment. A few short steps to the gate, years to catch up on, and the circumstances could hardly have been worse.

"How have you been, Jan? Was Will a good husband to you?"

"I've been fine and yes, Will was a good man."

"I never forgot you, you know."

"Nor I you. You were always kind to me," replied Jan, her voice barely audible. "And you? Have you been happy? How's… Lady Dawlish?" She nearly said "Mrs. Bird."

A woman's voice shrilly pierced the tranquility of the graveyard.

"Ah! There you are Colonel."

They had reached the gate and on the road beyond stood a barouche and two immaculately groomed horses. The driver sat motionless and stared forward with an expression of mournful boredom. In the open carriage sat Lady Dawlish, very finely dressed in pale greens and blues with an overly large brimmed bonnet sporting several long feathers. Her sharp features and pointed nose gave her a cold, uninviting countenance.

Janetta was certain that she heard a quiet groan rumble in Timothy's throat.

"Yes, my dear, I'm coming."

Janetta wanted to keep Timothy's arm but instinctively let it go at the precise moment that he subtly sidestepped away from her.

"My condolences Mrs....er," Lady Dawlish waved her hand in a small circle in the air to suggest that the name was on the tip of her tongue. It was obvious to Janetta that she hadn't a clue what her name was and that frankly she couldn't give a damn.

"Rayner!" snapped Timothy.

"Mrs Rayner," Lady Dawlish was oblivious to her husband's irritation, "It must be such a great loss to you."

Janetta was about to give her an appropriately genteel reply when Lady Dawlish turned her gaze back to Timothy.

"Come, my dear, we will be late for dinner. The Countess is expecting us at five and it would be unpardonable for us to be late."

Timothy Bird winced. It was plain to see that he'd had quite enough of this overbearing women but was resigned to suffer his lot. He turned to Janetta.

"Mrs Rayner," he said with polite formality, "do forgive me I must..."

"Of course," replied Janetta.

Then under his breath he added, "I'll be in touch."

He gave her a slight bow and walked through the gate to join his wife in the carriage. As they drove away Lady Dawlish didn't even acknowledge her.

"Focking 'ell," Michael had stepped forward to stand beside her, "now I've known some pretty focking scary women in my toim but that one takes the ruddy biscuit, so she does!"

Janetta gave a halfhearted laugh, put her arm through Michael's arm and hung on to it tightly.

"That she focking is an'awl!" she teased, mocking his Irish accent.

Two black funeral carriages waited to take Janetta and her family home. She walked with Michael as far as the first carriage where he opened the door and helped her climb in. She turned and looked enquiringly at Michael, who did not follow her into the carriage.

“I’ll see you you back at th’ ’ouse, Jan,” he said and walked smartly away from the carriage.

Janetta felt momentarily abandoned. She sat facing her children, all with long faces. Young Albert looked the most lost. He was only five and couldn’t quite comprehend what had happened to his father. He stared at his mother, watched a tear roll slowly down her face, and didn’t know what to say.

Janetta sat silently watching the shops in the New Road drift slowly past the carriage window and wondered how she could face all those people in her house expecting tea, gin and beer.

She was forty-seven and widowed for the second time. What were her chances of finding a man to support her now? How was she to manage with so many mouths to feed?

CHAPTER 32

Letting Go

The afternoon of the funeral was more than Janetta could bear. The house was full of well-meaning friends and neighbours all speaking in unnaturally low tones so that the room was filled with a monotonous hum of voices. Everywhere Janetta went she was stopped by women dressed all in black, who proceeded to tell her how sorry they were for her great loss and how much Will would be missed. Half the people hardly knew Will, and Janetta thought they were only there for the free gin and beer.

It was too hot in the small room and she gradually made her way through insistent well-wishers with sombre lowered glances, to the hall, where the stairs would give her an escape.

The children were all quiet and remarkably well behaved. The younger ones seemed overwhelmed by all the strangers in the house and sat in the corner eating slices of cake. May did her best to play host and relieve her mother of as many duties as possible. She refilled glasses, handed around plates of cake and sandwiches they could ill afford, and smiled sweetly at all who spoke to her in low and melancholy tones.

Janetta retreated to her bedroom, sat on the bed, threw her head back and groaned at the ceiling. Would they never leave?

A low cough announced that someone was standing in the doorway.

Janetta sighed to herself. Was there nowhere that she could find peace and quiet?

"Yes?" she said, making no attempt to disguise her annoyance at being interrupted.

"Sorry! I'll leave you be!"

It was Jos Wennlsoy their second lodger. Janetta liked Jos. He was a well-educated Irishman from Dublin, his accent being quite soft, and he worked as a photographic printer. Jos was only thirty-five but the twelve-year difference between them went unnoticed by Janetta. He was handsome in an awkward and untidy way. Janetta always wanted to run a comb through his unkempt mop of black hair and, despite the fact that she supplied him with clean, well-ironed laundry, he always looked as though he'd slept the night in his clothes. But he was a very quiet, kindhearted man who always made Janetta feel at ease when alone with him.

"No! It's all right, Jos. You can come in," she said holding her hand out to him. "It was too hot down there," she gave a slightly derisive nod at the floor to indicate her guests below, "I just needed to get away from that lot, that's all."

Jos stepped into the room, took her hand and allowed himself to be guided to her side. He sat on the bed next to her, almost too close to her. He didn't know what to say so felt it best to remain quiet. Sometimes, he knew, body language alone spoke volumes and, since he was a man who felt uncomfortable speaking his mind to a woman unless he was absolutely sure of her giving him a positive response, he remained silent.

Janetta nestled gently into his side. It was a gentle move, so subtle that he barely felt her do it. But when he felt the warmth of her body he knew it was a deliberate move on her part.

He could feel her right breast against his arm and the gentle pulsing of her breath. Nothing was said. He reached out and gently laid his hand on her leg just above her knee. The touch of her leg against his palm gave him a warm glow. She didn't flinch or attempt to pull away and he wanted the moment to last forever.

How could he ever remove his hand now? Why would he ever want to? How devastated would he feel if she moved away and he could no longer feel her breast gently rise and fall with each breath she took?

For several moments they sat together in silence, Janetta staring at the wall and he looking nervously toward the door. What would he do if someone looked in? His hand on her knee was an extraordinarily inappropriate position to be in, on this, of all days, and he was concerned about protecting Janetta from criticism if observed, but he desperately wanted to hold the moment.

They sat together silently enjoying the touch of one another's bodies. He couldn't resist turning his head to look into Janetta's face.

How beautiful she was with her aquiline nose and lips moistened with the red gloss she rarely used. She turned to look into his eyes and smiled, and in that very brief moment there was a silent communication between them that made Jos's heart skip a beat. Her beauty overwhelmed him and he swallowed as he fought hard against blurting something out that would make him look foolish or cause Janetta to be made uncomfortable. How could he tell her he loved her? She was his friend's wife, freshly widowed. He forced himself to focus on how incredibly inappropriate it was for him to express his feelings and so he broke contact with her eyes.

They sat there in comfortable silence for several more minutes before being interrupted by May.

"Mum," she said quietly from the doorway. Janetta gave her daughter a weak smile but didn't move away from Jos. Jos instinctively removed his hand from her knee. "Mum, there's a couple of people down in the 'all who 'ave just arrived," she screwed her face up in disbelief. "Said they wos my Aunt Jane and Uncle Tom."

Janetta's eyes widened in shock and then she let out a scream of excitement.

"Jannie! Jannie is 'ere! Gawd bless me soul!" she leapt off the bed and, abandoning Jos, rushed for the door. May stood aside to let her mother fly past her and run down the stairs.

May grinned at Jos and shrugged her shoulders as if to say, *"Your bet is as good as mine,"* before leaving the room to follow her mother downstairs.

Jos found himself alone on Janetta's bed. He was in a state of shock. What had happened there? In a few brief moments his entire perspective of his landlady, the wife of his departed friend, Will Rayner, the mother of five children and twelve years his senior, had been thrown right out of balance. He now saw her as the most beautiful woman he had ever known. Her dark hair and loving eyes had melted him and he now felt like a ship without a rudder. He realized he loved Janetta and for the first time in his life felt completely lost now that he was not in her presence.

He remained seated on her bed. His hand gently stroked the warm spot where she had been sitting; he looked down at the remains of her impression on the blanket and felt a lump rise in his throat. This was going to be a difficult thing to come to terms with, and he took a deep breath to clear his thoughts before rejoining the party downstairs.

Janetta's feet barely touched the stairs as she ran down to greet her sister in the hall. On seeing Jane she let out a scream of delight and threw her arms around her neck. Her other guests watched in shock at this display that must have appeared unseemly for a woman in mourning for a husband barely cold in his grave. Jane, more from surprise at the force of Janetta's approach than shock, staggered back a little and regained her balance by putting her hand against the wall. The two sisters hugged one another tightly for several seconds before Janetta let go with tears running down her face.

Jane held Janetta at arms length and seeing the tears, narrowed her eyes, pursed her lips and cooed at Janetta as if she were addressing a baby.

"Ohh! Jan my dear, I was so upset to hear of pooorrr Bill's tragic passing, that I said to Tom;" she raised her voice in replaying the moment, "Tom, we must go immediately. Didn't I say that, dear?"

"Immediately, was the very word you used my dear," replied Thomas, who was still standing behind her, just inside the front door, unable to find the room to advance further into the room.

"Go and pack I said," interrupted Jane, "there's no time to lose if we are to catch the nine o'clock train!"

"Nine o'clock train!" confirmed Thomas from over Jane's shoulder.

Janetta's attention switched to her brother-in-law, Thomas Vanson. He was still as distinguished looking as she had remembered but he looked more tired. He had put on a bit of weight about the midriff, had gray liberally sprinkled throughout his whiskers, and he wore a pair of wire-rimmed spectacles that enhanced his somewhat scholarly appearance.

Jos came slowly down the stairs, attracting Jane's gaze. She couldn't help wondering who this handsome young man was and what he was doing upstairs. Jos saw the surprised expression on her face and smiled at her. There was no room left in the small hallway so he stopped a couple of stairs up from the bottom. Janetta ignored her sister's questioning eyes and didn't bother to introduce Jos in order to increase the mystery. She had always loved to shock her sister and knew that Jane would draw the wrong conclusion.

The awkward moment was broken by one of Janetta's guests slowly getting out of her seat and tugging at her husband's sleeve.

"It's time we were leaving, dear, to allow Jan time with her family," she said, nodding her head towards Janetta. "C'mon!"

Her husband stood up and they made their way into the crowded hallway. One by one the other guests took the hint and also made their way out.

Jane and Thomas, who were effectively blocking the door, squeezed past everybody and made their way into the parlour, allowing space for the guests to say their goodbyes and give their last condolences before funnelling out of the front door.

When the guests had all finally left, the parlour seemed empty and quiet. Cups, plates and crumb-filled doilies littered every vacant flat surface. Chairs were left in disarray and the children sat quietly, still numbed by the loss of their father and the large number of people who had invaded the house.

Jos put his coat on, made his excuses and left as well. Janetta felt his absence and wanted to call him back. A shiver of panic went through her. She felt alone. Jos had become the closest she had to a sympathetic shoulder to cry on and he had left her alone with her family, who, Janetta felt, secretly disapproved of her.

She turned to her sister who was taking this opportunity to make a close inspection of the room. She didn't, or couldn't, hide her distaste at the sight of the decor. She ran her finger discreetly along a shelf, tutted and rubbed her fingers to remove the dust. Thomas flicked his tails to the side of his legs and sat in an armchair. Jane looked at him with a moment's annoyance and then, deciding it wasn't the time to chastise him for his manners, perched herself on the edge of a chair by the dying fire.

"Can I get you something?" asked Janetta, wondering what she could offer since they had been practically eaten out of house and home.

Jane shook her head and waved her hand dismissively, interrupting her.

"Jan dear," she said in a not unkindly manner. "Tom and I were talking on the way down here."

"We were!" nodded Thomas.

Jane closed her eyes and pursed her lips in frustration at being interrupted. Satisfied that her husband had said his piece, she carried on.

"We were so shocked to hear about poor Bill."

"Will," broke in Janetta, "he liked to be called Will."

"Will," Jane corrected herself.

"I said he was Will... Didn't I say he was 'Will' my dear?" said Thomas, eminently pleased with himself. Jane looked pained.

"We were saying, Jan, that now poor Will has passed on you will be feeling somewhat," she paused as if uncertain what words to use.

"Financially embarrassed," chirped in Thomas as he reached into the remains of the fire with a taper to light his pipe.

"Thomas really!" snapped Jane. She always called him Thomas when she was annoyed with him.

"No point in pussyfooting about, my dear. She's lost her income and something has to be done. I'm sure Jan doesn't mind us talking openly."

Janetta was dumbfounded. She didn't know what to say. They were right of course. Will's army pension died with him. All she had was the rent money from her lodgers and a pitifully few shillings she earned from doing the street's laundry.

Baby Jane coughed in the corner. She always coughed so the others in the family hardly noticed any more. Janetta noticed of course, but couldn't afford a doctor. Jane looked at the child and a crease furrowed the bridge of her nose.

"That child doesn't look well! Which one is it?"

"Jane," replied Janetta.

"She should see a doctor!"

"Yes, she will," said Janetta.

Jane seemed doubtful but pressed on.

"As you know, Jan dear, Tom and I have not been blessed with children, but we are..." she carefully considered the word to use, "comfortable, and are in the fortunate position to be able to give a child a good home and education."

Janetta was stunned for the moment.

"You want to take my kids from me," she said, horror struck.

"No dear," jumped in Jane, "not all of them! Goodness me no!"

"Will," shouted Janetta towards the kitchen door. Young William who had been helping his older sister wash the dishes, dropped the tea towel and came into the parlour.

"Take the little-uns outside to play," she snapped.

William recognized the tone of his mother's voice, so without questioning her, he quickly ushered his younger brothers Tom, Albert and the baby, Jane, out of the front door. When they were gone, Janetta turned back to her sister. May came out of the kitchen and leaned against the doorframe.

"Now then," said Janetta, her arms folded across her chest and her eyes wild with anger. "Just what did you mean?"

Jane looked sheepish and turned to Thomas for help. Thomas, seeing that his wife had now passed the baton to him, picked up the subject nervously.

"Jan dear, please don't take offence. We're only trying to help, you know," he said in as conciliatory a tone as he could muster.

"How," cried Janetta, "by taking my kids away from me. Am I such a bad mother? Eh?"

"No, no Jan not at all. It's simply that you have so many mouths to feed and we can offer one of your children… only one mind you, a very good home and education."

"Oh so my 'ome's not good enough now is it?"

Jane stood up, very put out by Janetta's refusal to accept their proposal in the spirit that it was offered. Her sudden movement made Janetta take a quick step back as if to defend herself against an oncoming blow.

Thomas looked up at her startled.

"Jan dear, we've upset you!" said Jane rather haughtily. "But we meant no offence. We'll return to our hotel now and leave you to think about it. Come along, Tom."

Thomas got up out of his chair and looked apologetically at Janetta.

"We meant no offence, Jan, I assure you." He repeated Jane's sentiment as he brushed past her and made his way to the door. "We'll be off now. We'll come again in the morning if we may. When you've had time to think about it. I'm sure you'll see that it makes good sense. You'll feel better then."

"I'm feeling just fine thank you, Thomas," snapped Janetta as she held the door open for them. Her sister and brother-in-law walked out into the street and Janetta closed the door behind them a little too hard.

"Bloody cheek," she snapped to nobody in particular. She looked at May who was still standing in the kitchen doorway. "Did you hear your bloody aunt? Bloody nerve she's got! Get me a drink girl… and make it a big one!"

May went back into the kitchen and opened a cupboard under the stone sink. There was a bottle of gin kept back from the guests. She half-filled a mug and brought it in to her mother.

Janetta was sitting by the fire extremely agitated and stared into the glowing embers. She took the mug, held it with both hands and took a big swallow of the warming gin.

"God I needed that! Put some more coal on, May dear," she said in a quiet and exhausted voice. "I'm cold."

"There ain't much left, mum."

Janetta looked up at her daughter and glared straight into her eyes. May avoided her gaze. "Alright, I'll get some," she said and went back out to the kitchen. When she came back in with the coal she saw her mother looked very tired.

"Are you alright, mum?" she asked

"Wot am I going to do, May?" she said very quietly. The storm inside her had been softened by the gin and now she was feeling depressed. "They're right ain't they? Can't go on without ya dad can we?"

"Yeh they're right, mum!" replied May as she placed a couple of pieces of coal onto the fire and slapped the dust off her hands. "But who should go?"

"Mmmm," Janetta let out a long low pensive hum. "Well she ain't taking my Albert!" she said and she took another swallow of the gin.

"Will's working now so he can stay and Jane is sick…you really should get the doc to look at her mum."

"I know, I know! But doctors cost money, girl."

"That only leaves Tom, then don't it!" said May. "He's a little shit anyway."

"Watch ya mouth, girl!"

"Well 'e is! We could do without 'is nonsense around 'ere! Anyway it'll probably do 'im good."

"Anybody would think yer don't like ya bruvver," said Janetta.

"Well 'e did nearly drown Bert t'other week didn't 'e! He's a bloody menace!"

"I ain't sending 'im because 'es a bastard to get rid of, but he is the obvious choice." Janetta gave a little quiet laugh. "He'll probably end up better off than any of ya and he's the least to deserve it. Little shit!"

May chuckled at the irony.

"You'd better call the kids in now, it'll be getting dark out there," said Janetta swallowing another mouthful of gin.

****

The next day, Jane and Thomas rapped on Janetta's front door. They both looked cold and apprehensive. When Janetta opened the door, Jane looked sheepishly in at her and in an uncertain voice asked, "Is it all right if we come in, dear?"

Janetta smiled at them and ushered them in out of the cold wind.

"It's not very nice out this morning," said Thomas as he took off his overcoat and handed it to Janetta, who hung it on a hook behind the door.

"Come in and warm yourself by the fire," said Janetta as she went to the fireplace and put another chunk of coal she could ill afford onto the small fire.

"Sorry if I was a bit sharp wiv ya yesterday," she said as she jabbed at the coals with a poker, "but it was a bit of a shock you know."

"Yes dear we quite understand!" replied Jane in a gentle manner.

"I think it very kind of you to offer this help," continued Janetta as she sat in her favourite chair, "and we think Thomas is the best choice. I spoke to him about it yesterday."

After she had got Jane and Albert to bed, she had sat down with May and William to explain the plan to Thomas. At first Tom just sat there and listened. He tried to take in everything his mother was saying. He tried to understand his big sister's apparent excitement on his behalf and his brother Will's protestations that he would rather go; all he could think of was that his mother wanted to get rid of him and that he was going to be sent away from his family. First he could feel a prickling at the back of his neck, tightness in his chest and a trembling in his lower lip and before long he was sobbing and protesting that he didn't want to go. He clung to Janetta's dress and screamed into her lap. His red face was streaked with tears, his nose ran and he sobbed with panic.

Janetta and May did everything they could to console him and eventually decided it was best just to let him exhaust himself with crying. Janetta stroked his hair and whispered soothing words to him. Eventually his crying subsided and he sat on the floor and whimpered.

It was May who changed Tom's opinion about going. She gently told him about his Aunt Jane's huge house in the country. She told him how he would go to a posh school and one day become rich. She told him how he would wear really nice clothes – which he really couldn't care less about – and have lots of wonderful things to eat such as ice cream and sweets and fruit fresh from the orchards. She found herself making up as much as she could about the wonderful new life he was going to have, but it was the promise of all the toys he could possibly want that finally appealed to him. If he could have all those toys, ice cream and sweets, then what on earth did he want to stay here in this cold draughty house for? He looked at his mother in her dowdy dress and unkempt hair compared to how beautifully dressed and well mannered his Aunt Jane and Uncle Tom were. He thought about his mother's drunken rages and his Aunt Jane sitting quietly sipping tea. He thought about a beautiful house and train sets and rocking horses and toy soldiers, and the idea of living with his aunt and uncle slowly began to look better.

"Good boy!" said Janetta, "then you must get up early tomorrow morning and put on your best clothes and pack whatever you wish to take. It's going to be a big day in your life, Tom. The first step to becoming a man."

****

Tom stood in the hallway wearing his cleanest clothes and carrying a small white sheet tied up in a bundle, which held his spare clothes. He had no toys with him. Janetta walked over to him, spat on her hand, and smoothed his hair down.

"Well you do look smart," she said. Or as smart as he'll ever be, she thought.

"Good morning, young man," said his Aunt Jane, who tried not to look too uncomfortable.

"Ah ya!" replied Tom and uncharacteristically bowed his head shyly.

Jane looked pleased at her new charge as Thomas opened the front door and led him out into the street where a carriage waited.

Janetta fussed about him. "Now you be a good boy now, and use the 'anky I gave ya, and eat wiv ya mouth shut. There's a good boy. Remember everyfing I told ya now."

"Yeh yeh, mum," whined Tom, who found it embarrassing, being fussed over.

Young Albert stepped out of the house holding his baby sister Jane's hand. Jane coughed as she watched Tom climb into the carriage. William gave him a brotherly slap across the head as he climbed the step. "Go on, glad to be rid o'ya," he said with a broad smile on his face.

Tom turned and poked his tongue out at William.

May bent forward and kissed him on his cheek, which made him shy away and wipe his face against his sleeve.

Janetta stood in the doorway and held her arms out to him.

"Give ya mum a hug goodbye then."

Tom put his arms around her neck and gave a squeeze. His little face peered over her shoulder and seeing William standing on the pavement he poked his tongue out at him a second time.

William returned the gesture, pulling an ugly face for good measure.

"Now don't worry about a thing, Jan dear," said Jane as she approached the carriage door, "he'll be just fine and we'll expect you to come and visit us on a regular basis."

Janetta smiled weakly and assured her she would although deep down she knew she probably never would. This was possibly the last time she'd see her Tom for many years and the lump in her throat prevented her from saying too much.

Jane climbed into the carriage and sat next to Tom who was preoccupied with studying the interior fabric. He'd never been in one before and the experience was fascinating him. Thomas Vanson got on board after first giving Janetta a very tight hug. He smiled and nodded at May and William.

"Goodbye to you all, goodbye!" he repeated amiably.

The coachman clicked his tongue and the horse moved off at walking pace. There was a last minute shouting of goodbyes from everybody at once. Tom stood up and stretched across Jane's legs to lean out of the window and wave to his family. In a couple of moments the carriage turned into the next street and was gone from view. Janetta and the other children were all left standing and staring at the empty street. Tom had gone.

"Com'on, kids, inside," said Janetta gently and held her arms out to usher them all into the house.

CHAPTER 33

The Guardians
28th June 1902

The rain had been falling all morning and the sky hung heavily over a sea of glistening grey slate roofs. The road, slick with sodden manure, was full of street vendor's discarded rubbish.

Janetta, her head covered by a thin shawl clasped under the chin by a large pin, hurried along the street with Jane sitting on her left arm, her little hands clasped round her mother's neck. Young Albert trotted beside her, being almost pulled along by his hand. His scruffy boots let in the water and his tattered, buttonless jacket flapped open and did nothing to keep him dry. He had no idea where they were going on such a wet day.

Jane whimpered as she kept her head down to stop the rain getting in her eyes. She coughed continually and her chest rumbled with every breath. Janetta's arm ached from carrying her.

She stopped to draw breath in a shop doorway. They had walked the last half-mile to Tewson Road, Plumstead from their apartment on New Road because she didn't have enough omnibus fare. Albert was tired and grumpy. They sheltered a few moments from the rain and Janetta stared across the street at the large gray stone building that faced them. It was a grim edifice. With its high walls, small windows and huge oak door it could easily have been mistaken for a prison. Today, in the dim light of the rain and the low-hanging smoke from thousands of coal fires throughout the city, the building looked frightening, even to Janetta. This was no prison yet it fostered as much apprehension as if it were. This was the home of the Woolwich Guardians, a pleasant sounding name for what was in fact the workhouse.

Nobody looked well upon the workhouse. It was the final refuge of the destitute. Those whose lives had left them in penury in their old age, with no means of support, could find a home of sorts within those bleak, cold walls. This was a house of the infirm, the downcast, the abject failures and the honest poor. Here they were expected to work for their keep. Within these walls the 'guests' toiled at the most menial tasks, like oakum-picking where they teased out the fibres from old hemp rope, broke up rocks for road making, worked in the kitchens or scrubbed floors.

Janetta hitched Jane a little higher on her aching arm and threaded her way between horse-drawn wagons to get to the other side of the street. She approached the massive black front gates of the workhouse and stopped short. What was she doing? Jane coughed again and Janetta looked into her pale thin face. Her daughter's sunken eyes were rimmed with red and she wheezed each breath. The Woolwich Union Workhouse may be a forbidding place but at least she could get a free doctor to look at her child.

She looked up at the arch above the door. Chiselled into the granite in large, deep letters were the words "The poor ye have always with you".

Janetta swallowed nervously, took another look at her fading daughter and banged the iron knocker hard against the door. The sound echoed inside, but nobody stirred. She banged again while drops of rain dripped off the stone archway and splashed on her hair and Jane's face. Jane screwed up her eyes and whimpered.

A faint voice somewhere in the halls behind the great door answered the knock.

"Alright! Alright!"

A bolt slid back, a small door within the larger gate opened and a woman in a starched blue dress and white apron looked out at them. She was a kindly-looking lady in her mid fifties, Janetta guessed, but she looked as if she would take no nonsense from anyone.

"Want a bed for the night do ya ducks?"

"Umm…no!" replied Janetta nervously.

The woman seemed surprised, "Oh! What is it then?"

The rain suddenly started coming down harder and the woman grimaced and looked at Jane and then at Albert, who was hiding behind Janetta's skirts. She gave a gentle smile to Albert.

"You'd better come in or you'll catch ya death."

She stood aside to allow Janetta to step through the small portal in the gate. Albert followed, lifting his legs over the gate's threshold.

The inside of the building wasn't much better than the outside. She found herself standing in an enormous hallway with a very high ceiling. Gray flagstones covered the floor and the walls had shiny cream tiles to a height of four feet and whitewashed brick above. Several open-flamed gas lamps hung from long pipes on the ceiling. There was an ominous hum of voices that emanated from endless corridors and the air was damp and cold.

"So what can we do for you?" the woman asked, but her eyes were on Jane, "When did that child last eat?"

"This morning," bridled Janetta who felt insulted at the insinuation that she didn't feed her children, "but she don't eat much," she added.

"She looks pretty poorly to me...poor little mite!" she cooed at Jane.

"Can she see a doctor?" Janetta asked.

"Mmmm!" grimaced the woman, "I'm not sure he's in today. Let's find out shall we?"

She turned to walk away but Janetta stayed where she was.

"Well, follow me then!" called the woman when she realized she wasn't being followed.

They walked deeper into the hall and turned right at the first corridor. Albert clung to her hand. Voices grew louder, but still she could see no one. The woman stopped by an office door and pointed to a bench.

"You sit there a moment and I'll find out from matron if the doctor's in the building."

She disappeared through the door and Janetta sat on the bench with Jane shivering in her arms. Albert sat on his hands, stared at the floor and swung his legs back and forth. There was a rustling of dresses and scuffling of feet and half a dozen old women came down the passageway. They looked dirty and unkempt. Their clothes were gray, drab and all alike. Each wore a blue striped dress and once white apron. It was the uniform of those whose degradation had forced them to make this place their home. They nodded to her as they shuffled past; their eyes were dull.

The office door opened again and the woman in clean blue came out.

"You're in luck, dearie," she said, "the docs doing his rounds now. I'll take the little'n shall I?" She reached out and lifted Jane from Janetta's arm.

"What's your name then?" she asked Jane who looked as if she was about to burst into tears.

"Jane…" Janetta was about to volunteer her full name but stopped short.

"Well you wait here dear and I'll take Jane to see the doctor. Won't be long!" and with Jane in her arms the woman walked off down the corridor. Little Jane looked at her mother, reached her arm out towards her and whimpered. The woman turned a corner and Jane was lost to sight.

Janetta and Albert sat quietly on the bench. Albert's legs continued to rock forward and back, the heel of his boot occasionally hitting the bench. She put her hand on his knee.

"Stop fidgeting!" she said. Albert settled down a little and said nothing. They sat there for about ten minutes and Janetta felt increasingly agitated. She knew that Jane had consumption. She also knew that she couldn't afford medicines and doctors and would be watching her daughter slowly die.

She stood up and paced up and down. Albert's eyes followed her in silence. Here, in this oppressive place, Jane would get looked after. She'd still die but at least she'd have professional attention. Janetta couldn't give her that. If she left now no one would be able to find her. They didn't know her name. Jane would be looked after.

Albert stood up, bored with the bench. He wandered back towards the main lobby. Janetta idly followed. They got to where the corridor turned towards the main door and there they stopped. Any minute now the woman in blue could reappear with Jane. Janetta fidgeted and paced.

She could walk right out of the front door now and get away before the woman came back. She didn't want to watch her daughter slowly die.

What could she do after all? Jane would die sooner without treatment and here she'd get looked after. She looked at Albert. He would be her youngest now. Little shy, quiet, Albert who was now amusing himself by tracing the grouting around the edge of the wall tiles with his finger.

She had made up her mind. She took Albert's hand.

"Come on then. We'll let the doctors look after Janie, shall we? We've got a long walk home."

She led Albert to the front door, praying that they wouldn't be seen. When she got to the door she stopped and looked back and listened. No footsteps followed her, so she undid the latch and pulled the door open. Albert looked back to find his sister but stepped through the door as Janetta pushed against his back.

"Out you go!" she said and then she followed him into the rain.

CHAPTER 34

The Long Night
Friday, March 20th, 1903

It had been a long afternoon and Albert was getting tired of walking. It was a typical March afternoon, cold and windy. Janetta had taken him on a short omnibus ride which he considered a treat and they had spent the last couple of hours walking around shops in a neighbourhood he didn't recognize. She hadn't bought much and it all seemed a waste of time to Albert.

The evening was getting prematurely dark due to the low clouds and Albert started whining that his feet were sore and he was hungry.

Janetta stopped by a public house and looked at it thoughtfully. Albert recognized that look. Just beside the door stood a wooden bench under the window. An old man with an iron-wheeled cart containing a brazier grunted "hot taters" to everyone who walked past. He looked ill and his clothes were tattered and grubby. Albert found himself staring at the man's feet because he had odd boots, one tied together with string. There was a three day stubble on his face and his blackened fingers peered out of the ends of old woollen gloves like claws.

"Sit ya'self down there then, Bert and I'll get ya somefing, shall I?" said Janetta, "wanna potata?"

Albert nodded shyly. Janetta went to the brazier while Albert sat on the bench. Two young men dressed in large checked suits and derby hats, swaggered up to the pub, their fingers tucked into their waistcoat pockets and cigars hanging out of the corners of their mouths. They looked cocky, full of "piss and vinegar" as his father used to say. One of them looked his mother up and down and grinned before opening the pub door. The sound of music and laughter within got louder. A shaft of warm air smelling of stale beer and tobacco wafted past Albert before the men disappeared and the door closed again.

Janetta came back with a newspaper containing two jacket potatoes.

"Careful, they're 'ot!" she said as she handed them to him. "I'll get ya some ginger beer shall I? Stay there." She disappeared into the pub and Albert tried to hold his potatoes but they were much too hot. He passed them from hand to hand and finally placed them on the bench next to him. The potato vendor watched him, amused. A few minutes later Janetta reappeared with a brown jar with Bolt's Ginger Beer in large black letters on its side. She helped Albert pull the cork out of the neck and then retreated into the bar after warning him not to wander off.

The pub was full of people and very noisy. The air was blue with cigarette and pipe smoke and the piano player hammered out familiar tunes while ale slopped from the glass vibrating on top of the instrument.

Janetta pushed her way to the bar and purchased a mug of gin. There was nowhere to sit and her feet were sore from walking. She sidled through the crowd to the opposite side of the snug where she found a small table against the wall with a young man sitting at it. She approached him and placed her gin on the table.

"Anyone sitting here, luv?" she asked.

The young man shook his head and gestured for her to sit down. She took the seat, turned her back towards the wall and leaned against it.

"Cor, blimey that feels good that does!" she said to nobody in particular, and she raised her knee above the tabletop and rubbed her ankle, "me plates are killing me, they are!" she continued, using cockney slang to describe her feet.

The youth smiled politely but didn't saying anything. Janetta took a sip of gin and then looked at her companion. He was about twenty-five she reckoned and very smart in a loud sort of way. His three-piece suit was mid-beige with a very large brown check pattern. His shirt had a starched high-neck collar and he wore a bright red tie with an enormous knot that bulged over the top of his waistcoat. She could see the chain of a fob watch looping between his two lower waistcoat pockets.

"You drinking all on ya own then?" she asked.

"Nah me mate is getting the drinks."

He had jet-black hair parted in the middle and smeared down with pomade and a small moustache. Janetta thought him quite handsome in a cocky sort of way. She looked at his hands. They were clean and soft but bore ink stains on the insides of the first two fingers on his right hand. She thought that he had very likely never done a days hard labour in his life. He was probably a clerk of some kind and spent his days sitting on his arse scribbling on papers, or else he was involved in something less than honest.

On the table lay two derby hats. One was brown and well-brushed, which matched his suit and the other was black and probably belonged to the friend.

The friend arrived with two pints of ale and sat down without acknowledging Janetta. He was dressed almost identically to his friend except his suit was a light grey with black check. Janetta watched them as she sipped her gin. Both were equally as handsome, full of themselves and overdressed which made them stand out like two peacocks in a chicken run, but neither seemed to care.

The new arrival took a sip of his ale and looked about the room, resting his eyes for a second or two on each young woman he could find. He noticed a pretty young girl by the door and nudged his elbow into his friend's side. The one in brown glanced at her as well and gave an approving smile.

"These boys are on the prowl," thought Janetta.

"You two are slumming it a bit tonight ain't ya?" she said. The comment implied they were dressed for a more upscale establishment. They both looked at her and Janetta got the distinct impression that they were trying to decide whether she was worth talking to. Their eyes looked her up and down, assessing her charms as a woman. She was almost old enough to be their mother but she knew that she still had her youthful beauty, despite the ravages of age and childbirth. Hard work and meagre food had kept her figure trim, her hair was still long and tonight at least, it was clean and well groomed. Just the streaks of gray and a few wrinkles betrayed her years but she still turned heads.

"This isn't ya usual place is it?" she guessed.

The man in brown spoke first. He leaned back in his chair removed the cigar from his mouth and, tucked his thumbs in his waistcoat pockets.

"Nah! Fred and me prefer the Crown, don't we Fred?"

"The Crown! Yeh!" echoed the gray suited companion.

"But you got to spread yourself around a bit ain't ya? See new sights."

A young barmaid walked past the table and both men followed her with their eyes.

"New sights is right, Charley," said Fred

"Let the ladies in this neighbourhood see what they could have," continued Charley.

"If they play their cards right," said Fred.

'Lord above,' thought Janetta, *'but these two do fancy themselves.'*

"Like the girls do ya boys?"

Janetta was teasing them now. The glow of the gin was working its magic on her and she was beginning to enjoy these two conceited 'boys'.

They both nodded and grinned mischievously.

"Pretty young thing ain't she?" she continued referring to the barmaid. "Course they don't know nothing do they. Ain't lived!"

She swallowed another mouthful of gin.

****

Albert sat outside and slowly ate his potatoes and drank his ginger beer. He was used to waiting outside public houses and thought nothing of his loneliness. He did miss Jane. Watching her always gave him something to do while he waited, but without his younger sister he had to amuse himself.

He stood up on the bench and tried to peer through the grimy windows of the bar. He couldn't see much through the dirt. The evening had closed in and the gas lamps were now lit inside. Human shapes moved about behind the glass and roars of laughter occasionally drowned out the piano, but there was no sign of his mother. He would just have to wait on his bench in the encroaching darkness.

****

The gin was really starting to get to Janetta by nine o'clock. She was now halfway through her third mug and the voices in the room were getting muffled. She had to concentrate hard on forming her words and staying awake.

Charley and Fred had long since forgotten about the other younger girls in the bar. Janetta had kept them entertained with stories of the Royal Artillery and her various lovers. She even told them about her brief encounter with Ellen Barry in Swansea, and she was amused by how enthralled they had been to hear of such a thing. She embellished the story enough to keep their eyes on her in amazement.

As Charley and Fred supped their ales and listened to Janetta, they forgot her age and began to see her as a very desirable woman. She'd been right, none of the younger girls had her experience.

Janetta was in her element. She had two handsome young men eating out of her hand. She noticed how they stared at her breasts so she stuck her chest out more. It had been so long since she'd been able to flirt and she was determined to make the most of these two popinjays. She delighted in teasing them. The more she played them, the more the lust crept into their eyes and the more Janetta felt like a young woman again.

She was drunk with gin and overjoyed with a sense of youthful irresponsibility. She was happy and couldn't give a damn about what anyone might think. She was having fun and why not. She deserved a little fun time. She had missed her men and tonight she was remembering the thrill of the tease.

She felt hot, her head was swimming and she needed to pee badly. She struggled to stand up.

"Where ya go'n, ducky?" asked Charley.

Janetta blew him a kiss, "Where you can't follow dearie! I 'ave to piss."

The two youths laughed and watched her as she struggled to stop the room from spinning.

"I'll be back and no drinkin' me bleed'n gin while I'm gone neither." She pretended to take a serious note of the line of the liquid in the mug.

She steadied herself, took a deep breath and made a real effort to walk in a straight line as she headed for the back door. When she stepped outside the cold night air hit her, but it felt good after the smoke, heat and noise of the pub. She thought she might be sick but the urge passed.

She found herself standing in a dark back yard surrounded by a high brick wall. One gas lamp glowed weakly, throwing shadows that flickered against the damp cobbled floor. It had been raining and everything glistened in the glow of the lamp. The yard was only a few feet square and a gate opened into an alleyway at the back. Against one wall was a brick outhouse and beside that an open-sided shed.

She lifted the latch to the outhouse, opened the door and was met by an almost overwhelming stench of urine and faeces but she barely noticed.

****

In front of the pub Albert sat on his bench and watched the people and traffic go by. He was used to being left on his own outside pubs. Usually he sat with Jane, but he hadn't seen her for a year. He sat with his collar up against his neck. The rain had been light but he still felt a little chilled. He swallowed another mouthful of his ginger beer and drew his knees up to his chest to keep warm.

****

The two youths were getting impatient waiting for Janetta to return and Charlie also needed to pee. He got up and made his way to the back door and out into the night. Janetta was still in the outhouse and so rather than wait for her, he walked out into the dark back alley and peed against the brick wall. He'd barely finished and got the top button of his trousers done up again before he heard the outhouse latch and saw Janetta step uncertainly back out into the chill night. She was singing to herself and hadn't seen him standing in the shadows.

It started to rain again. Janetta stood all alone in the yard, threw her head back, spread her arms out to the side and allowed the rain to splatter against her face. It felt so refreshing and cool that she suddenly laughed out loud and twirled like a schoolgirl.

Charlie stepped into the yard and out of the shadows, which made her start. She squinted into the gloom until she recognized who was standing there and then a bright grin crossed her face.

"Charlie!" she sang. "If it isn't the 'andsome Charlie. Have you come to pee as well? Do you need an 'and?" she teased and she reached forward as if to help him undo his fly buttons, but they were already undone and Janetta grinned at him and wagged her finger in his face.

"Whose a naughty boy then?" she teased.

Charlie caught her wrist and smiled at her while stepping backwards, pulling her under the roof of the shed. Janetta squealed with delight as she staggered forward into his arms. The shed was almost empty except for an oil drum and a couple of wooden boxes and he pinned her up against the dusty wall.

There was a clap of thunder and the rain began to come down in torrents hammering on the tiled roof and Janetta and Charlie paused for a second to watch the water cascade off the roof like a silver curtain. They both laughed and stared into one another's eyes. Charlie began kissing her. He was young enough to be her son but she couldn't care. He was a man and she really wanted him. Her head swam with gin, her body felt the glow of alcohol and his lips were pressed hard against hers. She was happy.

****

A shiver ran down Albert's back as he hunched on the bench. The rain was starting to come down really heavily now so he moved into the doorway and huddled into the corner as much as he could. He could hear the piano and singing inside. He took hold of the door handle and pulled it open an inch or two and peered into the smoke filled snug. He couldn't see his mother, just a sea of people laughing, talking, drinking, smoking and singing. The door burst open, knocking him onto his backside. A young man came out with a woman on his arm. She looked at him as she stepped over him.

"You all right, luv?" she asked but didn't stop to hear his reply. Albert nodded shyly as she hugged the man's arm tighter and huddled against him to find some protection from the rain. Albert picked himself up off the wet cobbles and went back into the shelter of the doorway.

****

Charlie reached down and started hitching up Janetta's skirts. He did it tentatively at first, gauging her reaction, but when she made no attempt to stop him he hoisted them up to her waist. Janetta folded her arms around his neck and allowed him to lift her off the ground by her waist. She wrapped her legs around his legs and waited while he fumbled to drop his trousers.

"Now what'ya fink ya doing, Charlie boy?" she teased. The question was rhetorical and Charlie only grinned.

"You'll find out in a minute! Won't ya?" he said.

The rain water that poured off the roof splashed on the ground just two feet from where they stood but Janetta was oblivious.

'So long', she thought, it had been so long and she wanted to savour every second of his invasion. Charlie gritted his teeth as he jerked his hips against her. She could feel the palms of his hands pushing against her buttocks as he encouraged her to rotate her hips while he pumped. Janetta's shoulders chafed against the brick wall but she didn't feel it. She squealed with delight and for the first time in a year she was happy. She forgot everything. She forgot about Albert waiting, she forgot the time and Will, and she forgot Fred who had been sitting waiting for them in the pub. She thought of nothing but the sensations in her body and she cared about nothing.

Footsteps ran across the rain-slicked cobbles but neither Charlie nor Janetta could give a damn. They pumped hard against one another as if it was the last time they'd ever have sex.

Fred ducked through the sheet of rain flowing off the roof and ran into the shed. He shook the water off his jacket, unaware that Janetta and Charlie were also in there. Janetta saw him but didn't care and didn't stop. A chill of excitement went through her at seeing the second young man. Charlie was gasping for breath as he continued to thrust at her. Fred, hearing the moans in the dark, struggled to focus on the two black shapes against the wall. It took him a moment or two to realize what he was seeing but when he did his face lit up and he came over towards them.

Charlie stopped thrusting and rested his head on Janetta's shoulder, exhausted. He was relieved to see Fred, as it gave him an excuse to relax for a moment. It was extremely uncomfortable and Janetta was getting heavy.

"Fred! Wan't a go?" he gasped.

“Swing her round, Charlie,” replied Fred as he fumbled with his buttons.

Janetta laughed out loud at the thought of having two men in the same evening. Charlie backed away as Fred came up behind her and fondled her breasts. She instinctively leaned forward against the wall and moaned contentedly.

As the gin swam in her head and the rain pounded on the roof, Fred found his rhythm and rogered her hard and fast. She gasped and cried out in the thundering night and yelled at him to push harder and faster. She was loving every second of it and never gave a thought to poor Albert sitting outside the front door.

There was a brilliant flash that for a second turned the yard into daylight and a sharp clap of thunder shook the shed roof startling them. Fred stopped as if caught in the act and then realizing what it was, all three burst into laughter. Charlie and Fred were exhausted and they all hugged one another tightly as they huddled in the shelter. Janetta was crushed between their chests but they kept her warm.

The wind blew a gust of rain into the shelter and she felt a cold splash against the side of her naked leg and buttock. Fred flinched as the rain hit him and he withdrew from her and retreated further into the shelter of the shed. Fred fumbled doing up his britches and Janetta slid down the wall onto her haunches.

“See yu next tim, eh luv!” said Charlie.

Janetta laughed at them. “Is that all I’m getting from yu? Call you selves men?”

But they weren’t listening. Charlie and Fred looked at the rain nervously, hoisted up the collars of their jackets and made a run for the warmth of the pub.

“I hadn’t finished yet,” yelled Janetta into the darkness, but they were already in the back door of the pub. “Bloody men!” she mumbled to herself and then started laughing again. “Gawd bless ’em.”

She lowered her bottom onto the cobbled floor, leaned her head against the bricks and closed her eyes. Her head swam and tiredness crept over her. The splashing of the rain faded from her hearing and she drifted into a cold and fitful sleep.

****

Slowly the pub was emptied and Albert had to keep avoiding the door. Each time the door opened and somebody came out he tried to look inside for his mother but he never saw her. He knew she'd be drunk. He'd seen this before. Usually somebody came out at closing time half-carrying his semi-conscious mother. They'd stagger off up the road towards the house and Albert would follow. Then they'd be met at the door by May, who'd help her mother up to bed while Albert warmed himself by the fire.

But tonight they were not at their usual pub. This was not their neighbourhood and there was probably nobody inside who knew his mother and would take care of her. Albert knew that the publican would throw her out at closing time and then it would be up to him to pull his mother round enough for her to be able to get them both home.

He was only seven and yet already he was becoming the man of the house in his brother's absence, and getting his mother home was to be his task tonight. He worried about it nonetheless because his sister May was working as a domestic and living away from home. She wouldn't be there to help him get his mother to bed.

The evening grew later and colder. Soon there were no more people coming out and Albert huddled in the doorway pulling his thin jacket tight against his chest. Eventually the door opened again and the publican came out to stack a couple of empty barrels on the cobbles. He nearly tripped over Albert sitting in the shadows.

"What are you doing here, lad?" he asked impatiently.

"Waitin' for me mum," replied Albert meekly.

"Ya mum?" he sounded surprised. "You sure she came in 'ere?"

Albert nodded.

"Well she ain't in 'ere, lad. Best go 'ome if I were you," and he went back inside. Albert heard a bolt slide on the door.

The rain was stopping but it was still cold. Albert felt a pang of panic at the thought of having lost his mother, but he knew she'd come back for him sooner or later so he decided to stay put and wait. It was only a matter of time before she was sober enough to remember him and then she'd be back. He huddled close into the corner of the door, tucked his knees up to his chest, laid his face against his knees and closed his eyes.

She'd come! He knew she'd come!

****

The morning light was gray and cold. The sun struggled vainly to find a chink in the overcast sky. Janetta opened her eyes and tried to focus on her surroundings. She didn't have a clue where she was and remembered little of the previous evening. She looked about her and couldn't believe her eyes. She had slept in a shed. No wonder she was cold. As she started to pull herself up, she felt a cold wetness on her bottom and discovered that she had been sitting in a puddle all night. Her dress was soaked, her bottom was frozen, and her head pounded. A faint recollection of the previous evening crept into her mind and she wanted to smile but her sour stomach pushed any pleasant memories from her mind.

She wished she could be sick and waited with her head against the wall. She stood on weak legs; her head pounded as she supported herself against the wall. She shivered violently and realized she had lost her shawl. She felt so ill she wished she were dead but she managed to keep her stomach down.

It was so early nobody else was about. A dog barked somewhere and a few birds sang their morning chorus in the grayness. She walked very hesitantly towards the back gate of the yard, lifted the latch and staggered out into the back alley.

She focused hard to look down the alley in each direction and to concentrate her mind. One way was very long the other seemed quite short and appeared to end in a main street. She slowly made her way toward the street thinking of nothing but getting home to her bed. She hadn't even thought about Albert. The sourness of her stomach, the looseness of her bowels and the pounding of her head all fogged her mind. All she could think about was her bed and some dry clothes. The longer she dithered about in the alley the worse she would feel, so holding her stomach, she brushed her wet tangled hair out of her face and headed slowly towards the main street.

CHAPTER 35

The Search for Janetta
Saturday, March 21st, 1903

Albert slept fitfully huddled in the doorway of the public house. He couldn't believe how quiet the town was throughout the night. The once bustling street was now deserted and the houses dark. A few cats meowed in the alleys and occasionally a dog barked, but otherwise the whole town slept in shadowed darkness. No traffic rumbled and clattered along the cobbled streets, no hawkers cried out their wares, no street musicians played on the corners. All was quiet and as cold as the grave.

Albert pulled his jacket tight over his chest and folded his arms. He shivered and his legs trembled as he curled up into as small a ball as he could in the corner of the doorway.

The dawn's light came gray and early, and Albert shivered having barely slept a wink. He was cold and hungry.

He was woken by the sound of horses hooves and iron-rimmed wagon wheels on the cobbles. When he looked about him he found the street was already filling with dozens of horse-drawn barrows containing fruit, vegetables, meats, breads, spices and a whole variety of household goods. It was market day and the vendors were setting up their stalls in the street ready for the day's business.

Albert stood up, his legs stiff from being bent and cold all night. He hoped his mother would arrive any minute to collect him. She'd remember where she left him and he hadn't moved. She'd be here soon; hung-over and irritable after her night on the tiles, but she'd take him home, give him some bread and a cup of tea for breakfast and he'd be warm again.

He looked at the clock that was set into the brickwork of a large four-storeyed building on the far side of the street. It was five o'clock. So many people were about at such an early hour and, he thought, they must have been up much earlier to get the market ready this soon in the day.

Then he thought about his mother again. There was no way that she would be awake this early. She would most likely sleep in late with a bad head and sour stomach, and then she'd have a long journey by omnibus to get there. No, he was in for a long wait, and he was getting hungrier by the minute.

About twenty feet from him was a barrow containing bread and a variety of buns. They were freshly baked and he could smell them. His stomach growled for his breakfast but he had no money on him. He tried to put food out of his mind and concentrate on keeping warm. The potato vendor was back and his brazier was already alight so he wandered closer and stood downwind of it, so that he felt the warmth of the fire. The potato seller gave him a toothless smile as he continued laying his potatoes out on the grill.

Albert grew steadily hungrier and looked longingly at the buns. He was not a thief and had never even considered stealing anything before, but his stomach wouldn't leave him in peace. He knew his elder brother Tom wouldn't have given it a second thought. He would have had the buns off the wagon in a second and would have laughed at the joke of it. Albert's conscience held him back though. Stealing was a sin and he was a good boy; everybody said so. He couldn't shame his mother, but how his stomach did growl with hunger, and how sweet the buns smelt.

He watched the baker potter about his barrow and chat with the sweet seller next door to him. Albert rehearsed his crime in his mind. When the moment was right he'd walk casually past the barrow and pocket a bun when the baker's back was turned. He'd be away before the baker even realized that one was missing. In fact, thought Albert, if I take a bun from the back edge of the barrow he'd probably never miss it.

He wandered closer to the baker's barrow and waited for his moment. His heart pounded in his chest and he started to tremble. He must be brave if he was to acquire his breakfast in this way and appear innocent.

Several minutes and a couple of false starts went by before he was confident enough to execute his plan; and then a miracle happened. The sweet seller called out to the baker that his horse had got loose.

There was a temporary enclosure set up on the corner where the vendors could tether their horses during the morning market. One horse had got loose and was trotting around the market with several men and boys in pursuit.

"Fucking 'ell!" exclaimed the baker and abandoning his barrow he took off after the horse.

This was Albert's moment; all the other vendors were watching the chase and enjoying every minute of it. He walked nonchalantly over to the barrow, grabbed a cinnamon bun and shoved it in his pocket.

It had been so easy. Nobody saw a thing and he was able to disappear into an alleyway and devour the bun before anybody noticed.

His hunger pains eased and he was able to go back to the pub doorway to wait for his mother. The horse was retrieved and everybody settled back to their morning chores. The street soon began filling with morning shoppers, and Albert was amazed at how busy the street became at such an early hour. The hands on the clock now pointed to seven and his stomach had already forgotten the bun. He felt it was time to get some more food.

This time would be more difficult. There were hundreds of people about now and the baker never let his stall out of his sight. Albert decided to wander around a bit to look at the other stalls and see if an opportunity presented itself. He wandered almost aimlessly through the crowds of people. Nobody seemed to notice him and his small body became almost invisible as he manoeuvred behind the ladies' full skirts.

After a while he found himself by a fruit stand. The costermonger was busy serving half a dozen women and seemed far too busy to notice a small boy standing beside the barrow.

Albert looked at all the apples, peaches and plums. He'd had apples several times and peaches he didn't like too much, but his eyes settled on a bunch of bananas. He knew what they were but had never had one before, and he decided that this was the perfect opportunity to try one.

He waited until the vendor turned his back and then, as quick as lightening, he grabbed a banana and ran. To his horror however, the banana didn't come away from the bunch, but instead the entire bunch ripped off the barrow, bringing several other bunches off with it. They hit the cobbles with a thud and several people turned to look at what had happened.

The barrow owner was on top of him in a second and grabbed the bananas from his hand. Before he had a chance to run a large hand grabbed his arm from behind.

"Got ya, ya feaving git," a loud gruff voice bellowed in his ear as a second man lifted Albert off his feet and held him by the scruff of his neck. "Last time you little bastards thieve my stuff."

"I've never stolen nuffin," protested Albert.

"Well we'll see what 'lilly law' 'as to say about that shall we," and he pushed Albert down onto a box and held him in place.

Within a couple of minutes a large crowd had gathered around the barrow, and somebody was shouting that he'd got a copper. Albert sat whimpering in a state of bewilderment. What had he done?

"I wanna go 'ome, I wanna go 'ome," he pleaded.

He was terrified by having a rough hand grabbing his collar and a booming voice behind him threatened prison and all sorts of awful retribution.

After what seemed a lifetime, a deep but not unkind voice broke in upon the chaos.

"All right! All right! Settle down," boomed a police officer and then turning to the gathered crowd "Quiet!" The crowd came to a hush and the policeman turned back to the barrow owners. "Right, let go of the lad." The barrow owner released his grip on Albert.

"He stole my fruit," growled the barrow owner, his veins standing out on his reddening temples.

"All right, George, just take it easy!" replied the policeman.

He stepped towards Albert and squatted down to his level.

"Now young man," his voice was business-like but gentle, and Albert felt himself relax a little. Albert hesitated.

"I ain't 'ad nuffin' to eat, sir. I'm 'ungry," he half whispered.

"What's your name lad?"

"Albert, sir."

"Where do you live Albert?" asked the policeman as he gently laid his hand on his arm to reassure him.

"Forty one New Road, sir," he replied.

“Lord, you’re a ways from home aren’t you? Where’s your mum?”

“Don’t know, sir, she left me last night outside the pub.”

The barrow owner broke in on the chat. “Well what are ya going to do wiv ’im then. I want ’im arrested. I’m fed up with losing my stuff.”

“Calm down now,” replied the policeman, “you haven’t lost anything this time, have you? I’ll take over now.”

“Yeh, well see ya do then,” said the stall owner dismissively, and began ushering them out of his stall. “Now I’ve got customers to see to,” then turning to a lady who was finger testing some fruit “lovely fresh pears them, luv, ’ow many would ya like?”

The constable drew Albert to one side.

“Well, young man, I’m going to let you off the thieving this time.”

Albert looked sheepish but felt relieved.

“I think the best thing to do,” continued the policeman, “is find your mum. Don’t you?”

Albert nodded shyly.

“Well it’s a long way, New Road, so I think the best thing to do would be for us to go to the police station and we’ll find someone to take you ’ome. How’s that?”

Albert felt relieved that he was no longer alone. He was grateful that he was in the hands of someone who would look after him and so he went happily with the constable to the police station.

****

The police station fascinated, yet slightly frightened Albert. It was a large building and in the foyer stood a high wooden fence with a desk raised up on a dais. Against one wall was a long bench on which several people sat waiting. The white tiled walls were covered in posters and handbills, most of which Albert couldn’t read. A duty sergeant with the largest moustache Albert had ever seen, sat at the desk writing in an enormous book.

“Sit there, lad,” said the constable who had brought him to this place. Albert sat on the bench and, a young woman with brightly coloured clothes and much too much makeup moved up a few inches to give him room.

"Well!" she said to Albert, "wot yoo in fa then? Squidger are ya?"

Albert knew that a "squidger" was a pickpocket and he shook his head.

"Leave him be, Patsy!" said the constable.

"I ain't 'urtin' the lad!" she replied with an exaggerated expression of innocence on her face.

The constable turned to the duty sergeant and mumbled to him in tones too low for Albert to hear. The large moustached sergeant leant to one side and looked past the constable directly at Albert. He pursed his lips, nodded to the constable and scribbled in a clean page of his ledger.

The constable came back to Albert. He looked briefly at the colourful woman on the bench and then leant forward as if to impart a secret to Albert.

"The sergeant there," he said pointing to the moustache, "is going to get you a mug of tea and slice of bread. Now you are to wait here, see, and soon a nice lady will come to the station and she'll take you home, all right?"

Albert nodded.

"Good lad," he said as he patted Albert on the shoulder. Then he turned back to the woman next to him.

"Now none of your nonsense, Patsy. He's a good boy this one and he doesn't need your kind of help. So keep yourself to yourself."

"Oh bleedin' charming innit?" she replied as if butter wouldn't melt in her mouth.

"The sergeant will keeping an eye on you Patsy, so behave."

Patsy crossed her arms, tutted and turned so her back was almost to Albert. The constable, satisfied, winked at Albert and walked back out onto the street. Albert was alone again.

It seemed as if he had sat in the police station for hours. All the people on the bench had been replaced by others and he'd been given two mugs of tea and slices of bread and butter. The second time he was also given a chunk of cheese, which he really enjoyed.

Albert noticed that the clock behind the desk said half past ten when a woman in a dark brown overcoat and woollen scarf round her neck approached the sergeant's desk and spoke to him in lowered tones. The sergeant leant forward to join her conspiratorial conversation and Albert saw him nod in his direction. The woman turned to look at him. She smiled, thanked the sergeant and walked over to where Albert was sitting. She sat down beside him.

"Well, young man," she said, "the sergeant tells me you're Albert Rayner and that you've lost your mummy."

Albert nodded shyly.

"I think we'll go and find her, shall we?"

Albert smiled weakly and nodded again. The woman paused for a second or two before pressing on.

"My name is Mrs Rudge."

Albert said nothing. There didn't seem to be any necessity for a response although he felt she was waiting for one.

"Tell me...Albert? Do you like being called Albert or do you prefer Bert? I expect your family all call you Bert, or Bertie."

Albert nodded again.

"Well Bert, it's a funny thing, but where I work there's someone else named Rayner. A little girl, Jane."

Albert's eyes lit up.

"You knows Jannie, miss?" he asked, "She was sick an' mum took her to see the doctor but I ain't never seen 'er again."

Mrs Rudge smiled gently at him.

"Yes, I've seen... Jannie. Well, well now! This is a fortunate day is it not, young man! We'll go and take you home and then, later, we'll be able to take Jane home too now that we know where she lives."

"Yes please, miss," said Albert enthusiastically.

"Good, well have you finished your tea? Then put your jacket on and we'll be on our way, shall we?"

Mrs Rudge took his hand and lead him back out into the crowded street.

"Stay close now. We don't want to get lost again, do we?"

They walked to the corner of the street and waited there until a horse-drawn omnibus came along and stopped to pick them up.

Albert climbed up the winding back stairs to find a seat on the top floor. He remembered his mother taking him up there yesterday and he enjoyed the view of the street so much better from the top. There was a seat at the front and he was able to look down right on top of the horse. He felt happy and secure with the kindly Mrs Rudge taking him home to his mum.

The bus ride seemed very long but Albert's attention was filled with all the sights, smells and sounds of the bustling high street. Before long he began to recognize various landmarks and he knew he was nearing his home.

Finally Mrs Rudge took his hand again, led him back downstairs and when the bus stopped at the corner of New Road and Beresford Street, they got off and crossed the road.

Mrs Rudge held Albert's hand as they walked up New Road towards number forty-one. They had arrived back in Woolwich and Mrs Rudge stopped and bought Albert a roll and small block of cheese for his lunch. Albert nibbled at the cheese as he trotted along close beside her so as not to get lost in the crowd. He was beginning to recognize places now. Familiar sights greeted him as he walked further up the busy street. He'd be with his mum shortly and he began to feel a little excited and relieved.

When they arrived at the building containing forty-one, Albert started to walk ahead of Mrs Rudge, pulling her as if showing her the way. They arrived at the door and Mrs Rudge rapped her knuckles on the flaking paintwork. They waited for someone to come, and Mrs Rudge looked down at Albert and gave him a wink and a smile.

The door was opened by a very scruffy, middle-aged women with a deeply wrinkled face. Albert immediately recognized her as Flora Chambers, the woman his mother was always trying to avoid. Flora Chambers was their landlady. He didn't like Mrs Chambers. She was immensely fat, dirty and smelled of body odor.

"Yeh," she said, obviously irritated by the interruption.

"Janetta Rayner?" asked Mrs Rudge hoping to God it wasn't. She vaguely remembered the woman who had brought Jane Rayner to the Guardians and she had been a strikingly handsome woman. This abomination couldn't possibly be her.

"Who wants 'er?"

"I'm Mrs Rudge, head matron at the Guardians. May I come in?"

She didn't wait for a reply but stepped straight into the small hallway, obliging Flora Chambers to step back to make room for her. Mrs Rudge entered the living room still holding Albert's hand.

Albert let go of Mrs Rudge's hand and called out for his mother. The parlour was empty so he ran into the kitchen.

"Muuuum," he yelled into the deserted kitchen.

"'Allo Bertie," said Flora, "come to find ya mum 'ave ya?"

"I didn't catch your name," said Mrs Rudge.

"Ya didn't ask. But I'm Flora and this is my 'ouse, see, and Rayner was me tenant." She shrugged her shoulders, "some tenant and all. Look at the state of this place."

Privately Mrs Rudge had to agree. The room was filthy.

"Ah! I see. And where is Mrs Rayner now?"

Albert ran between them and up the stairs; his boots clunked on the wooden steps "Mum where are ya?"

"Gone ain't she," said Flora to Mrs Rudge ignoring Albert's calls.

"Gone where, Mrs Chambers?" Mrs Rudge was beginning to get irritated by Flora Chambers' manner and had no intention of hiding the fact.

"How the 'ell should I know? Why should I care?"

Albert's boots could be heard running from bedroom to bedroom. "Muuum."

"Because I'm trying to find her Mrs Chambers, that's why."

"Well I don't know," said Flora defensively. She realized that this conversation wasn't going to end and this woman and boy weren't leaving until they got the information they needed, so she gave a sigh of resignation before continuing.

"Look!" she said, "she came 'ome this morning, didn't she. Been out all night she had. Looked in a right state she did an' all. Been sleeping rough I'd say. Bleeding slut she is and no mistake!"

"Mrs Chambers!" she indicated to Flora that she should lower her voice, "remember the boy!"

She turned and walked into the kitchen and Flora Chambers followed her sullenly. Satisfied they were out of earshot she continued.

"Now! You were saying, Mrs Chambers."

"Yeh well…she was. Right little tart! Carrying on down the pub every night with anyone in trousers she was; and the gin! She could drink any man under the table she could. I wouldn't mind, Mrs Rudge. She can do what she likes can't she? But not with my rent money, eh? Drank it all away she did. Bleeding cow!"

Mrs Rudge sighed. She'd heard this story so many times before. Poverty, gin and prostitution were epidemic among the lower classes and the workhouse was full of Janetta Rayners.

"So where is she now, Mrs Chambers?"

Flora Chambers shook her head and pursed her lips. "Dunno, I threw 'er out this morning…she came 'ome, as I said, in a right state. She was dirty, smelling of gin and sick as a dog, so I told her that if she didn't 'ave me money she'd 'ave to go. She was in such a state she 'ad no fight in 'er. She just begged me the kindness of allowing 'er to 'ave a bath." Flora laughed at this. "A bloody bath would ya believe?…Well I couldn't begrudge 'er that I suppose, so I said I'd be back in an hour and she'd 'ave ta go then."

"And you came back in an hour?" Mrs Rudge prompted.

"Yeh I came back alright. And a right shock I got an' all! There she was, clean, smartly done up in her best frock, 'er hair all done up posh like and 'er bag packed."

"Did she say where she was going?"

"Nah! And tell ya the truth I didn't really care. It's the little'un though I feel sorry for," she jerked her head towards the upper floor indicating Albert. "Sweet kid that one. Oh! An' 'is older sister, May, she was a real nice girl."

It had gone quiet upstairs. Albert has stopped calling for his mother.

"Do you know where I can find May?"

"No, she left home weeks ago, she did. Got herself a job in service somewhere. Canterbury I fink" Flora went suddenly pensive and paused for a minute before continuing with a concerned tone in her voice. "Funny thing you know about her," meaning Janetta, "got herself all dressed up she did, to leave like I said, but she 'ad a strange manner about 'er. Made me fink of those, wot yu call em? …Zombies. You know, awake, but nothing up 'ere." She tapped herself on the temple. "Then she just walked out of the 'ouse. Ain't seen 'er since."

"So you have no idea where she might have gone?"

Flora shook her head. "Nah! Nowhere. Pity, 'er 'usband was a lovely fella. Dead now of course. Will 'is name wos. Used to be in the army. Could see your face in 'is shoes, you could."

Mrs Rudge couldn't help but show her disappointment, but she had half expected this. She walked back into the parlour and up the stairs. She found Albert sitting on the bed. His feet dangled a few inches of the floor and his hands were clasped together in his lap. He sat quietly, his head hanging down and tears streaking his cheeks, but he didn't cry. He sat resigned to the fact that his mother wasn't there and crying, even for a seven-year-old, wasn't going to bring her back.

"Come along Albert," she said as brightly as she could, "let's go."

Albert lowered himself off the bed, took one last glance at the empty wardrobe where his mother's clothes had once hung, sniffed and followed Mrs Rudge back down the stairs.

Flora went before them and opened the front door.

"Well thank you, Mrs Chambers. Let me know if you hear from her again. You know where to find me."

Flora nodded.

"Bye Bertie," she said as Mrs Rudge let Albert back out into the street, and then closed the door.

Mrs Rudge stopped, took a deep breath and then looked down at Albert. He looked bewildered but said nothing. Tearstains streaked his little cheeks but he fought to hold them back. He didn't whimper or sniffle and he did not cry for his mother. He just stood by her side and held her hand. He stared at the closed front door with watery eyes. A feeling of anger built inside him but he couldn't let it out. Numbness crept through his body and he squeezed Mrs Rudge's hand a little harder for fear that she'd disappear as well.

"Well Albert," she said gently, "I think we should go and find your sister Jane, don't you?"

CHAPTER 36

A new beginning

Janetta stared into the brown cold waters of the River Thames and shivered although it wasn't a particularly cold evening. She stared into the small wavelets that lapped against the mud and felt…nothing. The river moved inexorably towards the sea; life, she thought, moves with it. The river was unconcerned about the world it left behind and so was she.

Her fingers fondled the few shillings she had in her coat pocket. These few coins were all that she had now. She leaned her elbows against the metal rail that guarded pedestrians against the river and lowered her head onto the back of her hands.

She'd wandered the streets all day. Her feet were sore but she didn't notice; she was hungry but didn't care. The sun was starting to go down and her mood sank with it. She felt so alone.

She hadn't seen William for weeks, as he was working away from home. May was living in her employer's house in Canterbury where she was a domestic. Young, sickly, Jane was in the workhouse infirmary and Thomas was somewhere in the West Country living with her sister. Now her dear Bertie was on the streets somewhere, probably cold and hungry. Probably crying for her. Probably lost. She felt sorry for Bert and a pang of remorse tore at her gut.

"It'll do the little bugger good," she muttered to herself "teach him to stand up for himself." But she wasn't sure she believed it.

He'd join the endless ranks of street urchins that roamed the alleyways of London, picking pockets and stealing to survive. But Albert was such a sweet-hearted boy. She doubted he'd survive such a hard life. He'd probably die of cholera or tuberculosis within a year or two and that brought a lump to her throat.

"Poor little blighter," she thought. *"I'll go to the police and find him when I'm on my feet."*

Her two lodgers had moved out. James Franklin had gone back to live with his wife and Jos Wennsloy had returned to Ireland.

She suddenly found herself crying for her husband Will. Why did he have to die? She felt angry with him for dying and leaving her with nothing but five children to feed. She felt betrayed.

Her fingers rubbed the coins together in her pocket. There were just a few shillings. Not enough to live on, especially if she had to pay rent. No, tonight her bed would be a bench by the foul-smelling river, but what was there to look forward to tomorrow? She stared at the water and shivered again.

"Oh Timothy!" she said out loud. If only Timothy was here. She thought back over the years. She'd had two husbands, both soldiers. First John, "pathetic creature," she muttered to herself, and then Will. She'd loved Will. He was kind, steady, hard-working, a good father and big hearted; weak hearted in the end, but there was no passion. They had been comfortable together but it wasn't enough. Life, she thought, must have passion, or else what is it all about.

Her thoughts went back to Timothy. "Oh God! But he was beautiful!" she said to the waters that passed her unhearing. He was her passion, her reason for living. But he had not married her. He married his rich, stick insect, Lady Dawlish; the wife he barely tolerated to maintain his position in society, *"and I am alone by the river,"* she thought sourly.

Her thoughts were broken by footsteps behind her.

"Looks very cold and uninviting to me."

It was a man's voice and she turned around, startled.

"I'm sorry, I didn't mean to sneak up on you."

It was a middle-aged man in the blue uniform Janetta knew so well. She instinctively looked at his arm to see his stripes. *"A sergeant major,"* she thought, *"a most respectable rank."* She looked at him intently. He wasn't an ugly man by any means. Some might say that he was quite handsome…in his way. His uniform was well pressed, his black boots shone and he stood tall with his shoulders pulled back, as you would expect from years of practice on the parade ground.

"It's quite all right," replied Janetta and she almost surprised herself by her perfect diction. She was out of practice controlling her speech and yet her ability to sound like an educated lady came back to her as if it were second nature.

"It's terrible how many bodies are fished out of the river every year," he said, peering over the railing and grimacing at the brown foul smelling water, "they say that fisherman sometimes fetch them up in their nets, right out to sea. Fancy that eh!"

Janetta laughed and shook her head.

"I do hope you didn't think I..."

"No...no, of course not, ma'am! I was just saying..."

"Yes quite," replied Janetta, "well you're correct of course. It's a terrible thing!"

She turned to look back at the river and there was an awkward pause.

The Sergeant Major cleared his throat.

"I'm Sergeant Major Henry Halfacre, Royal Artillery, at your service...ma'am!" he announced rather stiffly.

Janetta nearly burst out laughing. This officer was unaccustomed to talking to women and was feeling like a fish out of water. She decided to put him at ease and make him feel welcome.

"And I'm Janetta Rayner, Sergeant Major, very pleased to make your acquaintance."

Halfacre visibly relaxed and smiled. There was another pause. Then he continued, "Are you going on a journey, perhaps?"

Janetta noticed that his eyes were cast down at her carpet back.

"Ah, no...well, I mean yes, I was. My husband recently died and I thought I might as well go and visit my sisters. They live in Cornwall you know."

"Cornwall! Ah!"

"But I believe I've missed my train," she lied. In fact she had no intention of taking a train and no money to waste if she was to eat.

"Er...yes it's late."

"So I was just thinking about finding lodging for tonight in an inn somewhere," she said.

"Oh, well, um, perhaps I could walk you," he said nervously.

"That would be very gallant of you..."

"Henry, please, I insist."

"Oh well, Henry, I am very grateful."

Henry Halfacre picked up her bag and they began to slowly walk along the river path towards the town. *"This could be a little tricky,"* thought Janetta, as she had nowhere to go.

"So you're a widow, Mrs Rayner?" he asked.

"I am," replied Janetta.

"I, alas, have never been married. The Regiment always came first you see. But now…well I'm not young any more."

"You're not old, Henry. You're in your prime I'd say."

"You're very kind to say so ma'am."

"I think any woman would be proud to be your wife," she flattered him artlessly and she knew it, but this man was begging for a woman's good opinion and her words warmed him. He was no match for her cunning and she recognized a good 'mark' when she saw one. It was going to be so easy to seduce him and she knew she could play him right into her hands. She walked deliberately slowly as she had no place to lead her escort and she stalled for time.

"You think so…I don't know! There are plenty of younger men in the Regiment. Too much competition." He was laughing now and feeling slightly absurd at having this conversation with a complete stranger, but he liked this lady and felt oddly comfortable with her.

"Ah but you see, Henry," she replied "women like men with the experience that only age can bring." She doubted he had much experience with women, other than whores, but her flattery was working its charm on him.

"You think so, Mrs Rayner?"

"Janetta, please Henry… of course, I know so. What have these young men got, apart from muscles and a tight…" she pretended to be embarrassed and giggled, "I'm sorry!" she said.

"No, no, go on!" replied Henry, anxious to hear what she was going to say. They walked on a little further.

"All I'm saying, is that when it comes right down to it, women much prefer a man with experience. A man like you, Henry."

Henry Halfacre positively glowed inside at her words. Nobody had ever spoken to him like that before. This lady seemed sincere in her opinion of him.

"Look!" he said, "I don't live far from here."

"You don't live in the barracks then?" interrupted Janetta.

"No… I have a house. It's way too big for me I'm afraid. I have a housekeeper-cum-cook who "does" for me, but I have plenty of room."

"It sounds charming," said Janetta.

Henry Halfacre swallowed hard and took a deep breath. He'd never been this forward before and he realized that he could blow the whole situation with one inappropriate suggestion. But would he ever have the chance again?

"Mrs Rayner…if you don't think it improper of me to suggest it, I would be happy to put you up for the night…or two…you'd have your own room of course!"

"I should hope so," Janetta teased.

"Oh absolutely!"

Janetta stopped in her tracks and pretended to think hard about this proposition. It was of course exactly what she wanted; a new protector. She remembered sharing the bed of Colonel Wentworth. A sergeant major was no colonel but still…think of it; a nice house, a gentle protector, perhaps even the opportunity to go to regimental entertainments again. And he did seem a kind man. Careful not to be over anxious she continued slowly.

"Well…it would be very much appreciated, and you do look to be a gentleman…I suppose it would be all right if we assured the house keeper that I am simply a house guest. We both have our reputations to consider after all."

"Indeed yes! And you are quite safe with me, I do assure you."

"Well…in that case, Henry, I would be very much obliged by your kind offer."

Henry Halfacre beamed from ear to ear. He couldn't believe his luck. He was actually going home with a very beautiful woman on his arm.

"My dear lady, you will be very welcome and quite safe with me I assure you," he repeated.

Janetta chuckled to herself. *"Yes,"* she thought, *"but will you be safe with me?"*

"I don't live far from here. Take my arm, Mrs Rayner and I'll escort you home; and on the way you must tell me your life story."

Janetta smiled at him lovingly and cupped her hand under his elbow.

"Oh I'm afraid I've led a very simple and quite boring life, Henry. There's very little to tell."